FIRST HERD TO ABILENE
The Memoirs of H.H. Lomax

Book 5

PRESTON LEWIS

WOLFPACK PUBLISHING
— EST 2013 —

WOLFPACK PUBLISHING
— EST 2013 —

Published in the United States by Wolfpack Publishing, Las Vegas

Wolfpack Publishing
6032 Wheat Penny Avenue
Las Vegas, NV 89122

wolfpackpublishing.com

Paperback ISBN: 978-1-64734-014-8
eBook ISBN: 978-1-64734-009-4

FIRST HERD TO ABILENE

For Mike Cox and Beverly Waak,
Our Cruising Buddies

INTRODUCTION

This book marks the fifth volume in The Memoirs of H.H. Lomax and represents the most challenging manuscript to edit because it covers thirty-eight years of his life, a period longer than any other work in the series. First Herd to Abilene takes Henry Harrison Lomax from the end of the Civil War to three years past the turn of the century and, as in the earlier volumes, allows Lomax to weave another yarn about his encounters with some of the most memorable characters in the history of the Old West, folks such as James Butler "Wild Bill" Hickok, Calamity Jane, Jesse Chisholm and Joseph G. McCoy.

After the publication of Bluster's Last Stand in 2017, several readers contacted me wanting to know the background of Lomax's relationship with Hickok, as bad blood was alluded to in Bluster's. In going through the Lomax papers in the past, I had found multiple Hickok references scattered throughout almost 22,000 pages handwritten in pencil on Big Chief Tablets and on other sheets of cheap pulp paper. As I assembled a consistent narrative, I separated out the sections that related to Hickok and combined them with portions peripherally connected to Wild Bill but important for the context of a broader, more coherent story.

In cutting and pasting this volume together, I came

to appreciate even more both Lomax's knack for being at the right place at the right time and for his often humorous and sometimes sardonic look at others as well as himself. As with his previous published memoirs, Lomax's account generally lines up with the facts as best modern historians can determine, though discrepancies arise as you might imagine from a pioneer who compiled his recollections in the later years of a life that began in 1850 in Arkansas and ended in 1933 in Texas in the final irony of his eighty-three-year existence. Lomax held a grudge against Texas and Texans because of a tragic set of circumstances explained in this book.

As to the further origin and provenance of the Lomax papers from which I have compiled the five volumes in The Memoirs of H.H. Lomax, I will refer the reader to The Demise of Billy the Kid, The Redemption of Jesse James and Mix-up at the O.K. Corral. Those three books plus Bluster's Last Stand provide more substantial background on the derivation of his journals and how that wandering rascal H.H. Lomax winds up at the center of many of the most legendary events of the Old West. While some may question his credentials as a credible chronicler of the occurrences Lomax claims to have witnessed, no one can doubt his abilities as a humorous story-teller of the first rank. In the fall of 2018 I was honored to receive on his behalf the Will Rogers Gold Medallion Award for written western humor for Bluster's Last Stand. So, it's obvious Lomax had a way with words if not always with facts.

It has been a joy to work with The Memoirs of H.H. Lomax over the last two decades and to bring his perspective to the literature of the Old West. What has made it most fun is the fine people I have worked with in publishing these papers. I should like to acknowledge the contributions of Sally Smith, the first coordinator on the project, and Elizabeth Tinsley and Pam Lappies, the original editors. A special thanks goes to Billy Huckaby, the publisher of Wild Horse Press, for bringing the inaugural three volumes back into print and for publishing the award-winning Bluster's Last Stand. I should also like to thank Mike Bray, president of Wolf-pack Publishing, for picking up the Lomax memoirs and continuing them with this volume, which was immensely helped by the editing of Lauren Bridges.

A loving thanks goes to my wife, Harriet Kocher Lewis, who has endured my obsession with Lomax and supported me throughout the process. She and I have not only shared our lives together, but have also shared a wonderful set of offspring with son Scott and his wife Celeste and with daughter Melissa and her husband John. Their marriages have produced "The Grands," as we call our grandchildren: Hannah, Cora, Miriam, Carys and Jackson. They remain an ongoing joy in our hearts. Finally, I must thank the readers who have taken H.H. Lomax to their hearts or funny bones.

Preston Lewis
San Angelo, Texas
September 2019

Chapter 1

Over the years on the frontier, I came to loathe Texans more than any creature on two legs or four. Fact is, by charting the first major cattle trail to the railheads in Kansas, I made many Texans rich, but I never got so much as a thank you from a single one of those Texas cattle kings. Even worse, I received nary a cent for all the hard work I put in and all the risks I took to chart the route to Kansas. If I'd built a toll gate along the Lomax Trail and charged a nickel a head for every steer that tromped my path to the railroads, I'd've lived out my life in luxury. That, however, was not to be.

Not only did wealth bypass me but also the credit for my accomplishment as the trail came to be named after Jesse Chisholm, an old coot who never traversed the route from Kansas to South Texas and back. Even Joseph G. McCoy denied me proper recognition when he wrote of the early years of the trail-driving era in his book Historic Sketches of the Cattle Trade of the West and Southwest, never once mentioning me. If I hadn't spread word to the Lone Star State about his plans for Abilene, McCoy would've never seen a Texas longhorn, much less profited from one.

Besides making the acquaintance of Chisholm and McCoy, I also made an enemy of Wild Bill Hickok, who threatened to kill me over a misunderstanding after he rescued me from an impromptu lynching in Kansas. It didn't matter that I had likely saved him from shooting himself when we first met and that I had even combed nits out of his lousy hair at one point. When I finally faced Hickok after years of running from both his threats and the despicable rumors he had started about me, the reprobate might have survived if he had been paying less attention to me and more to the unsavory characters around his Deadwood poker table. Some folks claim Calamity Jane saved me from Wild Bill, though I disagree, as she was little more than a distraction to us both. Calamity Jane did take a fancy to me, most likely to make Wild Bill jealous, but I never cared for her as I considered Calamity the homeliest woman I'd ever laid eyes on. If you could assay ugly, she'd work out to a hundred dollars per ounce in her early days and five times that in her later years. On top of that, her mouth was no prayer book because it was usually filled with whiskey or profanities so rank she could make Satan blush.

Much as I disliked those folks, it was the Texans that angered me most. They were brash and arrogant, proud that they could call theirs the biggest state in the Union. Nobody, though, called Texas the smartest of the states. If Texans'd been bright, they'd've found Abilene, Kansas, without me having to do it for them. All they had to do was ride north until they encountered two parallel lines of iron rails over a bed of crossties. That, however, was beyond their limited mental capacity.

When I first rode across the Red River into Texas in 1867, the state wasn't on good terms with the Yankee government as a lot of dim-witted Texans were still thinking they'd won the War Between the States. They were proud how they had once been an independent nation and how they had whipped that great military power Mexico to earn their sovereignty. "Remember the Alamo!" they would say, but how could you forget it with them bringing it up all the time? Them being independent for a while held no sway with me as they weren't smart enough at independence to manage it alone and had to join the Union. Then fifteen years later, they wanted to try sovereignty again and failed at it once more, just like the other Confederate States, including my home state of Arkansas. Us Arkansans had sufficient sense not to brag about our failures. None of us pranced around chanting "Remember Appomattox!" even though that surrender was the start of my trek on the trail to becoming a promoter, guide and Texas cowboy — for a while at least.

I never intended to go to Texas but the War of Northern Aggression took a toll on our family, including two brothers, John Adams Lomax lost at Gettysburg in an unmarked grave and Van Buren Lomax killed in the battle at Prairie Grove, near our home in Cane Hill, Arkansas, and buried beneath a headstone I am proud to say that I purchased. My oldest brother Thomas Jefferson Lomax returned from Virginia minus an eye and my other two brothers, James Monroe Lomax and Andrew Jackson Lomax, came back home only briefly before heading on to Texas to make their fortunes. Of my sisters, the oldest, Constance Louise Lomax, ran away from home before the war to God knows where. I was born between my two youngest sisters, Melissa Irene and Harriet Lomax, who both remained around Cane Hill during and after the war.

As for me, my age and my momma kept me from joining the Confederate Army, but that doesn't mean I avoided the hostilities as tensions were high among the Unionists and the Secessionists with bushwhacking and other wickedness making our lives miserable for the duration of the conflict. Even though I never became a soldier, I wound up involved in some incidents, including the death of Southern partisan Beryl Fudge, that made it necessary for me to abandon northwest Arkansas for my safety. As war grudges lingered for years, I was marked for assassination by Fudge's surviving renegades, despite my supporting the Confederacy, if not all the mischief conducted in its name. The worst part of leaving Cane Hill was abandoning my girl, LouAnne Burke, but she was destined for sorrow if I had stayed, and I didn't want to make any young lady, particularly one as sweet as LouAnne, a widow. I've always wondered what might've happened had I remained at home and survived the post-war animosities. Perhaps I would've made something of myself.

As it was, I left Cane Hill in the weeks after Appomattox and headed north into Missouri. I didn't know many folks there except for the James brothers, who occasionally passed through our corner of Arkansas on some of their guerilla raids during the war. They lived in Clay County, north of Kansas City, in northwestern Missouri, so I started that direction. I should've known they weren't the best fellows to run around with, but I had nowhere else to go because neither Texas nor Indian Territory appealed to me, and I knew no one but them outside of Arkansas.

At that point, I didn't care much for Missouri folk either as they had failed to join the Confederacy like any sensible Southern state would've done. Maybe they were right, but it still galled me after all the sacrifices us Arkansans had made over the previous five years with nothing to show for it. So, I entered the state not knowing what lay ahead of me, but spending considerable time looking over my shoulder to make sure my past wasn't tailing me.

I had left Arkansas atop an Army mule I'd found during the war and named "Old Abe" for his habit of kicking and braying whenever someone mentioned the name of Jefferson Davis. Pa, known to the world as George Washington Lomax, had given me a carbine, a pistol with holster and cartridges sufficient to protect myself as long as I created no messes. I never planned to start any trouble, though it had a way of finding me. Momma had provisioned me with a bundle of grub, adequate to get me inside Missouri, but not nearly enough for the journey to Clay County. My money totaled three dollars and thirty-three cents, so I was either going to kill my food or impose on the kindness of folks for a free meal now and then. Unfortunately, I found few Missouri citizens willing to share their chow as they were too stingy to give you the time of day, much less some food. They were so suspicious of strangers they wouldn't trust a teetotaler to hold their moonshine, so I received little help putting vittles in my belly. Too, I didn't care to waste ammunition hunting game as I never knew when I might need a bullet or two to defend myself. As a result, the farther I rode from home, the hungrier I got.

So, anxiety set in as I approached Springfield, hoping to find either a meal or a job to earn me a few dollars for food. Nearing town, I came to a stream and dismounted to allow Old Abe to water and blow while I filled my canteen. I uncorked the container, took a swig, then lowered it by the strap into the rippling waters, watching the air bubble out as the cool liquid rushed in.

BOOM!

A gunshot exploded just around the tree-lined bend of the stream. I yanked the canteen out of the creek, and it flew over my head as I grabbed for my pistol, uncertain if I was in danger. Unperturbed, Old Abe kept drinking as I scanned my surroundings, grimacing when I saw the water flask snagged on the branch of an oak and wondering if a bushwhacker was lurking nearby.

BOOM!

I flinched again, then crouched and moved toward the bend in the creek, keeping myself hidden behind bushes and trees as I looked for my possible assailant. Whoever he was, he was a poor shot. Peeping between branches I spotted a lanky fellow with a broad frame that tapered into a narrow waist. His long chestnut hair cascaded down his shoulders as he jerked his twin revolvers from his holster, then shoved them back and repeated the process. He carried his revolvers butt forward and alternated cross draws with reverse draws. About every third or fourth time, one pistol flew out of his hand, fell to the ground and discharged.

BOOM!

If he wasn't careful, the damn fool was more likely to shoot himself or some gopher than this poor boy from Arkansas. Relieved that this fellow hadn't intentionally shot at me though his erratic draw remained a threat, I kept watching, as fascinated as if I were observing two rattlesnakes mating. The pistoleer picked up his wayward weapon from the ground, shoved it in his holster and then unbuckled the belt, walking over to his horse and laying the rig across the top of his saddle where he had left his frock coat. After lifting his hat and scratching his head, he straightened his vest, then pulled from his saddlebag a maroon sash he wrapped and tied around his waist. Then he yanked his revolvers from their nest and slid them inside the cloth. He took a deep breath, turned back toward the stream and practiced his draw again and again, his pistols sometimes snagging on the sash and him cutting loose a string of curse words. Odd thing was he never intentionally fired his weapons as he worked on his speed rather than his aim. Periodically, he dropped a handgun, usually from his left hand.

BOOM!

The gun's retort drowned out his profanity. I shook my head and started back to Old Abe, who was grazing on the grass by the stream, uninterested in the noisy fellow just down the creek. I picked up a broken limb and used it to retrieve my canteen from the tree branch. After tying the container to my saddle, I climbed atop my mule and guided him along the edge of the bank toward this man, who must have had lots of spare time to practice his gun artistry and plenty of money to waste on ammunition.

BOOM!

I rode to the bend and startled the idiot as he spun around and pointed his pistol at me. If his draw reflected his accuracy, I had nothing to fear as long as he aimed at me.

"Good afternoon," I called. I studied his cold eyes, his protruding lips that hid behind a thick handlebar mustache and his nose that was lengthy and wide enough to replace the cowcatcher on the front end of a locomotive.

He mirrored my stare. "Why aren't you on the road?"

"Had to water my mule. Where am I?"

"Wilson's Creek, near the site of the battle back in 'sixty-one, not far from Bloody Hill where so many fine northerners died."

"I'm new to these parts and looking for Springfield.

Don't know my way around. My name's Lomax, Henry Harrison Lomax."

He nodded. "Howdy, Lomax Lomax."

I shook my head. "It's Henry Harrison Lomax, not Lomax Lomax."

Shrugging and squinting those frigid eyes at me, he defended himself. "I thought you said Lomax Henry Harrison Lomax. That's Lomax Lomax in my books."

It was clear this fellow was no more well read than me. "Let's make it simple, friend, and just call me H.H. or Lomax."

"Okay, H.H.R. Lomax."

"No, just call me Lomax."

"Fine, Lomax, I'm James Butler Hickok," he announced, "but most folks call me Wild Bill."

From his protruding upper jaw, I would've thought Duck Bill was a more fitting name, but I didn't say such.

"You ever heard of me?"

"Can't say that I have, James."

"Call me Wild Bill. You sure you never heard of me? Wild Bill Hickok, scout, soldier and spy in the late difficulty."

"Which side?"

"The winning side."

His words grated my pride, but I kept quiet since his gun still stared at me. "I didn't spend much time during the war reading up on Yankees. Now what do you do?"

"Pistoleer, gambler, whatever'll make me a few bucks," he answered, lowering his pistol and shoving it back in his sash. "I'm out here pistoleering."

"Is pistoleering what you call dropping your gun?"

Hickok spat at Old Abe's feet and pointed at my holster. "I see you're heeled. You care to face off and determine who's fastest?"

"Nope," I replied, "but let me give you some friendly advice. Remove your cartridges before you practice so your pistol won't go off when it hits the ground."

Wild Bill rolled his eyes. "Gun doesn't have the same weight unloaded. I need the feel of a pistol ready to do business."

I scratched my chin, then expectorated at Hickok's boots. "You have a home with a bed?"

"I stay in a hotel, the Lyon House, but what's that got to do with my pistoleering?"

"Now I don't claim to be a pistol sharp, but I suspect it'd be safer and save your ammunition, even your life, if you practiced beside your bed. If you drop your pistol, it's less likely to go off when it falls on a mattress, and you won't have to bend so far to pick it up." I leaned over in the saddle toward him.

Hickok grimaced like he was trying to lay an ostrich egg. He removed his hat, exposing his full head of chestnut hair parted down the middle. As he scratched at his tresses, my nose detected a whiff of perfume. Did Wild Bill use toilet water in his curls? The fragrance amused me. I thought only women did that and not the reputable kind at that. Finally, he nodded at me. "That never entered my mind."

"I figure a lot of things never entered your head, Wild Bill, but I'm glad I could help out and even save you from shooting yourself."

"I'll have to practice by my bed tonight, Lomax."

"It might save a poor gopher his life."

Hickok grinned. "Now you wouldn't tell anybody about me dropping my guns, would you? I'd hate for someone to get the idea they can best me with a pistol."

"As a favor to you, James Butler Wild Bill Hickok, I'll not mention it to a soul. Is that why you come so far out of town to practice, so folks won't see you fumbling with your revolver?"

Hickok smiled for the first time in our acquaintance. "I appreciate the consideration, Lomax."

"Now, Wild Bill, you could do me a good turn by giving me two-bits for supper when I reach Springfield."

His smile melted away like grease in a hot skillet. "I loathe handouts."

"Look at it as payment for the sound advice that saved your life and the lives of countless gophers and ground squirrels."

Hickok slapped his hat back on his scented hair and

pointed his finger at my nose. "Don't be funning me, Lomax. You best stay on my good side."

"I can't hear you over my growling belly," I answered. "Two-bits and I'll repay you in a couple weeks."

Shaking his head, Hickok responded. "No handouts, Lomax. I need the money for my gambling debts and my clothes."

"Don't forget ammunition," I replied."

"It takes money to stay in fashionable attire, Lomax."

I'd never noticed a man talking about fancy garb before, just women. Hickok was a different type of fellow than I had ever encountered. His garments and scented hair bothered me as it seemed less manly and more Nancy. "I never had much but work clothes and a hand-me-down Sunday-go-to-meeting outfit," I offered.

"A fellow that can't pay for a meal certainly can't afford fine attire," Hickok responded.

"I can't eat britches, and I didn't realize I needed fine clothing until I met you, Wild Bill."

"It's what separates men from the beasts."

"Like gophers and ground squirrels," I replied.

"Tell you what I'll do, Lomax. I'll give you a chance at a free meal."

"What have I got to do?"

"Go to South Street near the courthouse square. On the west edge of the road across from the Lyon House is a saloon I give my patronage. Let the bartender know I sent you and ask him to show you the Rattle Jar."

"The Rattle Jar?"

"If your nerves are steady enough to pass the test, they'll give you a free meal. In fact, you might even lay a wager and make money for meals."

"What's the Rattle Jar?"

"Can't tell you because I don't want to fluster you, but if you beat the challenge, you'll get free grub, maybe more."

I shrugged. "What have I got to lose?"

"Nothing," he answered, "because you're broke and lack a reputation around these parts so you're not risking a thing, Lomax." Hickok pointed northeast.

"Springfield's that direction. Good luck, Lomax."

I tipped my hat to Wild Bill, nudged Old Abe's flank with my heel and headed off to Springfield and the Rattle Jar, whatever that was. Glancing over my shoulder once, I saw Wild Bill pull his pistol from his sash. I shook my head and kept moving toward town when behind me I heard a noise.

BOOM!

Another gopher had bitten the dust.

Chapter 2

Leaving Wild Bill behind, I rode across the battleground around Wilson's Creek where the land still showed subdued signs of the mêlée five years earlier. Old Abe meandered past shallow depressions where men had dug shelter or rounded craters where artillery shells had landed. Oak trees were pockmarked with bullet holes and some were splintered or blackened by exploding cannonballs. I passed a couple mounds where I suspected several soldiers lay buried in mass graves and spotted a few bleaching bones that may have been rooted out by feral hogs. I saw fragments of weapons and equipment that remained untouched except by the sun, the wind, and the rain.

Memories flooded me of the Prairie Grove battlefield where my brother Van had died and of Gettysburg where my brother John was buried in an unmarked grave like those I had passed. It saddened me to recall the hard days of the war and the losses of so many families and to realize that men such as my brothers would soon be forgotten. Only the generals lived on in memory, even after their deaths. Wilson's Creek had claimed the life of General Nathaniel Lyon, the first Union general to die in the hostilities, so he would be remembered even in defeat. Despite the beating his troops took from Missouri militia and Confederate soldiers commanded by Ben McCulloch and Sterling Price, Lyon knocked the vinegar out of the Confederates and, some said, saved

Missouri for the Union. I assumed the Lyon House, where I was headed in Springfield, was named after the dead Yankee officer. My spirits rose once I got beyond the faded signs of battle and away from the bad recollections that lingered from the conflict, even though I was still running from the war and its aftermath in northwest Arkansas.

Eventually, I came to a well-traveled road that took me the final miles to town. My throat went dry when I realized I had never been in a city the size of Springfield, which was said to have a population approaching three thousand inhabitants. Previously, the biggest settlement I had ever visited was Fayetteville, and it had less than a third the number of residents, though I figured they were of much finer stock than the Yankee-loving citizens nearby. Approaching the outskirts of Springfield, I ran into clustered cabins and dwellings. Folks there paid me no mind, unlike their country brethren who suspected something amiss by my mere presence. Spotting one old-timer sitting on his porch in a rocking chair and chewing tobacco to idle the time away, I reined Old Abe up, took off my hat and held it over my heart like I was attending a funeral.

"Afternoon, kind sir," I said. "Can you give me directions to the Lyon House?"

He leaned forward in his seat, eyeing me, then my mule. He squirted brown juice at Old Abe, then pointed at the "US" branded on the animal's flank. "You a Yankee?"

"No, sir, I'm from Arkansas."

"That don't mean you ain't a Yankee. And why are you riding a Union mule?"

"He's a deserter," I replied, realizing the only thing more stubborn than a Missouri mule was a citizen of the state, maybe because they were related. "Jackass," I said, referring to the old codger.

"Your mount's a mule, not a jackass." The fellow leaned back in his rocker and crossed his arms over his chest. "You're too dumb to know the difference."

"That's why I need you to give me directions to the

Lyon House."

"Just keep going, and you'll get there."

"Jackass," I said, tugging Old Abe's reins toward Springfield.

"It's a mule, dang you," he called after me.

"I wasn't talking about him," I replied as I yanked my hat down on my head.

The aged coot blasphemed me, and I cussed him back, but it turned out he was right. I kept riding and found the Lyon House after going through town and reaching the square where the three-story stone courthouse of Greene County stood watch over the northwest corner of College Street. Most towns I was familiar with built the courthouse in the middle of the plaza, but not these Missourians. They put it on the perimeter, the only reason I could come up with being they wanted no dim-witted citizens finding it or justice within its walls. I'd never seen so much city traffic as I rode around the quadrangle, bonneted women afoot, folks in buggies and wagons, men astride horses, Yankee soldiers in pairs and me atop my mule, the smartest being I had yet met in Missouri. I made one and a half trips around the square before I saw a sign for South Street, me being too distracted by the commotion from so many citizens and troopers to spot it the first time I passed. Aiming Old Abe down the lane, I traveled two blocks farther into the city and sure enough found the Lyon House on the east side of South, just as Hickok had told me.

I spotted across the avenue a tavern with an imaginative name on the sign over the door: SALOON. What these Missourians lacked in brains they made up for with a comparable shortage of imagination. I turned Old Abe toward a hitching post and halted him in front of the building, studying the entry with fogged glass insets and the windows painted with a blue-and-gray checkerboard pattern. The panes didn't let much light in, but they also kept nosey bodies from seeing inside. I had hoped to survey the interior and see if I could figure out what the Rattle Jar was. Having no such luck from atop my mule, I dismounted and tied him to the rail. I was still young enough to have had little saloon experience, so I checked that my pistol remained secure in case I had to shoot the Rattle Jar. I tugged my hat down, took a deep breath and started for the door, weaving my way between a married couple, a uniformed Yankee carrying a rifle, and an old biddy that looked at me and pronounced, "You're not old enough to go in there."

"Is your name Jenny?" I asked.

"Gracious no, child, why do you ask?"

"You remind me of a jackass, sticking your nose in other people's feed bags."

"Why you impertinent—"

"Good day, Jenny." I tipped my hat at her and twisted the knob on the saloon entry, taking another step toward manhood.

Nervous, I shut the door too firmly, rattling the glass in the windows and drawing the stares of the dozen fellows spread around the room. It was the fanciest drinking establishment I had ever seen, in fact the first I remember entering. It wouldn't be the last. What impressed me the most was a fellow in the corner pedaling a contraption connected to a chain that turned an overhead ceiling fan to help counter the summer heat. On top of that, several customers had drinks with ice in them. I quickly realized I could get accustomed to the luxuries of big city life.

I nodded at the stares aimed at me and headed to the bar. The crowd was mixed, some with coats and ties being either gamblers or bankers, there being little difference between the two professions, and other fellows dressed in working clothes and primed to lose their hard-earned money to the gents in suits and bow-ties, either at the saloon's card tables or at the bank's loan desk. All eyes in the room followed me as I approached the counter, where I saw on the nearest end a platter of roast beef and bowls of boiled potatoes, green beans, succotash and turnips. On the bar's far end was a tall keg or something covered with a stained and tattered brown quilt.

"Where you from, boy?" asked the bartender. "You

look a little young for my trade."

"That's what the old lady outside said, but I've years enough to hold my own."

"Where you from," he repeated without calling me boy this time.

"Arkansas, sir, Cane Hill, Arkansas."

"Yeehaw," shouted a fellow in work clothes. He stood up from a table in the back corner and marched my way, grinning like I was his long lost and rich brother. He swatted me on the shoulder. "Welcome to Springfield," he said, "I'm Davis Tutt from Yellville, Arkansas, and before that a soldier for the cause."

Tutt didn't look like a supporter of any cause but his own. He had a bushy black beard and wild eyes that befitted a horse thief more than a preacher. I didn't know what to say.

"Did you serve the Confederacy?" Tutt asked me.

"I was too young."

"Ah," he replied, "unharvested seed corn for the South. It's a shame you never got a chance to polish off a few Yankees."

Tutt's remarks drew groans from half the crowd and smiles from the rest, those in working clothes.

I figured I should introduce myself, but didn't want to give my full name, thinking I'd sound older if I used just my surname. "I'm Lomax."

"Well, Lomax, let me buy you a drink."

The white-aproned bartender stepped to the counter. "What'll it be, son?"

"Lomax," I corrected him.

"Okay, Lomax, what'll you have?"

"I'm not as thirsty as I am hungry," I said to the barkeep, then turned to Tutt, "but I'm broke. Could you help me for a meal?"

Tutt backed away. "It's bad luck to buy a fellow vittles when you've offered to purchase him a drink."

I'd never heard of such an omen, so I countered, "It's even worse luck to drink on an empty stomach." I felt the hard gaze of all the eyes still staring at me.

"Two bits for grub," the bartender offered.

"A fellow I met on the outskirts of town told me I could get a free meal if I handled something he called 'the Rattle Jar.' Any truth to that?"

The saloon keeper grimaced. "You don't look to have enough starch in your collar to conquer the Rattle Jar."

"I got more starch in my collar than I do food in my stomach, good sir. That's my problem."

The barkeep kept shaking his head. "I've seen men humiliated by the Rattle Jar and run screaming from this place never to return."

"Sounds like it's bad for business," I countered.

"Who told you about the Rattle Jar," Tutt interjected.

"Some fellow I ran into outside town, a guy named Hickok, calls himself 'Wild Bill'," I answered.

"Why that reprobate shouldn't be sharing the secrets of the jar," Tutt replied. "What did he tell you?"

"Yeah," echoed the bartender. "That's how I make money."

"He didn't divulge a thing, other than I could win a free meal if I survived the Rattle Jar. Being hungry and broke as I am, it sounded like a good way to fill my belly. What is it?"

The barkeep pointed to the opposite end of the bar and the quilt-covered keg. "That," he said as he crossed his arms over his aproned chest, "is the Rattle Jar."

Whatever it was, it didn't appear that imposing, regardless of what the filthy blanket hid.

Tutt shouted, "What do you think, fellows? Should we let the kid here take on the Rattle Jar or is he too young in the britches to face its horrors? I'm betting he can't do it!"

The saloon's patrons pushed themselves away from their tables, stood up and walked toward the far end of the bar. "Let him try," one of them said.

"Whatever it is," I replied, "I bet fifty dollars I can beat it."

"Whoa, there, son," said the bartender. "I thought you told us you were broke. If you've got that much money, you can afford to buy a meal or two without having to face the Rattle Jar. It could ruin your life!"

"Maybe I fudged a tad, good sir, but I'll work for you until the fifty dollars is paid, if I lose. If I win, I'll expect my winnings and a free meal."

The drinkers laughed.

"I don't think he's got the mettle to win, though he's good at bluffing," the barkeep said as he unraveled his arms from across his chest.

Tutt scratched his chin and started to speak when the front door swung open and banged against the window, rattling the glass. Instinctively, Tutt grabbed for his pistol, then let it slide back in his holster as everyone stood staring at the latest customer, James Butler Hickok.

"Has Lomax tried the Rattle Jar yet?" Wild Bill shouted.

"Nope," answered the bartender, "we're debating whether he's old enough to risk it. We don't want to scare him into girl britches."

"No matter his age," Wild Bill replied as he shoved the door shut, rattling the glass again. "He's got a smart head on his shoulders for his years."

I suppose I was sharp of mind for my age, but then Hickok wasn't a college professor, either.

"But does he have ice water in his veins?" Tutt asked, looking from Hickok to me and back to Wild Bill.

"I say he does, and I'll cover all bets that says he can't," Hickok said as he strode to the bar. He removed his hat and scratched his perfumed hair, then reached in his pocket and slapped greenbacks on the counter.

Tutt grinned and looked at me. "I've never lost gambling against Wild Bill because he's as poor a gambler as you'll ever find. Fact is, he owes me forty dollars I've yet to collect. He'd lose with his own marked deck, so I'll be betting against you, son, even if you are from Arkansas."

That made no difference to me because I was still hungry.

"Okay, gentlemen," called the barkeep, "we'll let young Lomax here face the Rattle Jar as Hickok's covering everybody's bets."

The other men divvied up how much of Wild Bill's money they would take. Tutt became the biggest investor in my failure, thinking he could cover twenty of the fifty dollar pool. All the others took lesser amounts, each man convinced I would lose against the jar. Only Hickok believed in me, which worried me because I had questioned his intellect.

The bartender yanked a pencil and pad from a drawer in the backbar and listed the wagers against me, then winked at Hickok. "It's you against the rest of us."

"No different than when I faced down the McCanles gang, me against the world," Wild Bill bragged as he scratched his head again.

"How many was it you killed, Hickok?" Tutt taunted. "Twenty? Fifty? A thousand? The number grows every time you tell the story. And you shot them all with what, only six bullets?"

Hickok scowled, took a step toward Tutt and cat-quick reached for his vest. Tutt flinched until Wild Bill yanked his watch from his pocket. He snapped open the cover and looked at the timepiece, then at his antagonist. "Time's a wasting. If we don't settle this within the next two minutes, I'm not playing, gentlemen. Let's quit blabbering and see what Lomax is made of."

"Sure," said the bartender, checking the figures on his notepad. "It adds up to fifty dollars so all bets are covered. Us against Wild Bill and the Arkansas Kid."

"Lomax," I corrected. "I ain't no kid."

Wild Bill shut the cover of his gold watch and slid it back into his vest pocket, rocking on his heels like a man who was as proud of his timepiece as he was of his attire.

The barkeep marched to the opposite end of the bar where the others had gathered. He picked up a corner of the quilt.

Hickok grabbed me by the sleeve, yanking me toward my destiny and maybe even my dinner.

Tutt followed, laughing and advising everyone, "This will be the easiest money I've yet taken from Wild Bill."

Hickok tugged tighter on my shirt until we reached

the end of the bar.

Uncertain as I may have been about what awaited me at the Rattle Jar, I understood past animosities poisoned Tutt's and Hickok's acquaintance and I, through no fault of my own, had found myself between these two volatile men, both just weeks removed from the recent hostilities that had torn the nation asunder. I would've favored Tutt because he was from Arkansas but he had bet against me. Even though I didn't much care for Hickok, he had wagered on my behalf.

At the end of the bar, the rivals eyed each other warily while the saloon's other patrons watched the bartender as he yanked the quilt from over the Rattle Jar.

Instantly, a wicked buzzing filled the air and I focused my gaze on a huge glass jar with a tin lid screwed on top. Inside, his tail vibrating furiously and creating a sinister drone, was the largest rattlesnake I had seen.

"Okay, Arkansas Kid, here's the Rattle Jar."

"Lo—mmm—max," I stammered.

"Lomax, this is Pepper. He's undefeated in matches against men and boys of all ages."

I shook my head. What kind of mess had I gotten myself into?

My hunger didn't bother me nearly as much as the fear that to win the bet I must stick my hand in the Rattle Jar with Pepper. After that, I figured I'd have more than stomach pains to worry about. I felt my knees wobble and my hands shake as I tried to decide which one I would sacrifice for a meal I could've now done without.

"Steady, boy," said Hickok, whose grip tightened on my arm.

I nodded and hoped I wouldn't faint, especially after Pepper flicked his forked tongue my way as he continued his—or was it my?—death rattle.

Chapter 3

I have to admit I was as troubled as a Godly man at a convention of Democrats as there was no way I was escaping without being defiled. As I stared at that serpent, Pepper glared back, flicking his tongue in my direction as if he lusted to taste my flesh or whatever he struck when the bettors unscrewed the tin lid and shoved my hand inside. I'd gotten myself in a bigger mess than a public outhouse, and I saw no escape from permanent injury or even death. If I turned yellow, I feared that reputation would trail me for the rest of my life, which looked like it wouldn't last much longer than sundown on this very day. I'd never figured a little Pepper with my meal might be fatal, but these town folks played me like a rube that'd never before been to the big city. I gulped and awaited my fate.

"You can do it," Wild Bill said as he gripped my arm. "A lot of my money's riding on it."

His comment about filthy lucre troubled me. If Pepper's bite didn't kill me, then Wild Bill's anger might if I lost the bet. I'd decided I'd rather get shot than snake bit so I prepared to tell Hickok to shoot me and send my belongings back to Cane Hill so the folks'd have something to remember me by, but the bartender spoke up and saved me the trouble.

"Okay, Lomax, here's your challenge."

I took a slow, deep breath to steady my nerves before deciding if I should go through with this travesty or bolt for freedom, forever ruining my reputation as a man. Hickok tightened his grip around my arm as if he realized I might high-tail it out of there.

"All you have to do, Lomax, is place your hand on the jar and leave it there when Pepper strikes. If you keep your fingers on the glass without flinching, then you and Hickok win everybody's bets. If you recoil or move your palm off the jar, you lose and the rest of us collect."

I let out a slow breath. "You mean I don't have to stick my hand inside?"

Everyone laughed, but me.

"Good lordy, no," answered the beer baron. "What do you think we are? Barbarians?"

"The thought had entered my mind," I replied. "I'm not accustomed to big city ways."

The spectators guffawed at my comment and my fear.

"Whenever you're ready, Lomax," the bartender instructed, "put your palm on the jar."

Even though I didn't have to stick my hand inside the Rattle Jar, I was nervous as a blind man lighting a candle in a powder house. I no longer feared dying from snakebite, but rather from Wild Bill's pistol. I realized I had to outsmart everyone to keep Hickok from plugging me for losing his money. "Okay," I said, "all I've got to do is hold my fingers on the Rattle Jar and not move them when Pepper strikes. Is that right?"

"That's it, son," indicated the bartender.

"Then I'm game," I replied.

Wild Bill released his grip on my arm and at once scratched at his hair.

Reaching toward the jar, I closed my eyes and clamped my hand against the cold jar. I squeezed my eyes as tightly shut as I could and felt two thuds against the glass. I withstood them without moving a muscle."

"He did it," Wild Bill shouted.

"No he didn't, dammit," cried the bartender. "He shut his eyes."

"That's right," clamored all the losing bettors. "Lomax closed his eyes."

"Can I move my hand now?" I asked, my eyes still shut.

"Sure," said the barkeep, "but you lose the bet?"

"What the hell," cried Hickok. "The bets are mine."

"He closed his eyes, didn't even watch the Rattle Jar," answered the bartender.

I crossed my arms over my chest and shook my head. "I asked you if all I had to do was put my hand on the glass. You said yes, but not a thing about my eyes."

"That's a fact," cried my only ally in the room. "You didn't tell him to keep his eyes open."

"That was assumed, Hickok. What's the point in betting if he shuts them?" the barkeep asked.

The other patrons grumbled, but they knew Wild Bill and I were right.

"Now pay up, everyone," Wild Bill insisted.

The losers groused even louder. "This ain't proper," shouted a fellow in a derby.

"Unfair, unfair," cried another spectator.

Hickok was licking his lips, anticipating his fifty dollars in winnings. "I won fair and square." He grinned like he was as rich as a Republican politician.

"Nope," said the bartender. "It's a disputed play so nobody wins."

Several booed.

I decided it was time for me to interject myself into the argument. I spoke with a newfound confidence in my ability to outsmart Pepper and the lesser intellects in the room. "Okay, let's go two out of three times. Will that work for everyone?"

The patrons grumbled among themselves, finally agreeing that it was the only fair way to resolve this problem. The bartender surveyed his customers as they nodded their agreement. "Looks as if everyone's on board, Lomax. Two out of three it is."

Nodding, I studied my opposition, then glared at the bar man. "Okay, fellows," I said, "let me make sure everyone understands the rules since I'm so dumb and don't know your city ways. I've got to keep my eyes open and put my hand on the Rattle Jar again. If I flinch from

Pepper's strike, you fellows collect the fifty dollars. If I don't, Mr. Hickok and I claim the winnings. Is that correct?"

All nodded their approval. "That's the rules," the bartender reiterated.

I slipped my hands from my chest, spread my fingers wide on my right hand and reached toward the jar. "Okay," I called, "does everyone agree my eyes are open?"

"Yeah," they answered.

"You sure?"

"Yeah," my antagonists repeated.

"Get on with it," scowled the barkeep.

With that, I lifted my head and stared at the overhead ceiling fan as I touched the glass, instantly absorbing three thumps against the jar.

"No, no, no," cried the barkeep. "You didn't look at Pepper." All the patrons but Wild Bill booed me.

I yanked my hand from the glass and lowered my gaze from the fan blades, staring at the exasperated bartender.

"You said I had to keep my eyes open. I did just that."

"But you were looking at the ceiling," he countered.

"Yeah," agreed the losing betters.

"He did what you said," Hickok interjected. "I win."

"No you don't," cried my fellow Arkansan Davis Tutt. "That wasn't right."

I cleared my throat. "I've done everything exactly like you asked, but you keep switching the rules on me. The way I see it, I've won two out of two challenges. Do you care to go three of five?"

"Hell, no," shouted Hickok.

"Hell, yes," cried Tutt.

The barkeep shrugged and looked at his other patrons. "What do you fellows say? You want to go three out of five?"

"Sure," answered one, "what have we got to lose?"

"Fifty dollars," said Wild Bill, rubbing his hands together.

Growing in confidence, I interlocked my fingers and

stretched my arms in front of me. The last few minutes had proven how much smarter an Arkansas boy was than these Missourians, who were too dumb to recognize their own ignorance, especially if they couldn't outsmart a kid fresh off a two-bit farm in Cane Hill, Arkansas. "Okay, let me make sure I've got this straight, I have to keep my eyes open without looking at the ceiling and then place my hand on the Rattle Jar again."

"That's right," replied the bartender, "and you can't look to your left or your right or at the floor or over your shoulder. You can't look anywhere but toward the Rattle Jar."

"Hand on the glass, eyes open, looking toward the jar, not up, down, left, right or anywhere else. Is that correct?"

"Yeah," everyone agreed.

"No more monkey business," scowled my Arkansas neighbor Tutt.

I looked at Wild Bill. "You're about to be fifty dollars richer."

He tossed his head and ran his fingers through his flowing hair. "This'll be the biggest pot I've ever won."

"Because you win so few," Tutt interrupted. "You still owe me forty dollars from our last poker game."

The bartender harrumphed. "You two settle your differences elsewhere. That's why I refuse to let you play poker in my place. You always find something to fight over."

Chastised, both men turned back to me.

"Okay, Lomax," Hickok said, "show 'em what you're made of."

"Just don't cheat this time, kid," Tutt growled.

"All right, fellows," I began as I wriggled my fingers. "I want to make sure I understand the new rules. I've won the first two times, doing what you said. Correct me if I'm wrong, but the latest rules are eyes open and looking toward the Rattle Jar. Hand on glass. No flinching."

Everyone nodded.

I took a deep breath, widened my eyes as far as they

28

would go and reached for the jar. As I was about to place my right hand on the glass, I lifted my left up in front of my eyes. I touched the container and felt Pepper's single thump against the glass without even the slightest flinch of my flesh.

This time the losers reacted with groans intermixed with a few chuckles as I removed my right hand and lowered the left from my eyes.

"That's three out of three," Hickok crowed. "Pay up, boys."

Tutt screamed, "That ain't right! Lomax cheated."

Shrugging, I looked at my antagonists. "Ya'll agreed I had to look toward Pepper, which I did until my other hand got in the way. Even so, I was looking toward the Rattle Jar. Nobody said I couldn't block my eyes with my free hand. Ya'll want to go four out of seven?"

"Naw," cried the bartender. "I'm calling it quits before Pepper gets a headache from banging the jar so much."

"But the money?" Tutt shouted.

"Ya'll can decide how to handle the bets. I did this for food."

The derbied spectator slapped me on the shoulder. "I've got to admit you're skilled at shading the truth. You ought to be a lawyer."

I shrugged. "I'm not that dumb."

The bartender pointed to the roast beef and vegetables awaiting on the opposite end of the bar and motioned for me to head that direction. He pulled out a plate and utensils from under the counter and handed them to me. "The meal's on the house."

While I loaded up my dish with as much as I could pile on, the saloon keeper retreated to the other end of the bar, picking up the brown quilt and draping it over the Rattle Jar so Pepper could take a nap.

"Show me your pad," Hickok demanded of the bartender, "so I can collect my money."

I took my food to a table, plopped in a chair and gobbled the vittles down while the bettors argued with Wild Bill about what they owed him. Tutt bickered the loudest, demanding that all bets should be nullified because I had cheated. Hickok countered that I had followed the rules as stated each time, repeated by me and agreed to by everyone. Consequently, Wild Bill contended he was due the winnings in their entirety. I was on my second helping of roast beef, boiled potatoes, green beans, succotash and turnips before the fellows accepted a solution.

Because of the unusual nature of my interpretation of the rules the bartender, displaying the wisdom of Solomon, decided that the wagers should be cut in half. Everybody's bet would be reduced by fifty percent and Wild Bill would walk away with twenty-five dollars instead of fifty. The compromise satisfied everyone save for Hickok and Tutt, who kept grousing at one another, as if they were more interested in antagonizing each other than settling the issue. As the barkeep read the stakes from his pad, each loser counted out half of his bet into Wild Bill's fingers. With so much money in hand, I feared Hickok would buy himself new pantaloons or other clothing without even giving me any consideration for my skill in outfoxing this horde of dumb Missourians.

The bartender reached the bottom of the list and announced, "That's all, Hickok."

Wild Bill counted his winnings and replied, "That's only fifteen dollars. There's another ten I'm owed."

The barkeep swallowed hard and shook his head. "That's between you and Tutt. I'm not getting in the middle of that."

Hickok eyed Tutt who had slithered to a table near the door. "Pay up," he commanded.

"You owe me forty dollars from our last poker game, Hickok. After you shell that out to me, then I'll give you your ten dollars."

"That bet don't have nothing to do with this wager," Wild Bill countered. "You've got the money so pay up."

Now to my way of thinking, Hickok could have just reduced his debt to Tutt by ten bucks and the dispute would've been resolved, but that wasn't how these two men settled their differences. They enjoyed poking each other with their spurs until they drew blood.

"You boys take your dispute onto the street," the bartender ordered. "I've done what I can to make this come out as fair as possible under the circumstances. It appears Lomax is smarter than the rest of us combined."

Several of the other patrons nodded, one shouting, "Hey, we had a few laughs out of this, so drop it boys and let's have a drink."

Tutt pushed himself up from his seat, shook his head at me. "I can't believe you turned on a neighbor from Arkansas."

"You bet against me," I reminded him.

"But you cheated," Tutt insisted.

"I outwitted the bunch of you."

The barkeep laughed as did others, then pointed at the entrance. "Drop it, Tutt, or take it outside."

Tutt shoved his chair aside and exited the saloon onto the busy streets of Springfield, leaving the door open. Another patron quickly closed it, and the spirits in the room lifted instantly. As I worked on my second plate of grub, three of the imbibers who had bet against me came over and slapped me on the back, thanking me for the fun I had provided on an otherwise bland day, even if their laughs had cost them money.

Hickok strode by and sat down opposite me. "I reckon I owe you some cash."

"I couldn't cover the entire bet, just three dollars and thirty-three cents, so give me four dollars and we'll call it even."

Tugging at his mustache, Wild Bill nodded. "Tell you what I'll do, I'll give you five for bringing me good luck."

"It's a deal," I replied, proud that in less than a couple hours in Springfield, I had more than doubled my money. This city life might have potential for me to get rich.

"Besides that," he added, "I'll let you share my room in the Lyon House. We can partner up for a while."

"I'm obliged," I said. "You gonna be practicing your pistoleering any in your room?"

Hickok glared at me, then looked from side to side to see if anyone had overheard my comment. That's when

I realized Hickok was a touchy fellow about his affairs and other people knowing his business. For that reason, he practiced his gunplay miles outside of town. Indeed, I had promised him back at the creek that I wouldn't tell folks I'd seen him working on his draw, then broken that promise, even if accidentally, in conversation.

Satisfied that no one had overheard my offhand comment, Hickok growled at me through clenched teeth. "Those are things we don't talk about when others are within hearing distance."

"Gotcha," I replied. "Wasn't thinking."

"As long as you keep bringing me good luck, I can overlook your mistakes, but don't let it happen again, Lomax."

"Sure thing, Wild Bill," I said as I finished the dregs from my second plate of food. I had a full belly, eight dollars and thirty-three cents to my name and a roof over my head for the first time since I left Arkansas.

Hickok waved at the bartender and ordered a beer. He pulled his timepiece from his pocket and checked the time as he awaited his drink.

"Nice watch," I said.

"It was my father's. My only possession of his."

After the bartender arrived with his mug, Hickok stowed his timepiece and sipped at his beer, mired in thought as the barkeep took my plate and utensils.

"How long have you known Davis Tutt?" I asked.

"Since the war ended and we both wound up in Springfield. We don't agree on much."

"That's plain to see. What kind of gambler is he?"

"About the worst around," Hickok answered. "Only reason he wins is because he cheats."

"Then why don't you quit playing cards with him?"

Hickok lifted the mug to his mouth, took a healthy swallow, then looked at me over the rim as he sat the goblet back down on the table. He studied me, as if trying to decide if he could trust me with the answer.

I prompted him. "Why play poker with him?"

"I intend to catch him cheating."

"If you know he cheats, why do you need to confirm his deceitful card playing?"

"So I can kill him," he replied as sincerely as if he was teaching a Sunday School lesson.

I decided in that instant not to play any cards with James Butler Hickok.

Chapter 4

The Lyon House was the finest facility I ever spent a
night in, even if I slept on the floor in Hickok's room.
On top of that, they had out back a stable made from
saw-milled lumber and sturdier built than a lot of the
houses we called homes in Arkansas. Old Abe took to
his quarters and didn't mind the company. Of course,
he had better roommates than I did.

After considerable thought, I decided rooming with
Hickok, even for free, was risky, especially if he practiced
his gun handling. On the other hand, the Lyon House
was as luxurious as any place I had ever stayed, boast-
ing fine carpets, polished glass lamps, shiny spittoons,
upholstered mahogany furniture and a registration
desk that could have doubled as a bar in a small saloon.
Hickok introduced me as his cousin to the proprietor, a
slender fellow with narrow eyes, a thin nose and a wisp
of a mustache, and insisted that I be allowed to stay at
no charge. As Hickok was reputed as a bad man to fool
with, the Lyon House owner agreed my temporary stay
presented no concerns.

Examining me with those lean eyes, he clasped his
hands in front of his suit coat and said, "Welcome to
Springfield, Mr. Lomax."

No one had ever called me mister before so I was
proud of my elevation to adulthood.

The proprietor pointed to a large school bell on the
polished counter. "Any time you hear the bell ring, Mr.

Lomax, it means the sheriff or marshal has entered the hotel. If you are taking part in any unseemly activities, you should suspend them until the law officers leave the premises."

"What he's saying," said Hickok, "is that if you are in a poker game upstairs or bedding the preacher's wife, you must conclude those activities so as not to defame the good name of the Lyon House. The proprietor keeps a room upstairs for poker away from public view. City ordinances don't always favor gambling so it's where we can play cards without the law looking over our shoulders."

I nodded. "That's good to know, though I won't be up there."

Hickok shook his head. "Yes, you will."

"I don't have enough money to gamble."

"You won't be betting," Hickok informed me. "You'll be my lucky horseshoe, my good luck totem." He turned to the proprietor. "Did you hear that Lomax defeated the Rattle Jar this afternoon? Three times, he did it. Not once did he flinch."

The hostler looked at me with a new found respect. "Congratulations, Mr. Lomax. We are delighted to have you staying with us."

Hickok pointed down the hallway. "Let me show you our room."

I followed him past the swanky furniture along cushioned carpets that made my feet feel like they were walking on a feather mattress. I could grow accustomed to this hotel living.

At the door to No. 10, Hickok fished a key from his pocket, put it in the lock and released the pin for us to enter.

"Why didn't you get a room upstairs since it would take the law longer to climb the steps?"

"You always want one on the first floor, Lomax, in case you have to leave by a window. Mine looks out on a side alley."

Apparently, Hickok possessed a bad conscience. As for me, mine was clear, at least for the moment. It wouldn't be by the time I departed Springfield in a week.

We entered the room, dimmed by a drawn shade that vibrated from the breeze seeping through the open window. Hickok closed and latched the door behind him, then pointed to a bed with the thickest mattress I had ever seen in my life. "It's big enough for us to share," he announced. As I considered the invitation, Hickok yanked off his hat, tossed it on the bed and scratched his head with the fury of a gopher trying to dig a hole.

I'd bunked on the same mattress with my brothers growing up, but not with a fellow I'd only met hours earlier. That fluffy bedding was sure tempting, but his head-scratching worried me. "I'll just toss my bedroll on the floor as I'm so accustomed to sleeping on the hard ground, I don't want grow soft for when I have to leave."

Hickok grimaced as he yanked at his hair. "Damn head lice!"

Now I knew for certain I wouldn't be dozing with Hickok as I didn't want to depart Springfield with a colony of varmints in my hair.

"You ever had lice, Lomax?"

"Not that I remember," I answered. "In Arkansas we had a cure. First time a momma found a head louse on her baby boy, she plucked it and gathered everyone around the family Bible. When they'd all assembled, she dropped the louse on the Good Book and popped that little booger. Once past that ritual, the little boy was free of lice for life, so my momma said. Don't know if it worked on girls, but it did on boys because I never had lice."

"We didn't have a Bible that I remember growing up," Hickok said.

"Perhaps you're doomed."

"I've tried everything to get rid of them. No luck."

"I've heard the only sure way is to shave your head and soak it in vinegar for a week until it kills all their eggs, the nits."

"Nobody's cutting my hair, no Indian, no white man, no black barber, nobody."

I shrugged. "Only other way I know is to get a nit

comb and run it through your hair for several days and then rinse your head each night with vinegar. As much hair as you've got, I wouldn't guarantee that."

Hickok nodded. "I may want to try that. It's the second good idea you've shared with me today."

"What's the first?"

Turning his back to me, Wild Bill stepped to the bed and yanked his revolvers out of their holster, practicing his draw and returning the pistols to the leather. He repeated the process three more times until the gun flew out of his hand and landed softly and silently on the mattress. "It didn't go off," Hickok said in amazement.

"Gophers and ground squirrels throughout Missouri are celebrating a brighter future," I answered as I looked around the room. Beside the bed stood a shaving stand with a pitcher and wash basin on top and a mirror tacked to the wall. Near the window rested a four-drawer dresser with a couple spare hats atop it. In the adjacent corner sat a two-door, solid oak wardrobe that must have weighed a hundred and fifty pounds. I strode over to the furniture piece, passing two matching oak chairs, and grabbed the handles to open both doors. Squeezed into the cabinet were pants, frock coats, shirts and vests, more outfits than my mother and sisters had combined. On the positive side, they didn't have nearly as many lice as Wild Bill did. I reached for the arm of one coat and saw it was stained. I inspected a couple shirts and discovered they were dirty. It seemed Wild Bill spent more money buying clothes than laundering them. At least Momma kept clean what few garments we Lomaxes owned, and that was likely why lice had never plagued our family.

Hickok continued drawing, re-holstering and scratching his head as if I wasn't even there.

Bored, I decided I'd go out back to retrieve my bedroll and rifle. "I'm heading to the stable to bring in my things," I announced.

Hickok stopped his gunplay, turned around and nodded. "That's a good idea. While you're out, would you do me a favor?"

"Sure thing."

"Let me give you money so you can stop by the druggist and buy a nit comb and a gallon of vinegar. We're gonna try out your remedy for the head lice."

I feared this "we" stuff, but didn't know how to avoid his expectations. "Sure you don't want me to get a set of shears and a razor to shave it bald. That's the only guarantee."

"Nobody's cutting my hair, Lomax!"

"I suppose you're right. It didn't turn out well for Samson."

"Who?"

"Samson."

Hickok looked as perplexed as a preacher in a whorehouse.

"You know, Samson and Delilah?"

He scratched his head again, trying to scrape together a coherent thought on Samson rather than trying to kill a louse for a change.

I wasn't a Bible scholar, but I knew the story of Samson and was surprised Wild Bill had no inkling of the strongest man in history. "It don't matter," I said. "I'll get your vinegar and nit comb for you."

Hickok nodded. "I'd be obliged." He stopped scratching his head and practicing his draw long enough to fish a couple dollars out of his pocket. "This should cover it." He handed me the money, turned to the bed and yanked his pistol free of its holster without dropping it on the mattress.

"I'll be back in a bit," I said as I exited the room and closed the door behind me. I stopped at the desk and asked the proprietor for directions to the nearest druggist. He directed me to an emporium on the square. I stepped outside and off the hotel porch where a couple fellows sat in rocking chairs, discussing the fate of the world. Retracing my steps to the square, I found a pharmacist about to close up shop. I slid in before he could lock the door and told him I needed a nit comb and a gallon of vinegar. He retrieved the comb and charged me a dime, but informed me he didn't carry vinegar.

The druggist said he would sell me a gallon of rubbing alcohol, but I'd always understood that prolonged use of vinegar was the only sure way to destroy lice and their nits so I declined his offer and scurried outside, hoping to find a grocer before he closed.

As I slipped the comb with the narrow teeth in my pocket, I looked around, spotting a mercantile across the square. I dashed the seventy-five yards to the store and ran in out of breath, though I realized I could have walked when I saw a sign in the door that the merchant would stay open for another hour. I asked for a gallon of vinegar, but the clerk said he was sold out of that size, though he could give me a two-gallon tin. Deciding two gallons were better than one as much hair as Hickok had, I bought the tin for forty cents and lugged it back to the hotel.

Reaching the Lyon House winded, I stepped up on the porch where the two fellows who had been discussing the world's problems stopped their conversation and eyed me. "Can't afford whiskey?" the nearest one asked. I was too breathless to respond so I went inside with their laughter trailing in my wake and made my way to Hickok's room. As I opened the door and walked in, Hickok spun around from the bed and jerked his revolver from its holster.

"Don't shoot," I screamed, "and don't drop the pistol either."

"You shouldn't startle me," he answered as he shoved his revolver back in its scabbard.

"I figured you'd expect me when you sent me on your errand." I dropped the tin of vinegar by the washstand and pulled the nit comb from my pants pocket, placing it on the stand by the wash basin. Then I plucked Hickok's change from my britches and offered the bill and coins to him.

"Put it on the bed," he said, scratching his head.

"Fine," I said, "but now I'll fetch my bedroll and my carbine. Don't pull your gun on me when I return."

He gave a half-hearted nod as I exited the room and headed out the back door to the stable. I still couldn't believe that the hotel folks had used such fine lumber for a stable, but they had and Old Abe was sure proud to be residing in those luxurious quarters. "E-e-e-e-onk! E-e-e-e-onk, onk, onk!" he brayed.

"And, good day to you, too, Old Abe. I came to get my carbine, my bedroll and my saddlebags," I announced as I entered his stall and fetched my belongings. As I stroked his neck, he nuzzled against my face until I could slip past and gather my possessions. I squeezed back out of the stall. When I was clear, I decided to see if this high living had affected Old Abe's sensibilities. I shouted, "Jefferson Davis."

Instantly, my mule brayed and kicked his rear legs, his hind hooves flashing in the air, quick as lightning and just as devastating if you were in the way. I was glad to see this fancy Yankee living wasn't changing his outlook on life or on old Jefferson Davis.

I toted my belongings back to Hickok's room and dropped the saddlebags and bedroll in the hallway as I twisted the doorknob slowly and pushed the door open with the barrel of my leveled carbine. As it swung silently on the hinges, I tip-toed into the room as Hickok shoved his pistol back in its holster.

"I'm back," I said.

Hickok jumped and spun around, his hand instinctively going to the butt of his revolver, then stiffening when he realized I had the carbine pointed at his gut. "Damn, Lomax, don't sneak up on me."

"Hell, fellow, what do you expect me to do? I come in normal and you almost shoot me. I enter quietly and you think I'm sneaking up on you. What do you want me to do, have a bugler announce my arrival every time?" I lowered my weapon.

Hickok laughed. "My past has taught me to be cautious."

I leaned the carbine up against the wall. "I'm stepping back into the hallway to get the rest of my stuff, Hickok, so don't shoot me when I return in five seconds." I retreated outside and grabbed my possessions before re-entering the room. Wild Bill remained calm this time. "That's more like it," I told him. "Why are you so jumpy?"

Hickok stared at me, then sat down on the edge of the mattress. "It goes back to the McCanles fight four years ago."

"That's the one Davis Tutt mentioned in the saloon."

Hickok nodded. "Nasty affair. I shiver whenever I recall it, and sometimes I even dream about it and wake up in a cold sweat. Dave McCanles headed a gang of desperadoes, murderers and regular cut-throats, and McCanles was the biggest scoundrel and bully of them all. Worst of all, he was a Reb sympathizer, and after the war started we had had run-ins enough to boil our blood." Wild Bill's words dripped venom every time he mentioned his foe.

"I was scouting for the Union Cavalry when I stopped at Rock Creek Station in southern Nebraska. I was talking to the manager's wife when I heard the gang ride up. I recognized McCanles voice when he pointed out my horse and told his men he would get me." Hickok's lips tightened like his face as his fingers patted the handle of a revolver.

"You okay?" I asked.

He shrugged. "It gives me goose bumps, thinking how close I came to dying that day, especially since I only had one revolver on me. I tell you this, after that day I've gone nowhere without a pistol on both hips. McCanles came in, revolver drawn, but I was waiting with a single shot rifle from the station and shot him when he pointed his gun at me. Then his men rushed me. There were seven, eight or nine of them. With my pistol I shot five with six slugs, then the rest rushed me, shooting me with bird guns and attacking me with gun stocks and knives when we all ran out of ammunition."

I could tell the memory upset him. "No need to continue."

Wild Bill shook his head. "Once I start something, I finish it. I broke one of their arms, stabbed another fellow with my knife and took the shotgun away from a third scoundrel and beat him to death with it. When I finished, there were eight or nine dead."

"Damn," I said. "I never heard of such a fight. How bad were you hurt?"

Scratching his head, he grimaced. "I took eleven buckshot, some of them I still carry in me to this day. I was cut in thirteen different places, some wounds potentially fatal, but the doctor pulled me through it after several weeks of care."

"It was the closest call I've ever had, including my time with the Army during the War of the Rebellion."

I let out a deep breath. If it was true, Hickok was tough enough to sort bobcats for a living. I was ready to change the subject for Bill's sake as well as mine so I moved to the window to lift the shade and let in more light from the dying afternoon sun.

"When do you plan to attack your head lice and nits? It's gonna take you a long time to get 'em out."

Hickok looked from me to the tin of vinegar on the floor. "I figured you'd comb them out for me, Lomax. It's your idea."

"Yeah," I protested, "but it's your head."

"I can't see the back of my head, can I? Besides that, I'm providing you a room at no charge."

Much as I wanted to argue, I knew he had me. Just like these city folks to take advantage of a kid fresh off an Arkansas farm.

Now Hickok decided to change the subject, at least until the morning. "Won't be long before supper time. We'll start in the morning," Hickok announced. "You hungry?"

"Not especially, not after two heaping plates for lunch at the saloon, but I learned on the ride up here to never pass up food because you don't know when you might get more grub."

"Then nothing fancy tonight," Hickok said. "We'll go to the library. There'll be snacks up there."

To be honest, I was unfamiliar with libraries. "Can you explain what a library is?"

"It's a place where they keep books."

"Then what's a library got to do with food?"

"Nothing, but you'll see in a few minutes."

Other than the Bible, we didn't have many books back in Cane Hill. Too, I wasn't much of a reader or book man, but I had never been in a library before, so I had to see one. "I'm game," I replied, not knowing I had just taken the first step in a series of events that would result in me leaving Springfield in a week and Wild Bill standing trial for murder.

Chapter 5

Our trip to the library turned out to be nothing more than a climb up the stairs of the Lyon House. Wild Bill wore striped pants, vest, frock coat, and gold pocket watch with matching chain. He left his twin pistols in the room as weapons were banned in the library. Wild Bill looked good enough to attend a funeral, even his own. At the far end of the hallway, Hickok rapped the door with his knuckles. "Wild Bill and friend," he announced. Momentarily, I heard the groan of a latch being pulled and saw the door cracking, an eye staring at us to confirm Hickok was who he said he was.

"Welcome, Bill" said our host, who admitted us, though he eyed me suspiciously as he closed the door and slid the bolt back in place.

Inside I looked around. It wasn't much of a library with just a single bookcase and a hundred and fifty substantial but well-worn volumes sitting on the shelves. Beside the bookcase stood a four-drawer dresser identical to the one in Hickok's room. A round table covered with green felt occupied the middle of the room with six wooden chairs around it and a thick book at each seat. One fellow sat at the table, playing solitaire with a new deck of cards. Around the wall sat other chairs for spectators.

Hickok introduced me to Taylor, the doorman, and Chris, the card player, then clawed at his head and the little tormentors that made him to itch. Taylor stood a full head shorter than me with thick black hair and glasses while Chris was gaunt with close-cropped brown hair.

"Are you the Lomax that took on the Rattle Jar today?" Taylor asked.

I nodded.

"We heard about that," Chris said. "We won't put up with such chicanery when we play poker."

"I didn't come to gamble," I answered. "I wanted to see the library."

"A bookish fellow are you?" Taylor asked.

"Lomax is my lucky horseshoe," interjected Hickok. "I won all the bets on the Rattle Jar thanks to his iron nerves."

"More like his cheating folks out of their good money," Chris replied.

Hickok laughed. "He followed their rules each time he won. If they'd specified all the stipulations before he started, they might have prevailed. Even losing, they left laughing."

"Davis Tutt wasn't grinning when he left from what I've heard," Taylor said. "Fact is, he's still mad about it."

"Is he going to be here tonight?" Hickok asked.

"Don't know," Chris said as he gathered up his cards and shuffled the deck. "If he shows up, I don't plan on being caught in the middle between you two."

"No need to fret," Hickok answered. "I'm not playing with him until he pays me the ten dollars he owes me for betting against Lomax."

"Tutt says you owe him forty dollars." Taylor walked around in front of Hickok to take his full measure.

"That I won't deny, and I'll pay him the forty after he coughs up my ten bucks."

"Why don't you subtract the ten from what you owe him and give him thirty bucks, square all of this up?" Chris asked.

"Because he's won so much of my money in the past, I want the pleasure of seeing him pay up for a change."

"This'll lead to nothing but trouble," Taylor observed.

Hickok shrugged. "Only if Tutt starts it."

"This is your gambling room, not a library, isn't it?" I asked Bill.

My roommate laughed. "You're real quick on the uptake, Lomax."

"You might say it's both," Taylor explained. With a sweep of his arm, he directed my attention to the shelves. "There's much hidden in books." He stepped to the table and picked up one. "If the law comes while we're gambling, we start reading as soon as we hear the front desk ring the bell."

"Open the book, Taylor," Hickok ordered.

The short fellow spread the jaws of a thick book, and I saw that the center of the middle pages had been cut out. "When the hand bell jingles, we put our cards and our stakes inside the books, turn the pages to the beginning and are reading at our table when the sheriff or marshal walks in."

"You might call this our reading circle," Chris said.

"Who hides the pot?" I asked.

"The dealer takes it," Hickok explained. "We don't let the dealer play to avoid any accusations of cheating."

"Ya'll got it figured out," I said, "but I thought Bill told me there would be food."

All three pointed to the dresser. "Top two drawers," Hickok and Taylor said.

I ambled over to the cabinet and opened the top drawer, finding a bowl of boiled eggs, a platter of biscuits and a tin of jerked beef. Shutting that drawer, I pulled the second and saw a big container of popcorn and a smaller one of peanuts. I grabbed a handful of popcorn and plopped it in my mouth while I looked around for a plate or a bowl for a sizeable helping.

"Any dishes?" I asked.

"Nope," said Chris, "you have to make do."

I strode over to the bookcase and removed a thick volume from the top shelf. Expecting to find its innards gone, but no one had taken a knife to its inside pages. I grabbed another, then one from the second shelf and both volumes were still intact. "Are any books fixed other than those on the table?"

"Grab one from the bottom shelf. They've all been scalped," Taylor said.

I took the biggest volume I saw from the lowest shelf, opened it a third of the way and saw the great cavity inside. Stepping to the dresser, I opened the second drawer and scooped our four handfuls of popcorn to fill the void in the volume. Then I retreated to a seat along the wall and ate my popcorn while I waited for the poker to begin. I had never enjoyed a book as much as the one I was holding in my lap.

While I was munching on my snack, Wild Bill sat at the table facing me. As I learned was his habit, he pulled his gold Waltham watch from his vest pocket, released it from the chain, snapped open the cover and put the timepiece on the table by his book. With the watch in front of him, he kept up with the time he was losing as well as the money he would forfeit if he was as bad a gambler as Tutt had indicated. He and Chris played betless blackjack until others arrived. All Hickok did was scratch his head and lose each hand of the cards. I wondered if he could even count to twenty-one as the dealer would have wiped him out had they been playing for cash. Four other men eventually showed up to play. Fortunately, Davis Tutt was not among them. They were introduced as Lester, Hardy, Morris and Peter. The fellows took their place at the library table while Taylor retreated to the dresser to fetch a boiled egg, then came over and sat by me.

As Taylor peeled his hen fruit, the gamblers got out their money and placed it by their books as Chris dealt the cards. Hickok dumped his ten dollars on the table by his watch and nodded to his opponents. What little conviviality there had been turned serious once the poker began. From where I sat, I watched Hickok's face and movements. Now I was no card sharp, but I have to say he was the worst gambler I ever saw. A blind man could've read his expressions without having to see his hand, he was that obvious. He cocked his head, licked his lips and grinned on good deals and lowered his chin and scowled on poor hands. Wild Bill was the only gambler I ever saw that could cheat and still lose his shirt, pants and boots with his own marked deck. When he wasn't giving away his hand, he was scraping his head. Those lice must have been worrying the devil out of him.

On his good hands, his opponents folded, yet he seldom tossed in a poor draw, so his challengers stayed in and called his bluffs. If all Yankees were as bad at bluffing as Wild Bill, I wondered how they won the War of the Rebellion, as Hickok called it.

"Everybody likes to play poker with Wild Bill," Taylor said as he finished eating his egg. "He has a great skill at losing, always scratching his head like he can't figure out what to do before the play or how he lost afterwards."

"Too much piss and not enough vinegar," I answered, knowing I'd give him a vinegar shampoo in the morning. As touchy as Bill was, though, I wanted no one else to know he had head lice or he might shoot me intentionally rather than accidentally.

I finished a couple more books of popcorn before Wild Bill went bust. He stretched his arms and yawned, then scratched his head. "Fellows, I fear I must retire."

The others groaned because the source of the easiest money they had made in days was calling it quits. "We've got time for you to take out a loan," said Hardy.

"We enjoy your company, Bill," Peter added.

"Your luck's bound to change," Lester noted.

Taylor nudged me with his elbow. "I thought Lomax was your lucky horseshoe."

Hickok looked my way and shrugged. "I did too."

"Maybe Lomax is only lucky when he's playing with snakes," Chris said, grinning as he looked at me. "Perhaps he can bring his vaunted good luck and cash to the table the next time we play. His money'll spend as well as Bill's."

"I'm no match for you boys," I answered as I stood up, turned my open book downward and slapped it on the spine to knock out any popcorn flakes onto the floor. I returned my tome to the bottom shelf and stepped over to Hickok, who was staring at the spot on the table where his earlier winnings had waited to make more. Those spoils were now in the pockets of Lester, Hardy, Morris and Peter, and all he had was his watch, which he picked up, hooked back on its chain and slid into his vest pocket.

"Good evening, gentlemen," Hickok said as he and I departed.

After we exited the library, Wild Bill admitted he had lost his gains from the Rattle Jar bets earlier in the day. I didn't answer because I feared being overheard as we walked down the stairs. Once we got back to his room, I would cut loose on him. As I locked the door behind us and he lit a lamp, I let him have it.

"You're the worst gambler I've ever seen, Bill."

Flames flared in his eyes as he shook the glow from the match and replaced the globe on the lamp. "What do you know about gambling? You're just a snot-nosed kid from Arkansas."

"Maybe so, but I didn't lose any money in the library. Watching you gamble is like reading a book. When you get a good hand, you cock your head and grin or lick your lips. When you have a poor deal, you lower your chin and frown or scratch your head."

"I can't help it, not with these head lice."

"Then we're starting tonight, not waiting until the morning."

"Starting what?"

"The treatment, Bill. Strip to your union suit and I'll comb the nits out of your hair."

"That can wait until tomorrow."

"Not if I'm staying with you. I want to get rid of them before they migrate to me and make my life a mess."

My roommate grumbled but undressed, though it took awhile with all the clothing he had adorned himself with. After attending his business in the chamber pot, he sat in the chair I had move by the light. I grabbed the nit comb and started at his forehead, working my way down strands of hair that reached to his shoulder. I worked for two hours, extracting the nits and holding them over the lamp to fry. When I finished, I filled the wash basin with vinegar and had Hickok rinse his hair in the tart liquid. He complained about the aroma as it wasn't as sweet as the perfume he preferred.

"That tonic water may be to lice what good whiskey is to you, Bill. So soak yourself with the vinegar and drive those vermin out of your hair forever."

"It stinks."

"Good. Perhaps it'll scare the lice away. Maybe they'll find a new home on Davis Tutt. You'd be okay with that, wouldn't you?"

"I need a drink," he answered.

"Swallow all the vinegar you want," I said as he dipped the top of his head in the wash basin and ran his vinegary fingers through his chestnut locks.

"No, check the bottom dresser drawer. I've got whiskey in there."

I dropped the nit comb in the basin and crossed the room opening the drawer and finding six bottles of whiskey lying side by side like brown-glass sentinels. The flasks held more expensive liquor than I had ever seen, much less tasted. I grabbed one by the neck and carried it to my roommate. "Hell, Bill, why don't you soak your head in whiskey after this. You've got plenty."

"No, sir," he shot back. "I'm using it myself. I not even going to share it with you, no more luck than you brought me tonight." He took a towel and dried his head.

"You do what I say, Bill, and by Friday, five days from now, I guarantee you'll be a winner."

"That's big talk for a snot-nosed kid from Arkansas." He yanked the bottle from my hand, twisted the cork out of the neck and took a healthy swig. His hair reeked of vinegar and his breath of liquor, which was better than I smelled after the time I'd spent on the trail to Springfield.

I returned the chair to its place, rolled out my bedroll near the window and lay down to enjoy the gentle breeze as it entered the room. Bill suckled on his bottle, then blew out the lamp. I had a restless night, uncertain what the next day would bring and whether Hickok would throw me out of his room or continue the treatment for the lice.

Bill awoke in a decent mood. "Lomax," he whispered, "are you awake?"

"I am now," I answered. "What is it?"

"I want another treatment this morning and one this evening."

"It'd be easier on me to shave your head and get out of town as fast as I could."

"Not if I caught you, it wouldn't."

"Fine, I'll do it, but you've got to pay for me a bath this afternoon."

"There's a communal tub down the hall. I'll have the proprietor reserve it and heat water for you."

"I need a change of clothes, too."

"Okay, Lomax. We'll get whatever you want."

"No," I replied, "I'll get it myself, but if I'm gonna do this, I want to get an early start, like now."

"Fine by me," Hickok answered, throwing back the covers and sitting up on the edge of his mattress.

I crawled to his bed and pulled out the chamber pot, attending my business, then getting up and placing the chair by the window where I could enjoy the cool morning breeze. Hickok fished the nit comb out of the vinegar-filled basin and brought it over. Again, I started at the forehead and combed over the top of his head and down the back all the way to the shoulders, the vermin eggs much fewer than the previous evening. This time I scraped them off the comb onto the window sill and used my boot to smash them before brushing the residue outside. While I finished up, Wild Bill stepped to the basin without complaint and again rinsed his head and hair in the vinegar.

As I dressed, Bill toweled off his hair and began combing it to speed the drying. He smelled like the trash can behind a Chinese kitchen.

Needing fresh air, I told him I planned to head to the square and find a clothier for some new duds. He said he wanted to help me out.

51

"No," I told him, "I'll manage on my own." I feared he would dandy me up in his style of fancy clothes, but I lacked both the funds and the inclinations to walk around Springfield or anywhere else in such attire.

"Let me loan you money," he offered.

"I don't care to be indebted to anybody. Besides that, didn't you lose everything?"

He walked past me to his wardrobe and pulled open a door, sticking his right hand in and exploring the pockets of one of his frock coats. "This is my bank," he said, pulling out a handful of bills and offering them to me. "Most of these pockets have money in them. I never know how much and don't care as long as the bills are there."

On my person, I had eight dollars and thirty-three cents. I knew that like I knew my own name, and I was astounded that anyone was so casual about money, especially someone that seemed to lose it so easily. I hesitated to take the cash.

"Go ahead," he implored me.

"I'm not borrowing from you."

"Then it's a gift," Bill said, shaking the bills at me. "Buy your needs on me."

Nodding, I took the currency and thumbed through nine dollars. I had more than doubled my wealth, I thought, as I shoved the money in my britches pocket. "Okay, but I'm buying clothes for me, not for you, and it's not a loan."

"Agreed," Hickok answered.

"And, you'll arrange for me a bath here this afternoon?"

"I will. Just look at the money and the bath as payment for treating the head lice and helping me to win at the poker table."

"You haven't won yet, Bill."

"Yeah, but you promised I would by Friday."

"Bill, I was just prattling on, trying to get your attention. It wasn't a guarantee or a promise."

"Maybe not to you, Lomax, but it was to me."

I gulped. "What happens if you don't win?"

Hickok grinned. "Let's just say you'll be wearing new clothes for your funeral."

Chapter 6

In a clothier next to the courthouse, I purchased my new duds with care, wondering if I'd wind up by Friday wearing them forever in a pine box buried in Missouri dirt. I bought a pair of long johns, two shirts, two pants, two pairs of socks and a straw hat for eight dollars and thirty-five cents. The clerk took my money, handed me my new headgear and wrapped my other purchases in brown paper and twine. I tucked the bundle under my arm, put on my new bonnet and stepped out onto the square to enjoy the sun and the people who seemed to be everywhere. Strolling by the courthouse, I admired the three-story building's arched entry and the four stone columns that rose above the entrance to the roof. The county structure, unadorned with any marker designating its importance, stared solemnly across the square at neighbors sporting gaudy sign boards for confections, clothing, guns, hardware, groceries, leather goods and tinware.

None too eager to return to the hotel and Hickok, I strolled around the square, enjoying the flurry of activity as men, women and children scurried about their business or leisure, a grocer wrestling a fifty-pound sack of flour into a wagon, a little girl playing with a paper doll, two fellows arguing over politics, riders heading in all directions, and a portly woman carrying an umbrella over her head and complaining about the heat. Cane Hill had never generated so much commotion as this.

Tired of lugging my new outfits around, I headed back down South Street toward the hotel, but stopped instead across the way in the saloon where I had survived the vaunted Rattle Jar. When I stepped in and closed the door, the bartender greeted me as I was his first patron of the day.

"Well, if it isn't the Arkansas Kid, the cunningest fellow in Missouri. Did you return to face Pepper again?"

I grinned. "Depends on how much you folks are willing to bet this time."

"Nobody in this place is betting a thing with you until we can hire a lawyer to draw up the rules and get your signature to abide by those rules and accept the outcome. Pepper was so woozy after the beating you gave him that he still can't crawl in a straight line."

"You need a smarter rattlesnake," I suggested.

"Or a dumber customer," the barkeep countered.

"Let bygones be bygones. I came for a bite to eat."

The proprietor glanced at the clock on the backbar. "It'll be another twenty or thirty minutes before we bring out any food. This lunch will not be on the house."

I patted my pocket. "I'm good for it."

"Have a seat, but keep your back to the wall as a lot of my customers might like to take a shot at you."

Grabbing a chair against the far wall, I looked at the pedal rig that powered the ceiling fan. "Where's your man that runs the fan?"

"Cooking the food."

"What's on the menu and how much?"

"Two bits, paid in advance, for fried chicken, mashed potatoes, green beans and gravy. Water's free but a beer or whiskey costs you extra."

I dug into my britches and fished out a quarter, flipping it toward the bartender, who snatched it out of the air and slid it in his pocket. "I'll take a water with ice in it."

"That'll cost you a nickel more."

"I thought you said the water was free."

"It is, but the ice isn't."

"Well, good sir, I've got a question for you."

"Shoot."

"What forms ice?"

"Water."

"So, if the ice is water and water doesn't cost a cent, why must I pay you another nickel to have frozen water in my water?"

"Damn, Lomax, is all you do argue?"

"And win bets."

"Okay," he conceded. "Free ice water today, but not the next time or the time after that or ever again."

I removed my new straw hat and placed it on my bundle of clothes, then smiled. "You win."

Grumbling, the bartender sauntered into the back to check on the food. When he disappeared, two customers came in and shook their heads when they saw me.

"Not him again!" said one.

"Good day to you as well, gentlemen."

They laughed and grabbed a table on the opposite side of the saloon near the Rattle Jar while I remained at the end of the counter where the food would be served. The bartender returned with my ice water. I sipped the drink, and it was like swallowing liquid heaven. The amenities of big city life could sure grow on a fellow, I decided.

When I sat the glass down, the bartender eyed me, then smirked. "I thought you was Wild Bill's lucky horseshoe."

"I am."

"That's not what I heard after last night's action in the gambling room. I hear the fellows cleaned him out."

"Bill's luck's a changing. I promised him he'd be raking in the bucks by Friday."

"This Friday?"

I nodded.

"God, himself, couldn't change Wild Bill's luck when he's sober, much less when he's drunk."

"He was sober last night."

"And still lost from what folks say."

"He'll get better."

My liquor-dispensing antagonist shook his head.

55

"He can't get any more sober than sober, but he can damn sure get drunker than drunk."

"My luck'll rub off on him."

"You're damn cocky for a kid fresh out of Arkansas!"

"No, just smarter than you Missouri rabble."

The barkeep turned at the sound of platters being placed on the counter as his cook and pedal pusher brought in the first of the food. My debating pal retreated behind the bar and pulled out a plate for me. "I'd give you a dirty one but we've washed them all, same with the utensils."

"Obliged as always," I said as I stepped up to the bar and put three chicken breasts on my dish as the cook returned with bowls of mashed potatoes and green beans. I helped myself to the vegetables as he brought out the gravy and biscuits. I broke two of the biscuits apart, slathered them with gravy and returned to my table, taking my time to eat lunch. As I ate, several regulars entered and acknowledged my return, but none came to join me.

I dreaded facing Hickok again so it was about an hour after high sun before I gathered my new hat and my bundle to head to the hotel. Knocking on the door to No. 10, I announced myself, then entered. Wild Bill stood by the bed, practicing his draw. The first thing I noticed was that he was no longer scratching his head that often. The treatment was working, at least I hoped it was, if I was to get him to concentrate on his gambling.

"Took you a long time to buy clothes," he said, shoving his gun in his holster and checking his timepiece.

"Decided I'd eat lunch at the saloon across the street. They love me over there."

"I bet they do the way you outsmarted them." He pointed at his gold watch. "It's ten after one. You're scheduled for the bath tub for an hour, starting in twenty minutes. They'll provide soap and towels. You have little more than peach fuzz for whiskers, but if you want to take my razor and strop you're welcome to it."

"Just as well," I answered. "Don't know the next time I'll have a chance to bathe."

Hickok gestured to his shaving gear. I nodded, went to a chair and untied my bundle of clothes. I undid my gun belt and left my revolver behind. Next I picked a set of the clean duds, removed my new straw hat and left it atop my remaining garments. I grabbed Bill's shaving utensils and trudged down the hall to my first bath in Missouri. A hotel attendant had filled the iron tub with hot water and was waiting for me when I arrived. He pointed to the soap and towels, informing me I had to be out in an hour, then exited. I placed my fresh clothes on a stool and took the shaving implements. Slapping the razor against the strop, I honed it for a moment and left it balanced on the edge of the tub. Next I undressed and I slid into the hot liquid, feeling better at once, even more so when I lathered up my hair, my face and every inch of my body. I scrubbed and washed and shaved until the water had cooled, finally forcing myself out to dry before the hostler returned to evict me. I ran my fingers through my hair because I had forgotten to bring my comb, then dressed in my new clothes. As I strolled back to my room, I felt as handsome as a barber's cat. At least I'd die clean if I didn't improve Hickok's poker luck.

That evening, we returned to the library with the same cast of characters. I didn't give Bill any instructions as I wanted to watch him one more night before mapping out a gambling gambit. The only excitement other than Hickok losing another fifteen dollars came when the hand bell rang at the hotel desk. I shut my book, trapping inside the popcorn I was enjoying. All the gamblers scraped their cards and pots into the cavities in their books and were innocently reading when the knock came from the hallway. Chris unlatched the door and let in the sheriff of Greene County.

"Evening, gentlemen," he announced. "Just checking how things are going with your reading circle."

"Fine," replied Taylor. "A good book is like a warm woman, hard to put down."

"Uh huh," noted the lawman, walking around eyeing everyone in the room and checking the waistline of each to make sure no one carried a pistol. "I need to confirm no one's armed. We all know how reading can lead to trouble, don't we?"

"Whatever you say, Sheriff," Hickok responded.

As the sheriff rounded the table, he pulled up opposite me. "Don't believe I know you, son? Are you an avid reader?"

I held up my popcorn-filled volume. "This book is most fulfilling. And my name is H.H. Lomax."

"So you're the one that conned the bettors on the Rattle Jar. I was expecting a smarter looking fellow."

I was expecting a better mannered sheriff, but I didn't think it wise to say so at the moment. "I can't help it I have the look of an honest man."

"Is it true you fancy yourself as the Arkansas Kid?" he continued.

"It's not a name I use, good sir, but one given me by the sore losers in my bout with Pepper and the Rattle Jar. I refer to myself as Lomax."

"I'll remember that, kid," he said as he marched on, completing his circle of the room.

"Back to your books fellows, but remember no gambling in here. A place has to be licensed and pay a fee to the city and county to run any game of chance. The Lyon house isn't registered."

"Nor should it be for a simple reading room," Taylor said.

"Yeah," replied the sheriff as he exited.

Chris jumped up to close and latch the door.

I opened my book, but Taylor shook his head. "Do nothing until the clerk rings the handbell again. After several impatient minutes, the clang from the front desk resounded up the stairway, and everyone resumed gambling or eating popcorn. Hickok finished the night another fifteen dollars down by the time we left the library. I combed his nits again, and he rinsed his hair in vinegar. I told him my plan for the next evening. When he got what he thought was a great hand, he was to control his emotion and rather than grin and raise his head, he was to grimace and lower his chin.

"And don't do any drinking between now and then because I've got to have your mind clear to fight your instinct to gloat over what you think is a good hand," I instructed him. "Say something to clue me in when you get a solid draw."

He scratched his chin. "How about 'I'm gonna have to shoot Lomax, if my luck doesn't improve'?"

Flinching and shrugging, I said. "That'll gain my attention and everyone else's."

"Then that's what it'll be," Hickok informed me, and I didn't argue for fear he would plug me.

The next evening we gathered in the library with the same players as the previous two nights. My primary fear was that Davis Tutt might show up and throw our plans awry as I wasn't sure Hickok could concentrate on cards with Tutt in the room. The first thing I noticed after Hickok placed his gold watch on the green felt beside his stake was that he seldom touched his head. The treatment was working and the infernal itching was receding so that a man could focus on his cards rather than his vermin.

Card play proceeded as usual with Hickok on the losing end, his resources gradually declining, until he slapped the table with his palm and announced, "I'm gonna have to shoot Lomax, if my luck doesn't improve!" His words captured everyone's attention. Taylor seated beside me elbowed my ribs and Chris, Hardy, Peter, Morris and Lester glanced my direction before looking back at Hickok, who grimaced, bit his cheek and lowered his chin. He played it masterfully. I just hoped he had a good hand.

Hardy smelling blood raised the pot and everyone stayed in. Hardy took two cards, Peter three, Morris three and Lester, who was so confident of Hickok's poor poker sense, called for four cards. Hickok took but one. After everybody examined their hands, Peter increased the ante two dollars with everyone else matching except Lester, who folded. When they showed their hands, Hickok displayed a full house of aces over jacks. Only Hardy came close with another full house, eights over threes.

As Hickok pulled in his first big pot of the evening, he looked my way. "I won't be shooting you after all, Lomax."

"Thank you, Bill. That means a lot, that and your undying friendship," I replied.

Hickok stayed in the game another half hour before calling it quits. He lost some of the winnings from the big pot, but still came out six dollars ahead.

Back in the room, I combed his hair, needing only an hour to finish and then let him rinse it in vinegar again. I explained my plan for the next night was for him to control his emotions so he could show what he wanted them to read rather than his natural reactions. The goal was to make sure he could give them false looks to throw them off the trail of his hand, good or bad. He was not to worry about losing or winning, as long as he didn't bet too much, and he concentrated on controlling his mannerisms.

"Why waste another night?" Hickok wanted to know.

"You need more practice managing your reactions to the cards. We'll do it in two nights. That'll be a Friday when we might have a few more readers and money in the library."

"This better work, Lomax."

"Your rivals don't have to see your cards, when they can read your face. Control your reactions tomorrow night, and it will work the next night when we can make a killing."

Hickok shrugged as he finished drying the vinegar off of his head. "How long do we need to keep up with the treatment?"

"Two more days," I said, "so you should be free of lice and undisturbed come Friday night."

We retired to bed and awoke Thursday anxious for the evening card game to begin. Once again, it was the same crew as the previous evenings. Hickok lost a couple bucks by the time he quit, but he managed his emotions as well as I could expect, and he never once scratched his head the whole night.

Back in our room, I worked his hair and found no

more lice eggs on the comb. He rinsed with vinegar, and we repeated the process the next morning. I had Hickok find a deck of cards, and we practiced poker hands the rest of the day. As I watched him play, I told him whether I thought he had a good or bad draw. By the end of the afternoon he was better at hiding his emotions than he had been that morning.

After concluding our practice, we walked across the street to the saloon and paid two bits apiece for supper. Most of the customers teased Wild Bill for having such an unlucky totem as me following him around. I wanted to tell them wait until tomorrow, but I kept my mouth shut.

As we were finishing up, Hickok called to the bartender. "Give me a bottle of your best whiskey."

"No, Bill," I cried.

He waved for the barkeep to go ahead with his assigned task. "It's for after the poker game, not before."

I sighed in relief as he paid for the bottle, and we exited the saloon. We both took deep breaths as we walked up on the hotel porch and entered the Lyon House. We marched to our room, left the whiskey bottle on the bed and unbelted our holsters and leaving them on the mattress. Bill studied himself in the mirror over the washstand.

"I need a tie," he announced, retreating to his dresser and extracting one which he knotted and straightened around his neck. He looked at his reflection a final time, winked at himself and announced, "I'm ready."

So was I.

After I exited, Bill locked the room, and we marched up the stairs, knocked on the library entry and waited to be admitted.

Taylor grinned as he opened the door. "We feared you had chickened out on us."

"Not, Wild Bill. He's ready for anything you fellas can throw at him."

As Taylor locked up behind us, I saw four new faces sitting along the wall plus the regulars at the table and one man taking a boiled egg from the food cabinet.

When the fellow turned around, I gasped.

Standing there with a big grin slashing across his unruly black beard was Davis Tutt. Barely had I realized Tutt had joined us than Bill did too, freezing where he stood.

"Howdy, Hickok," Tutt said. "I've come to collect my forty dollars."

"Damn," I whispered. Since Tutt hadn't shown up for the previous nights in the library, I had not prepared myself or Wild Bill for this possibility. I feared someone might die. I hoped it wasn't me!

Chapter 7

"If you've got enough money to play poker, Hickok, you've got plenty to pay me," Tutt said.

"Not tonight and not before you pay me the ten I'm owed from the Rattle Jar," Wild Bill replied.

As Taylor latched the door behind us, I studied Tutt then the others, making sure no one was armed. They weren't or at least they didn't have side arms at their waists. Who knew what might be hidden beneath their coats or tucked in their boots?

Tutt cracked the boiled egg in his hand and removed the shell, dropping the pieces on the floor as he moved toward Hickok. "Take your ten from the forty you owe me, then you can pay me thirty."

Stubborn as a constipated Missouri mule, Hickok refused to budge. "Give me the ten and I'll settle with you on the forty-dollar bet."

I figured this was headed to no good, so I stepped between the two men. "Gentlemen," I said, "maybe we best call it quits for this evening."

Hickok shook his head. "I'm playing tonight, but not against Tutt until he pays me what he owes."

Tutt took a step toward me, reached over my shoulder and waggled the egg in front of Hickok's nose. "Fine by me, Hickok, I won't play cards or checkers or anything else with you until you pay up. But I intend to stay here and back every hand played against you."

I grimaced, figuring Tutt's intrusion would ruin

Hickok's concentration and spoil our play to take the boys for all the money they had.

"What you do don't concern me until you pay up, Tutt."

Tutt pulled his arm from over my shoulder and snapped a bite of the boiled egg, chewing it vigorously as he backed away.

Taylor slid between Tutt and me. "Okay, fellows, I'm dealing. We'll start with the regulars who've been here the last few nights. The rest of you take a seat against the wall. You can fill in when the players tire or go broke."

"That's fine," Hickok said, "as long as Tutt stays out of the game while I'm playing."

"You'll be busted well before I get in the game, Hickok."

Grumbling, Wild Bill grabbed the first chair at the felt table, and I scurried to a perimeter seat where I could see his face and study his expressions. Chris claimed the place next to me. As Hickok settled into his seat, he pulled out his gold Waltham, unhooked the chain as was his habit, flipped open the cover, and sat the timepiece by his book. Then he retrieved a wad of money that must've been fifty or more dollars. I couldn't believe he had that much stashed in the pockets of his clothes in the wardrobe cabinet.

As Lester, Peter, Morris and Hardy settled into their places, Tutt took a seat behind Hickok. That pleased me as Tutt would not distract Bill, unless Hickok thought he was trying to peek at his cards and signal the others. As the five gamblers nodded their readiness, Taylor slipped into the dealer's chair and grabbed a new pack of cards. He broke the seal and riffled the pasteboards before passing the deck to each player to inspect. When the cards made their way back to him, he mixed them again and dealt out the first round.

I remained too nervous to fill me a book with popcorn, fearing that if I left my seat someone else might take it. With Tutt behind him, Hickok seemed edgy, glancing over his shoulder occasionally but never scratching his head for lice. I wondered whether the tiny vermin or Tutt would have been the greater distraction. After the first two hands, I realized both were equally annoying because Hickok telegraphed his cards by his reactions and lost several dollars both times. As Hickok shoved his second losing hand back into the slush pile, he glimpsed my way and winked. Was he signaling me he knew what he was doing? Was he setting his opponents up before he took all their cash? I prayed he was that shrewd, but I doubted it.

Then Hickok began to play like he was a gambling god! He hoodwinked them hand after hand after hand, bluffing and winning with inferior hands and stinging them with strong draws. It wasn't that his cards were that good or bad as much as his rivals were misreading his every action. Within an hour, Hardy and Lester had lost all their cash, and Peter and Morris verged on bankruptcy.

At one point, Chris leaned over and whispered, "Maybe you are his lucky horseshoe after all."

"We've been practicing," I answered.

As Hardy and Lester pushed themselves away from the table, Tutt jumped up behind Hickok. "Keep your seats, boys."

"We're broke," said Lester.

"No you're not," Tutt replied. "Since Hickok's too yeller to play me, I'm staking you fellows to take his cash for me."

"I can't afford to borrow money to gamble," Hardy said.

"Me either," Lester added.

"I've got a hundred and eighty dollars here to bring Hickok to his knees. And since he's too much a coward to take me on, I'm sharing the money with you fellows. Clean him out and you can repay me."

"What if we lose?" Lester asked.

"You won't," Tutt assured them, "but even if you do, you won't owe me a cent."

"Are we gonna play or talk," Hickok interrupted. "My cards'll grow cold if we don't resume."

"That's what we want," Tutt responded.

Lester and Hardy shrugged, settling back into their chairs as Tutt counted out sixty dollars apiece to stake them and gave thirty each to Morris and Peter to enhance their chances of taking down Hickok. What perplexed me as much as anything was where men of Tutt's and Hickok's character came up with that kind of money. I considered myself an honest fellow, but I'd never come across that kind of cash honestly and wondered how Tutt and Hickok did it.

Hickok scratched his head a couple times, adding to my worries, especially after he resorted to his old ways of signaling his hand and lost modest pots on the first three rounds. Behind him, Tutt smirked, but Hickok gave me another wink, either that or his eye was twitching with worry.

The following deal, Hickok took a thirty-dollar pot and continued like an avalanche after that, winning every four out of five hands. The wide eyes and frazzled looks on the faces of Peter, Morris, Hardy and Lester showed they were as bewildered as Tutt, whose grubstake was gradually evaporating from the stakes of his allies and reappearing in the growing stack of money beside Hickok's gold Waltham.

Hickok never eased his assault on Tutt's money, even if it was being gambled by other men. The rush of winning and the thrill of hearing his adversary's groans and curses at each lost pot invigorated Hickok. Once he looked at me and nodded. "I knew you'd bring me good luck, Lomax, if I kept you around."

I nodded, though I feared we were all hurtling down the tracks for a train wreck. "Don't get too cocky, Bill, because you luck can always change."

Nothing that night, however, changed Hickok's fortunes. In two hours, he had not only cleaned out all of his four rivals' money but also that which Tutt had provided them. He so dominated the game that no one else claimed a seat vacated by Lester, Hardy, Peter or Morris.

When Hickok pulled in the final pot, Morris threw down his cards and shook his head, embarrassed to have been cleaned out by Hickok.

"Dammit," cried Tutt, standing up from his chair and banging his fist against the wall. He strode to Hickok's side. "Give me my forty dollars, Hickok."

"Pay me the ten you owe me first, then I'll hand over your forty."

"Just give me thirty."

Hickok shook his head. "Not until I get my ten."

Tutt threw up his arms. "I don't have ten dollars now. You got it all."

Hickok grinned, relishing Tutt's insolvency. "You should've paid me before you bet your money against me." Still seated, Hickok gathered his winnings.

Stamping his feet, Tutt leaned over and snatched Hickok's gold Waltham from the table.

Hickok reached instinctively for his absent sidearm, then threw his bills on the felt and pushed himself up from his chair. "Give me my watch."

Tutt shook his head. "I'm keeping it until you pay me the thirty you owe me."

"I'll give you the forty I owe you once you give me the ten I'm due from you."

It was a silly argument, but stubbornness always trumps logic when two hard-headed sons of bitches butt heads.

"Give me my watch," Hickok demanded.

Tutt backed away from the table. "Not until I get what's owed me."

"You're biting off a bigger chaw than you can chew, Tutt. Money's one thing, but taking an heirloom like that can get a man killed."

Tutt held the timepiece up to the lamp, snapped the cover shut and grinned. "Looks like a cheap watch to begin with."

"It was my poppa's. Don't matter what it's worth; it means a lot to me."

"Forty dollars is what it's worth, Hickok. It's yours when you pay me my forty bucks. You got the money right there," he said, pointing to the bills on the felt.

"Once you give me my watch back and the ten dollars you owe me, I'll settle the rest with you."

Tutt shoved the Waltham in his pants pocket. "You'll come around, or I'll sell your watch for what I can get."

"You best not sell my timepiece," Hickok warned, "and you best not show it to folks like it's yours because it's not. If you do, I'll find you, and I'll be armed."

"So will I," Tutt answered. He spun around, unlatched the door and strode down the hall, the heavy footfall of his boots on the stairs resounding in the room. Stunned by the exchange, the others stood there, fearful of doing anything that might turn Hickok against them. As Hickok retook his seat to gather his winnings for a second time, the losing gamblers stepped meekly away, grabbing their hats and disappearing in the hall until only Hickok, me, Chris and Taylor remained.

"This doesn't bode well," Chris said.

Taylor nodded as he gathered the cards and shoved them back in the box. "Nothing good'll come out of this. Why don't you pay him thirty dollars, Bill, and get it back?"

"It's the principle. Now he owes me ten and my watch. He best not brag about it as I'll not be shamed by him bragging about taking my timepiece."

Chris shrugged. "Glad we don't allow guns in the library or it might've all ended right here this evening. I saw you reach for your gun when Tutt taunted you."

"Habit," said Hickok, "but a good instinct to have if a man wants to survive." He looked at me. "You are my lucky horseshoe, Lomax." He held up his winnings and smiled. "Over three hundred dollars here. The most I've ever won at poker."

"Not everyone's thrilled, Bill," I answered

"That don't matter as long as I am. Tomorrow, I'm gonna treat you to the biggest steak in Springfield."

"You plan on inviting Tutt to join us, maybe settle things before they get out of hand?"

"I won't break bread with that scoundrel." He stood up, pocketed his earnings, and marched out the door.

I followed him to our room, wondering if his hard head was bullet proof. He marched inside, not stopping to light a lamp. As I nursed a match to the kerosene lamp, Hickok threw his winnings on the bed and picked up his gun belt, quickly fastening it around his waist. By the time I had put the globe back on the lamp, Hickok grabbed his hat from the bedpost and yanked it down on his head. "I'm going out for a drink," he announced.

I pointed to the new bottle of whiskey he had purchased earlier in the day to celebrate our expected poker earnings. "What about nursing on that bottle?"

"Not tonight. I intend to discover if Tutt's mouthing off over taking my watch." He opened the door.

"What about your winnings, Bill?"

"Do with them what you want? I've got more important matters to handle." With that, he marched out in the hall, pricklier than a rattlesnake on a hot skillet. I figure he was mad enough to beat Pepper in either a staring or a biting contest.

"Good night," I said, but meant, "Good God, what had we gotten ourselves into?" I closed the door and stared at the bed. While I had never handled dynamite, I felt like I was juggling an entire case between Hickok and Tutt. The least I could do was hide his money, so I gathered it all up and carried it to the wardrobe. Opening the doors, I pulled on each of his four frock coats and stuffed a few bills in the various pockets of the four jackets. When I finished, I placed the coats back in the furniture piece, but an idea struck me at that moment. What if I took ten dollars and offered it to Tutt to pay off Hickok at the same time he returned the timepiece? While I didn't care much either way whether Tutt or Hickok got killed, I was mighty worried about being shot when the blowup came.

I decided it was too dangerous to go to looking for either of them in the dark so I went to bed, aiming to get up in the morning and diffuse the situation before somebody, especially me, got hurt. After blowing out the lamp, I retired to my bedroll for a restless night. After midnight, I heard Hickok enter our room because he knocked the whiskey bottle onto the floor and cursed like he had just invented profanity. I detected the aroma of liquor, but couldn't decide if the flask had broken or if

Bill had returned pickled.

Though I listened to him return, fall into bed and start snoring, I did not hear him leave the next day. When I woke up about mid-morning, he had disappeared. I dressed and decided to determine if my contraband ten dollars could resolve the predicament, even if my play was dishonest. First, I had to find Tutt and hope Hickok didn't see me with him. I figured it would take me a couple hours to run him down when I stepped out on the front porch of the hotel. There in facing rocking chairs sat Hickok, his clothes rumpled from having slept in them, and Tutt, his eyes and beard as wild as ever. Five other men stood or squatted around them, cajoling them and trying to turn down the temperature on their dispute.

"It's about time you got up," Hickok said, "though I don't know the exact hour since Tutt stole my poppa's Waltham."

Tutt grumbled. "Lomax is the jackass that started this whole row. If he hadn't cheated at the Rattle Jar, there wouldn't have been any doubt who owed what because I would've prevailed as usual."

"Don't be insulting my lucky horseshoe, Tutt. Thanks to him I won more money last night than in any other poker game I've ever bought into. Most of my winnings was your money, Tutt."

Tutt spat at the wooden slats between him and Hickok, his anger building. Hickok's right hand slipped to his waist and the butt of one of his revolvers. The men nearest the two antagonists backed away.

"Pay me what you owe," Tutt commanded.

"You give me the ten I'm due, and I'll give you the forty I lost to you."

All of this was so convoluted I thought my head might explode, so I complicated matters even more.

"Bill, how about, you loan Tutt ten dollars right now so he can give you your Rattle Jar winnings? Then you can give him the forty dollars you owe him, and he can pay back the ten you just loaned him."

Both men scratched their heads at my genius.

"When that's done," I continued, thinking I was exhibiting the wisdom of Solomon, "Tutt can return your watch, Bill. What do you think?"

"That's about as confounding as trying to untangle a barrel of rattlesnakes," Tutt observed.

"And just as stupid!" Hickok retorted.

"Finally," I announced, "you two agree on something."

"Lomax," Tutt continued, "We agree that you are about the stupidest jackass in all of Missouri."

"Then that's two things you both agree on." I turned to Hickok. "Why not allow someone other than Tutt to return his ten dollar Rattle Jar wager and your watch this afternoon?"

Hickok shot that idea down like a quail on the wing. "He's gotta return it himself because I want to see him squirm just as he's relished collecting debts from me."

Tutt shook his head and slowly pushed himself out of his rocker, careful to keep his hands away from his revolver so Hickok wouldn't jump to any confusions about his intent. He stuck his hand in his britches pocket, pulled out Hickok's timepiece, opened the cover and checked the hour. "Won't be long for lunch," he announced. "This morning's been a waste of time." He snapped the watch shut and walked past Bill, down the steps and across the street to the saloon.

Hickok sat there, sizzling in his seat like bacon in a frying pan. "This has been as useless as having your feet under the table but no food on your plate." He arose angry and brushed by me, heading inside. I figured it would be easier to kiss a cougar than to douse his anger, so I left him alone and headed to the square for a bite of lunch rather than going across the street and eating at the saloon with Tutt. Hoping to find Tutt in the afternoon and convince him to give me Hickok's Waltham, I didn't care to risk Bill spotting me with his rival so soon after their spat on the porch.

I strolled toward the plaza, which teemed with activity, it being a Saturday and folks having come to town from miles around to buy supplies, attend to their business and relax at the watering hole or eatery of their choice. The best I could tell, I had five eateries to choose from on the square and selected the one—Honey Creek—with ten folks standing in line for the eleven o'clock opening. After I took my place, another seven people fell in behind me, some talking about Davis Tutt's boasts of appropriating Wild Bill's gold watch and others bragging about the eatery's excellent pie.

Promptly at eleven o'clock, the proprietor opened the door and everyone scurried in, me parking at a small table for two and reading the menu written on a chalk board on the wall. I smiled because they listed cherry pie among their offerings. I loved my momma's cherry pie when she could afford cherries, so I ordered meatloaf with boiled potatoes, collard greens, beets and brown bread as a preliminary to the pie. When my meal came with a glass of water, I told the waitress to bring me a slice of cherry pie, then dug into lunch, which at twenty-five cents was bland and overpriced, but at a dime a sliver the cherry pie was the closest a fellow my age could get to heaven, short of getting under a young lady's blouse. The dessert tickled my tongue so I ordered another piece and relished it as much as the first. As other folks were waiting for tables when I finished, I paid my forty-five cents to the waitress and left with a full belly.

For almost five and a half hours, I wandered around town, looking for Davis Tutt. I retreated down South Street to the Lyon House and saloon, checking them both out, then back to the square to look around. Finally, I spotted him near the courthouse and dashed across the quadrangle, yelling "Tutt, Tutt, hold up a minute."

Reaching him breathless, I held up my hand for him to give me a moment to let my lungs catch up with my brain.

"What do you want, jackass?" Tutt scowled. "You doing Hickok's dirty work?"

I inhaled a full breath and spoke. "I hope to make things right so no one gets hurt. Even if you bet against me on the Rattle Jar, I'm still from Arkansas like you. I feel I owe it to you."

"Is this some Hickok trick?"

"No, I swear it's not. I've got ten dollars I can give you to repay Bill and return his watch."

"I'll not grovel in front of Hickok. I'm sick of his damned Yankee attitude he's better than us. You understand me, boy, don't you?"

"Sure, but if you won't let me give you the ten bucks to pay off your debt, will you let me buy the watch for ten dollars? I'll return it to Hickok and you can do what you want with the money."

Tutt scratched his chin, then bore into me with his wild eyes. "This isn't a trick, is it?"

"No, sir. I'll give him the watch this evening. I won't tell him I bought it, just that you meant no harm by taking it and that you want to settle up each other's debts and put this behind you."

"How do I know you won't trick me?"

"Think about it, Tutt. If I don't give him the watch, all you'll need to do is get word to him what I've done. After that, I reckon he'll come after me for betraying him."

"Okay, Lomax, I'll go along," Tutt said, "but only because you're from Arkansas. If you swindle me on this, I'll let Hickok know, and we'll both come gunning for you."

"Believe me," I said, "all I want to do is get out of the middle of this so I don't have to worry about either of you.

We both dug into our pockets, me extracting the ten dollars in greasy bills I had borrowed from Hickok and Tutt handling Wild Bill's gold Waltham. We swapped the items and shook hands to seal the deal.

"You give him the watch this evening, Lomax. I'm depending on you."

"I'll do it as soon as I find him, promise."

Tutt counted the money while I slid the Waltham in my pants pocket. "There's eleven dollars here," he said, offering me one back.

I shook my head. "You keep it for good luck."

He grinned, "Why, thank you, Lomax."

Turning about, I started across the square again, so proud of myself that I decided I'd stop at Honey Creek and treat myself to another piece of cherry pie. I had to wait ten minutes for a table, but when I got one near the window, I told the waitress to bring me a piece of pie. I had my dime ready for her when she returned.

"You're lucky," she said. "This is the last one, though our blueberry pie's just as good."

She placed the plate on the table in front of me, and I gave her my dime which she exchanged for a fork. I studied the bright red pie filling before I attacked it with the utensil. I'd finished half of it, when a wide-eyed pedestrian burst into the eatery and shouted, "There's trouble. It's Hickok and Tutt."

I jumped up from my chair, grabbed the rest of my pie and shoved it in my mouth as I ran across the room and out the door. Across the square, I saw Tutt standing outside the courthouse, followed his gaze and spotted Hickok at the far corner of the plaza. They were yelling at each other, though I couldn't make out what they were saying.

I bolted across the square, waving my arms in the air and hoping to stop any gunplay.

"Stoppppp!" I yelled, but the pie muffled my cry.

In that instant, both men drew their revolvers.

BOOM!

Chapter 8

I froze, waiting for a second shot and making certain neither of them turned their pistol on me. Though I heard only one gun retort, I saw smoke belching from both revolvers, so the antagonists must have fired simultaneously. I looked from Tutt to Hickok to Tutt, who dropped his revolver and staggered four steps toward the courthouse. He leaned against the stone archway, then lurched back to the street and collapsed.

As soon as he fell, spectators on the opposite end of the plaza screamed, and a mob of men, pulled their guns, starting for Hickok, who spun around and leveled his pistol at them. They stiffened or let their side arms slide back into their holsters.

"More of you'll die if you don't put your shooting-irons to bed," Hickok cried. "It was a fair fight, as fair as possible when you're facing a skunk."

I glanced from Hickok to Tutt, who lay sprawled on the street in front of the courthouse. Now, I panicked. If I hadn't stopped for a slice of cherry pie and instead returned the watch first, the shooting might never have happened. On top of that, I had the disputed Waltham in my pocket, and I feared I might take the blame for the killing. The timepiece burned my conscience like a hot ember. Fearing for my life, if my good intentions and my craving for cherry pie became known, I bolted toward Tutt, uncertain what to do.

Three men squatted beside him, one rolling Tutt

over on his back. His face was blanched with his eyes rolled up until the pupils disappeared behind his half-open eyelids. One fellow poked a finger Tutt's ribcage and the scorched hole heart high. "Here's where the slug entered," he announced. A man on the opposite side lifted Tutt's left arm and grimaced. "It's a bloody mess over here where the bullet came out. There's nothing anybody can do for Davis, save bury him."

As both fellows stood up, I slipped my hand in my pocket and palmed Hickok's timepiece as I slid the Waltham out.

The two men who had inspected the wounds looked toward Hickok still holding the crowd at bay with his revolver. "Hell of a shot," said the first. The other nodded. "I'd say two hundred feet or more."

I cleared my throat. "And all over a watch."

When the two fellows looked at me, I squatted beside Tutt and slid my hand with its hidden load inside the deceased's pants pocket. "This must be it," I said, extracting my fingers and standing up, opening my palm for the gathering crowd to see the Waltham.

"Don't you think you ought to leave the watch on him for the law to resolve?" asked a spectator placing his hat over his heart.

Shaking my head, I told them, "We best return it to Wild Bill before someone else gets killed over it."

"Perhaps you're right," the observer responded, placing his hat back on his head.

Holding the timepiece between my fingers now for everyone to see, I started toward Hickok and the crowd on the opposite corner of the plaza. "Here's your watch, Bill, here's your watch," I cried several times as I trotted across the plaza. I wanted to make sure plenty of people heard me.

Hickok glanced over his shoulder at me, then turned his attention back to those who might wish him harm.

Stopping beside him, I extend the Waltham between my thumb and trigger finger for everyone to see. "It was in Tutt's pants pocket, Bill. I figured I should get it to you before it disappeared."

With his free left hand, Hickok snatched the timepiece from my hand, like a pond frog snagging a fly out of the air. "Obliged, Lomax," he said, looking oddly at me. He studied me for a moment, rather than those that meant harm. "How close were you to Tutt when he fell?"

"On the other side of the square," I responded. "Why?"

"You've got blood on your face."

I swiped my trigger finger over my cheeks and lips, then looked at the sticky red residue. It was cherry filling from the pie. I stuck my finger in my mouth and sucked off the remains of the dessert.

"Damn, Lomax, you're a blood-thirsty son of a bitch," Hickok said as others groaned and turned away, repulsed at what they thought I had done.

I shrugged. "I was trying to help out."

Hickok looked from me to the thinning crowd, any friends of Tutt among them backing away and deciding to let the law handle Hickok and his blood-savoring partner.

An officer in a cavalry uniform marched up and announced himself. "I'm Colonel Albert Barnitz, post commander here in Springfield. I witnessed the whole thing and am holding you for the civil authorities."

"You'll have no trouble from me, Colonel, as long as you don't try to take my guns. A few men here are intent on harming me."

Barnitz pointed to the courthouse. "There's the sheriff. Let's head that direction."

Hickok slid his revolver back in his right holster, and I accompanied him and the colonel as they crossed the square, counting my steps as I went. Though people moved out of our way, most stared in awe at a man who had killed his antagonist at such a range. By the time I reached Tutt's body, I estimated the distance at seventy-five yards. It was the best pistol shot I would ever witness in my life on the frontier, and I knew I had caused it.

As we approached Tutt, a doctor kneeled over his corpse, unbuttoning his vest and shirt, exposing his bloodied chest and confirming the bullet had entered Tutt's right side between the fifth and seventh ribs, just below the nipple, and exiting between the same ribs on his left side. Hickok's aim was as steady as it had been deadly.

The sheriff eyed Hickok. "This your doing?"

"I told him not to wear my watch in public," Bill replied.

"No cause to shoot him," the sheriff answered.

"He drew on me. It was self-defense. He'd been bragging about taking my watch and was parading it around town to humiliate me."

The doctor glanced up from the body to the lawman. "There was no timepiece in his vest or pants pockets."

I interrupted with an alibi for my own actions. "That's right, Sheriff. I knew the Waltham had created bad feelings so I pulled it from his britches pocket and ran it to Hickok to avoid any more trouble."

The sheriff turned to the accused. "That true?"

Hickok nodded, sliding his hand into his trousers and extracting the timepiece that had caused so many problems. He held Waltham up for the lawman's inspection. "Lomax gave it to me after the shooting. I'm obliged to him."

"Wish I could've returned it sooner," I said. "Maybe it would've avoided all of this."

Hickok shrugged as he slid his timepiece back into his pants pocket. "Who knows?"

I knew, but I didn't say so aloud.

"If it hadn't been this," he continued, "it would've been something else as Tutt and I didn't geehaw too well. He'd threatened me many times."

"We'll let a jury to decide, Hickok," the lawman noted. "At some point I'll need to take your guns and arrest you."

Hickok placed his hands on his hips near the reversed butts of his twin Colt Navy revolvers. "You can arrest me, but I can't let you take my guns until I'm in your office or jail."

Colonel Barnitz glanced at the sheriff. "Should I call

soldiers to disarm and arrest him?"

"I'm not resisting arrest," Hickok responded. "Sheriff, I'll go with you, now or later, but I won't give up my guns, not until I'm out of sight of Tutt's friends that might want revenge."

"I can have troops here in a few minutes," Barnitz repeated.

The sheriff wagged his head. "No need, Colonel. I can handle it from here as long as Hickok promises to hand over his weapons at my office."

"I do," Bill answered.

The doctor stood up from Tutt and retreated far enough to retrieve the dead man's hat from the street. He returned and placed it over Tutt's face. "That'll do until we can get an undertaker."

"Thanks, Doc," the sheriff said. "I'll want the coroner to examine the body. If you'll notify the undertaker, I'll advise the court. You can stay free, Hickok, until I get the coroner's report and submit it to the judge for a warrant, but you must promise not to leave town."

"I'm not going anywhere, but back to my room to remain out of sight for a spell."

"You give me your word?"

"I do, Sheriff."

Lingering nearby, Colonel Barnitz spat his disgust at Hickok walking away free, spun about and marched off.

The sheriff looked at me. "Did you witness the shooting, Lomax? You may need to testify."

I shrugged. "Sort of. I was in the eatery having a slice of cherry pie when folks came in saying trouble was brewing between Tutt and Hickok. I stuffed the slice in my mouth and ran out, yelling stop. They drew their pistols and fired so close together I only heard one gunshot."

"Why'd you yell stop," the lawman inquired.

Did he suspect my role in the shooting? I answered carefully. "I thought it was too much trouble over a watch, something I could fix, but I was too late."

"Cherry pie?" said Hickok, staring at me with narrowed eyes and a glint of a smile under his thick mustache.

The sheriff glanced at Hickok then back at me, so I pointed at Honey Creek. "Their blueberry pie is better," he said, turning to my roommate. "Now, Hickok, I'm letting you go back to the Lyon House. Don't leave the city limits unless I tell you otherwise. I'll come for you when a warrant is issued. I don't want any trouble."

Bill nodded. "If that day comes, I'll go to jail, but I intend to wear my guns to your office for my own protection. If you allow me that, there'll be no trouble, Sheriff."

"Agreed," the sheriff said as he twisted around to stand over the body.

Hickok and I walked toward the hotel, me staying a good three feet from him in case a Tutt ally took a pot-shot at Bill.

"Cherry pie," Hickok laughed. "I thought you were a blood-sucking leech when you licked the filling off your finger."

"It was delicious," I said, "though if I hadn't been eating pie, I might've been able to stop the shooting."

"You couldn't have changed a thing, and now I don't have to look over my shoulder all the time for Tutt. I'm walking and he's not. It turned out fine to my way of thinking."

"You still might get hung for murder."

"It was self-defense. You did me a favor not running out sooner or I might have shot you and been in real trouble."

Maybe I felt better and maybe I didn't as it bothered me to have contributed to a man's death, even one as loco as Tutt. I decided never to tell Hickok the full story, but I began to wonder if Tutt had informed anyone he had given me the timepiece to return to Hickok. If the dead man had told someone, and things came to a trial, I feared I might have to testify. Then what would I do? If I told what really happened, I might be charged with something or become the target of Tutt's allies. If I lied after taking an oath on the Bible, I figured I'd go to hell, and I didn't care to spend eternity in such a warm climate.

Back at the hotel, we locked ourselves in Hickok's room. I explained what I had done with his winnings from the previous night, except for the eleven dollars I'd given Tutt, and asked Wild Bill how much money he thought he had altogether.

"Maybe five hundred dollars," he replied. "I don't figure I'll have enough to make bail, if I'm arrested. If I am, you'll have the room to yourself for a spell."

"It won't be the same without you."

Hickok laughed. "You know what's not the same?"

"No," I replied.

"The head lice, those little boogers aren't pestering me anymore."

"I've noticed you're not scratching your hair as much?"

"You think I can perfume my hair again."

"I'd wait until after you learn if you're going to jail for a while."

We didn't say much after that, Hickok locking the door and wedging one of chairs under the knob for extra security. I retired to my bedroll and slept as good as a fellow could with pie in his stomach and a dead man on his conscience. We slumbered late the next morning and might have rested until noon except for the banging on the door as lunch time approached.

"Hickok, it's the sheriff. I've got a warrant, and I've come to arrest you," he called.

Jumping up from my bedroll, I headed for the entry, rubbing my eyes all the way. I pulled the chair from under the door handle and unlocked the latch. The sheriff entered and looked at Hickok, sitting on his mattress and stretching.

"Morning, Sheriff. I didn't expect you so early."

"It's almost noon, Hickok. Put on your clothes and your guns like we agreed, then I'm taking you to jail." He offered Hickok the papers in his hand. "Here's the warrant."

Bill shrugged, his long hair bouncing as he did. "I trust you, Sheriff. Give me a minute to attend to matters." He slid off the bed, used the chamber pot, and pushed it back in place.

"You might empty that before I return, Lomax," he said as he dressed. He put on his two-holstered gun belt and his hat. He looked at himself in the mirror over the shaving stand and smiled his approval. "Okay, sheriff. I'm ready to go. What's my bail?"

"Two thousand dollars."

Hickok whistled. "I can't cover that so I reckon I'll be staying at your place a while. What kind of food do you serve in your fine establishment?"

"The cheapest the county can buy."

Slapping the sheriff on the back, Hickok marched down the hall and out of the Lyon House with the lawman. That was the last time I would see Hickok for two years.

Uncertain what to do, I pondered my situation. I was tired of being Hickok's lucky horseshoe and him thinking I was little more than a servant he could order to dump his slop jar. As I dressed, I considered my options, which were dim, and my Springfield prospects, which were dimmer. I strapped my gun belt around me, not knowing if one of Tutt's avengers might come after me, but hoping I'd have the mettle of Hickok if one did. Deciding it wasn't wise to make a decision on an empty stomach, I left the hotel and returned to the Honey Creek eatery for lunch, dining on chicken and dumplings, corn on the cob, red beans and cornbread and topping that off with two pieces of the fatal cherry pie, all for forty-five cents.

Back at the Lyon House, I gathered up my clothes, tucked some in my saddlebags and rolled up the rest in my bedroll. I filled my canteen and checked my pistol and carbine. After I loaded, I was down to a mere three cartridges in my gun belt and knew I would have to buy more ammunition. I put on my new straw hat and looked at myself in the mirror. I didn't cut the figure that Hickok did, but then I never cared to look like a dandy. Uncertain if I must pay for stabling Old Abe, I retreated to Hickok's wardrobe and extracted twelve dollars from a frock coat.

I toted my saddlebags, bedroll and canteen out of the room and down the hall, hoping to pass the proprietor without being seen, but that was like trying to slip sunrise past a rooster. He eyed me with suspicion, but never said a thing. Outside I checked with the stable hand and asked about the charges, but he said stabling came with the room. Old Abe perked up when he heard my voice and stamped his feet as I approached his stall. Dropping my gear on the hay-strewn ground, I un-tethered my mule, fitted him with his bridle and I lifted my saddle off the stall plank. I threw it atop his back, quickly cinching it up and tying my saddlebags, bedroll and canteen in place.

As I passed the hotel desk on my way back to Hickok's room, the proprietor asked, "Are you leaving us without paying?"

"Nope, I'm looking at selling my gear to cover any costs that Hickok can't manage."

"Since he's been arrested, you're gonna have to pay for your lodging because he may not be able to pay his own bill, much less yours, if he is hung."

"It was self-defense," I replied. "I saw it."

"Any truth to the rumor that Tutt gave you the watch to return to Hickok, but you never returned it to him until after the shooting?"

As my knees went limp, I realized I had made the right decision to leave Springfield. "Where do rumors like that get started?"

"That's what Tutt's friends are telling folks," the proprietor informed me.

"They're sore Tutt wasn't a better shot." I strode on toward Hickok's room.

"If I was you, I'd be careful, especially around Tutt's pals. It'd be a shame to be shot over a rumor."

"Don't worry, friend, I won't let them shoot me before you get paid. For the time being, I'm gonna take a nap."

"My only advice to you, Lomax, is don't leave town without paying for your lodging."

"Wouldn't dream of it."

The first time I entered Hickok's room, I thought he

was the dumbest man I'd ever encountered. As I was about to depart, I realized he was smarter than I had credited him. After all, it was Wild Bill who recommended a first floor hotel room for an easy escape out a window if needed.

I went inside, grabbed my carbine and glanced around for anything I'd left. Satisfied I had all my belongings, I walked to the window, drew back the curtains and lifted the shade, before raising the glass. Sticking my head outside, I looked both ways down the twelve-foot gap between the hotel and the adjacent millinery shop. When I was satisfied no one was looking, I stuck my leg out, then my torso and other leg, all the time holding onto my carbine. I paused a second, looking toward the street to see if anyone had noticed, but the pedestrians and riders paid me no mind. I strode to the back of the Lyon House and turned the corner toward the stable. At that moment, I realized I still had Hickok's twelve bucks in my pocket. While I knew I should return the money, I didn't because I was more fearful of being spotted by the proprietor or one of Tutt's acquaintances than breaking one of the Commandments. Fortunately, the hired hand was running an errand when I reached the stable and my mule. I slid my carbine in the scabbard and led Old Abe out of the best quarters he'd ever called home. Once in the afternoon sunlight, I mounted my mule, pointed him away from South Street and tried to make myself as inconspicuous as I could until I got to the edge of town. Though I needed ammunition, I decided to wait until I put another county or another state between me and Springfield.

Over the next three weeks, I looked over my shoulder a lot, wondering if the law or any of Tutt's pals were searching for me. I made my way toward Kansas City, Independence and the James Brothers, who were the only other folks I knew in Missouri. Wherever I could on my trip north, I found newspapers to follow the legal proceedings back in Springfield. Fifteen days after the killing, Hickok stood trial, and the jury acquitted him two days later. I read every account I came across

whenever I could borrow or steal a paper, always looking for any mention of my name. Not a single story ever
listed me, pleasing me greatly. The farther away from
Springfield I rode, the better I felt about myself and life.
I grew confident I might live to be an old man, despite
my encounter with James Butler Hickok and Davis Tutt.

It would be more than two years before I encountered Wild Bill again. On that fateful day, he became
my lucky horseshoe for a change.

Chapter 9

I bounced around Missouri and Kansas the next two years, taking up with the James Brothers for a few months, much to my regret. What I learned during those weeks was that their momma was the meanest woman God ever put on this earth. I discovered Jesse took after his ma the day he shot Old Abe in the ear because I'd given my mule a Yankee name. Jesse hated those northern bastards so much, he'd shoot an innocent animal. I also realized I was not cut out for bank robbing as Jesse forced me to take part in his first foray into the banking business. I was lucky to leave the James's with my belongings and a fine horse they offered to replace Old Abe.

After I escaped the clutches of Jesse, Frank and their nasty mother, I worked for the railroad as it made its way west toward the Pacific. That's where I first met William F. Cody, better known as Buffalo Bill in later years, and hunted buffalo with him, though I spent more time skinning animals than shooting them as my aim did not satisfy Cody. Because I wasted so much bullet lead in the effort to down bison, Cody nicknamed me "Lead Eye Lomax." I admit I wasn't a terrific shot, unlike Buffalo Bill, but shooting a Sharps Big Fifty was comparable to inviting a mule to kick your shoulder time after time after time. Following that I worked a while on a rail-laying crew and didn't care for work so strenuous. I finally decided the railroads would reach the Pacific with or without me and gathered my belongings, mounted the gelding I'd escaped from the James boys on and followed the iron rails eastward, uncertain where I was headed or even why I was traveling that direction in the early spring of 1867.

My journey took me across the Flint Hills of Kansas to Dickinson County and Abilene, a scab of a county seat that clung to the east side of Mud Creek, a tributary of the Smoky Hill River just south of town. The Kansas Pacific ran by the burg but railway investors didn't think enough of the place to build a depot. I agreed as Abilene was little more than a dozen log huts when I first rode into town looking for a place to stay. The good folks of Abilene were so lazy that none strolled the street when I arrived and, further, they thought so poorly of outsiders that their little six-room hotel offered cots rather than beds with mattresses. The best I could find was a tall hickory between the community's westernmost shack and Mud Creek. I noticed three apple crates on the west side of the tree so I directed my gelding to the opposite flank. Hobbling my bay under branches just showing buds, I planned to unfurl my bedroll and sleep on the ground after I found a saloon or an eatery where I might buy a cheap meal. I had a hankering for cherry pie, but feared someone could die if I had a slice. As I walked down the dirt trail, a chained dog snarled at me, my official welcome to Abilene. The primitive structures lacked windows and were indistinguishable as homes, businesses or vacant. I finally saw one that had the word "liquor" carved in the door so I strode over, uncertain whether to just enter or knock. I knocked.

"The door's unbarred," growled a throaty voice. "Come on in, you idgit."

Cautiously, I opened wooden slats and entered, my eyes adjusting to the late afternoon dimness broken only by a flickering candle in each of the room's four corners. I was baffled whether the place was a saloon or a carpenter's shop as there were a couple planks across empty barrels for a makeshift bar on the left side of the room and saws, planes, mallets and levels on the right.

Raw lumber leaned against the wall behind two saw-horses that held what looked like a coffin in the making. Maybe this was an undertaker's abode. Though I'd heard a voice after I knocked, I didn't spot a soul when I first walked in, but the proprietor popped up from behind the rough burial box brushing sawdust off his apron. He eyed me, then stepped around the pine box and swiped his hands against his denim pants.

Taking off my hat, I nodded at my host. "Is this a saloon or a funeral parlor?"

"Tain't neither. I'm out of whiskey, and I don't have a body. What do you want?"

"I'm passing through, looking for grub or a place to stay."

"You're on your own, kid. There's not enough folks for an eatery, much less a hotel, though one reprobate keeps six bug-infested cots for visitors. If whiskey'll satisfy your hunger, you can try Josiah Jones's place just down the road. He carries overpriced liquor."

"More interested in food. Need to keep my wits about me."

"Are you wanted by the law?"

"No, sir."

"Are you crazy?"

"Not that I know of," I replied, uncertain what may have given this carpenter or barkeep or undertaker such an idea.

"Good. I prefer a lawbreaker to a loco fellow such as the last pistol that arrived in town."

"You must not get many visitors."

"No, you and that crazy pistol both arrived today. That perturbs me, so many folks coming on the same day. Soon riffraff will overrun Abilene. Abilene's fine the way it is."

Pointing to the coffin, I asked, "You expecting a departure?"

"Can't say for sure. Old man Haney's been sickly for months and this new arrival's been delirious so he may be touched in the brain."

"That a fact?"

"Yes, sir. He got off the stagecoach this morning."

"Not the train?

"Neither the westbound nor the eastbound stop here. It's a stage, horseback or afoot if you're planning on visiting Abilene. Like you, he's been looking for food and lodging."

"That doesn't sound crazy to me."

"Yeah, but this pistol's talking about making Abilene the biggest city in Kansas and attracting thousands of Texas cattle to town and then shipping them on the railroad to Chicago and New York. You ever known of such nonsense? To begin with, we're inside the dead line?"

"What dead line?"

"The western border of Dickinson County. It's the quarantine line that longhorn cattle are forbidden to cross."

"What difference does it make?"

"Texas or Spanish fever is what they call it, something them ugly longhorns bring with them. Once they mingle with our local livestock, they pass on the malady to our cows, calves and beef stock. Our animals get drowsy, don't eat, poop blood, then bloat up, lie down and die."

"Never heard of such," I offered.

"Homesteaders around here hate Texans and their cattle. Folks damn sure don't want any longhorns crossing their land. And this loony man wants to bring thousands up here, at least that's what he's telling folks. Says he's expecting more baggage on tomorrow's stage. That's too much baggage to stay in Abilene. The crazy fool even set up apple crates under a tree and calls them his office."

"A big hickory tree between here and the creek."

"That be the one."

What the crazed visitor called his office would be my hotel for the night, assuming he was sensibly insane, not a maniac that might slit your throat while you slept. None of this made sense, but I decided not to linger in Abilene, not with crazy visitor and eccentric barkeeps or undertakers or whatever this Kansan was. "Thank you for your time, sir. I'll be leaving come morning." Returning my hat to my head, I exited the log structure.

Outside the late afternoon sun cast long shadows. I glanced westward, seeing a man in a suit and tie sitting on one of the apple crates opposite my gelding. He was looking at a scroll of paper he had unwound on the two crates that served as his desk and then glancing north and east past the town and then south and west across the creek and past the railway bridge that crossed it. I strode over desiring to determine if he was as loony as other men I'd met since leaving Arkansas, fellows like Hickok, Cody, Tutt and my railroad boss.

As I neared him, he glimpsed me when he pulled his head up from the papers, which I identified as local maps. Seated as he was, I didn't make out this height, but he was a lanky fellow I judged to be near thirty years old. He had brown hair, dark eyes, a beak of a nose and narrow cheeks that sloped to a narrower chin overgrown with an unruly brown goatee. He wore a black tie and a gray suit that still showed the marks of stage travel, a dusting of grime over his coat.

Arising from the crate, he removed the rocks at the corners of the maps and quickly rolled them up, tying them together with a strand of twine. "Afternoon, lad," he said. "I'm Joseph G. McCoy of Springfield, Illinois, final resting place of our great martyred President Abraham Lincoln."

"My name is H.H. Lomax of Cane Hill, Arkansas. I once had a mule named Old Abe until Jesse James shot him in the ear back in Missouri."

"Not the Confederate brigand Jesse James, I hope?"

I shrugged. "Brigand's a new word for me, but Jesse James the outlaw is who I mean."

McCoy pointed to the three apple crates. "Welcome to my office."

Nodding my approval, I aimed my finger at my bay. "It's as fine as the hotel and stable where me and my mount are staying."

McCoy laid the rolled maps on one of the apple boxes

and tugged at his goatee. "That's a good looking bay horse. Where'd you come by it?"

"The animal came from Kentucky by way of Frank James."

"Brother of the scoundrel Jesse James?"

I dipped my chin to acknowledge the accuracy of his statement.

"No offense, lad, but I'm not sure I care to associate with friends of the bank robbing scoundrels."

"The horse compensated me for losing Old Abe, the greatest mule that ever lived. I named the bay for Robert E. Lee, calling him Relee in hopes Jesse James wouldn't shoot him like he had Old Abe. I never wanted to throw in with the James brothers to begin with, though necessity dictated it for a spell. I escaped from them as soon as possible, more than a year ago and hope never to run into any of them again, especially Dingus, as I called Jesse."

"Tell me H.H.—"

"Just call me Lomax."

"Okay, Lomax, do you have vision?" With a sweep of his arm, McCoy pointed east of town and north of the railway. "What do you see?"

"I see a pitiful town, railroad tracks and prairie grass."

"You have sight, lad, but not vision."

I scratched my head like I had Hickok's head lice.

"You know what I see? I see pens that will hold thousands of cattle, a railroad siding to load those animals into hundreds of stock cars and locomotives pulling them to Chicago and New York and everywhere else back east."

Rubbing my eyes, then shaking my head, I stared again in the direction he pointed, but I observed none of that. "I must need spectacles."

McCoy shook his head. "No, lad, you don't need glasses, you're just looking at the present. I'm looking to the future."

"Are you crazy?" I pointed to the saloon keeper's and undertaker's place. "A fellow in there says you're loony."

McCoy laughed, then walked over and put his arm around my shoulder. "Lad, would you care to touch the future?"

"Never thought about it."

"Well let me tell you where this nation is headed, and how Joseph G. McCoy is going to take folks there."

That's when I had the first inkling that McCoy could talk the ears off of a circus elephant. He went on for so long, I realized he could even jabber the varnish off of furniture. He told me how easterners had tired of eating pork and mutton and how they now wanted beef on their plates and in their stomachs. Texas, he continued, was teeming with cattle that had run wild during the War of the Rebellion when men had gone off to fight rather than manage their herds. A pound of beef in Texas was worth five cents at most when that same weight in New York City would bring five to six times as much.

"Last year in Texas, lad, cattle commanded six dollars a head at best, but more likely four or even three dollars apiece," McCoy told me, lifting his arm from my shoulder. "Yet in Chicago, New York and other cities north and east, you can sell that same beef for as much as forty dollars a head. That's a fine return, once you get the cattle to market."

All the figures McCoy spouted left my brain a simmering. He threw out numbers like a locomotive spewed smoke, soot and cinders. "Okay," I said, "you can buy cattle for less in Texas and sell them for more up north, I get it, but how are you getting the cattle there?"

"Vision," he replied, pointing east with his forefinger as he was too genteel to have a trigger finger.

Though I gazed beyond his hand, I still couldn't see his future—or mine.

"Can you imagine livestock pens teeming with cattle, all bellowing in the evening air?"

First, he had asked me to spot something that wasn't there and now to hear sounds that were never made. I hoped he didn't expect me to smell all the manure that wasn't there. At that point, he was full of more bull dung than his imaginary pens.

"Can't you envision it, lad, the loading chutes ready to spew out cattle, the railroad siding thick with stock cars, the locomotive steaming to start the trip north, the hotel to house the cattlemen during their Kansas stay before returning to Texas as wealthy men?"

I answered him as if I was responding to a Baptist revival preacher. "I believe, reverend, I believe!"

McCoy looked at me funny, then laughed. "I suppose I'm as fervent as a traveling parson at times, but making money, lots of filthy lucre, is my religion. You familiar with faro, lad?"

Still young enough not to have been corrupted at that stage of life, I shook my head. "Momma though poorly of games of chance."

"God bless her, lad," McCoy said, "but you know who wins the most at faro?"

Shrugging, I indicated I had no idea since I didn't even understand how to play the game.

"It's who owns the table and the faro layout. Don't you see it, lad, Abilene is my faro table and layout?"

Looking around me, I found no livestock pens, much less a single faro table. "This place is so small the train never stops here."

"Exactly, lad. I need an isolated town, not too big. One with decent water and good grass. Too, Abilene is directly north of the old Indian trail and trader path that's the best route from Texas."

McCoy kept talking up the advantages of Abilene, but what I saw and heard was a fellow driving a freight wagon and team toward us. I shrugged. "I still don't get it."

"Pardon me a moment, lad, while I deal with this gentleman." McCoy waved his arms and pointed his finger at a nearby spot. The driver followed his directions and reined up just past the apple crates, then bounced from the seat and unhitched the horses. As he did, McCoy reached in his coat and pulled out a pocketbook which he opened and counted out ten dollars. From what I could tell, that was but a fraction of the cash the promoter carried in his wallet.

I suspect I'd grow bowlegged carrying that much money. Even if McCoy was crazy, he wasn't broke.

The driver turned the loose team around like he was directing plow horses and stopped beside McCoy, who gave him the bills. "The tarp's under the seat with a spool of twine and your bags are in the back," he said, taking the money and slipping it in his shirt pocket. Then the fellow clicked his tongue and the animals started back home.

Right proud of himself, McCoy pointed at the conveyance. "What do you see, lad?"

"A wagon without horses."

"Vision, vision," McCoy shouted. "It's our hotel!"

Throwing up my arms, I cried, "You've been staring at the moon too much."

"Vision, lad," he repeated. "As you have likely determined, no quality accommodations are available in Abilene for visitors such as ourselves. I've rented this wagon to sleep in and a tarp to cover the top, should the weather turn ugly. It's better than sleeping on the ground."

This crazy promoter had a point.

"And, you're welcome to share it with me, if you let me finish my proposition."

"You don't have head lice do you?"

"Absolutely not, lad! Do you? And why do you ask?"

"No, I don't, but I shared a room with a fellow that did, and that turned out poorly."

"Then will you listen to my proposal?"

"Sure," I answered, having nothing to lose.

"Say a Texas cattleman has eighteen hundred head of cattle that bring four dollars a head, assuming he can even find a local buyer. He'd make seventy-two hundred dollars. But, say he drives the same number to Abilene, and I offer him twelve dollars a head. That'd come to twenty-one thousand and six hundred dollars."

"The cattle aren't walking to Abilene on their own," I said.

"You're a smarter man than you look, Lomax," McCoy said. "You're talking about overhead."

I glanced up at the sky, but noticed nothing.

"You're meaning costs," he continued. McCoy started a long explanation that a cattleman needs one cowboy for every three hundred head of cattle. He must also hire a cook, a horse herder and a foreman, so that's nine men total he pays a dollar a day for seventy-five days on the trail. That comes to six hundred and seventy-five dollars. McCoy said he estimated the cattleman's other expenses at two dollars a head for another outlay of thirty-six hundred dollars.

I had nothing to add to the conversation because my head handled calculations much slower than McCoy's as he was schooling me in cattle arithmetic.

"Then say he loses three hundred animals on the drive and arrives in Abilene with fifteen hundred head. I give him twelve dollars a head; that comes to eighteen thousand dollars."

Holding up my hand like a school boy in class, I waited until he stopped. "But what if you only offer four dollars a head."

McCoy wagged his finger at me like it was a baby rattle. "No, no, no, lad, because I can sell a steer for twenty-four dollars or more in Chicago or New York. I want to build a reputation as a fair dealer so other cattlemen will come to Abilene. They'll get rich selling in Abilene and I'll grow prosperous selling in Chicago and New York and Philadelphia and Boston."

I feared I'd never get rich if I had to do so many calculations in my head.

"Now, taking away this Texan's expenses of four thousand, two hundred and seventy-five dollars for trailing the herd to Abilene, that leaves him with thirteen thousand seven hundred and twenty-five dollars profit, almost double what he might've made on the entire herd in Texas, even if he had found a buyer."

"Are you herding the cattle to Chicago yourself?"

"Goodness no, lad. The Kansas Pacific will handle it from here in stockcars that'll carry eighteen to twenty head apiece to all the states back east."

The more McCoy talked, the nearer my head came

to exploding from all the figures and calculating he did in his brain. If the promoter didn't stop, I feared my skull might burst, and I would keel over and die, right there, and be buried in Kansas in that unfinished coffin back in Abilene's combination saloon, carpentry shop and funeral parlor.

"So, what's this have to do with me, Mr. McCoy?"

"Lad, I'm glad you asked."

I was too since he stopped throwing so many numbers and calculations at me.

"What I need presently is an energetic fellow with a good horse to ride to Texas and distribute handbills in towns all the way to San Antonio. You'll spread the word of my plans to ranchers. With your youth and your bay, you fit the bill for what I need, even though I'm not fond of your time with Jesse James."

As I mulled over his offer, I remembered my conversation with the barkeep-carpenter-undertaker. "Haven't Texans driven cattle to Kansas and Missouri before?"

"Yes, lad, they have, but they've had no central market guaranteeing to buy their stock. I intend to be that buyer. You might call me the middleman in this arrangement."

"In the middle of what?"

"Between the Texas cattleman and the rich markets back east. We all stand to profit."

"What's this I'm told about a dead line and Texas fever?" I asked. "Abilene's inside the quarantine line so how are you gonna get around that?"

McCoy grinned. "Nothing I can do will change the fever, but I've taken the quarantine line up with the governor. I suspect he'll look the other way as should others when they realize how much money and business these cattle will bring to Kansas, even for homesteaders."

Dusk was approaching, making it harder for me to glimpse McCoy's vision of stockyards, loading chutes and cattle cars loaded with Texas longhorns that were nowhere to be found.

"What's in it for me?"

"A hundred and fifty dollars, half now and the rest when you return. If you can convince a rancher to follow you back to Abilene with a herd, I'll give you a nickel a head for each I buy. If you get back before September with the first herd from Texas, I'll give you a dime per head. That's a lot of money for a lad your age, Lomax, enough to start you a business or maybe buy a farm of your own."

Before darkness overtook us, I looked at the nothingness where McCoy envisioned the future.

"I don't know, Mr. McCoy. What if I get a Texan to bring a herd, but when we arrive there's no stock pens, no loading chute, no cattle cars, no fancy hotel, no nothing because when I look at your vision I can't see a damn thing. Besides that, I understand Texans are meaner than a momma bear with a sore tit."

"You drive a hard bargain, Lomax. I'll raise your pay to two hundred and fifty dollars with a hundred and fifty up front and the balance when you return."

"Let me sleep on it," I answered.

"Fair enough," he said. "Now let's set up camp."

Chapter 10

My partnership with Joseph G. McCoy began that night, even though I didn't realize it. He shared dried apple slices with me for supper, then in the dwindling daylight arranged the back of the wagon so we might retire. He sat his carpetbag on the seat and pushed his trunk to the side where he opened it and pulled out bedding. Placing blankets on the floorboard with a pillow at the wagon front, he told me he would sleep there. After dropping the tailgate, he instructed me to arrange my bedroll on the opposite flank of the conveyance with my head to the back. I did so after caring for my gelding, all the time listening to the promoter chatter about the future, his dreams, and his plans to change the nation.

What I wanted was for him to change the subject. Even in the darkness he saw a vision I could never make out. When I fell asleep, he was still nattering. When I awoke the next morning, he was chatting to himself on his dream for Abilene and the cattle industry as he called it. If I could've rounded up his words, herded them to Chicago and sold them for what he believed they were worth, I might've become a millionaire.

After a breakfast of more dried apples, I took in the vast, vacant prairie land around us. Despite a solid night's rest, I still did not envision the empire that McCoy had created in his mind. "Where do you plan to build your dream?"

The schemer pointed northeast of town. "Over there.

Water is better here by the creek, but the footing is not as good for a railroad siding. I figure I must purchase two hundred and fifty acres or more."

"You haven't purchase land yet?" I asked, concluding that McCoy was crazy.

"That's why I'm back in Abilene, lad. I intend to buy what acreage I need, convince the railroad to construct a siding while I start laying out pens and loading chutes, plus a fine hotel for cattlemen and an office for myself, something more dignified than three apple crates. I'll initiate building by June, July at the latest, and ship out my first livestock in early September if you do your job well."

"But even if I bring back a herd of two thousand cattle, that won't be enough to support a town and business."

McCoy nodded. "You're smarter than I thought, lad. That's right. I'll send out a couple other fellows to find any herders bringing beef into Kansas and funnel them here."

"Wait a minute," I said. "How am I gonna earn a nickel or dime per head bonus if you direct those already on the trail here, and they beat me to Abilene?"

"Our agreement will stand because you'll be the first to intentionally drive cattle here from Texas. You'll earn the bonus, provided your livestock arrive by the first of September."

I couldn't decide whether or not to trust him, especially when I stared at the vast expanse of empty prairie land surrounding us. Besides that, several things made little sense. "Mr. McCoy, there's not enough folks in Abilene to build your dream by June or July."

"We'll bring in the workers we need in plenty of time to complete construction."

"How?"

"Money," McCoy said smugly. "Money talks."

I agreed because money was always speaking to me, usually saying "goodbye." I eyed him long and hard, trying to intimidate him into laughing and admitting he had been funning me from the get-go, but he stood there as serious as a preacher presiding over his momma's funeral. My mind whirled with the possibilities, most with poor endings such as me getting shot by a cattleman who came on my word and found it no different than the emptiness I was staring at or getting hung from the hickory tree which shaded my breakfast.

McCoy gauged my skepticism. "Trust me, lad. You'll make money from this. You'd be a representative of the Great Western Stock Yards, as I plan to call this endeavor. I'll be handling affairs in Abilene while my two brothers in Springfield will secure buyers in the big cities."

My doubts grew. I'd thrown in with the James brothers out of desperation and that had not turned out well, and here I was a day away from throwing in with the McCoy brothers, who might rival the James boys for thievery except that they stole with pen and paper rather than by gun.

McCoy acted amused by my misgivings and that a kid of my limited experience should even question his business sense. "The afternoon stage should have a couple crates of supplies for your trip to Texas. You ever been there?"

"Nope."

"I hear Texans are a rowdy bunch, taking after their cattle, the longhorns. You know how to get to Texas, don't you? You head south through Indian Territory, cross the Red River and there you are."

It sounded simple enough, but many miles separated Abilene from Texas, not to mention rivers and creeks, prairie dog holes, rattlesnakes, thunderstorms and, worst of all, the Indians, maybe not so bad for the five Civilized Tribes, but most definitely for the Comanche and Kiowa, who still believed white men were encroaching on their lands, even though they didn't build houses or fences to mark their property or file a deed with the county.

"How far must I spread these handbills in Texas?"

"I'd say San Antonio, a little over seven hundred miles from Abilene. You should arrive there in four weeks or less, spend a month raising a herd and have three months to return before the first of September. The farther south you go, the more word will get out in Texas about the Great Western Stock Yard and the more profits we'll all make."

McCoy had figured out more angles than a billiards player and remained confident enough in his scheme to succeed, assuming he wasn't a big-talking crook. If he paid me most of my earnings up front, I couldn't complain. "Let me consider on it more."

"I'll need an answer by sundown, Lomax, or I need to find someone else because time is running out on us, if we are to make my schedule."

I nodded, though I knew it was me, not we, that must fight all the hazards, human and natural, between Abilene and San Antonio and back.

Satisfied, McCoy patted me on the shoulder. "That's fine. Let's walk around Abilene until the stage arrives."

We left our makeshift quarters and his outdoor office, strolling along the rutted road that linked the dozen log cabins and crude buildings that made up Abilene. We passed the cabin that housed the saloon with no liquor and the coffin with no corpse. "There's a crazy fellow that lives in there," McCoy noted.

"He thought the same of you," I said.

The promoter shook his head. "He's crazy. I have vision." As we passed each structure, McCoy identified it and its occupants. He pointed out the store, the stage stop, each home and the saloon of Josiah Jones.

"He's another strange fellow, that Jones."

"Crazy, too?"

"No, just odd. Raises prairie dogs to sell to passengers on the stage."

"Any market," I asked, "for prairie dog meat in Chicago or New York or Philadelphia? It'd be easier than driving cattle."

"Ah," said a gratified McCoy, "my vision is rubbing off on you."

"So, it's a good idea?"

"Absolutely not. It's a terrible suggestion, but you're thinking like a lad that will one day find your vision, that idea that will both make you rich and help mankind."

It sounded like a load of malarkey, what McCoy was saying, but he kept on yammering about opportunities available to a man smart enough to grab them. Try as much as I might, I didn't come up with another idea beyond shipping prairie dogs back east. By noon time, McCoy treated me to lunch at Josiah Jones's saloon, but it was little more than a dill pickle fished out of a briny jar and a handful of soda crackers so stale that they tasted like leftovers from the war—the Revolutionary War.

The stage arrived a half hour early and left two wooden crates for McCoy. We each toted one back to his office, me the heavy crate and him the lighter one. Winded, I dropped mine atop an apple crate, and McCoy placed his on an adjacent box. "This is what I've been waiting for and what you'll need in Texas." He retreated to the wagon and dug around in his trunk, returning with a Bowie knife.

"That's an impressive blade for a Yankee," I observed.

"It's come in handy a time or two in my travels?"

"Gutted a fellow have you?"

"Goodness no, lad. Opening tins, cracking walnuts, even shaving once when I misplaced my razor. Now I'll use it to pry the lid off of our handbills." He worked the knife beneath the wooden top and pried the container open, the wood and nails groaning as he separated the cover from the rest of the box. Leaning the top against the crate he pulled a handbill from the stack and placed the knife atop the other sheets so the breeze wouldn't scatter them. He held up the flyer for me. In big, bold print across the top was emblazoned CATTLE MEN READ THIS!

Before I read more, he turned it around as if he didn't think I knew my A-B-Cs. He recited the lines on the circular:

Texas Cattle Wanted!!
Fair Prices Paid by the Great Western Stock Yard
Abilene, Kansas

Joseph G. McCoy, Proprietor

Cattle Received Beginning August 1867
Cattle Pens Enclosing 200 Acres & Multiple Load-
ing Chutes
Fine Hotel Accommodations at Reduced Rates for
Cattle Men & Hands

Favorable Rates from Kansas Pacific Railroad
Convenient Rail Siding Adjacent to Pens
Contact Proprietor for Rates and Details

As he announced his handbill, I looked around and, despite his vision, I saw no pens, or loading chutes, much less a fine hotel. Nor did I spot a railroad siding or understand how those facilities could be built by September first.

"Good words, reverend," I offered.

"So you believe?"

"If seeing is believing, then no. If not seeing is believing, then yes."

"Ride to Texas for me, lad." A hundred and fifty dollars when you leave and the other hundred when you return."

"What if I don't return?"

"You're richer by a hundred and fifty dollars, and I'm better off by the hundred I'll save."

"You sure this'll work? Rumor has it that Texans are so dumb they can't read."

McCoy shrugged. "That's what I've heard about Arkansas folks. I don't know if you can read, lad, but you're not dumb, naïve but not dumb."

"My momma didn't raise an idiot. I can read, though I must admit I'm having a difficult time seeing your vision."

"Go to Texas, come back in the fall. It will be here, I promise. Will you ride for me?"

I debated if this was an opportunity or a chore, but it was easier work than laying rails or skinning buffalo and not nearly as dangerous as robbing banks with Jesse James or standing near Wild Bill Hickok when he practiced pistoleering. Finally, I nodded. "Okay, I'm in."

My new employer clapped his hands. "Wonderful, lad. You can head out in the morning, and I'll see you again this fall."

"I hope to find your pens, chutes, rail siding and hotel when I return because I'd hate to disappoint a crew of dumb Texans, no telling what they might do."

"Not to worry, lad. Let's get to moving as we've things to do." With that he placed the lid back on the handbill box and used the knife to open the other crate. Inside were a few hand tools, some bulging leather sacks the size of a big tobacco bag, three sets of canvas bags with shoulder straps. McCoy picked up a tack hammer and one sack. "Here's a bag of tacks and a hammer to place these handbills anywhere they might draw attention, post offices, courthouses, telegraph poles, any other place they're visible."

I took the materials and walked over to my riding gear, dropping them beside my saddle.

McCoy trailed me with one of the canvas bags. When I turned around, he was standing in front of me, holding the canvas by the shoulder straps. "I suppose I should call these haversacks," he said lifting it by the bands and draping it over my head so that one pouch rested on my chest and the other against my back. "He lifted the flap on the front container. You can carry the handbills in these pouches while you travel and conveniently remove them when you need one. Or, you can drape these over your saddlebags on the back of your horse."

He lifted the canvas from over my shoulders, returning to the box of hand bills. "I had three thousand printed," he said. "I'll give you two-thirds of them and split the remainder between the two riders I hire in June to direct any herds already on the move to Kansas."

He filled both sides of my haversack with posters, then loaded the other two shoulder harnesses. I took the first canvas pouch, heavy with his handbills, and laid it by my saddle.

McCoy spent the rest of the day giving me instructions and showing me a map of the best route to Texas and back. "It follows an old trail that a trader has traveled over the years doing business in Indian Territory. His name is Chisholm as I recall. Last I knew he had a post around the junction of the Big and Little Arkansas Rivers, ninety or so miles south of here."

The Chisholm name sounded familiar, but I failed to place it. McCoy was filling me with so many details, I lacked the time to linger on the fellow's moniker. My boss explained how I must remember rivers and watering holes because cattle needed to water daily, if possible. He said to note good grazing areas and identify a route that provided adequate water and forage.

"That can be tricky on your return trip," McCoy said, "if other herds have passed ahead of you and eaten the grass, so always look for multiple options."

I absorbed as much information as possible, but the promoter kept saturating my mind with so many facts and instructions that I felt like I was getting a diploma from a cow college. I managed okay unless he brought up costs, profits and figures which he manipulated in his head while I was still ciphering on my fingers. McCoy, I admit, possessed book smarts, but I worried he might be a promoter with a vision but no results.

His instructions carried us until dusk when he fished out two tins of peaches from his trunk, cutting the lids open with his Bowie knife. I took one tin and pulled out the peach slices with my finger, savoring the flavor and sipping the thick sweet syrup.

"Any questions about the task ahead?"

"When do I get paid?"

"I can pay you now," he offered, "but I'd suggest I compensate you in the morning when the light's better so you can see I'm not shortchanging you."

Uncertain whether to be impressed with his honesty

or concerned over his larcenous idea, I nodded. "That'll do."

After finishing supper, McCoy and I retired to the freight wagon to prepare our bedding for sleep. He looked at the sky where clouds were building to the west with occasional glimmers of lightning and low rumblings of distant thunder. "We best tie the tarp over the top of the wagon in case we get a shower tonight," he told me. I helped him retrieve the tarpaulin from under the seat, unfold it and pull it over the sideboards. Using his thick-bladed knife, he cut lengths of twine to run through the grommets and secure the cover to wheels. Then we crawled into the wagon, McCoy on the left side, head to the front, me on the opposite flank with my face resting on the open tailgate. If it rained, I would have to inch deeper under the tarp, but the showers passed us by.

"Goodnight, Lomax," McCoy said.

"Same to you, Mr. McCoy."

"Now that we're partners, just call me Joe."

"Goodnight, Joe."

I expected McCoy to keep jabbering but he must have depleted his stock of words while giving me instructions because shortly I heard him snoring. Without his blabber tiring out my ears, I fell asleep quickly, resting so well that McCoy crawling past me to get out of the wagon come morning never disturbed me. The sun had cleared the horizon when I awoke and yawned. I clambered from bed and headed toward the creek to attend to my regular business. I wondered if I was making the right decision going to Texas. While I had been in hostile country before while working on the railroad, other men had always accompanied me. Now, I was to be riding alone through Indian Territory and, even worse, into the Lone Star State. The way McCoy described it, I would traverse land controlled by the five Civilized Tribes: Cherokee, Chickasaw, Choctaw, Creek and Seminole. While they worried me, I was petrified of running into a party of Comanche or Kiowa as I knew enough of Texas to know they were still fighting settlers in some areas. Even scarier was the thought of encountering Texans.

When I returned to the wagon, McCoy awaited me with cash in his hand. He counted out one hundred and fifty dollars in my fingers. "There's a hundred more when you return, more if you bring cattle." In the morning light, I confirmed he paid me fair and square. I shoved the money in my pocket and strode to my bedroll, where the promoter had rolled the tarp back. I gathered my things and fixed my bedding.

I carried my belongings to my hobbled mount and bridled and saddled Relee. He nickered and threw his head like he was tired of hobbles and ready to ride. After securing the bridle and cinching my saddle, I put the hammer and tacks in my saddlebags and tied them to my mount, then slid my carbine into its scabbard. Most importantly to McCoy's way of thinking, I draped the canvas haversack of handbills over the bay's rump.

As I finished with my mount, McCoy carried over a gunny sack. "There's a couple pounds of dried apples inside plus a can of peaches for you." He'd tied the neck with a double loop of twine so I could hang the supplies from my saddle horn. I turned to shake his hand. He grasped it, pumped it hard, then pulled from my grip and threw both arms around me, hugging me as if I was a long-lost but rich relative. "Good luck," he said. "My vision won't succeed without you."

"I'll do my best," I replied, pulling myself from his embrace and bending to unhobble Relee. After putting the hobbles in a saddlebag and tying the flap, I grabbed the reins and saddle horn, then pulled myself atop my bay. I looked at McCoy and the tiny burg that was Abilene, wondering if I would ever again see the promoter or his vision for the town. With that, I turned Relee south, directed him across a shallow ford in Mud Creek and headed toward San Antonio and my first wholesale encounter with Texans, a breed whose stupidity, greed and depravity was exceeded only by that of politicians and lawyers.

As I rode away from Abilene, I studied the land forms

and the grasses and the water holes that might help me on the return trip. With spring taking hold, the landscape was a luscious green with wildflowers blooming and creating carpets of yellow buttercups, splashes of red honeysuckle and begonia and splotches of purple wild violets.

Mostly, I avoided the sod houses of homesteaders, but those I encountered were cordial, even sharing an occasional meal with me. Their smiles, though, darkened when I explained I was hoping to lead a herd of Texas cattle back to Abilene come summer. They feared losing their milk cows and calves to Texas fever and pointed out I was inside the quarantine line so I would have to pass to the west, a thousand miles westward being their preference. I informed settlers I would accommodate their wishes as much as possible, but several made it plain they intended to greet any trespassing longhorns or herders with shotguns and rifles. One feisty lady homesteader informed me she'd fight them off with a broom, if she had to, but first she'd knock me senseless with a frying pan. Like I say, they were good folk unless you riled them.

On the afternoon of the fourth day, I approached the Arkansas River where it met the Little Arkansas and where the Indian trader operated his main post. On a rise overlooking the confluence, I saw a structure that was part soddy and part log cabin with a trio of Indian ponies tethered in front. I pulled out my revolver and checked the load because I was nervous around Indians, even peaceful ones. When I confirmed my pistol was full, I slid it back into my holster and rode forward, pulling up at a hitching rack on the opposite side of the door from tribal mounts.

As I dismounted and tied Relee to the rail, I caught the guttural sounds of negotiations going on inside. The room was dimly lit and reeked of wood smoke, leather, coffee and Indians. The braves scowled at me, then continued their conversation with a gaunt old man with dark leathery skin beneath a crown of white hair and a drooping white mustache. His dark eyes flitted from the three to me and back. Dressed in a tawny buckskin jacket and britches, he spoke their language as easily as his visitors did. He wiggled his hand, signaling he would be with me shortly. As he raised his right arm to gesticulate at his customers, I spotted a silver bracelet that looked out of place on his wrist. After five minutes, the Indians spun around and headed for the door, one of them commenting in his indecipherable tongue as he passed. His friends snickered as they exited the door.

"What did they say?" I asked the old man.

'He laughed. "He said you smell like a buffalo's butt."

I edged to the window to make sure the three didn't take my bay.

"Don't worry," the fellow assured me. "They won't steal your horse."

"Just being cautious," I answered. "I haven't been around many Indians."

"I can tell you're new to these parts. My name's Jesse Chisholm," he said as he walked past the counter to shake my hand."

Offering him my fingers, he clasped them strongly for his age and shook vigorously.

"My name is Lomax, H.H. Lomax."

"Not a common name. Fact, I can recall meeting only one other Lomax, way back in forty-nine when everybody suffering with gold fever headed for California."

Swallowing hard, I bit my lip.

"His name was George Washington Lomax. How do you forget a man whose name honors our first president? You ever heard of him?"

I nodded. "He's my pa."

Chisholm stepped up and threw his arms around me, clinching me with a bear hug before releasing his grip and grabbing my shoulders to look into my eyes. "Your poppa," he said, "saved my life!"

Chapter 11

Somewhere deep in my memory, I vaguely recalled Chisholm's name, likely because my pa must have mentioned it after he returned from his trek to California. Leaving Arkansas with visions of becoming wealthy and providing a more comfortable life for his family, Pa came home dead broke.

The Indian trader inspected me from head to foot, then released his grip on my shoulders. "Welcome to my place, young Lomax. I am honored by your presence, and pray your pa is alive and rich from his Californy sojourn."

"Last time I saw him was two years ago, but he was still breathing. He made it back home from the rush, but the only things he returned with were a tintype of Momma he had carried with him and an American flag that had flown over Sutter's Mill."

Chisholm pointed to a bench squeezed between goods stacked against the wall. "Take a seat."

"How did Pa save your life? Rescue you from Indians or fight off a bear?"

"Nothing so dramatic, but much braver. My ma was a Cherokee and my poppa Scottish so I've always traveled freely and safely among the Indians. Even the Comanche took a liking to me." He paused and pulled up his right sleeve, pointing to the silver bracelet three-quarters of an inch wide on his wrist. "The Comanche gave me this as a sign of respect since I've translated for them at various treaty negotiations, me being fluent in fourteen Indian languages. Fact is, I'm helping gather tribes for another parlay at Medicine Lodge this summer."

Jesse got sidetracked. "What about Pa? How did he save you?"

"When everybody was charging across the plains to reach Californy, your poppa and his party reached a trading post where I had been doing great business with the gold-struck sojourners, hundreds of them over four months. The night your poppa and compatriots arrived, I took with the cholera, a dreadful disease. I was fevering and delirious, fighting the runs and the vomiting. I had enough sense about me to know the others wanted to steal my goods for the journey. Your poppa stood up to them while they argued it didn't matter because I was going to die anyway. He insisted stealing was a sin, even from a dying man, and if they thought otherwise, he'd started west with the wrong bunch. He refused to let them rob me, and he refused to leave me alone to die."

Pride of Pa washed over me.

"The others left the next morning. They may have taken a few of my goods outside of your poppa's sight, but they didn't clean me out. Your poppa stayed with me six days, hauling water from the creek for me to drink, forcing food in me even when I couldn't keep it down. When he finally departed, I was better though still weak. So the gold-seekers wouldn't pester me or steal my supplies once he took off, he found a stick of burned firewood and used the char to write SMALL-POX on the door. That discouraged intruders and gave me time to recover. I'd died if your poppa hadn't stayed with me, young Lomax. He deserved to find a fortune in Californy."

"He always said he got to the gold fields a week too late to register a paying claim. Odd thing is, the other ones in his party just disappeared. He saw no sign of them on the Pacific Coast and none of them ever returned to Cane Hill, Arkansas. Don't know if Indians killed them or they died of thirst in the desert or froze to death in the mountains. You may have saved Pa's life as well."

"I'm proud to hear that. Odd how our lives turn out

sometimes," Chisholm said. "What brings you to these parts?"

"A fellow named McCoy hired me to ride to Texas and promote Abilene as a destination for longhorn cattle. He plans to build stock pens, loading chutes, a railroad siding, a hotel and other facilities to attract Texans and their livestock to his town. I'm to tack handbills up between the Red River and San Antonio and bring back a herd by the first of September. Mr. McCoy said you'd know the best route."

"Can't say I've met this McCoy."

"He knows of you."

Chisholm shrugged. "Mr. McCoy has given you a dangerous task. You'll be going through Indian Territory, right? You haven't been around Indians much, I can tell."

Nodding, I answered, "That's a fact. When I worked with the railroad, I saw a few from afar, but I rode with other men and had no trouble."

"They have a greater sense of honor than the white man," Chisholm said. "Their word is good, but the government's isn't. Every tribe has been betrayed on treaties, and they distrust any white man crossing the lands ceded to them by the government. Sometimes, they attack innocent folks, especially those in small parties, and your party can't get any smaller."

I gulped. What had I gotten myself into?

"They expect a toll from anyone crossing their land. When herders near their territory, the various tribes extort cattle or something else from them."

Though I had plenty of money in my pocket, a hundred and fifty dollars to be exact, I didn't plan on bribing my way across Indian Territory. "Maybe I can slip past them."

Chisholm laughed. "They'll find you. Getting by them is harder than slipping a pork chop past a starving dog. Near impossible, it is. But ol' Jesse here'll help you. It's the least I can do for the son of the man that saved my life."

The old half-breed motioned for me to follow him

behind the counter through a door that led to a cramped space that tripled as kitchen, bedroom and storeroom with a small woodstove, a table and two chairs, a cot with a buffalo robe for mattress, a stack of bison hides in the corner and a mixture or crates, tins, and kegs filled with trading goods. I took a seat at the little table.

Joining me, Chisholm spent the rest of the evening, save when an occasional Indian arrived to barter, explaining how to navigate Indian Territory and its inhabitants. "Don't show fear when you encounter a brave. If he sees weakness, he might harm you." He instructed me in basic Indian sign language, giving me the gestures for several words.

"For 'friend,' you hold your right hand at neck level and raise it to the top of your head, palm outward with your first two fingers extended and your last two bent, like you're ordering two beers," he said. "For 'hunger,' place either hand palm up at your navel with your little finger against your belly and move back and forth like you're sawing yourself in half. Don't rub, your belly, saw it."

I practiced the signs with my arms and hands, careful to mimic Chisholm's movements so no Indian would mistake my intent. He gave me the gestures for "give me," "horse," "yes" and "no." My sign vocabulary was small, but functional.

After instructing me in rudimentary sign language, Chisholm explained options for getting to Texas. "I blazed a path from here to the Red River. It's rutted and worn enough you should be able to follow it to the border. Can't be as helpful about Texas because I haven't traveled there as much. I did some work for Sam Houston, I did, but that was years ago. Like me, he had a foot in the Indian world, he just didn't grow up in a Cherokee camp as I did."

Between McCoy's advice on the business of the cattle trade and Chisholm's instructions on the practical side of trail life among Indians, I picked up a basic education for my sojourn. At that point, however, I'd never met a Texas longhorn, as cantankerous a breed as ever walked on four legs, so I can't say I was an authority on trail driving. I came to learn that longhorns carried as belligerent a temperament as the Texans that claimed them, but at that moment I thought I was smart enough for the task before me.

As darkness approached, Chisholm instructed me to take my bay to the river to water him good, then put him in the corral in the back of the trading post. He said I could leave my gear, including my carbine, in the shed by the pen as the Indians wouldn't steal anything. I asked how he had could guarantee no theft, and he told me they knew not to anger him or he might move his post to another less convenient location for them.

I exited the trading post and untied Relee, leading him to the river bank and letting him water. While he drank, I pulled my carbine from its scabbard because I had less faith in the Indians than Chisholm did, especially after one had said I smelled like a buffalo's behind. Maybe so, but he and his two buddies weren't a bouquet of roses, either. When Relee had sated his thirst, I led him back to the tiny corral where two pintos watched our approach. I unloaded the canvas haversacks and saddlebags from the bay's back and hung them on nails in the shed, then retreated to my horse and removed the tack, carrying the saddle, blanket, bridle and carbine to the shelter, leaving them there, though I admit I preferred to take them inside where I could see them.

When I re-entered the trading post, Chisholm smiled and nodded. "You'll do."

Uncertain what he meant, I shrugged and asked, "How so?"

"You gotta build trust to get through Indian Territory. I told you to leave your gear in the shed, though I suspect you'd rather store it in here where you could guard it. You went against your instincts and did what I suggested. That's the faith you'll need riding through their country. You're decent stock, just like your poppa."

"Thank you, Mr. Chisholm."

"Jesse's fine, young Lomax, so join me in the back, and we'll have supper."

I followed him into the rear room where he had added wood to his stove and was heating a pot of leftover beans and a pan of cornbread. Figuring I should thank him for his hospitality, I excused myself and retreated outside to the shed and brought in the gunny sack containing the remaining dried apple slices McCoy had given me.

Sitting at Chisholm's table, I pulled out the brown paper bundle that held the fruit and opened the wrapping, exposing the deformed and discolored apples. "Here's something to add to our fare."

Chisholm looked over his shoulder and grinned. "You done with that tow sack?"

I nodded.

"Let me borrow it then as I've got a use for it."

"Sure, take it," I answered. "I won't need it now."

He deserted the stove, grabbed the bag and toted it to the counter where he left it. Returning to his station over the bean pot, Chisholm said, "Next time you see your poppa, tell him I still remember him and thank him for standing by me during my bout with cholera."

"I'll do it, though I'm not sure when I'll return to Cane Hill as there've been strong animosities there against me since the war."

Grabbing a rag, he brought over the pan with the cornbread, then the pot with the beans. "I didn't boil no coffee," he apologized.

"I drink coffee only when I have to."

Chisholm fetched a couple of tin plates and tin forks and joined me at the table. He scooped out brown beans onto my plate and added a slice of cornbread. After he helped himself, we attacked supper. The beans were too salty and the cornbread was too stale, but it was food and it filled our bellies. After consuming his offerings, I pushed the apple slices to him, and he grabbed about half. I retrieved the brown paper bundle and popped a piece of the dried fruit into my mouth, glad to have it to offset the bitter saltiness of the beans.

While we ate, Chisholm told me more to expect on my trip, landmarks to watch for, rivers that hid quicksand, locations where rattlesnakes thrived, and more things than I could ever remember. He had grown up close to the earth and his Indian forebears. When he finished, Chisholm offered me his bed for the night, but I responded I'd sleep in the corner on the stacked buffalo robes. He nodded as he stood up and took our tin plates, dropping them in a box by the stove to wash later. Stepping out to the counter, he instructed me to get comfortable on my bed while he gathered items he'd need the next morning. I told him I wanted to purchase a carton of ammunition for my revolver and my carbine before I left. He promised to remember.

As the Indian trader conducted his business in the front, I pulled off my boots and slumped over the stacked of buffalo hides, nestling into place and enjoying the best night's sleep since leaving Abilene. I awoke the next morning to the aroma of Chisholm cooking saltpork in his frying pan and boiling coffee in his blackened pot. Noticing my stirrings, he greeted me. "Morning, young Lomax. The way you snored, you must've slept well."

"Jesse, I admit, I rested peacefully. Breakfast smells delicious and the hospitality's been great, but while I'd like to spend another night on your buffalo robes, I can't lose too many days and still get back to Abilene by September first."

"You've a lot of riding ahead of you."

I got up, pulled on my boots, and grabbed my hat to go to the corral.

"There's a couple cartons of ammunition for you up front," he said as I slipped out of the kitchen and past the counter where the two boxes sat atop three Harper's Weekly Magazines and beside two bulging gunny sacks.

Outside I walked behind the shed to attend to my regular morning business. When I returned, Relee was watching me, chewing on hay in the feed trough while the two pintos circled the small pen. I entered the shed and grabbed my bay's bridle and saddle, which I heaved atop the upper fence rail. Opening the gate wide enough for me to slip through, I marched up to my gelding, slid the bridle over his head and led him from the corral.

After latching the gate, I tied Relee to a fencepost and saddled him, cinching him up tight for the ride ahead. Next I retrieved my carbine, canteen, saddlebags and bedroll, then tied them to Relee. I picked up the double haversack of hand bills and draped it over the saddlebags and Relee's rump.

Satisfied that my bay was ready for the miles ahead, I returned inside to find at my place on the table a dozen pieces of bacon on the same dirty plate I'd eaten from last night. The old fellow spent little time washing dishes. Chisholm brought over a piece of cold cornbread which he dropped on my dish. This didn't compare to eating a cherry pie in a Springfield's Honey Creek, but on the other hand, the eats here were free, and no one had died—at least not yet.

Chisholm poured me a cup of coffee and sat it down at my place. "Go ahead and eat so you can hit the trail. I'll have breakfast later. I've still got beans left over from last evening, if you'd like, though I haven't warmed them."

Remembering the frijoles' saltiness, I passed on the offer. "This'll be fine." The cornbread was even staler than the night before, but the bacon tasted mighty fine. His coffee was strong and bitter, but I drank it as didn't care to offend his hospitality. He offered me another cup, but I waved it away. "How far am I from Indian Territory?

"About forty miles," he said. "You can make it in a day and a half easy."

"How will I know I'm there?"

"You'll spot all the scalps hanging from the trees," he said. "You can't miss them."

I gulped.

"I'm pulling your leg, young Lomax, funning you. You'll do fine as long as you remember the things I've taught you."

"I'll try," I said after I swallowed my last bite of bacon. I wiped my hands on my shirt and arose, checking the holster at my side and marching out of the kitchen behind Chisholm. At the counter, he picked up the two cartons of ammunition and handed them over. "What do I owe you?"

"It's all a gift from me as the only way I can repay your poppa for standing with me when I stood at death's door. I've got more things for you." He pointed to the magazines. "You want to take those, there's a couple from last year and one from February."

"I'm not much of a reader."

"Me neither," he replied, "but they come in handy when I visit the outhouse. Beats corncobs or prairie grass or nothing."

Now I had to admit that I'd used a handbill or two on the way down to Wichita to wipe away nature's mess, but I'd never considered using a publication. "I think I'll take up reading after all, Jesse."

"It has its advantages," he answered as I took the three magazines and shoved them under my arm.

"Your gunny sack and one of mine go with you, young Lomax," he said. "I've packed trinkets, necklaces, awls, pieces of mirrored glass, beads and other items that flatter the braves and squaws. It'll provide you something to offer as gifts for crossing their land. In the other sack I've put a can of soda crackers, a jar of preserves, some jerky, a tin of matches, a ball of twine and a few additional items you might need like an old pocketknife as I didn't see a blade among your belongings."

"I've got money. I can pay you."

He waved my offer away. "Your poppa paid me in advance."

I grabbed the trinket bag; he took the food sack; and we marched outside to my bay. I dropped my gunny sack and moved the haversacks so I could untie the flap on my saddlebag and stuff the ammunition and the three magazines inside, before re-securing the flap and reloading the haversack stuffed with the handbills. At first I wasn't sure where to hang the two gunny sacks, then realized the twine and the pocketknife offered the solution. Opening Chisholm's sack, I retrieved the knife and ball of string. I cut a five-foot length, returned the twine to the sack and put the knife in my pocket. Next I

looped and tied one end of the twine around the mouth
of one sack, then the other end around the second bag. I
slid one gunnysack over the saddle and looped the twine
many times around the saddle horn. Satisfied that the
knots and twine would hold, I turned around and shook
Chisholm's hand.

"Thanks for everything."

"No, thank your poppa for helping me eighteen years
ago."

I patted the pistol in my holster, snugged my hat and
untied Relee's reins from the fencepost and climbed
aboard my gelding. "Maybe I'll see you when I return
late summer."

"I hope that works out for us both." Chisholm
paused, then said, "Hold on a minute." He reached with
his left hand for his opposite wrist and clamped onto
that silver bracelet I had noticed the day before." Slowly,
almost reluctantly, he removed it. "Take this and wear it
everywhere between here and San Antonio." He lifted
his arm for me to grab it.

"It looks like silver. Is it?"

"Yes, indeed. The Comanche gave it to me in gratitude for the work I'd done on their behalf. Most tribes
know what it represents. If they recognize it, they won't
bother you." He shook his hand at me. "Take it."

I slipped it from his fingers and slid it over my right
hand until it settled on my wrist. "You sure they won't
steal it?"

"No Indian will, but there's a lot of white men who
would for the silver. They'll give you more problems
than any tribe."

I thanked him again and started toward the Territory. Relee traveled with a skittish streak, annoyed as we
rode. It took me half a day to figure out that the gunny
sacks hanging from the saddle horn were heavy enough
to rub hard against him. When I stopped to eat a couple
strips of jerky, and let my bay graze, I reassessed our
traveling loads. Though it pained me to do it, the only
solution was to hang the burlap sacks instead of the haversack over the saddlebags. I knew the twin pouches

with the handbills would be just as annoying hanging from the saddle horn so I opted to wear the haversack over my shoulders because I had no other choice. I slipped the flyer carrier over my head. It was awkward, climbing into the saddle, but remained the best solution to Relee's discomfort, even if it added to mine.

By nightfall, we neared Indian Territory, and I expected to cross over by noon the next day. I'd heard so many horror stories of Indians, I slept poorly that night, thinking a war party was slipping up on me intent on taking my scalp. Even so, I awoke the next morning with my hair intact and continued my journey to the Territory.

I don't know when I entered Indian Territory because I saw no sign, no scalps hanging from trees, no burned out homes or anything, nor had I seen another human being all day. Maybe this leg of my journey would be as easy as kicking a dead horse. My overconfidence was premature, though. Late afternoon as I rode over a knoll and approached a tree-lined creek, I heard a swish and a thump. Something had struck me. I looked down.

An arrow protruded from my chest.

Chapter 12

The shaft, of course, had plowed into the front haversack pouch packed with handbills. I understood that, but my attacker did not. My mind raced with what to do next. If I rode on, he might shoot again and strike flesh rather than paper. After seeing an Indian emerge from behind a clump of trees astride a pinto, I decided to trap him. I wobbled in my saddle, slid off the side away from him so he could not so easily see me hit the ground. I collapsed in the spring grass, laying spread eagle and holding Relee's reins with my left hand so my horse wouldn't bolt and leave me stranded. With my right, I inched my revolver from the holster, cocked the hammer with my thumb and waited. I squinted my eyes, leaving them cracked enough to watch my assailant riding toward me uncertain of my fate. As the brave approached, Relee fidgeted, jerking his head back and pulling the reins free, trotting off two dozen yards as my foe neared.

Now I saw my assailant, who seemed older than me but still young, drawing closer on his pinto, his bow with another arrow aimed at me. I tried to hold my breath and remain motionless when he reached me. My ploy worked because he lowered his weapon, removed the arrow and put it back in his quiver. He came so close I feared his pony might step on me, before the savage tugged on the reins and slid off his pinto to stand over me, glowering at his "kill." When he pulled his knife,

I realized he planned to scalp me. Warily, he stepped toward me, straddling me at the waist, lifting the knife and leaning forward to give me a haircut.

As he did, I opened my eyes and lifted my pistol, pointing it straight at his nose. His eyes widened as big as a wash tub. I thought he fixated on my gun barrel, but my sleeve had slipped back down my arm, revealing Chisholm's silver bracelet. Then I realized the amulet more than my pistol terrified him. He tossed his knife aside and backed away, picking up the reins to his pony and handing them to me as I sat up, my revolver following his every move. My assailant stood more horrified than me, twisting his head from side to side.

"Nooo, nooo," he mumbled and gestured "no" with his hands, then retreated four steps from me. He walked toward Relee, placidly grazing on the new spring growth. Reaching my bay, the brave took the reins and returned him, giving me the leathers as he grabbed the guides for his own pony. He picked up his knife and inserted it in his sheath. I sat looking at him and trying to figure out the power of the silver bracelet. My attacker offered me his hand so I released the hammer on my pistol and shoved it in my holster. Taking my fingers, the warrior helped me to my feet. Maybe he wasn't such a savage after all.

When he reached to pull his arrow from my haversack, I pushed his fingers away and gestured the sign Chisholm had taught me for friend. This Indian mirrored the signal. He pointed to his wrist then mine, mouthing gibberish I couldn't decipher. I lifted my gun hand, and he took it with his left hand and rubbed it with his right, then bent and kissed the bracelet. His actions confused me, though I suspected he revered the amulet and feared he had offended its powers. He released me and retreated warily, fearful of affronting me or my silver wrist charm.

"I'm H.H. Lomax," I announced.

He shrugged and repeated more twaddle that made as much sense as a spoon did to a catfish. My Indian friend pointed again at his arrow in my chest.

"No," I said, "I keep."

"Nooo, nooo," he said.

I never determined what tribe he was from or what dialect he spoke. For what I knew, "nooo" meant "yes." I had no idea. Figuring to show him I carried no grudge, I stepped to my mount and untied the gunnysacks from the saddlebags. I opened the sack with the trade goods, stuck my hand in and pulled out a beaded necklace, offering it to "True Shot" as I named him.

My newfound friend grabbed the trinket and whooped aloud as he waved it overhead. When he finished swinging the bauble, he took his other hand and widened the necklace into a loop that he slid over his neck. I studied him, taking in his long braided black hair, his bronzed skin and dark eyes, accentuated by the beaded headband. He wore buckskin leggings and a loin cloth, but nothing covered his muscled chest. He smiled at me as the necklace fell in place.

I grinned back, thinking the brave and I were about to part ways. After re-tying the mouth of the gunnysack, I secured it to the saddlebags. I extended my hand, shaking his when he grasped mine.

"So long, True Shot," I said. "It's been a pleasure to meet and survive you."

"Nooo, nooo," he said.

I mounted Relee, difficult as it was supporting those haversacks filled with paper and now toting the extra burden of True Shot's arrow. As I pointed my mount south, True Shot leaped atop his pony and pulled in beside me. I figured he planned to abandon me shortly, but he accompanied me for miles.

Deciding company that didn't understand me was better than none at all, I jabbered to True Shot as much as McCoy did to me when we first met. I told my new companion I was from Cane Hill, Arkansas, and was headed to Texas to bring longhorn cattle back through his land.

"Nooo, nooo," he said, still as befuddled as when I shoved the barrel of my gun in his nose. As I spoke, he nodded, occasionally throwing out a sentence that made as much sense as a pencil did to a dog.

We both rode south, me gabbing and him listening to my every word like a revival-attending sinner on the verge of salvation. As dusk approached, my partner gestured wildly and reined his horse away, riding off toward another tree-lined creek. I figured I'd seen the last of True Shot, but I was as wrong as a husband arguing with his wife about anything . About fifteen minutes later, he reappeared, holding in the air an arrow with a cottontail impaled on the end and several pieces of firewood under his arm.

Pointing with the shaft toward the creek a half a mile ahead, I assumed he was directing me to a favorable spot to camp overnight. When we reached the site, I dismounted, removing my haversack and placing it on the ground so the arrow aimed skyward. As I removed gear from Relee's back, True Shot jumped from his saddle blanket, striding to a circle of blackened rocks that had been used as a fire pit. He stuck his arrow in the soil and dumped the wood in the depression, except for one small limb which he whittled with his knife to create the shavings necessary to start a fire. Satisfied he had enough wood slivers, he surveyed the surrounding area and strode to clumps of dead grass, yanking fists full of the dry plants to help with his blaze. He carried the straw back to the pit and pulled a flint and a piece of steel from the warbag on the side of his pinto. He bent and struck a rock to metal, trying to capture a spark to ignite a flame.

The way he was going, it might take all night before we got a fire and supper, so I dug through the second gunnysack Chisholm had given me and found the tin of matches. Pulling one out, I eased over to True Shot, who was begging for fire to take hold. I squatted beside him and remained there until he looked up at me. At that moment, I flicked the end of my match with a thumbnail and the stick flared. True Shot jumped back. "Nooo, nooo," he said as I touched the flame to the grass, kindling and wood. A fire took hold of the yellowed grass and wood chips. When my match went out, I tossed it aside, but he jumped for it, picking up the blackened wand and trying to bring it back to life by flicking his thumb against its tip. As the match was no Lazarus, True Shot failed, then watched in amazement at how quickly my fire grew. He looked at me for enlightenment.

I figured I'd flatter him with a scientific explanation. "It's magic," I said.

My companion nodded as if he understood, then yanked the hare-bearing arrow from the ground and slid the cottontail past the metal point. Yanking his knife out, he stepped to the creek waters to clean our meal.

Since he was handling our meal, I walked Relee to the stream for water. When my bay had his fill, I hobbled him and let him graze around camp. As True Shot was taking care of our supper, I laid out my bedroll and retrieved a magazine that Chisholm had given me. I had no interest in perusing it, but I was getting prepared for the morning when I suspected reading material should come in handy.

True Shot returned with the skinned red meat impaled on a stick. I thought I saw him licking his lips and wondered if he had been eating the cottontail's entrails. Rather than sicken myself wondering if this young brave had snacked on the lesser parts of the rabbit, I distracted myself by thumbing through the magazine. To my wonderment, I ran across an article by a fellow claiming to be Colonel G.W. Nichols writing about my former roommate James Butler "Wild Bill" Hickok. Not only that, the story purported to tell the actual events surrounding "the McCanles Massacre," as the piece described Hickok's showdown with that Nebraska gang, and the shootout with Davis Tutt. I cringed in disbelief. I moved closer to the fire for better light, and I plowed into the article, scanning it as fast as I could, and then re-reading it slower for details. This story left me sicker than True Shot's eating habits, the account coming no nearer to the truth than as I was to the moon just cracking the horizon.

Now I couldn't speak for the veracity of the description of the McCanles fight, but I was there at the Springfield gunplay and the facts were as dead wrong as Davis Tutt himself. I studied the article, looking for my name and was relieved not to see it, but offended that Colonel Nichols had misstated the truth as flagrantly as a politician on the campaign trail. He made Hickok sound like an ignorant hayseed with the words he put in Wild Bill's mouth. The February 1867 issue of Harper's New Monthly Magazine taught me never to believe what you read. I was torn between throwing the issue in the fire, using it later when nature necessitated or saving it for posterity. As much as anything, the article reaffirmed my belief that reading created more problems than it solved, especially when you had writers that made up "facts" to help sales.

As I returned the magazine to my saddlebags, True Shot roasted our supper over the fire, which hissed and spit as the juices and fat from the flesh dropped into the flames. When he was done, he offered me the shaft with the meat on it. I bit into the cottontail, burning my tongue as I chewed. I offered the spit back to True Shot, but he waved it off. By his gesture, I took it that the rabbit was mine, save for the entrails. I let it cool off before taking another bite, then pulled the meat away from the bone as I enjoyed the taste of fresh game. Finishing everything I could pluck from the bone with my fingers or my teeth, I tossed the remnants into the fire. I wiped my hands on the grass, then went to the food sack and extracted the jar of peach preserves Chisholm had given me. I unscrewed the lid and dipped my finger in the wide-mouth jar, extracting a dollop of the yellow fruit and placing it on my tongue to savor the sweetness. When I offered the jar to True Shot, he grabbed it and followed my lead, shoving two fingers into the jelly and removing a big wad. His eyes lit up when he stuck his fingers in his mouth and sucked off the preserves. He smiled, nodding rapidly as he chewed. Next he stuck three fingers in the jar, fished out a third of the container's contents and crammed the preserves between his lips. He offered me the jar, but I waved it away, deciding there'd been too much of his hand in the preserves for my taste.

"You keep it," I said.

Though he didn't understand my words, he recognized my intent and attacked the contents with his fingers again, getting as many preserves out of the jar as his digits reached. When he had extracted everything he could, he broke the jar against a rock in the pit and licked the preserves off each piece of glass before throwing the shards in the fire, smiling the whole while.

By the time he finished, darkness had shrouded the country, only the crescent moon and our fire offering any light. The day had been difficult, me being attacked by and then befriended by True Shot, and now on the verge of retiring for the night, I worried that this had been a ploy to disarm my concerns so my Indian friend might kill and scalp me while I slept.

I hobbled Relee near my bedroll, hoping that he might whinny or neigh to alert me if True Shot crept up on me while I slept. Removing my boots and gun belt, I placed my revolver by my side to defend myself if you-know-who approached my head or hair. I crawled atop my bedding and waited. "Good night, True Shot. I hope you don't scalp me overnight."

"Nooo, nooo," he replied.

For a spell, I wondered if I would still be alive come morning or what tribe True Shot claimed: Comanche, Kiowa, Cherokee, Seminole, Chickasaw, Choctaw, Creek or another variation that escaped me. I dozed off and fell into a deep chasm of slumber. I slept awhile, but was awakened by someone stroking my hair. My assailant was so close I felt his hot breath upon my forehead. I inched my hand toward my revolver, slowly lifting, cocking and swinging it at my assailant.

"Caught you," I said, ready to fire.

My assailant whinnied and snapped his teeth. It was Relee. He had been licking my head, I assumed for the salt from dried sweat. "Get," I said, slapping at his jaw with my pistol, releasing the hammer, sliding the weapon back in its holster and returning to sleep, though much less soundly. I arose with the sun and True Shot, who attended his business, though not with the benefit of reading material. After we finished heeding nature's call, we broke camp, loaded up our horses and headed south, nibbling on strips of jerky for breakfast. Each day I wore the haversack with the arrow in it as a joke that no one but me understood.

After that first night, I never worried about True Shot, though I never understood him either. I motioned the word friend to him and he nodded, returning the same sign. He stayed at my side the entire journey through Indian Territory, except for when he might ride away for an hour and return with other Indians, who stared at me from afar while he rejoined me. Sometimes the curious lined the trail as we passed, never speaking or threatening us. I came to believe leaving the arrow in the haversack and wearing it each day impressed the Indians that I was invincible to their weapons. Perhaps they wanted to see the bracelet. Or, maybe they thought I was stupid. I never knew because I didn't understand their language. If they understood mine, they never so indicated. When the Indians were close, I gestured the word friend and they mirrored it back, but otherwise they remained stoic. By the third day, I was distributing among them many of the trinkets from Chisholm's burlap sack.

Each day as I rode, I tried to remember the Indian trader's details about terrain, water and forage, things that would be helpful on the return. The land was mostly prairie with occasional patches of trees and periodic streams. The country held few secrets as you could see so far in any direction. Periodically, I saw hovels and soddies I took belonged to the Indians, but I was never sure.

Day after day we headed south, making good time as we rode twelve to fifteen hours a spell, stopping only to let our mounts graze or water and to pass out more trinkets to a few Indian families that gathered to watch me go by. The farther we traveled, the more comfortable I grew with True Shot. We visited a lot with each other, never understanding a thing, but enjoying the sound of another human's voice. There were things I wanted to learn, but doubted I could ever find out.

"Why'd you shoot me the day we met, True Shot?"

"Nooo, nooo," he replied.

"Why'd you stay as my guardian angel? Was it the silver bracelet or my natural charm?"

"Nooo, nooo!"

"What tribe do you belong to?"

"Nooo, nooo!"

That's the way most of our conversations played out each day. On occasions when we had time before sunset, True Shot would slip away and bring back game, mostly rabbits, for supper though one evening he returned with a turkey, and we dined well on the roasted bird.

The days ran together so I lost track of how long it had been since I departed Chisholm's post, but I made good time through Indian Territory because with True Shot at my side, I never fretted about Indians slipping up on me. Chisholm's trinkets helped endear me to the tribes. Riding with the arrow in my chest, I may have been to the Indian Territory spectators the main attraction in a freak show like the ones that visited Fayetteville when I was a boy.

"Why haven't you scalped me, True Shot?" I asked.

"Nooo, nooo," he answered.

I nodded. "I thought so."

No matter how much brain muscle I put to the problem, I never figured out how word spread among the tribes faster than we could travel. For several days, a crowd always watched us pass at multiple places along the trail. Sometimes just men on ponies gathered to observe. At other times whole families, all afoot, stood by and gazed. Their inscrutable faces, even those of the children, puzzled me. Perhaps they expressed awe or fear or boredom, I never knew and would never know. The farther south we rode, however, the fewer Indians came out to meet us, perhaps because I ran out of trinkets and baubles to offer them.

Then one afternoon we topped a small ridge and before me spread a wide river with red sandy shoulders and muddy sandbars sprinkled throughout its meandering course. We reined up our horses and stared. The burgundy waters rippled rather than rushed downstream. It had to be the Red River, the boundary between Indian Territory and Texas. I'd seen muddy streams before, but never water so loaded and red with sediment. I figured if you strained a tub full of the water, you'd wind up with a thimble of liquid and a ton of soil.

True Shot pointed across the water. "Tay-hass," he said, "Tay-hass."

"Texas," I repeated.

He nodded.

"Thank you," I said and made the friend sign.

Then he pointed to his pony and held the reins as if he was turning the animal around. I took it to mean he would not cross with me.

Tay-hass, nooo! Tay-hass, nooo!"

"I understand," I answered, nudging my horse forward.

True Shot followed me until I neared the water's edge, but rode up grabbed my reins and yanked them back. "Nooo, nooo!" he cried. With his fingers flat at chin level in front of his face, he slowly raised his arm until his hand was over his head. Twice he repeated the gesture which I took it to mean I would sink in quicksand.

I nodded, and he took my reins, leading my bay farther downstream and pointing first at the water's edge and second across the river. Try as I might, I discerned little difference between the two crossing points, but I trusted True Shot. I reached out to shake his hand. He clasped mine and pumped it. I smiled and released his grip, grabbed the arrow impaled in my haversack and wiggled it free. When I returned the shaft to him, he grinned and shoved it in his quiver.

To thank him for his guidance, I dismounted and untied the empty gunnysack that had held the Chisholm's trade goods. I offered him the empty sack and then the second burlap bag which still carried a few soda crackers, jerky, the ball of twine and the tin of matches. I knew I could re-supply in Texas.

"Gift," I said. "It's yours. Take it."

Hesitating, True Shot pointed to the bags and then to himself.

I nodded. "Yes!" Then I tied the mouth of the food bag shut and with the ends of the twine took his hand and wrapped the string around his wrist so he understood the bag and its contents were his.

He shouted more Indian gibberish, jumped off of his pony and grabbed me. I'd been shot with an arrow by an Indian that now hugged me. It was an odd world, I thought. When he finished, True Shot untied the twine from his wrist, shoved his hand inside and extracted the match tin. Twisting the lid open, he pulled out a match and used his thumbnail to flick it to flame.

"Magic," I said.

True shot let the flare burn to his fingertips before tossing the match in the water. He closed the tin and shoved it in the bag before tying the burlap to a leather strap on his pinto's flank. He draped the empty tow sack over his saddle blanket for added padding.

Then I mounted Relee and crossed the river along the route True Shot indicated. The ripples never reached my boots in the crossing. As I emerged, I turned and saw True Shot watching me. I waved, and he gestured back, jumped on his pony and galloped over the rise out of sight, screaming the entire way.

Relief washed over me that I had made it through Indian Territory alive. My first action after my Indian Territory companion disappeared was to dismount and relieve myself. Now I was in Texas, the home of actual savages, the Texans themselves.

Chapter 13

As I looked back across the Red River at Indian Territory, I took pride in reaching Texas with my scalp and
with Joseph G. McCoy's hundred and fifty dollars in
my pocket. I had as much cash as any kid of my caliber
in the state because Texas still suffered from the war's
aftermath, as money was tighter than a banjo string and
tempers flared like fat in a fire because Texans couldn't
accept they had been whipped with the rest of the
Confederacy. Being so far west, Texas had borne less
than the other Southern States, but Texans didn't see it
that way. As yet, the state hadn't been re-admitted to
the Union, so U.S. soldiers not only fought Comanche
and Kiowa, but also recalcitrant Texans who wanted to
relive the past rather than face the future.

Two miles south of the Red River, I came to a tiny
burg named Salt Creek. With a population hovering at
a hundred souls, Salt Creek looked like a city compared
to Abilene. I rode into town inspecting the squat buildings and the thin people that stared back at me. I opened
the flap on the top haversack and pulled out a couple
handbills as I entered town, offering one to a gentleman
crossing the street in front of me. He scowled. "What
are you peddling?"

"The future," I answered, "a vision to make Texans
rich." I handed him a poster.

He wadded it up and threw it on the ground. "I can't
read."

"You own any cattle?"

"I own nothing since them damn Yankees took everything but my thoughts!"

While I doubted this fellow ever had an original thought, I asked him if he knew of any cattlemen looking to sell their stock as a market was opening this fall in Abilene, Kansas.

My friend spat on the ground. "Kansas is a Northern state," he grumbled. "Why would any decent Texan want to trade with a Yankee?"

"Because those Yankees have money," I suggested.

"Remember the Alamo," the fellow said, before continuing his journey from one side of the street to the other. He was the first of hundreds to offer me that salutation as I made my way across Texas. Though that battle was over thirty years past, I suspected the Texans saw the adage as redeeming past glories without acknowledging recent defeats.

On a live oak at the southern edge of town, I dismounted, gathered my hammer and tacks, then nailed my second handbill to the tree. I figured one flyer on the oak and another in the street were all this place deserved, so I rode on. Two posters down and fourteen hundred and ninety-eight or so to go, not counting the ones I used for reading material.

I spent the night outside Salt Creek, got up the next morning and continued to search for Texas towns and sane Texans. There was a shortage of both. I greeted occasional riders, asking if they owned stock or knew someone that did. If so, might they be interested in driving the cattle to Kansas for a ready market? Most waved me off, while others took flyers, though I suspected they planned to use them for onetime reading material. "Remember the Alamo!" they said and rode on.

In a few days I crossed a bridge over the Trinity River into Fort Worth. With a population I estimated at seven hundred, it was the biggest Texas community yet for me. A fine stone courthouse sat vacant and unfinished in the square, another victim of the late war. I posted flyers on trees on each side of the plaza and asked about for stockmen. Still suspicious of nosy strangers so soon after the hostilities, most Texans ignored me or sent me off with the standard answer: "Remember the Alamo!" I left posters at the jail and post office and continued moving south, hoping to interest at least one Texan of Abilene's potential and praying McCoy was constructing his vision so I wouldn't get hung by a cattleman thinking I had double-crossed him. While I slept under the stars at night, I tried to take one meal a day at a local eatery everywhere I peddled my flyers. With the restaurant proprietor's permission, I tacked a handbill on the wall and moved on.

From Fort Worth, I kept moving south, working the little towns in the ninety miles to Waco, sometimes called "Six-Shooter Junction," a nickname I learned multiple Texas communities proudly claimed. Waco boasted a population of more than a thousand souls, though few paid me any mind, gossiping instead about the local grand jury decision not to indict an upstanding resident for killing a freedman. I left handbills at the courthouse, post office, a couple churches, an eatery, several stores and in the hands of the few fine folks that would take them.

I kept my bearing headed toward San Antonio, aiming next for Austin, the state capital a hundred and ten miles south. In every town I passed through, I tacked at least one handbill to a tree or on a public bulletin board wherever I found one. The deeper I traveled into the state, the more stray longhorns I encountered. They amounted to dollars on the hoof for anyone driving them to market. Perhaps McCoy had hit upon a grand vision after all, but I wondered if any Texan possessed the smarts to take him up on it or the courage to drive cattle more than seven hundred miles on my promise the stockyards would be there.

With a population hovering around four thousand, Austin was my biggest Texas city yet. I didn't find the state capitol building that impressive, though I left a flyer tacked to the main door, but I admired the two-story

Governor's Mansion with its six columns and wide ve-
randa. It left me wondering why politicians always got
mansions and the rest of us had to sleep on the ground
under the stars while we were passing out handbills
to drum up business elsewhere. I spent three days in
Austin, putting out the word about Abilene, Kansas, as a
cattle market and distributing a hundred and fifty flyers.
Everyone agreed Austin was a fine city except when the
Texas Legislature was in session. During those months,
the capitol held more crooks and swindlers than the
state pen.

Leaving the capital city, I began the final leg of my
trip, the seventy-five miles to San Antonio, stopping
at each town along the way and trying to drum up
business for McCoy and Abilene. Few Texans took me
seriously. Maybe it was my youth or lack of Texas blood
as that breed tended to be clannish, clinging to their
own kind, generally slow, dumb and suspicious. What
made it even more exasperating was the closer I got to
San Antonio, the more I spotted wild cattle, many with
horns as wide as locomotives. The longhorns were as
thick as the prairie dogs I had seen in Kansas and Indian
Territory. The stock represented fortunes on four legs.

By the time I reached San Antonio, I estimated two
hundred flyers remaining, so I planned to saturate the
town, which boasted eight thousand residents. It was
a squat town with more adobe and limestone buildings
and dwellings than any other Texas place I had visited.
Teeming with Mexicans, San Antonio had been established by the Spanish a few centuries earlier. I admired
the dark-eyed, raven-haired, tawny skinned señoritas
that graced the streets, but my Spanish fluency fell short
of True Shot's knowledge of English, so I never met a
one of those Mexican beauties.

I turned down one street that led me to a plaza
where an abandoned mission stood silently overlooking
the traffic and commerce. The walls and the chapel's
serrated top were crumbling and splotches of black
stained the sides as if someone had tried to burn down
the limestone perimeter. I approached the dilapidated

structure, passing Mexican vendors offering food, baskets and pottery to Hispanic and Anglos, afoot and on horses.

Stopping at the deteriorating edifice, I decided to post a flyer on the crumbling building. I dismounted and retrieved my hammer and tacks. Approaching the front door askew on rusty hinges, I pulled a flyer from my haversack and tacked it on one side of the crooked door and then a second handbill on the other side. As I admired my posting, a female voice startled me.

"Beg your pardon, sir, might I speak with you?"

She already had, but I turned around and examined a woman in her mid-twenties with hair the color of straw peeking out from under a calico bonnet. She had wide eyes that took in everything and a petite nose that guarded full lips.

"Sure, ma'am, but what's this place?"

"It's the Alamo."

"Remember the Alamo!"

"That's the one, sacred ground where many Texas heroes died." She smiled. "I have a proposition for you."

Until that moment, no woman had ever propositioned me, especially one so striking. I didn't know what to say, but she continued before I answered.

"I want to paint you," she announced.

Her offer stunned me. "Do I need a coat of white-wash?"

Shaking her head, she laughed, then took my hand. "Follow me."

Grabbing the Relee's reins, I followed her to the edge of the plaza where an easel stood with a canvas colored with a rendering of the Alamo. On a stool sat what I learned was a palate, a paint-splattered board with four brushes. "I'd like to paint a portrait of you."

"Why me?"

"I see strength in the set of your jaw, determination in the curl of your lips and independence in the depth of your eyes, all characteristics of a great Texan," she said.

Now I was stunned because I never figured I looked so mean, so stupid and so ugly as to be confused for a

Texan. "I'm from Arkansas, just arrived in San Antonio and hired by Joseph G. McCoy of Abilene, Kansas, to distribute handbills on an emerging cattle market."

Rather than be discouraged by my response, the painter grew more intrigued. "Show me a flyer. I'm Madlyn Dillon."

Lifting the flap on my haversack, I pulled out a sheet and handed it to her. "My name is Lomax."

She studied the handbill intently. "Mind if I keep this?"

"You whitewash longhorns, too?"

Miss Dillon laughed. "On occasion as my father runs cattle. Like everybody else, he can't sell them for what they're worth, times being so hard."

"Maybe he should drive a herd to Kansas. I can guide him to Abilene."

Cocking her head at me, she smiled. "I'd be more inclined to discuss that with my father, if you allowed me to paint you, Lomax."

Shrugging, I told her, "I can't waste time for whitewashing until I've posted my handbills."

Insistent on painting me, Miss Dillon asked for a dozen more leaflets. "Father can pass flyers to his acquaintances. I can't pay you to sit for my painting, but I can help distribute these."

"No offense, ma'am, but I doubt your circle of friends would do Joseph McCoy much good. I figure they are better at sweeping floors than herding cattle."

Smiling, she answered. "Mr. Lomax, I'm not town folk and have lived on a ranch my entire life, even helping run things while my father was fighting Yankees. I may not have done as well as him, but I managed. He indulges my painting, the one luxury he affords me. We are in town for the day before we return this evening to the ranch."

"Not meaning to be rude, ma'am, but I've got work to do, and time's a wasting."

"Might I offer a suggestion, Mr. Lomax? Distribute as many flyers as you can, then return here an hour before sundown. Father and our foreman will pick me up at that time for the journey home. It's a three-hour ride, but the full moon will light our way."

"I'll think on it," I said.

"Be here on time because Father waits for no man, woman or beast."

Nodding, I mounted my bay and started across the plaza, looking for places to post the handbills and men to accept them. I tacked them on trees, on the sides of wooden buildings as long as the owner wasn't around, and on an occasional signpost. After dining in a Mexican eatery where I consumed my fill of flour tortillas, frijoles and fried beef, I left a dozen flyers on the counter. While I didn't care to be whitewashed, distributing hundreds of posters across Texas now bored me, and Miss Dillon was the first Texan, male or female, interested in McCoy's vision.

As the day drew to a close, I still had forty handbills left, but I had wearied of hanging them everywhere, so I headed back to the plaza. A wagon sat by the site where Miss Dillon had been painting, and two men helped her load her easel and materials in the back of the wagon.

A smile worked its way across her face when she saw me approaching. Drawing up my horse, I dismounted. She scurried over. "I feared you might not return," she said, leaning over and kissing me on the cheek. The younger of the two fellows scowled at me while the older one shook his head. "Father, this is the gentlemen I spoke of, the man who's distributing the flyers around town. His name is Lomax, but I didn't catch his given name."

"Henry Harrison," I offered, "but I prefer Lomax."

Her pa extended his hand and shook mine. "I'm Saul Dillon. Most call me Colonel Dillon because of my rank in the late difficulties." He pointed to his helper. "That's Sainty Spencer, he served in the Confederate artillery. The cannonades left him hard of hearing."

"I'm not deaf," Spencer corrected as he walked over and offered me his paw. I clasped it and took in his receding hairline, his lively eyes and his cautious grin. Soon I discovered the farther I stood from Miss Dillon, the wider Spencer's smile grew so I gathered he was sweet on her. By his look I figured him to be four or five years older than the artist.

"Were you an officer, too?"

"Captain by the end of the war because we had lost so many fine men before me."

"So Colonel Dillon outranked you," I observed. "With a name like Sainty you surely outrank him in the eyes of God."

The three laughed.

"Never thought of it that way," Spencer replied. "Momma believed I wouldn't turn bad with such a holy name."

"He's not worried about outranking me in the eyes of God, just in the eyes of my daughter," the colonel offered.

When Madlyn blushed and Spencer glanced at his boots, I confirmed he was fond of her and begrudged her kiss on my cheek. I wondered if her desire to paint me would antagonize him even more.

"My daughter tells me she's invited you to our ranch as she wants you to sit for a portrait, says you possess the classic face of the rugged frontier Texan."

"I'm from Arkansas."

Madlyn responded. "That doesn't matter to the artist—"

I feared, however, that it might concern her suitor, who stared at me with suspicious eyes.

"—as we take the subject and create a new identity that matches our own vision for him."

The high-faluting explanation perplexed me, and I decided I was the only person west of the Mississippi that didn't have a vision. First, McCoy in Kansas and now Miss Dillon in Texas saw things I couldn't even spot with field glasses.

"Don't worry, Lomax," interjected her father, "I don't understand what she's talking about. I buy her paint and canvas so she can amuse herself. I'm more interested in this handbill of yours. So, if you don't mind putting up with Madlyn's foolishness with a paintbrush, I'd like to

PRESTON LEWIS

invite you to our place to talk business. We can discuss this fellow McCoy and the facilities he's built for shipping cattle to markets."

Planned, I thought, was a better description than built, but I decided not to disabuse the colonel of his notion. "I've seen nothing like Mr. McCoy's vision for Abilene and the future."

Dillon liked my response until I elaborated.

"The first herd to Abilene will enrich the first stock herder that takes the gamble."

The colonel crossed his arms over his chest and grumbled. "We're not herders. We prefer the name cattlemen to separate us from the sheep herders and pig farmers."

"Yes, sir, Colonel," I amended, "the first Texan to reach Abilene will be known for his pioneer daring, his business sense and his new wealth." I hoped this pioneer wouldn't be remembered for lynching me, if he found an Abilene as sleepy as the one I had left weeks ago.

Sainty finished loading Madlyn's art equipment, then helped her into the seat. "We're ready, Colonel, when you are," he announced.

Dillon nodded. "Let's head for home." He pulled his lean frame into the wagon box and sat down beside his daughter while I mounted. Taking the reins, the colonel rattled them, and the team started forward, me riding on his side of the wagon and Spencer on Miss Dillon's.

Passing the jinxed fortress, I uttered, "Remember the Alamo!"

"Remember the Alamo!" answered the trio in unison.

"A sad day in the annals of Texas," Dillon said.

"Did you lose kin at the Alamo?" I asked.

"My folks arrived in Texas the year after the War for Independence, so we didn't lose kin. Wish the same could be said for the more recent hostilities."

I nodded. "I lost two brothers."

The Colonel sighed. "The Yankees took my three sons as well as my wife from a broken heart. Madlyn's all I've got left, her and cattle I can't sell. I had a family any decent person would've been proud to call his

140

own, but the boys are gone now, one at Shiloh, another at Chickamauga and the third at Franklin, all buried in unmarked graves the best we can determine. It's a damn shame to lose one son and not even know where he lies. Imagine facing that not for just one or two, but all three of your sons. It was more than their momma could take. She died in May, six months after our last boy fell. And others suffered more than us."

We headed northwest out of San Antonio as the sun died for the day, casting a red tint across a horizon where hundreds of longhorns grazed or watched us pass. As the sun disappeared a full moon took its place and we rode in the moonlight.

Dillon pointed at the sky and the glowing orb. "They call that a Comanche Moon because the Indians liked to attack settlers on such nights. Bitter, often fatal outcomes resulted from those raids, either folks massacred or taken captive. We hired a girl orphaned by Comanche after the war to help Madlyn with chores."

His discussion made me glad I was still wearing Chisholm's Indian bracelet, though I wondered if any Comanche might see or recognize it in the glow of the moon.

"You'll meet Ruth when we get home. I reckon she's your age now. I kept her on so Madlyn could paint, but Ruth has no place else to go."

The moonlight ride sat well with me, the first time I'd had an extended conversation since True Shot and I parted. These folks, even though they were Texans, understood English. I conversed with the colonel while Madlyn talked in low tones to Sainty, who heard her okay, making me wonder if he was a sly one, just acting deaf to eavesdrop on conversations not meant for him. I glanced at Spencer. He grinned, nodding like he realized I had figured out his secret.

"Hard as the war hit us," Dillon announced, "we came out better than most, though I can't say for how much longer. Right now I can put food on the table and buy Madlyn her painting supplies, but I'm not sure for how much longer. Folks say I've indulged her expensive artistic inclinations, but it keeps her mind off the loss of her brothers and her mother and gives her something to worry over other than suitors hoping to inherit my land."

Glancing at Sainty, I caught the flash of a grin across his face. I gathered he heard more than he let on. "I've never known an artist," I said.

"I suppose she's got talent because her canvases show what she's painting, most times better than they actually are, but I don't know the value her paintings have, same as all those cattle in the distance."

"What she needs is a buyer, someone like Joseph G. McCoy of Abilene, Kansas," I said. "I doubt he's in the market for paintings, but he'll purchase cattle from enterprising cattlemen."

"We'll talk commerce tomorrow, Lomax, but I want to know more about you."

As we rode toward his place, he questioned my experience and my acquaintance with McCoy. I told him of growing up in Arkansas and having to leave LouAnne Burke behind for her safety and mine. Figuring parts of my life since Cane Hill might worry him, I neglected to mention things like robbing a bank with Jesse James or eating a piece of cherry pie and causing a man to die on the square in Springfield, Missouri. The colonel appeared satisfied that I could handle myself despite my youth and might be capable of guiding a herd back to Abilene.

Our three-hour ride passed quickly, and when we topped a final rise, I saw in the gentle valley below a modest limestone dwelling, a smaller stone structure and a wooden barn with pens, holding a dozen horses. The front room of the house was lit until a dog barked, then the lamp went dark.

"Ruth, it's us," Dillon shouted, "back from San Antonio."

Momentarily, the light returned, then the door

opened and a young woman emerged on the porch holding a lantern. In the lamp's glow, she appeared as an angel in gingham, with long brown hair, brown eyes and a smile that could melt granite.

"We brought a guest, Ruth," the colonel announced.

"A handsome one," she said as she stepped off the porch toward me.

I knew then I would enjoy staying on the Dillon place.

Chapter 14

In the full light of the next day, Ruth was even more becoming as she served us a breakfast of bacon, scrambled eggs and biscuits. "Good morning, Mr. Lomax," she said as she set a tin plate in front of me. Unless I was imagining things, my plate had an extra slice of pork and a bigger helping of eggs than the others. Ruth placed their meals on the table as they took their chairs. Last to arrive was the colonel, accompanied by a Mexican he introduced as José Muñoz. We shook hands, and Muñoz seated himself beside me.

"José and Sainty are hired help," Dillon said. "They're all I can afford."

"And we ain't getting rich in his employ," Sainty added.

"Mejor que nada," Muñoz said, then translated, "Better than nothing." He grinned at me as his dark eyes took my measure. He had a hawkish nose and the thickest, blackest hair I'd ever seen on a man, his mane hanging down to his shoulders and covering his ears.

As I reached for the salt shaker with my hand, Muñoz stared at the silver amulet on my wrist, then looked at me with a questioning gaze. "Where'd you get that bracelet?"

"A gift from an Indian trader."

"Can I see it? It appears to be Comanche."

I slipped off the wristlet and offered it to him.

"José was captured and lived among the Indians for

three years," Dillon informed me. "He speaks their language and several other dialects as well as Spanish and English, which he can both read and write. José's smart enough to be a city lawyer."

Muñoz took the silver band and studied the engravings. He looked up at me. "You're favored."

"What do the markings mean?"

"Roughly translated, 'the bearer is a friend of the people'."

"What people?"

"The Comanche and their allies."

Sainty whistled, and Dillon shook his head.

"It got me through Indian Territory unscathed, save for an arrow in the chest," I said.

Ruth gasped.

"And it'll be your ticket for a safe return," Muñoz said.

"Even with cattle?" the colonel interrupted.

Muñoz nodded. "Yes, sir."

The colonel looked at me. "Well, then, we've got plenty to discuss, Lomax."

"Not until I've painted him," interjected Madlyn.

Muñoz returned the bracelet, and I slid it over my wrist as Ruth joined us at the table across from me. Dillon asked that we bow our heads so he could bless the food. After everyone mouthed "amen," Ruth looked at me. "We don't get many visitors, Mr. Lomax. What brings you our way?"

"Miss Dillon says my distinguished looks deserved to be immortalized in one of her paintings—"

"It is a handsome face," she said.

"—but I'm in Texas promoting Abilene, Kansas, as a cattle market." While I hoped she meant it about my looks, I figured she had too few guests to compare them to. Even so, I couldn't deny that San Antonio women took to my appearance. "Thank you," I replied, then grew bold. "Nowhere between Kansas and Texas have I seen a face so pretty as yours."

Ruth blushed.

"Why, Mr. Lomax," said Madlyn, "aren't you a charmer. Sainty could take lessons from you, but remember you're mine until I'm done painting you."

"I'll give you today," I responded between bites, "but I must return to Kansas by September first, preferably leading a herd of longhorns."

"Give her—and me—two days," Colonel Dillon said, "and if I like what I hear you can guide my cattle to Abilene."

"Goody," said Ruth.

When we finished breakfast, I insisted on helping Ruth clear the table and dry the dishes.

"That's mighty decent of you, Mr. Lomax," she cooed.

"I've got first claim on Lomax," responded Madlyn.

"You can set up your easel," I informed her, "and I'll join you when I'm done."

"Meet me on the front porch where the light is most flattering." Madlyn followed the men from the room, leaving me with Ruth.

"Thank you, Mr. Lomax."

"You can call me Henry."

"I like that name, Henry. It's a strong name, a manly one."

I carried dishes to the wash pan and she heated water on the woodstove. Never one to think it my place to do girl's work, I enjoyed helping Ruth, as comely, charming and smitten with me as she seemed to be.

As we washed and dried tableware, we discussed our lives, both tinged with sadness from the loss of loved ones, either from Yankees or Comanches, and both of us being alone in life, her by the massacre of her folks and me by choice, having left home so my family and betrothed might survive the lingering animosities caused by the Yankee invasion.

"Did you ever have a girl?" she asked.

I nodded. "LouAnne Burke was her name, but assassins tried to kill me, and I feared she would get hurt so I had to leave her behind."

Ruth understood the pain. "I had a boyfriend, but the

war took him."

"Battle?"

"No, disease, though we never knew for sure what malady. I wanted to die. First my folks getting killed and next the boy I always expected to be my husband dies. The Dillons helped me through it, but at times it was hard being alone. I feared God was punishing me here on earth by taking my loved ones and leaving me by myself."

"You're too pretty to stay by yourself all the time."

Ruth blushed. "Thank you, Henry."

"You ever thought about marrying and settling down?"

"It's crossed my mind, if I ever found someone new, but there's a restlessness in me that's hard to tame, though I bet I could with the right girl."

Ruth looked at me with her shy eyes and smiled as softly as an angel's kiss. "I hope we have time together before you leave, Henry."

"I'd enjoy that," I said. The colonel entered the kitchen door and interrupted our conversation. "Madlyn says she's ready for you on the porch, Lomax."

"I'll be there in a minute." When Dillon retreated, I dried my hands, folded the towel, and laid it upon the dry dishes. "I've enjoyed visiting, Ruth. We can talk later."

She took my hand with her left and patted it with the right, splashing water on me. She giggled and I laughed. "Sorry," she snickered as I grabbed the dish cloth and re-dried my fingers. She smiled as I headed for the porch.

Emerging from the front door, I sat on the stool as directed by Madlyn while the colonel pulled up a rocking chair.

"Keep out of my line of sight, Father," she ordered. "Don't distract me from my work so I can capture his rugged yet handsome features."

"Should I stay beyond hearing range, too?" Dillon asked.

"Don't be silly."

Dillon dragged his rocker behind his daughter as she

positioned my shoulders and twisted my head to the right, then lifted my chin. Stepping back, she cocked her face, examined me and said, "That'll do. Try to keep your head at that angle. It shows determination."

My gaze reflected more pain from the tilt of my neck than resolve, though I wished for a mirror to examine my profile. As I sat there like a freak show exhibit, I decided artists resembled politicians as they didn't see the world as the rest of us did. While acceptable for painters, it remained a terrible trait for elected officials.

As Miss Dillon adjusted her easel and took up her brush and palette, the colonel read over one of McCoy's flyers. "I've never heard of Abilene. How far is from here?"

"Seven hundred miles, plus or minus thirty," I replied.

"Keep your lips shut when you talk," Madlyn commanded, "or this'll take all year."

"Yes, ma'am," I mumbled through a tight jaw.

"Through Indian Territory, right?"

"I crossed the Territory without a hitch," I muttered through stiff lips.

"Be still," Madlyn reminded me, as she stepped over to crack my neck and reposition my head the way she wanted it.

"But you had the bracelet. José thinks that's what saved you."

"That and my rugged determination," I burbled, pulling Madlyn's leg.

"Don't move," she commanded, missing the humor. I bet Ruth would've caught it.

As best I could between lips that were not supposed to move, I explained how cattle in Abilene would bring triple or quadruple Texas prices, even more in northern cities.

"What we're doing is feeding Yankees, and I have a longstanding anger for them."

I nodded. "Yankees have money. Look at it as picking their pockets."

"Quit moving," Madlyn scolded me.

"Could Abilene handle twenty-five hundred head?"

"Joseph G. McCoy wants cattle by the tens of thousands."

"And he's got the facilities to accommodate them?"

Here I had to shade the truth. "I've seen nothing like his vision for Abilene and the Great Western Stock Yards."

"I need to put a pencil to it."

Thinking I had gotten the colonel to bite, I next had to set the hook and reel him in. I tried to remember McCoy's talk on the finances of such a drive and started to explain the promoter's example with a thousand head, comparing the sale price in Texas with that in Kansas and then the cost of men and goods to get the longhorns to Abilene.

"Arithmetic is not your strong suit," Dillon said when I stopped, "but I can do the ciphering, and it adds up profitably, providing you're correct on what cattle will bring up north."

I grimaced. "I'm shooting as straight on prices as I am on the McCoy's facilities,"

"Freeze yourself," Madlyn scolded.

"That's enough palaver about Kansas, or Madlyn may kill us both," the colonel decided, arising from his chair. "I'll check with Sainty and José, get their thoughts on going to Abilene."

"Good," said Miss Dillon, "now my subject can concentrate on his pose."

"When it comes to painting, we're all your subjects Queen Madlyn," Dillon said as he sauntered away.

I regretted the colonel's departure as our conversation kept me focused on something other than posing like a statue. In a few minutes, Ruth floated around the side of the house, slipping up behind Miss Dillon and sitting in the rocker as quietly as a mouse.

"What's come over you, Lomax? There's a glimmer in your eye I haven't seen since you sat down."

"A pretty little bird roosted behind you."

Ruth smiled and giggled.

Madlyn looked over her shoulder. "I didn't hear you

come up, Ruth."

"I was afraid to disturb you, Miss Dillon."

Grinning, Madlyn said, "I get it, Lomax, your pretty bird comment, but keep your focus on your pose."

"I won't be here long, Miss Dillon, as I'll start preparing lunch shortly. And you do what she says, Henry. I'm anxious to see her finished portrait and decide if it captures you."

"Henry, is it?" said Madlyn.

"Lomax to you, Miss Dillon," I replied. "Ruth can call me whatever she likes."

"I take it you relish her cooking," Madlyn said. While she painted, I eyed Ruth, admiring the softness in her eyes and the gentleness in her lips. Her gaze and her smile had more than compensated for the long ride to Texas and all the rude Texans I had encountered along the way.

When Ruth slipped away to resume her meal preparations, Madlyn noted her departure. "The glimmer in your eye disappeared as did the little bird. Any connection?"

Knowing I would see more of Ruth in the coming days, especially if the colonel sent a herd to Kansas, I smiled. "I can't say I understand your meaning, Miss Dillon."

"I'm sure you don't, Henry," she answered.

Sitting there bored from posing, I rejoiced when the colonel approached with Sainty and José as high sun neared.

"Aren't you done with Lomax yet?" Dillon asked.

"Never rush art," she replied.

"How come you've never painted me?" Sainty wanted to know.

"You lack Lomax's lean frame and determined demeanor."

All three walked behind Madlyn, studying her progress.

"It doesn't resemble him a bit," said Sainty, "but the ears ain't long and pointy enough."

"Hush, Sainty."

Dillon looked at the painting. "I'd say it's a fair likeness. What do you think, José?"

Muñoz ran his fingers through his thick mane and nodded. "I agree with the colonel."

"I'll judge for myself when I get up."

"No, you can't," said Madlyn. "It's bad luck to view your portrait before it's finished. Don't you dare look."

Ruth stepped out the front door and onto the porch. "Lunch is ready."

"Remember that pose," Madlyn said as I jumped from my stool. She stood between me and the canvas to make sure I didn't peek.

The painting interested me much less than Ruth. I strode to her, offering my arm. "Let me escort you."

She accepted my offer with a giggle, and we strolled inside to the kitchen. As she removed her arm, her hand brushed against the top of my mine. Her fingers were those of a working woman, more stiff than soft, but that was the only thing rough about her.

As the others walked in, Ruth announced, "I've changed the seating." She pointed me to the chair next to hers where Madlyn had sat at breakfast. Sitting by her during lunch was more fun than looking at the back of Madlyn's canvas.

After we seated ourselves, the colonel offered grace, actually thanking God for bringing me their way. It flattered me knowing someone had put in a good word for me upstairs. After everyone said amen, Dillon removed the lid from a pot and picked up a ladle he dipped inside. He pulled out a serving of red beans and ham hocks and dumped it into the top bowl in a stack by his place. He passed the bowl to me, and I took my spoon, thinking I'd taste the fare first to compliment Ruth's cooking.

As I slipped my spoon into the vittles, Ruth nudged me. When I turned to her, she shook her head slightly. I left the spoon where it was and waited as Dillon passed a bowl to each diner. When Ruth received the last bowl, she nodded and I picked up my spoon simultaneous with the others. "Good eating," I said.

"Thank you," Ruth replied as she offered me a platter of corn dodgers. I grabbed the biggest piece and took a bite as I passed the dish to the colonel. Her corn dodgers were as tasty as the beans and ham hocks. I nodded at Ruth, "Very good."

Ruth smiled. "Thank you, Henry."

"Henry?" Sainty asked.

"Lomax to everybody but Ruth," I informed him.

Ruth's lips lifted into a smile. "I'm pleased you're enjoying lunch."

The colonel crumbled his corn dodger into his bowl and mixed it up with the beans before he took his first bite. Then he turned to me. "Lomax, I've talked it over with Sainty and José, and we're gonna drive a herd to Abilene, if you'll lead the way."

I felt rich because I'd make more money off of old Joseph McCoy. Then I looked at Ruth, who lowered her gaze and stared at her bowl. I frowned even though I still had a hundred and fifteen dollars from McCoy's down payment on the Texas trip. With the hundred I'd get on my return plus five or ten cents a head on the cattle, I'd be sitting as pretty as Ruth beside me.

"What are you paying?"

Dillon took another bite, cogitating as he chewed, then swallowing and answering. "I've figuring to do first before I can answer. It depends on the men and supplies we'll need."

"Mr. McCoy says it takes one hand for every three hundred cattle. Driving fewer than a thousand head isn't worth the effort but anything over a thousand should turn you a decent profit. Besides the cow hands, you'll need someone to handle the horses, a foreman and a cook."

Dillon nodded. "Sainty'll be trail boss, and José'll be the wrangler."

Ruth raised her chin, "Could I go as the cook?"

I shook my head at her, but Colonel Dillon ignored her.

"We need to reach Abilene before September to get the best price as I don't know how many cattle Mr. McCoy will buy after that date," I informed Dillon. "I figure we have ten days, maybe two weeks maximum before we must start north."

Dillon looked from me to Sainty and José.

Spencer nodded. "We'll do what we have to do. Hiring men's the first task, then rounding up and branding unmarked cattle. There's more unbranded than branded."

"What about horses, José?"

"Probably three per man, minimum. I may have to break a few before we leave, but they won't be cattle savvy by then."

Dillon shrugged. "Do the best you can."

Muñoz nodded.

"As for men," the colonel pondered, "we'll ride to San Antonio this afternoon and hire a crew. I'm thinking three thousand cattle so we'll go with ten other hands. What about a cook?"

"I'll do it," Ruth offered again

"No," said Dillon. "A cattle drive's no place for a woman or an old man such as myself."

Ruth looked at me like she was apt to cry.

The colonel pointed at me. "Lomax, you'll accompany me and Sainty to town. We'll take horses instead of the wagon to save time."

"What about my painting?" Madlyn asked.

"It'll wait, Madlyn. This drive is crucial for us to keep the ranch, much less buy your paints and canvases." Dillon turned to Sainty. "I'm worried about finding a cook."

"I could—"

"No, Ruth. I'll not hear of it," Dillon scolded. "Anything else you boys can think of?"

"What about us women?" Madlyn said.

Her father answered. "I'll stay here and keep an eye on things. Between you, me and Ruth, we'll be fine. Sainty'll be in charge on the trail. The future of our place will be in his hands. If he succeeds, I'll consider his request for your hand, Madlyn."

"If there's nothing else, men, let's get at it," Dillon said, rising from the table. "We've got horses to saddle. José, handle mine if you please, and I'll be out in a few minutes after I fetch my satchel and writing papers. Let's leave in a half hour, men."

Sainty and José burst out the back door toward the barn. Madlyn bolted up and shot into the next room, her head in her hands trying to hide her moist eyes. Ruth sat there, a tear rolling down her cheek.

I assisted her to her feet. Instinctively, I hugged her, and she melted into my arms. "I wanted to help with the dishes again."

"That would've been nice," she sniffed.

"I'll spend every spare moment with you before we leave."

"It's like you're a whirlwind that's rushed into my life and is now spinning away, Henry. I've dreamed of something good happening to me since my folks died. I thought you were it, and now you're being taken from me."

"We'll be together before I leave, and I'll come back and find you, Ruth, I promise. When I return, I'll have enough money to buy a place of our own."

She nestled into my chest. I felt better than I had since abandoning LouAnne Burke in Cane Hill two years earlier. I lifted my finger to her chin and raised her head until I could look into her soft brown eyes. While I knew it was forward of me, I lowered my mouth and kissed her. She fell even deeper into my embrace.

"I'll be back, Ruth, I promise." Though she struggled to hold onto me, I finally pushed myself away from her. "I've got to saddle up for town." I broke from her grasp and ran outside, wishing I could stay with her forever.

Chapter 15

The colonel, Sainty and I reached San Antonio by mid-afternoon in time to spread the word that Dillon was hiring cowboys to push a herd north, though we didn't say how far north. We passed along the news wherever possible, greeting men on the street, announcing plans in a handful of saloons, putting the call out in stores and even confessing our intentions at a Catholic church. The colonel stated he would interview men in front of the Alamo the next morning and, if hired, they were to be ready to ride that afternoon.

Dillon fretted about soliciting hands in drinking establishments because he feared they might have drinking or gambling urges on the trail. As we searched for recruits, he told Sainty to prohibit liquor, cards and dice as they caused trouble. As the afternoon drained away, we entered one store where Dillon instructed Sainty and me to buy gear for the sojourn, including two pairs of leather gloves and a gum blanket or a slicker for rainy days, plus anything else we might need on the drive. While I had thought a bottle of whiskey, a deck of cards and a pair of dice might be fun, I settled for gloves, slicker, shirt, work britches and a new felt hat, which set me back a little, but I planned to recoup the cash when I reached Abilene. I decided to purchase a surprise for Ruth. Uncertain what she might prefer, I decided on a blue-and-white checkered calico apron.

"No need for an apron, Lomax, because you won't be

our cookie," Dillon scolded.

"It's for Ruth," I replied.

Dillon winked. "I know."

Sainty nodded his approval, relieved I was thinking of Ruth rather than his girl. "I suppose I should get Madlyn something," he said and wandered away.

Dillon asked the storekeeper if he knew of any willing cooks for the trail north.

"No good ones," the merchant answered.

"A bad one's better than none at all," the colonel replied.

"Well, there's Charlie Bitters. He cooked for officers in the Army of Tennessee, I'm told. Some say his cooking cost the Confederacy the war, as the generals never thought straight after eating his meals. Other veterans report his slop's why John Bell Hood ordered the doomed assault at Franklin, as he went loco with the stomach cramps."

"Any other possibilities?" Dillon asked.

"Maybe a few Mexican cooks, but their fare doesn't always suit a white man's tongue."

"Bad food tastes better than none," Dillon responded. "I'll pay a cook two dollars a day, twice what my hands'll earn. I figure he'll be ninety days on the drive. That's almost two hundred bucks."

"I'll put the word out."

"We'll need supplies before we leave. If I hire a cook you've suggested, I'll buy trail provisions from you so you stand to make a good profit."

The storekeeper perked up. "If one tells you Alamo Mercantile sent him, then you'll know he's my man."

After the colonel and the merchant shook hands, we departed, me with my new duds and Ruth's apron and Sainty with his gloves and a handkerchief for Madlyn. We rode to the edge of town to bed down, slept the night and arose as the horizon was tinting with the light of another day. We returned to the plaza, tethered our horses to a post twenty yards from the Alamo and waited by an oak tree.

Immediately, a fellow leading a dun gelding approached us. "Are you gentlemen hiring hands to work cattle?"

"That we are," answered Sainty.

"I'm Martin Michaels , and I'm interested in work."

"We're heading to Kansas. Must arrive by September first. You had experience handling longhorns?" Sainty asked.

"Branded some and steered others. I've driven cattle, though never that far."

Dillon stepped up to the applicant. "Do you use gloves?"

The applicant nodded.

"Do you smoke?"

"No, sir. Never have. Why buy something you're gonna set fire to?"

"I'm fine with him, Sainty, if you are."

The foreman clasped Michaels' hand. "You're our first hire."

"I'll work hard for you."

Then Sainty pointed to me. "That's H.H. Lomax. He's our guide. Goes by Lomax."

Michaels shook my hand, and I directed him to an adjacent oak. "Wait there until we finish hiring, then we'll start to the ranch." I watched Michaels amble over to the tree, hobble his dun, then pull from his saddlebags a pencil and a pad of handbill-sized paper. He leaned up against the tree trunk and scribbled in his notebook.

Several others, some men and some boys, approached, seeking employment. The colonel asked each one if he could provide a horse and if he smoked or used gloves. Asking about a mount seemed logical, but the other two struck me as odd questions, especially after suggesting Sainty and I buy leather protection for our hands. Eventually, I recognized his pattern. He'd hire a smoker or a glove wearer, but never a smoker who wore gloves.

Sainty's second hire was Tom Errun, born in England to a British Army officer who wanted him to continue the military tradition. Rather than be shipped overseas to the far reaches of the British Empire, he sailed the Atlantic for Galveston where he could start Texas adventures of his own choosing. Tom neither smoked nor wore gloves. Though a good horseman, he had never worked cattle. Sainty surprised me by hiring him, saying Errun struck him as a quick learner. The Englishman had as much to learn about cattle as we did of his vocabulary, as he used words in odd ways, saying "biscuits" when he meant "cookies" and "marmalade" for "jelly." Too, he spoke words such as "gigglemug" and "tora-loorals" that left us perplexed when we first encountered them and amused when told their meaning. Errun joined Michaels in the shade.

Harry Dire was a slight fellow wearing wire-rimmed glasses and speaking so softly you barely heard him most times. He promoted himself as a great roper, a necessary skill on a cattle drive, but we had no way of confirming his claim as men promise anything to get paying work. But Dire spoke the truth, as we learned that he could rope and hogtie a gnat blindfolded. "A man needs to fondle his rope to guide its aim," he told the colonel. Though that sounded odd, Sainty hired him after learning he smoked but shunned gloves as they interfered with his roping aim.

Sainty and Dillon rejected several other fellows before a Negro stepped up to them. He removed his hat, placed it over his chest and announced, "I be Silas Banty, and I be looking for work. I've roped and branded calves and yearlings. What I don't be knowing I can be learning."

"Do you smoke?"

"Not unless I be on fire," he answered, then slapped his knee with his hat. "I be funning you, sir. Now I do be smoking on occasion, but I be too poor to smoke regular like rich folks."

"Do you use gloves working cattle?"

"No, sir, I don't. Can't afford 'em."

Sainty nodded and pointed to the others. "You're hired. Join the others."

"Thank you, sir. You won't be regretting it. I be making you a fine hand."

Dillon counted four hires and shook his head, then looked up at the sun. "We still need six more and noon's approaching."

"We'll manage," Sainty replied.

I sauntered to the colonel and inquired what difference it made if a smoker wore gloves.

"A man can't roll a smoke while wearing gloves. I don't mind a hand taking the time to pull gloves on and off or a man spending time with cigarette fixings, but I don't want him wasting time doing both, he loses focus."

His thinking made sense, I decided. Men came in ones and twos the rest of the morning, including Trent Parsons, an ex-Confederate soldier in his mid-thirties. He smoked, but didn't wear gloves, indicating that they made it hard to turn the pages of his Bible.

"You a religious fellow?" Sainty asked.

"Ever since Shiloh, where I took three bullets to the torso. I promised God I'd take up the Bible every day if he'd let me survive my wounds and the awful carnage I witnessed there. I managed somehow, but I was selfish, thinking of myself and not my family. I never asked God to protect my family. I survived, but my wife and three boys were killed by Comanche. A dead family and my place burned to the ground made my homecoming worse than the war."

The colonel, Sainty and I stared silently at Parsons, knowing we were helpless to reduce his sorrow. "You're hired, Parsons," Dillon finally said, pointing to the tree. "Wait over there."

Next a Mexican sidled up to us and spoke in Spanish to Sainty. I made out his name as Pedro Ramírez, but little else. He likely smoked because the top of a tobacco pouch dangled out of his shirt pocket. Sainty nodded and directed him to the tree.

Then a short man with a narrow build, greasy gray beard and matching, unruly hair walked up. Unlike our hires, he came afoot with no horse trailing him.

"You got a mount?" the colonel asked.

"Nope," he spat out.

"Then we can't use you," Dillon replied.

"Alamo Mercantile sent me. My name is Charlie Bitters. I'm your cook."

"I'll decide that," said Dillon.

Sainty and I squinted at Bitters as the colonel eyed him from head to foot. I pegged him as being too skinny to be a decent cook. As Dillon studied him, Bitters took out a tobacco pouch and papers from his pants and rolled a cigarette, which he lit with a match he struck against the stubble of his beard.

"I'm told you'll pay two dollars a day for a good cook."

I figured Bitters was only worth two-bits daily.

"It true your cooking lost the war for the South?" Dillon asked.

Bitters expelled a cloud of cigarette smoke in the colonel's face. "I prefer to think I freed the slaves." He pointed to the previous hires. "Looks like you've taken one slave already. He can thank me later for his emancipation."

Dillon scratched his chin, then tugged on his ear, before surveying the plaza for other possibilities. Seeing none, he nodded. "Do you understand you'll be cooking three meals a day, gathering firewood, setting up camp, washing dishes and breaking the site come morning?"

"Done it before for more men than you've got there, general."

"Actually, it's colonel, Charlie."

"Everyone's a general in my book. It's easier than remembering names, general."

"Tell you what, Charlie, you come back this afternoon, and I'll tell you my decision."

"You won't find a better cook than me," Bitters said. "I'll be at the Alamo Mercantile, if you want me."

Dillon crossed his arms over his chest. "I expect you to return here, if you want the job."

"I've been here once, and I won't return. You know where to find me." He spun around and walked away, his head in a cloud of cigarette smoke.

Dillon shrugged. "Surely, we can find another cook."

"Whatever you say, general," I answered.

Sainty laughed. "I might stomach his food on the

trail better than his charm."

The colonel shrugged. "We still need four more hands and a biscuit shooter."

We waited half an hour for the next inquiries, which came in a flurry. The first two were Chuck Muscher and Toad Beeline. Muscher was tall and lanky, always looking down his nose at folks and flashing a sickly smile as sincere as a Democrat's promise. He claimed to be of New York lineage, a superior stock to that which he found in Texas. Muscher said he smoked, but never wore gloves. He avoided a single word when a hundred would do. Fact was, I didn't trust his angular face and his lying eyes. But Sainty and Dillon had fewer reservations, so they hired him.

Beeline seemed a better sort, though I distrusted him for accompanying Muscher. He smoked but went gloveless and understood handling cattle better than most we hired. So, Sainty sent him to join the others.

As noon passed, another black fellow walked up, leading a black horse with a threadbare saddle. "Bartholomew Henry O'Henry's my full name, though most folks call me 'Bart.' Be you gentlemen hiring folks?"

The colonel nodded. "Do you smoke or wear gloves when you work?"

"No, sir," he said, swatting his shirt pocket, where I thought he hid the string from a tobacco pouch. "I don't uses no gloves," he continued, even though I swore I spotted the fingers of a pair sticking out of his pants pocket.

"Were you ever a slave?" asked Dillon.

O'Henry scowled, his eyes narrowing. "I don't talks of those days."

"Your name is not typical of a freedman. It sounds too distinguished. Are you an educated man?"

"I do reads some, I does. My name I gaves myself. It sounds more honorable than the name I be borned with."

"Fair enough, Bart. You're hired," Dillon said.

"Bless you, sir," he said as joined the others.

Two more glove-wearing smokers were rejected before a cowboy ambled up and introduced himself as Jurdon Mark. He had thick dark hair and a well-trimmed mustache, but mostly he exuded confidence, like he could win a rigged poker game. He didn't smoke, didn't drink, didn't wear gloves, didn't fornicate and didn't curse, unless it was absolutely required. Mark grinned more than he frowned, laughed more than he cried and spoke more than he listened. He was one of those fellows that got along with everyone. In fact, Mark could've sat down with Satan and God and had them laughing and slapping each other on the back as long as he steered their conversation away from religion. His wit, it turned out, kept trail animosities from spilling over and interfering with the job.

"You cut out for a long ride to Kansas, Jurdon?" Sainty asked.

"There's enough Texan in me to ride through hell and fight the fires with a thimble full of water," Marc responded, then added, "Remember the Alamo!"

Actually, the old fort was hard to forget with its walls towering over us in the plaza.

"Then join the others," Sainty said, pointing to the shade tree.

"Obliged," he answered as he sauntered by and introduced himself to every other hand on the crew. No other new hire had done that.

Sainty pointed his index finger at each man as he tallied up the total. "That's it. Ten men, Colonel."

"Except a dough-roller," Dillon responded. "I've my doubts about Bitters."

"He freed the slaves," I interjected, though Sainty and the colonel thought a funeral was funnier than my observation.

"No food's worse than awful food," Sainty offered.

Nodding, the colonel knew what he had to do, but he showed less enthusiasm than a man walking in front of his own firing squad. "I'll mosey over to Alamo Mercantile and offer him the job. Don't know that I have a choice. Sainty, you and Lomax round up the men and start for the ranch. I'll join you when I can close the deal with Bitters." The colonel untied his horse, mounted and headed toward store.

Sainty walked over to the shade tree and studied his new hands. "Is everybody agreed to ride for the colonel for a dollar a day from here to Kansas?" They nodded. "Do you all understand there'll be no liquor, cards or dice on the trail to Kansas?"

"What about marbles?" Mark asked. "Can we play marbles?"

Everyone laughed except Sainty, who was ambushed by question. "I suppose you can as long as there's no gambling on the outcome."

"Good enough," said Mark, "as no one can beat me."

"Any questions of a more practical nature?"

"When do we gets paid?" shouted O'Henry.

"When do we eat?" cried Errun.

"At the end of the drive," answered Sainty.

"I can't be waiting that long for vittles," snickered Banty, a slash of white teeth appearing across his black face.

"No, you're paid at the end of the drive," Sainty corrected. "You'll eat daily, once we hire a cook."

"Hope it ain't, Charlie Bitters," shouted Parsons. "He was the best-named cook in the Army of Tennessee and the worst hash burner."

"He may be our only option," Sainty answered.

"God bless our souls," Parsons replied. "Everyone knows his cooking was so pitiful it cost the Confederacy the war."

"Bitters said he was doing it to free the slaves," I answered to Sainty's dismay.

O'Henry scowled.

Banty laughed and danced a jig. "Then I be eating anything he cooks."

"Slavery ain't nothing to be laughing at," O'Henry bellowed, shaking his fist at the Silas.

"I be free to laughs at whatever I likes," Banty said. "That's what freedom be about."

Ramírez said something in Spanish that none of us could translate, and Dire appeared to comment, but the sound didn't carry enough for us to understand, his voice being so delicate.

"Lomax, hold your tongue and don't stir the pot," Sainty chastised.

"Remember the Alamo!" I answered.

Sainty shook his head. "It'll be a long seven hundred miles to Kansas. How many of you have lariats?" Half of them raised their hands. "We'll fix that at the ranch. Any of you need to notify kin you'll be leaving before we start for our place?" Sainty surveyed the bunch, and when none indicated any goodbyes were necessary, he ordered everyone to mount up.

As the crew got up and stretched, I went over to Martin Michaels, who had been the quietest among them, and tried to see what he had been doing with the pencil and pad.

"You keeping notes?" I asked.

"No, sir." He showed me the top page. "I like to draw, sketch things. It doesn't pay much, but it helps me avoid liquor, cards, dice, not to mention loose women and rabid preachers."

While Dillon and Sainty had been interviewing applicants, he had been sketching them and me. "That's a great likeness of the colonel and the foreman," I said.

"And you," Michaels responded, closing the cover of the tablet, then walking to his horse. "You've got strong jaw lines and a determined gaze. You're the best subject of the three."

I was becoming an artists' delight, I thought. "Then you're gonna love Madlyn Dillon."

"Whoa, Lomax, you've no business talking of Miss Dillon, not while I'm courting her," Sainty informed me.

"Michaels is an artist like Miss Dillon," I answered. "They'll have plenty to talk about."

"No they won't," he replied.

Whispering to the pencil artist, I informed him, "Sainty hopes to marry into the ranch. It's easier than building an empire from scratch."

"I heard that, Lomax," Sainty shot back. "Don't pay him no mind, Michaels. Lomax wasn't my hire, but the colonel's."

Scratching my head, I looked at Sainty. "You're not artillery deaf. I bet you could hear a flea fart."

Sainty cupped his hand to his ear. "Huh?" He laughed. On the trail, I realized I'd have to keep an eye—or was it ear?—on Sainty.

Michaels grinned as he returned his pad to his saddlebags and mounted. I pulled myself atop Relee and reined him around to study my trail mates for the next three months. Already they were grouping up with Michaels, Errun, Banty, Parsons and Mark clumping together while O'Henry, Dire, Muscher and Beeline gathered with each other.

Poor Ramírez stood apart from the rest. Fortunately, he would have Muñoz for company on the trail, but I thought I'd ride with him to make him feel welcome. I'd ridden through Indian Territory with True Shot and never had a clue what he said. Even though I wouldn't understand Pedro, I might pick up a few Spanish words for later. Reining my bay next to Ramírez, I grinned and pointed a finger at my chest. "Me, Lomax."

He smiled. "Lomax! Pedro es mi nombre."

We didn't make much sense to each other as we rode out of San Antonio, but we tried to talk. Colonel Dillon joined us a half hour later.

"I've hired us a cook," he announced.

"Is it Charlie Bitters?" Parsons called.

"He's the best I could find."

Everyone groaned.

"He didn't have a horse so we'll pick him up when we send a wagon back to town for supplies. I've got a line of credit at the Alamo Mercantile, so you boys will eat well."

"If Charlie doesn't burn, scorch, singe, sear or char our meals," Parsons answered to the laughter of everyone.

While the others were pondering our cookie—or biscuit as Errun might call him, I thought of the cute brown-haired cook back at the ranch house. I wondered if Ruth would enjoy the apron I bought her.

Chapter 16

We reached the ranch a half hour before dusk. As I dismounted, Ruth ran out to greet me and threw her arms around me, giving me a hug. The fellows hooted and whistled.

"Lomax, I didn't know you had it in you," Jurdon Mark said.

"A distinguished jaw line and determined eyes always attract the ladies," noted the artist Martin Michaels, as she released me and turned to inspect the new hands.

"Fine tora-loorals," Tom Errun observed, whatever the hell that meant.

Everyone was amused except Sainty, who looked miffed that Madlyn had not welcomed him back.

"Colonel," Ruth announced, "I've cooked a big pot of beans for everyone's supper. It's simmering on the stove, ready to serve any time. I hope that meets with your okay."

Dillon nodded as the hands whistled their approval, though I suspected their delight had less to do with the menu and more with her good looks or her tora-loorals, whatever they were.

"Can't she be our cook?" asked Trent Parsons. "We'll look out for her, gather her firewood and set up and break camp for her."

"It's too dangerous on the trail for a woman. Ruth stays here with me and my daughter."

Everyone groaned.

"No time for complaining," Sainty announced. "There's plans to make and work to do so we can start north in a week, ten days at most. We'll get lariats for those that need them, decide if José needs any help with horses and assign chores for tomorrow."

Dillon blessed Sainty's outline with one exception. "Lomax stays with me as I have some tasks for him. Since he's the guide, I don't want to risk him getting banged up."

Bartholomew Henry O'Henry moaned. "Why he be getting off easy?"

"Yeah," chimed in Chuck Muscher and maybe Harry Dire if he had spoken louder.

"Because he's more important than you to the Five-D's future."

All three sulled up like toads.

"If you fellows don't care for the way Sainty or I run things," the colonel continued, "you can leave now. If you do, I won't owe you a single dollar as you haven't done a thing but complain."

I learned then that some folk would find something to bitch about even if God slipped a thousand dollars in their pocket. They complain about the money being placed in the wrong pocket or the bills being too greasy or some other reason.

"You understand the colonel, Black Bart?" Sainty said.

"Don't calls me Black Bart!" O'Henry shot back.

"Full name's Bartholomew Henry O'Henry, isn't it?"

The former slave nodded.

"We'll call you 'The Irishman,' or 'Irish' for short," Sainty informed him.

"If he's Irish," said Jurdon Mark, "I'm a Chinaman."

"Okay, China, that's what we will call you," Sainty replied.

Everyone chuckled, save for Irish, Dire and Muscher, who scowled at the rest of us. They'd barely hired on and already were causing problems.

"Now everyone, save Lomax, head for the barn," ordered Sainty. "I'll introduce you to José Muñoz, our wrangler." He repeated his comment in Spanish.

Pedro Ramírez grinned. The men rode away under the colonel's stony gaze. "Some of those fellows are bad hires," Dillon said, then turned to me.

"Lomax, I want you to take Ruth and the wagon into San Antone tomorrow to fetch our cook and trail supplies. Ruth'll buy what we'll need here, but Charlie Bitters can cook for the men as that's too much work for her."

"Yes, sir," I replied. "Glad to."

"Thank you," Ruth said.

"Where's my daughter?"

"She's been painting on Henry's portrait. There's a lot to finish."

Nodding, Dillon rode to the barn to check on his foreman and his hands.

I tied Relee to the hitching post and shoved my hand into the bundle of Alamo Mercantile purchases I'd secured to the back of my saddle. Turning away from Ruth, I slipped my fingers into the new outfits until they felt the roll that was the apron. Extracting the gift, I offered her the bundle. "I bought something for you." I smiled.

Ruth clasped her hands in front of her bosom. "No boy's ever given me a gift before." She took rolled cloth, unfurled it and laughed. "It's beautiful, Henry, and blue is my favorite color. You should be here in the early spring when the bluebonnets bloom. They're gorgeous."

"I thought you could use it in the kitchen."

"Oh, no, Henry, it's too pretty to risk dirtying when I'm cooking. No, I'll wear it elsewhere, but not there." She hung the big apron over her neck and tied it at her waist, then stepped over, wrapped her arms around me and kissed my cheek. "You're so thoughtful."

"You like it?"

"Absolutely, Henry. I love it!

"Can we go for a walk before it gets dark?"

"Sure," she answered, "I'd be flattered."

We strolled hand in hand around the house, enjoying each other's touch. We ignored the hands at the barn where Sainty was introducing them to Muñoz and instead headed for a big oak tree where I noticed a square whitewashed picket fence. "What's that?" I asked.

"Let me show you," Ruth answered, pulling me that direction.

Reaching the fencing, I realized the pickets marked the family graveyard. Four markers faced us, one for Dillon's wife, the rest for his sons. "Weren't the Dillon boys lost in battle?"

"They were, but the colonel insisted each have a tombstone to mark their time on this earth, even if they lay elsewhere. He had stones carved at great expense for them and later for his wife. They are four of the five D's he named the Five-D Ranch for. He was the other."

"I count six, the parents, the three boys and Madlyn."

Ruth smiled. "His daughter arrived after he registered the brand, so the colonel decided not to change it, telling her as she grew older that she was the fifth D, rather than himself. Every evening before sunset, Mr. Dillon comes out here to talk to Martha and his boys. Sometimes he says he can almost hear her voice on the breeze. It's sad." Her eyes moistened.

"What's the matter?" I asked, putting my arms around her.

"At least his family got tombstones, my kin didn't. I'd gone to fetch water when the Comanches attacked. I hid in the creek until dark, then ran to neighbors. It was awful what they did to my parents, my sister and my two brothers. I was the oldest child, and after the attack, I'm the whole family. At least Mr. Dillon thought enough of me to take me in and help me."

I kissed her cheek. "I'm sorry."

"It's been hard with little joy in my life until you arrived, Henry."

I stroked her hair, and she rested her head on my shoulder as we stood silently by the Dillon family plot. Until then, the only girl I had ever fallen for was LouAnne Burke, back in Cane Hill, but we hated each other to begin with and only gradually grew to appreciate each other. So, I thought it took time to fall for someone, but everything happened so suddenly with Ruth, as if we were destined to be together. I wondered if it was because I was the first young man her age she'd been around since her family's massacre. A thousand questions stampeded through my mind, but I had to admit I truly liked her as she was genuine without a stitch of guile anywhere in her.

Eventually, she lifted her head and announced that she must return to her chores. We walked hand in hand to the kitchen door as darkness overcame the land.

"I've enjoyed the time with you, and I'll look forward to our to ride to San Antonio tomorrow. I fear things are tight for Colonel Dillon, and he needs to let me go, but is too decent to cut me loose. Perhaps he's trying to push us together."

I squeezed her fingers. "It's been sudden, Ruth. We've only known each other a few days, but I wouldn't object to being hitched to you."

She stopped and flung her arms around me and leaned against my chest. The time would come to talk about our future together, but at that moment we clasped each other and enjoyed the closeness. Ruth burst from my arms and sprinted to the back door to keep me from seeing her cry. We had but a few more days with each other before I left for Kansas, but I promised to return for her, no matter what I thought of Texas and Texans.

Walking to the front of the house, I untied Relee and led him to the barn where the men stood around a lantern discussing the next day's chores. As I passed the hands, they snickered and whispered, except for Jurdon Mark. "Where you from, Lomax?"

"Arkansas," I replied, uncertain the relevance.

"We'll call you 'Arky'," he announced. "Everybody's getting a new name like Irish." Mark grinned. "Irish loves his new moniker."

"Don't calls me a monkey, China," O'Henry protested.

"I said 'mon-i-ker,' it mean's name."

"That's a fact, Irish," said Martin Michaels, turning

to me. "I'm known as 'Sketch.' They considered brand-ing me 'Draw,' but feared I'd shoot anyone that called my nickname."

They'd compiled more nicknames than I could ab-sorb so I went inside the barn to manage my bay. When I returned to the house, the hands stood at the kitch-en door receiving bowls of Ruth's beans for supper. I marched around to the front porch where I made out Madlyn rocking furiously, her arms crossed over her chest.

"Father says you're gonna be too busy to sit for my painting. Is that true?"

"I suppose, if that's what the colonel said."

"So unfair. I invited you here for the portrait, and I want to finish it before you go."

"I'll be back in the fall."

"To see Ruth, not me."

"Still, I'm returning."

"The portrait can't wait."

"Sure it can," announced the colonel as he emerged from the house onto the front porch. "Everything is counting on this drive, Madlyn."

"What do you mean?"

"We're cow rich but cash poor. If this drive fails, the ranch goes under. A lot's riding on Lomax and Sainty. If they don't sell the herd and return with the proceeds, we're flat busted. Cattle bring less than your paintings, and they bring nothing. I've indulged your whims since your mother died, Madlyn, but I don't have the patience or the money to do so any longer. I was never sure if Sainty's been courting you or the ranch. Now we'll find out."

"I didn't know we were faring so poorly, Father. I can sell paintings."

"Nobody's got money for such frills, Madlyn. I've sheltered you from the facts because I hoped they would change. I can't even afford trail supplies without taking out a line of credit at Alamo Mercantile."

"I didn't know."

"And I didn't tell you because I thought it would turn

around. It hasn't. Lomax is our last hope."

Grimacing, I prayed to God that McCoy was building his Abilene stockyards.

"What can I do?"

Dillon stepped to Madlyn and patted her shoulder. "For now, start helping Ruth. She's ladling out beans at the back. Help her with the cleanup."

She arose, wiped tears from her eyes and headed inside.

"Sorry you had to hear that, Lomax, but it's the truth. If this doesn't pan out, we'll lose the Five-D. If it weren't for the family graves, I could deal with going broke and starting over, but I can't lose the earth that embraces Martha and the memory stones for my boys."

"I understand, sir." Again, I prayed that McCoy was progressing on his vision.

The colonel hung his head and retreated inside the house.

I plopped in the colonel's rocking chair and considered all Joseph McCoy and Jesse Chisholm had imparted. I hoped I remembered enough to reach Abilene. Driving longhorns would be a challenge, but returning the money back to Texas was a test I had never contemplated. The fate of the Five-D ranch depended on me. I was young and scared, fearful I couldn't bluff my way out of this like I had the Rattle Jar in Springfield.

If I failed, I stood to disappoint not only myself and Colonel Dillon, but also Ruth, who looked to me for her future. I had not realized how many needed me to succeed. I remained in the chair all evening, first rocking my worries away and finally going to sleep in the cool night air.

The colonel called me to breakfast early the next morning. I entered the kitchen to find Ruth dishing out bowls of mush for hands at the back door.

Sainty burst in and sat at the table. "José won't be joining us. He's eating with Pedro."

"Madlyn," cried the colonel, "come to breakfast."

She joined us and took her seat, though downcast.

"What's a matter, Madlyn?" Sainty asked, patting her hand.

"Nothing I care to discuss," she answered.

When she finished serving the hands, Ruth offered us a bowl of oatmeal. Before she sat, Ruth lifted her new apron from the peg on the door and put it on. "Look what Henry bought me," she said. "Wasn't he sweet?"

Though everyone nodded, no one spoke as the colonel bowed his head for grace. He acknowledged God's blessings, scarce though they had been the last two years, and thanked Him for sending me to the Five-D. He sought blessings for the ranch, for the drive and those who made it, beseeching God that all return safely and prosperously. Everyone said "amen," and we ate.

"How'd we do on our hands?" Dillon asked.

"Good on most, bad on others," Sainty replied. "Irish, Muscher and Dire are troublemakers. Several others may be a mite green on handling cattle, but they've got the capacity to learn."

Dillon and Sainty discussed the plans for the day and the coming week. After breakfast, Ruth and I would head to San Antonio to get our cook and trail supplies. Muñoz still had another six horses to break. Sainty said he would split the crew in half and send them in opposite directions to roundup up all the Five-D cattle they could find and any unbranded ones they came across. Any that hadn't been branded would be marked before they hit the trail. After two days of rounding up cows and driving them toward headquarters, the men would start branding. Once that was done, they planned to start for Abilene. It was serious talk, and everyone realized it because so many futures depended upon the drive's success.

After breakfast, I helped Ruth carry bowls to the wash pan. Before she poured hot water from the stove into the vessel, she removed her apron and hung it back on the peg behind the door. Then she joined me and cleaned the dishes, which I dried. A few minutes later, Madlyn and Sainly returned through the back door, carrying tinware the hands had used for their meals. They placed them on the counter and returned outdoors.

"That's never happened before," Ruth noted.

"What?"

"Madlyn helping with the kitchen work. She assisted

last night, too."

"She's worried over ranch finances."

"It's about time," Ruth said. "The rest of us under-stood, but she's so focused on her paintings she can't see the obvious. You've a lot of responsibility, Henry. I know you can do it, but I wish you could stay here."

"If I succeed, I stand to make good money, especially if I deliver a herd by September first. It'll be money we can use to start out. I've got more than a hundred dol-lars on me as is."

"A hundred dollars? That's more money than I've ever seen in my entire life."

"I'm due another hundred plus up to a dime a head when I get a herd to Abilene. That money could buy plenty more aprons."

Ruth giggled. "The one you gave me is enough. I'll think of you each time a wear it."

She had a way of saying things that made me feel important. When we finished the dishes, Ruth put her apron back on and grabbed a piece of paper and a pen-cil from the counter, finishing the list of supplies she'd need from the store for the next month. She looked it over, nodded and turned. "I'm done."

We slipped out the front door and I picked up my hat by the rocking chair, adjusted my gun belt, and marched to the barn with Ruth. As we approached, Muñoz and Silas Banty led the hitched wagon from the shelter.

The one-time slave removed his hat and smiled at her. "That be a fine supper and breakfast you fixed for us, ma'am," he said. "I be Silas Banty."

"Thank you," she replied. "I'm Ruth. Pleasure to meet you, Mr. Banty."

"You be calling me, Silas, nothing more, Miss Ruth "

Ruth smiled. "I will, Silas, and you call me Ruth."

Banty helped her into the wagon while I jumped into the seat beside Ruth and took the leather lines. "Thanks, José and Silas, for readying this rig."

"You be careful on the road, Lomax," Muñoz said as he pulled a slingshot from his pants pocket. "Want to take my slingshot for protection."

I shook my head and the reins, then the wagon lurched toward San Antone, as the Dillons called it, and Alamo Mercantile. The empty wagon creaked and rattled as we rode behind a pair of gray mules. An hour from the ranch, Ruth grabbed my arm and gasped. As she did, I saw four bare-chested riders emerge from a line of trees west of the road.

"Comanches," Ruth said, squeezing tighter on my arm.

I cursed myself. While I was wearing my revolver, I had left my carbine with my tack. Maybe I should have borrowed Muñoz's slingshot. "If trouble starts, you jump in the back and lie down so the sideboards will screen you from them. I'll make a run for it, if we must. Don't show fear."

"I'm scared," she whimpered. "These could be the ones that killed my family."

"Stay as calm as you can." I considered my options. Running was out because their ponies would catch our mules and wagon. I hoped to avoid a fight, but prepared for one anyway, patting my revolver and remembering Chisholm's bracelet. It had saved me from True Shot. Might it work on this quartet?

The four braves, each carrying a bow, straddled the road on their pintos and approached, their faces as impenetrable as stone. As we drew within thirty yards of each other, I tugged on the reins and stopped the mules. I stood up on the floorboard while holding the lines with my left hand and raised my right so they could see the amulet.

They looked at one another, confused. Three reined up their horses, but the fourth rode ahead cautiously. Afraid the brave might spook my team, I tied the lines and set the brake. I pulled my sleeve back for the warrior to note the wristlet as he came closer.

Ruth breathed in pants, terrified of the warriors' intentions.

The Comanche rider drew up beside the wagon and stared at me and Ruth, who shuddered. He examined my right wrist as I made the Indian sign for friend. I pulled off the bracelet for him to inspect. He directed his horse nearer, leaned over and grabbed my wrist, holding onto my gun hand, leaving me defenseless and Ruth vulnerable. The warrior studied the engravings and released his grip, stuck his arm through his bow and gestured friend back at me. He signaled his compatriots, and they advanced at a lope, drawing up near him. He pointed at the bracelet, then his allies. I lifted the bracelet for them to examine as well. They spoke excitedly as they checked the wristlet, nodded to each other and signed friend to me. I mirrored their signal. They backed their horses away and rode past the wagon. I retook my seat, untied the reins, released the brake and resumed our San Antone sojourn.

"Don't look back," I whispered to Ruth. "That shows distrust."

She grabbed my arm and pulled herself closer. "I fear any moment they might shoot an arrow in our backs," she said.

I offered her my right hand. "The bracelet has power over the Comanche.."

Ruth studied the charm. "Is this silver?"

"I think so. Do you remember José saying the engravings mean the bearer is a friend of the tribe?"

"Whatever it means, Henry, you were so brave to face them."

Pride washed over me that she felt safe at my side, and an idea struck me. If we got married, I could have a jeweler melt the bracelet and create wedding rings for us both with enough silver left over to make Ruth a fine necklace.

When we reached Alamo Mercantile, Charlie Bitters was waiting. He had told the clerks what we needed, and they loaded the goods as soon as we arrived. I oversaw the operation as Ruth entered the building to order things from her list. It took ninety minutes to complete everything and total up the amount the colonel owed. It was substantial. As I helped Ruth up in the spring seat, Charlie climbed in back on top of the supplies, and we turned for the Five-D.

I quickly learned that Charlie Bitters could talk you to death. Sampson may have killed a thousand philistines with the jawbone of an ass, but Charlie Bitters could talk that many Comanche to death with his own jawbone. But annoying as he was, I understood it best not to antagonize the man that would fix my meals for the next three months. Our ears needed a break by the time we reached the ranch.

I drove wagon to the house where I helped unload Ruth's supplies, then I turned the reins over to Bitters and told him to drive it to the barn and organize his utensils and staples for the long ride to Kansas. While I'd hoped to stay around the place and court Ruth for a few more days, the colonel had other ideas. At supper he ordered me to accompany him and the cook out to the growing herd the next morning. After Ruth's early breakfast, the colonel and I hit the trail before dawn.

Charlie Bitters followed us in the supply wagon, which rattled with the pots and pans he had hung from hooks he had screwed into the sideboard. With all the clanging and jingling we couldn't have slipped up on a deaf fellow if our lives depended on it. The noise did drown all jabbering that Bitters polluted the air with. Fact was, Bitters could talk an unabridged dictionary to death. The colonel, Sainty and I rode ahead to give our ears a break from the clatter of the utensils and the chatter of our cook. As this was before old Charlie Goodnight developed the chuck wagon, Bitters lacked the convenience of a cabinet to organize the tools of his trade and the food he would prepare with them. The colonel worried how the other hands would react to Bitters and whether his cooking was better than no grub at all. He estimated we faced a fifty-fifty chance of a mutiny.

We rode an hour until we came to the gathering point for the herd. Sainty greeted us and told Bitters where to set up camp. The foreman estimated the hands had driven in more than two thousand cattle, there being so many, and he expected another thousand by the end of the next day. He said they could start branding in two days, rather than three.

The news pleased the colonel. "Every day saved gives us more leeway on the trail."

As the hands were scattered bringing in cattle, no one complained about the cook's arrival. The colonel and I offered to help drive in cattle, but Sainty waved us off. "They need the experience." We offered to help Bitters, but he was set in his ways and didn't want anyone interfering with them. Besides that, Bitters had himself to talk to.

So Dillon and I returned to the ranch. The colonel would ride out to the hands each morning and would return home each evening while Sainty stayed with the workers. Because so much was riding on me, Dillon let me take it easy around the place and spend time with Ruth. We talked and dreamed about our future together for the next two days, the best times we ever spent together.

The second night after my foray to the herd, Sainty came home with the colonel to spend the night. At supper Dillon announced that he wanted me to try my hand at branding the next day. The other hands all showed certain skills at herding and roping cattle, but O'Henry lacked even elementary talents and was assigned to brand the cattle, Sainty informed me.

"He lacks touch," Dillon explained. "He doesn't let up on the iron, burning deep into the flesh, causing bad scabbing. It's like he's trying to burn both hips at the same time. Think you can handle it?"

"I'll give it a shot."

"Good. We'll ride out with Sainty in the morning."

"Yes, sir," I said, looking at Ruth. Her eyes brimmed with disappointment.

Chapter 17

As the colonel, foreman and I rode out the next morning, Sainty explained the feel of branding, the skill that O'Henry had failed to master. "You need a brand that will last, Lomax, not a hair brand," the trail boss noted. "A hair brand won't survive the season, once the hair grows out. So, you must burn through the coat and into the flesh so that is permanent, but not so deep it'll fester. O'Henry burns too deeply, as if he takes pleasure in hurting the cattle."

"Why didn't you put him to doing something else?"

"We need ropers to catch calves, flankers to pin the beast for branding, an ironman to maintain the fires and red-hot irons and others to keep the herd from drifting and to cut out unbranded cattle for the ropers. I tried Irish at everything, but he couldn't rope, couldn't cut a beef from the herd, nor pin a calf down, much less a yearling. He couldn't even keep a fire alive."

"Why not let him go?"

"The colonel and I discussed it, but we're running out of time, and I might not find anybody better. He's a known quantity, even if he is a poor hand. We'll put him to gathering firewood to keep the fires burning and the ironman happy. When we start north, he'll ride drag behind the herd. He'll be among his own kind as cattle string out on the trail, the lazy and stupid bringing up the rear. Irish reminds me of a catfish, all mouth and no brains."

As the sun cleared the eastern horizon, we spotted in the distance the dust kicked up by cattle, horses and hands already work. Longhorns bawled, mounts neighed and cowboys yipped, yelled and whistled. Fine dirt powdered the air and mingled with the smells of singed hair, wood smoke, cow dung and sweat from animals and men. Several of those aromas would follow us for the next ninety days as I retraced the trail to Kansas.

Beyond the working hands grazed the herd, over three thousand longhorns. Though I had seen thousands since entering Texas, I'd never observed so many so closely grouped. They were a lanky breed, their horns spreading up to eight feet on steers and less on cows and bulls. Other horns turned majestically and symmetrically upward, while some drooped, corkscrewed or snaked in opposite directions like the work of a drunk sculptor. I wondered if McCoy was taking into account the breadth of the horns when building gates and chutes to load the animals in stock cars. The beeves' coats came in muted shades of blue and slate, brown and red, yellow and white, and tan and black with splotches, spots, speckles and splatters giving each bovine a look unlike any rival strain. The longhorns bawled and bellowed, stomped and stammered their displeasure with the hands.

With so much racket, our approach went unnoticed. Sainty headed straight for O'Henry, who brandished a glowing iron that he buried in a yearling's side, holding the scorching metal against the animal's flank for an ungodly length of time. Sainty jumped from his horse and yanked the hot poker from Irish's hands.

The colonel pointed at the scorched mark. "It doesn't take that long to get a lasting brand, Lomax. There's raging anger in O'Henry, and I don't care if he was a slave all his life."

As we approached the branding fires, José Muñoz jogged over, leading Sainty's horse. When Dillon and I dismounted, Muñoz took our reins. "I'll handle your mounts," the wrangler said, then led them away.

"Muñoz is a good hand," the colonel offered. "Anticipates what needs to doing and does it. No lollygagging on his part."

I nodded, glad to have Muñoz on the drive. Not only was he a solid worker, he had the thickest head of black hair I'd ever seen on a man. I figured that lush mane offered an asset in Indian Territory if a brave got a hankering for a scalp because Muñoz's would look better at the end of a lance than my thin, mousy brown locks. "Gracias," I said as the wrangler walked away with the two horses.

"De nada mucho," he replied over his shoulder.

As the colonel and I approached the fire, Sainty told O'Henry the news. "Lomax is taking over your iron."

Irish shook his head. "What?"

"Lomax will be branding from now on instead of you."

O'Henry looked from the foreman to the colonel and spat at the owner's boots.

Sainty bolted to Irish and shoved his hands against his shoulders. The fellow stumbled backward, but maintained his balance. "You'll respect our owner or you'll be out of here."

"I been doing a good job."

Shaking his head, the colonel differed. "Not from what the foreman says."

"That's right," Sainty echoed.

Dillon pointed his finger at Irish's nose. "No more insubordination."

"Don't knows what that means," O'Henry responded.

"It means resisting orders," Sainty answered.

"I's not taking white man's commands no more!"

"You will if you want a job," Sainty interjected. "Just because you're no longer a slave doesn't mean you'll not take instruction from another man be he white, black or polka dot, unless you don't care to eat for the rest of your life."

O'Henry clenched his jaw and knotted his fists.

Sainty pointed to an ax by the fire. "You'll be gathering and chopping wood until we're done branding cattle. Any extra firewood give to the cook."

The former slave stared at Sainty until Dillon scowled. "Get moving."

Finally, Irish grabbed the ax.

Sainty eyed him, his hand slipping to the butt of his revolver in case O'Henry turned the ax against him or the colonel. Seeing Sainty's narrow eyes and his fingers tapping on the pistol grip, Irish eased away, heading for a line of trees along a creek a quarter of a mile distant.

"You might want to saddle your horse so you can drag whatever you chop instead of toting it back yourself," Sainty suggested.

"Hey, general," yelled Charlie Bitters at O'Henry, "bring me wood for my fire."

The hands split on whether the cook's request was a decent gesture or a despicable threat, based on his poisonous reputation as a grub grabber.

"That man be having a mean streak in him," said Silas Banty. It struck me he could be referring either to O'Henry or Bitters.

"Okay, Lomax," said Dillon. "It's time to start earning your keep."

I looked at my branding crew. Banty and Tom Errun were working as flankers, while Trent Parsons handled the irons and Martin Michaels roped. "I ain't done this before," I announced, pulling my gloves out of my pocket and sliding them on.

"You can't do worse than O'Henry," said Parsons, stoking the fire and adding a new log to keep the embers and irons glowing. "Like Silas said, Irish has a mean streak in him."

Dillon crossed his arms and watched as Banty and Errun downed an animal. Parsons handed me a white-hot branding tool. Holding it, I felt the heat of the iron on my face as I walked over to the squirming steer. Taking a deep breath, I shoved the poker against the animal's flank. The mammal flinched and bawled at the scalding metal. The odor of burning hair assaulted my nose. Fighting the instinct to yank the iron from the yearling's flank, I counted to four, then lifted the poker and looked at Dillon.

"Not bad, Lomax," he said. "Maybe a tad longer. When I'm counting, I go with a five count. It's a lucky number since you're branding for the Five-D Ranch."

"I went with a four count. I don't care to get a reputation for cruelty like Irish."

Dillon nodded. "That's good. Use a five count or possibly a six count, but no more."

As the flankers released him, I studied the black mark on the steer's hide, recognizing the colonel's brand as a numeral five with the open curve in the number closed in to make a D.

As I stared, Parsons called, "Get a move on it, Lomax."

Sure enough, Michaels was dragging another victim over. I returned my used iron to the fire and waited for Parsons to hand me the next one as Errun and Banty pinned my fresh target against the ground. Grabbing the next branding iron from Parsons, I shoved it against the yearling's flank, counted to five and removed the poker. Time after time after time I repeated that routine until I lost track of how many animals I had tattooed with the Five-D brand. I started just after dawn and seldom broke pace, not even for Parsons to smoke.

The other crew took at least three breaks before lunch time, the process coming to a stop as Pedro Ramírez, Toad Beeline, and Chuck Muscher lit up and exhaled clouds of smoke. Their roper, Harry Dire, smoked as well, dropping everything when the rest of his crew did. As the others wasted time burning paper and tobacco, Jurdon Mark stepped over and helped our flankers hold our prey. O'Henry still fumed when he dragged logs to our fire. He attacked the firewood with an ax like he was whacking off the head of a snake or an enemy, such as me. He occasionally looked my way and scowled as cutting wood was harder work than branding cattle, at least for the man that was handling the iron.

Around one o'clock Charlie Bitters rang the triangle announcing lunch was ready and waiting. We celebrated the break, though we approached the cook wagon like men marching to their execution. The smells of the roundup smothered the aroma of his fare so we didn't know what to expect. He ladled from his pot a serving of beans on tin plate for everyone and added a slice of cornbread that he had baked in his Dutch oven. Both the colonel and Parsons insisted on blessing the food before anybody ate, and we obliged, figuring divine intervention might counter the poison we were about to consume. All of us looked at each other to decide who would risk his life by taking the first bite. Finally, Jurdon Mark shrugged and lifted a spoon of red beans to his mouth. As China lived long enough to take another bite, we dug in. Cookie's beans were edible, too salty to my taste, but not so much so to pass on seconds, and his cornbread was tasty, moist just as I liked it. Bitters made the round with the coffee pot.

England native Tom Errun shook his head. "Do you make tea?"

"I only make tee-tee, but otherwise it's coffee," Bitters said.

"If I buy tea will you prepare it, Charlie?"

"It's coffee or nothing, general" Bitters announced.

Errun sighed. "It'll be a long trip to Kansas,"

"That's the truth," O'Henry scowled, "as the foreman ain't fair."

"You'll do what you're told on this drive, Irish" Sainty reminded him. "For now, you chop wood and when we start north, you'll ride drag."

"Nothing's worse than riding drag," Dire observed in his soft-spoken way.

"Being broke's worse," Sainty answered.

"Why're you picking on Irish?" Muscher asked.

"Somebody's gotta ride drag. You want to join him?"

Muscher remained silent.

"I've been watching both crews," Sainty continued. "Lomax's bunch works harder and faster. No smoke breaks since Lomax took up the branding iron. His crew'll get favors, them and Jurdon Mark. While the rest of you were smoking, he was helping the others brand."

Toad Beeline mumbled something, but nobody

understood it. Toad never said much and when he did speak he said even less because folks had a tough time deciphering his words. I suspect it was a hard burden to carry, having a name such as Toad.

"That's unfair," Muscher shouted.

"So's life," Sainty answered.

"That be damn straight," O'Henry noted.

"Glad we agree on something, Irish."

"Not fair that some men be born slaves and some men aren't," O'Henry snarled.

"We be born slaves, you and me," Banty countered, "but now we be free. Be counting your blessings and be living like a free man, not like a slave to the past."

O'Henry spat at the ground. "Show me your back."

Banty shrugged. "What?"

"Show me your back," O'Henry said, tossing his plate aside and jumping up. He unbuttoned his shirt and pulled his arms out of his sleeves, letting his tucked shirt fall to his waist. He spun around for everyone to see.

We gasped. Ribbons of pimpled, purple scars ran from his shoulders to his waist and overlapped until not a smooth patch of flesh was visible on his back. What I thought was the chip on his shoulder was actually the mutilation of his back and his pride. The disfigurement sickened me.

"That's what my master done to me, whipping me like a dog," Irish said. "Then he pours salt in my wounds."

"It be past us, Bart," said Banty. "You gotta be forgetting it."

"Maybes it passed you, Silas, but I can't puts on a shirt without remembering it. I can't finds a woman who's not sick to her stomach when she sees me withouts a top." O'Henry pulled his shirt back over his arms and buttoned it.

Parsons nodded. "You're right to be angry, Irish, but the Bible says you should forgive those who have wronged you or your hate will consume you, not your enemies."

"What do you knows of the Good Book? You and

your kind fights to keeps me and Silas in slavery. What do you knows of pain?"

"I've got three slugs from Shiloh in my chest, and doctors say they could shift any day and kill me. As for misery, I'd take your scars if I could have my wife and boys back. The war freed you, so you came out ahead. There's not a man here untouched by the war." Parsons looked from face to face among the men. "Raise your hand if you lost someone."

I looked around and everyone but Muñoz and Ramírez lifted their arms.

"We've got miles to travel together," Parsons said. "We need Christian compassion if we are to survive."

"My master say he bes a Christian man, goes to church all the time," O'Henry answered, "but he ain't never showed me no compassions."

Dillon stood up in the wagon box and banged his spoon against his tin plate. Everyone turned to him. "We can't change the past and the damage done by the war. Arguing over it don't help matters. Finish your meal and get back to work."

"Remember the Alamo!" Jurdon Mark offered.

"Remember the Alamo!" the rest of us echoed.

O'Henry sat back down, picked up his plate and shoveled beans and cornbread into his mouth. He stared at the horizon as if he was looking into the past. Irish had good reason to be angry, but the huge cow chip he carried on his shoulders wasn't placed there by any of us nearby. None at lunch had ever owned a slave unless the colonel had, though I doubted that. While everyone sympathized with O'Henry for his beatings, we had nothing to do with them.

Bitters worked his way among us, offering boiled prunes from a blackened pot to finish our lunch. He dropped a pair on my plate. I stared at them.

"They'll help your bowels, general," he said. "If John Bell Hood had eaten his prunes, he'd known not to order the attack at Franklin. A horrible afternoon and evening that was in Tennessee, and some stewed prunes might've prevented it."

Cutting a bite from one of the brown orbs that reminded me of a legless cockroach, I slid it in my mouth and chewed, doubting it would help either my brains or my droppings. As I chomped on my medicine, I listened to Bitters complaints about Hood's battlefield generalship as he dropped stewed prunes on the tin plates of any hands that would have them. To hear the cook tell it, Hood was the worst general of the Confederacy, an officer who had risen above his mental talents and put thousands of young Confederates in their graves as a result. "General Hood was as worthless as a one-legged runner in a foot race," Bitters said, then laughed. "Fact is, after Chickamauga, he just had one leg, but he never had a brain. After dispensing prunes, Bitters collected the tinware for washing, grumbling about Hood.

My crew headed back to work while the other hands took a smoke before picking up the irons and branding the cattle with the Five-D tattoo. The afternoon was tedious like the morning, only hotter as we branded hundreds of animals amid the noise, dust and commotion of roundup. By evening the colonel returned to the ranch house. Too exhausted to complain about Bitters' cooking, I collapsed on the ground and accepted the plate proffered by the cook, more beans, cornbread and stewed prunes. My mouth was too tired to taste whatever flavor Bitters had left in the food, and my nose was too full of dust to inhale any aroma from my supper, assuming he hadn't cooked away all the flavor and fragrance to begin with.

"We deserve better chow than this slop," Chuck Muscher said, tossing his plate on the ground and drawing an instant glare from Bitters.

Poor as his cooking might have been, I knew better than to rile our biscuit roller.

Jurdon Mark arose, picked up Muscher's plate and handed it to Bitters. He walked over to his bedroll and returned with a large pouch. "Marbles anyone?"

"They'd be better eating than supper," Harry Dire said, barely loud enough for us to hear him, though the cook did, scowling at him.

Mark shook his head. "A game of marbles will take our mind off our miseries."

"I'm in," I said, preferring to shoot marbles than listen to O'Henry complain about anything and Bitters bitch about General Hood.

Squatting, Mark emptied the bag, scratched a circle in the ground, and I shot marbles with him. Trent Parsons pulled his Bible from his bedroll to read to himself while Martin Michaels took his pad from his saddlebag and drew in his sketch book. The others from my crew gathered around me and the marbles while the smokers clung near O'Henry, rolling and smoking their cigarettes, then complaining about the food. After a spell, we retired to our bedrolls and slept as well as our aching muscles and the hard ground allowed.

The next four days followed much the same routine as we branded cattle for the trail herd. Sainty debated with the hands that had worked cattle before whether it was best to drive to Kansas a mixed herd that included bulls, steers, yearlings, cows and even calves, or one made up of mature steers. A mixed herd traveled slower, but was less likely to stampede than one of steers, but the steers brought a better price at market. Since they couldn't keep up with a herd and delayed their mommas who fell back with them on the trail, calves would have to be shot to keep from slowing the herd. Killing a calf was like throwing money away. While it didn't matter at branding time because the colonel wanted his mark on all the cattle on his property, Sainty must decide before we left so we could divide out the cattle for the drive.

When I wasn't aching from the bone-tiring work, I missed Ruth and regretted having to leave her. But with the money I'd already made and what I was yet to collect, I knew I would be able to grubstake us to a decent life if we got hitched. After four days of marking every cow on four legs with the Five-D brand, we headed back for the ranch house.

Sainty decided we would take beeves to Kansas rather than a mixed herd so he assigned the others to divide out the mature steers and move them north of headquarters and a bit closer to Kansas before we started the drive. The foreman ordered me to accompany him and the colonel back to the place to prepare to head out in two days. I smiled knowing I could spend part of that time with Ruth.

Chapter 18

Standing on the porch in her blue-and-white calico apron, Ruth spotted me and waved as we approached. Her smile widened like a Texas moon as she greeted me. "Welcome home, Henry. I've missed you."

"I'm glad to be back," I answered.

"The colonel told me yesterday you'd be returning this evening so I made a special supper."

As I dismounted, Dillon and Sainty directed their mounts to the barn. Certain they weren't looking, I dropped my reins and reached to hug Ruth, but she resisted.

"Your clothes are so dirty. I don't want to sully my apron." Instead of hugging me, she leaned forward and kissed me on the cheek, then stepped back and shook her head. "You've been working hard, I see. I'll wash your clothing tomorrow. For now, tend your horse and clean up for supper."

Ruth retreated to the kitchen while I headed for the barn as Dillon and Sainty exited. Inside I quickly removed the saddle and gear from Relee and hung them on the stall along with my gun belt and carbine. After tossing hay for my gelding to eat, I led him outside to the water trough to drink. I doused my head and face in the cool water, cleaning myself as best I could. When I finished, I guided my bay inside to his stall and pulled my spare shirt, pants, drawers and socks from my saddlebags to change. I struggled to get my boots off as my feet had swollen from days without removing them. Once I freed my sweaty feet, I changed clothes except for footwear, as I wanted my feet to breathe for a spell. I grabbed my dirty clothes, my clean socks and boots, then walked barefooted to the front of the house, dropping dirties and boots on the porch and sitting in the remaining rocking chair to relax with the colonel and the foreman.

"We'll head north in three days," Sainty announced.

"One thing's been bothering me," the colonel said as he stared my way. "If this McCoy fellow's got these wonderful stockyards with railroad connections in Abilene, how come I've never heard of them, Lomax?"

I swallowed hard, praying that McCoy had started the facilities. I shaded the truth a little. "He was starting his vision when I left, Colonel. Can't say how much progress he's made, but he printed flyers and paid me to promote his dream in Texas. The stockyards will be there."

Dillon rubbed his chin. "They better be. I've told Sainty to shoot you if they're not."

"No he hasn't," the foreman sputtered, then paused, "though that's not a bad idea!"

"Ya'll let me do the worrying," I replied. We pondered our futures in silence until Madlyn called us to eat. I rose stiffly on aching muscles and hobbled to the kitchen.

Ruth hugged me this time, though she had removed her apron. "You've cleaned some. Where's your dirties?"

"On the front porch."

She pointed to the wood stove and a pot atop it. "I'm boiling water so you can bathe after supper. I'll wash your things tomorrow."

As they took their seats, the colonel, Sainty and Madlyn seemed amused by Ruth's courtesies. They grinned when I sat down as we waited for Ruth to place the final dishes on the table. After she seated herself beside me, Dillon offered grace, beseeching God to watch over those heading to Kansas and to bestow upon all a safe and prosperous journey. I silently prayed the stockyards would be there. After the amens, we dug into a pot roast and vegetables that Ruth had spent all day making. The tender meat melted in our mouths, and the onions, potatoes and canned tomatoes flavored the pot juices. She rounded out the meal with the fluffiest biscuits I'd ever eaten and some green beans she had canned the previous fall. After we finished her roast, Ruth announced she had splurged and made a cherry pie that afternoon. She cut it and brought each of us a modest slice. While the colonel and the foreman discussed the drive, I relished Ruth's dessert but enjoyed her presence even more. She remained the prettiest thing I would ever see in Texas. Her smile could part the clouds on even the darkest day.

I hadn't pictured myself as the settling down kind, but Ruth disabused me of that notion. As the others left the kitchen, she told me to stay as she stepped outside and returned with a tin washtub large enough for me to sit in with my legs over the sides.

"While I'm doing dishes, you can bathe," she announced, as she placed it opposite the counter where she did her cleanup.

While I needed a bath, I wasn't certain this was proper. "You sure you should be in here?"

"It's my kitchen," she informed me. "On top of that, I had brothers so I've seen their tack."

"But you ain't seen mine." I protested as she carried boiling water over and poured it.

"Henry, I'm not planning on looking."

"If I had the chance, I'd look at you."

"Why, Henry? I can't believe you'd do such unless I gave you permission," she said returning the pot to the stove and grabbing a pail from the counter. Take this to the cistern and fetch water so you don't scald your behind. The sooner you're clean, the earlier we can walk."

Seeing no point in arguing, I made two trips to the cistern until I got my bathwater cool enough to bathe in. As I undressed, I told Ruth, "Now you pay attention to the dishes."

"Yes, Henry."

I turned my back to her and stripped. When I was

naked as the day I was born, I grabbed the sides of the tub, squatted over the water and lowered my bottom into the liquid. The warmth felt good and cleansing until I realized I lacked soap. "Ruth," I called, "any soap?"

"You need soap, Henry? I can't help since you won't let me look."

Sighing, I shook my head. "You win. Would you bring me soap, a cloth and a towel? Close your eyes."

Ruth gathered my needs, shut her eyes, and felt her way around the table.

"A few more steps," I told her as she neared. When I reached for the soap, her eyelids popped open, and she smiled. My hands fell to my waist, covering my tack. "I told you to shut your eyes."

"And I did," she replied, "but you didn't tell me to keep them closed."

I had met my match. Like me, she had the clever skills to defeat the Rattle Jar. "You win. Just leave the soap and cloth on the floor."

Smiling as she bent down to place my cleaning needs by the tub, she leaned over and kissed my forehead.

Never had I been kissed while naked until then. Though it was a nice feeling, I was still embarrassed as I tried to cover my growing problem. "Now get back to your dishes!"

She spun around and tittered as she returned to the counter and her chores.

I lathered up and washed my hair, face, neck and torso, then my legs to the knees. Next I rinsed all the dirt out of my ears, as Ruth asked me about my plans for the future.

"Can't say for certain," I said, "as it depends on other factors."

"Such as?"

"You!"

"I hoped you would say that." Ruth spun around, a broad smile on her face.

"Don't look," I cried, still blushing to be bathing in front of such an attractive young lady.

She grinned even wider, returning to her dishes and

humming. "I'll miss you."

"Promise me one thing," I said.

"What?"

"That you won't turn around right now. If you do, close your eyes and keep them shut!"

"What if I placed a towel over my head instead? Then could I turn about?"

"Whatever," I said, as I pushed myself up enough to stand beside the tub, then stick my feet in the water to wash my ankles, calves, and swollen feet. After I finished, I bent to grab my towel. Before I could snatch it and cover myself, Ruth giggled. I turned and saw her standing with a towel across head like a scarf, covering her ears but not her face or eyes.

"Ruth!"

"I've got a towel over my head, just like I promised."

I yanked my towel around my waist and dried myself as modestly as possible. Though embarrassed by her peeping, I enjoyed her playfulness. Stepping out of the tub, I turned my back to her and bent down to dry my calves.

She sniggered. "You've got a cute bottom, Henry."

"I not certain about that, but at least it's clean." I yanked on my drawers and my pants. As I buttoned my shirt, Ruth pulled the towel from her head and dried dishes. "Where do you want this bathwater emptied?"

"Dump it in the garden. You never know when we'll get another rain."

I lifted the tub by the handles and started for the back, careful not to slosh any of the dirty water onto the floor. Ruth opened the door for me and I eased outside, walking barefoot to the garden a dozen paces away. I apportioned the bathwater among a dozen yellow squash plants. By the time I returned to the kitchen, Ruth had finished the dishes and donned her apron. "I've a surprise for you," she announced.

"Do I get to watch you take a bath?"

She playfully swatted my shoulder. "No, Henry. It's better than that!"

At my age and inexperience with females, I thought

nothing rivaled seeing a pretty young lady naked. "What could beat that?"

"I saved a piece of cherry pie for you."

"Let's go," I teased, "so I can return for pie."

She swiped at my shoulder again and shook her head. "Henry! You're a mess."

"But a clean mess," I replied as I walked barefoot out the back door, Ruth by my side.

We strolled around the house, talking about the future and how our lives might merge. We wound up beneath the spreading live oak tree, holding hands and looking at the darkening sky.

"It would be nice to dream of a life with you, Henry, but I fear you won't return. You'll find a pretty girl in Kansas and forget about me."

"I'll come back for you, Ruth. I'm not sure what we'll do when I return, but I'll be back."

"You promise?"

"I do."

"Will you be true to me on the trail and avoid girls of bad repute?"

Nodding, I said, "Come with me and I'll prove it." After visiting the porch to put on my clean socks and boots, I led her to the barn. At the stall where I'd stored my belongings, I dug into my saddlebags and found the tobacco pouch I kept my money in. Extracting the bag, I untied the mouth and spread it open. I stuck my finger and thumb inside and pulled out a roll of cash, all I had remaining from Joseph G. McCoy's initial down payment for the trip to Texas.

Even in dim light, Ruth discerned the cash and gasped. "I've never seen so much money."

Counting out what I thought was fifty dollars, I handed the money to Ruth. "I don't have a ring to give you, but hold onto this. It's fifty dollars." I shoved the remaining bills back in the pouch, tied it, and inserted it my saddlebags. "Should the colonel let you go, spend it for your needs. What you save we'll spend together when I return."

"Oh, Henry, that's so thoughtful."

She reached up with both hands and pulled my face to hers. As she kissed me full on the mouth, I felt the bills pressing against my cheek. Pride rushed through my body because I had provided for my sweetheart, who needed me more than any person I ever met. When she broke the kiss, she slipped the money in her apron pocket. We exited the barn and strolled back to the kitchen where I ate my pie slice, which was twice the size of the pieces she served at supper. Sated and clean but exhausted, I retired, happy to be sleeping on a bed instead of the ground.

The next two days became a blur of preparation as we rode out daily to the herd, which the colonel had positioned five miles north of the ranch house. The drovers separated the steers from the bulls, cows, yearlings and calves, which they drove a dozen miles away, allowing the trail animals to graze on the grass and drink all the water they wanted. At night the hands accustomed the steers to bedding down together and to bunch up more than was customary.

José Muñoz tended the remuda, which would provide spare horses for every man. As wrangler, Muñoz knew which animals were skittish, which swam rivers well, which easily cut animals from the herd, and which were most comfortable with a roper plying his trade. Always with a smile on his face, unless O'Henry was around, Muñoz took Pedro Ramírez under his wing, trying to help him learn enough English to get by on the trail north.

As for Charlie Bitters, he jabbered to himself, likely because the others didn't want to talk to him after sampling his cooking. He organized his food wagon where he could find things in a hurry and still leave room for all the drovers' bedrolls. After that he jury-rigged a tarpaulin sleeve beneath the wagon bed to toss firewood inside whenever he found it. He screwed a coffee grinder into the tail end of a sideboard and nailed a worn out pistol holster into the sideboard within reach of the driver's seat. Bitters seldom wore his pistol, but kept it in the wagon scabbard to shoot any varmint—four-legged or two-legged—that created a problem.

On one trip, Sainty asked me to ride the herd with him as he looked for sick or cantankerous animals that might cause problems on the trail. "Cattle are like men," he told me. "Some are leaders, but most are followers. You've always got a handful of troublemakers, those that don't carry their load or start unnecessary commotions. I'm trying to cull out the mischief makers before we start out."

Being new to longhorns, I offered little help to Sainty, but rode along to learn. He identified four he wanted driven off, a brown splotched steer, a muley gray one, a brindle and a red-faced animal. Sainty cut them from the herd and instructed Silas Banty and Toad Beeline to drive them a couple miles away. If they followed them back, he ordered Banty and Beeline to shoot them.

"Those were definite bad boys," Sainty said as his two hands drove them away. "With them gone, one or two others will take their place. We must watch for them on the trail."

When Banty and Beeline returned, Sainty gathered all the drovers in a circle and explained how we would proceed in two days. As trail boss Sainty would ride up front with me as guide and scout. Martin Michaels and Tom Errun would lead the herd in the point positions. Jurdon Mark and Trent Parsons came next in the swing posts, followed by Toad Beeline and Silas Banty in the flank posts. Bartholomew Henry O'Henry, Chuck Muscher and Harry Dire brought up the rear as drag riders tasked with keeping stragglers moving and preventing any from escaping. Sainty assigned Pedro Ramírez to fill in where needed and to help Muñoz with the remuda.

"Any questions?"

"Yeah," Muscher cried. "Why am I riding drag?"

"Because I said so," the foreman replied. "If you don't like it, draw your pay."

"Other questions?"

When nobody else raised a concern, Sainty looked over the crew and reminded them their main chore the next two days was to prepare the herd for the trail and to identify any troublemakers.

"You be rid of the four biggest problems, but there be one you might be watching," said Banty. "He be a mottled one, a black circle around his left eye. I be calling him 'Eye Patch.'"

"You heard him, fellows, watch out for Eye Patch. Thanks, Silas."

"Anything else?" Hearing no other issues, Sainty sent them back to work.

As the cowboys dispersed, I asked the foreman if I might seek a favor of Martin Michaels. He told me it was okay. I turned to catch him. "Martin," I called, "wait up."

"What do you need, Lomax?"

"A favor. You're good with your pencil sketches. Would you draw a picture of me?"

He shrugged. "Fine with me if it's okay with the boss."

"Okay by me," Sainty answered, "just don't take all day."

"Thanks," I said as Martin climbed from his saddle and took his sketch book and pencil from his saddlebags.

"How you want it," Martin asked. "Atop the horse, full body?"

"Chest up."

"Then get down and pose for me."

I dismounted Relee and stood there holding his reins as Sketch held his pad with his left hand and rapidly drew with his right. My handwriting was so bad I could barely read my own signature, so Martin amazed me with how he produced an identifiable likeness on a sheet of paper so quickly. He looked from me to the drawing and back.

"I hope this'll do," he said, as he flipped the pad around for me to see.

It was like seeing my reflection in a mirror. "That's perfect, Martin. How do you do that?"

He shrugged. "I can't explain it."

"Do I owe you anything?"

"If I need a favor down the trail, I'll let you know."

"Obliged," I said.

Martin tore the sheet from his pad and handed me the drawing. I slipped it in my saddlebags, trying not to wrinkle it, uncertain when to give it to Ruth. The colonel, Sainty and I returned home that night to another of her tasty meals. After I helped her with the dishes, we headed outside and strolled hand in hand about the place, discussing our pending separation.

She kissed me a couple times, but seemed melancholy.

"What's the matter?"

"I fear I'll never see you again, Henry."

"You've got my fifty dollars, so I'll return."

She grinned. "You miscounted in the dark. You gave me sixty dollars. I owe you ten."

"Keep it, all the more reason to return for you. And, I promise you'll see me again."

She buried her head into my chest. "I haven't known you long, Henry, but now I don't know what I would do without you."

We stayed together as late as we dared, then retired so we could arise the next morning to handle our chores. Ruth had a hearty breakfast for us all, and the colonel, Sainty and I left before sunrise, reaching the herd and hands, making final checks. Just as Banty had predicted, Eye Patch had been skittish, unnerving some of the other steers.

"Was he the only one?" the foreman asked.

Banty nodded.

"We'll give him a day or two on the trail to see what happens."

After issuing final orders for our departure the next morning, Sainty pointed me and the colonel back to the ranch. As I had come to expect, Ruth ran out to greet me when I arrived. After tending my horse and gear so everything was ready for the start of our trip, I took the drawing out of my saddlebags and carried it with me to the kitchen where Ruth fried our supper.

Hiding the sheet of paper behind me, I announced, "I

have something for you, Ruth."

"What is it?" she asked as she turned around.

"Remember you said yesterday you'd never see me again? Well, I told you I'd prove you wrong." I pulled the sketch from behind my back and held it by the corners in front of her face.

"It's beautiful, Henry. Looks just like you."

She took the paper, examined at it, then placed it on the table and threw her arms around me, crying softly on my chest. "I'll look at it every day and hold it dear until you return."

"Believe my promise, Ruth, I will return. I'm uncertain what we'll do after that, but I'll come back as God is my witness."

Chapter 19

Though us men arose early the next morning, Ruth and Madlyn were up even earlier, working together to prepare breakfast by lantern light. Sainty and I walked to the barn, saddled our mounts, loaded our gear, and led our horses to the front porch where we tied them to hitching posts. Returning to the kitchen, we ate a hearty meal of scrambled eggs, bacon, biscuits and wild plum preserves. The women waited to partake, Ruth sitting across from me in her apron, mostly smiling but occasionally frowning, and Madlyn parking next to Sainty, offering her best wishes for a safe journey. The colonel came to the table midway through breakfast. "A lot's depending on you two," he said.

Miss Dillon glanced at me. "I'll finish your portrait when you return, Lomax."

"Can I have it when you're done," Ruth pleaded.

"We'll see," Madlyn answered.

Dillon stared at his foreman. "Don't let the hands forget who's in charge."

The trail boss nodded. "They know."

Turning to me, the colonel said, "Lomax, you're second in command, if need be."

"Thank you, Colonel. I'll get the herd to Abilene."

Sainty and I finished our plates and took a last sip of coffee. Standing up, we stretched, knowing days of hard work lay ahead of us as well as months of separation from our girls.

The colonel picked up the lantern and led us through the house and out the front door, hanging the light from a porch post nail. Outside I walked to the end of the planks with Ruth clinging to my arm. I embraced her, and she hugged me in return.

"I'll miss you," she whispered.

I broke her hold enough to slide my hand beneath her chin and lift it with my finger. I brushed the back of my fingers against her cheek and felt the moisture of her tears sliding down her soft flesh. "Don't cry."

"Why not, Henry? I haven't known you long, but you're the best thing to walk into my life ever. I can't bear losing you for these coming months."

Knowing no comforting words, I put my hand behind her neck, pulled her toward me and kissed her forcefully. I wanted to assure her I would not forget her.

Ruth mirrored my affection, then pulled her head from mine. I see her glistening eyes in the soft lantern light. "Though it may be forward for me to say, Henry, I want to tell you something: I love you." She kissed me again, and I returned her devotion in equal measure.

"I love you, too," I answered.

"Oh, you don't know how much I wanted to hear you say that!"

"Okay, Lomax," called Sainty, who required less time than me to bid farewell to his girl, "we best be riding."

I pulled myself from Ruth's hug. Holding hands, we stepped off the porch together and approached Relee. Once again I kissed her, brushing away her tears. I released her hand and climbed atop my bay.

Reining my gelding around, I reassured her, "I'll be back this fall, I promise."

"And I'll be waiting for you, Henry."

Though Madlyn and the colonel walked back inside, Ruth stepped beneath the light as Sainty and I started for Abilene. She stood in the lantern's glow, growing more angelic the farther I rode from her. My last glimpse of her burned into my memory, the lantern casting a halo around her pretty head. Deep in my heart I understood Ruth was a better woman than I deserved, but I vowed to make myself into a man she would be proud to call her husband. I glanced over my shoulder a final time, but the light and Ruth had disappeared. Her sweet memories would carry me to Abilene and back.

Sainty and I reached the herd as a sliver of sun topped the horizon. All the hands had saddled, and most sat atop their mounts as we approached. The cook loaded up his wagon with utensils and gear while José Muñoz and Pedro Ramírez hitched his team of mules to the rig.

"It's good they're up and moving," Sainty said. As we neared camp, the foreman aimed for the drovers segregated in two groups, the workers and the shirkers. I rode over and joined Michaels, Errun, Banty, Parsons and Mark, who I believed would earn their pay.

Sainty ambled toward O'Henry, Dire, Muscher and Beeline. When the trail boss spoke, he eyed them, each one either making or smoking a cigarette. "We've miles ahead of us. Put aside any differences, as your job is to drive these cattle to Kansas without losing a one. If you slack off or don't follow orders, I'll dock your wages."

"That ain't fair," O'Henry blurted out.

"Fair's got nothing to do with it," Sainty said. "You'll follow my commands, and when I'm not around, you'll take orders from Lomax."

"I can't abide Arky," Muscher shot back.

"Put it aside, Chuck, because you'll do what either of us order you to do."

Dire said something, but spoke so softly I couldn't make it out.

Sainty turned to Michaels. "Did you get a count, Martin?"

"I came up with twenty-one forty-seven, and Tom counted twenty-one fifty-five."

"Close enough," Sainty said, "we'll average it out to twenty-one fifty and that's how many cattle I want to get to Kansas. Are there questions?" Hearing none, he nodded. "Let's get started. Remember the Alamo!"

"Remember the Alamo!" echoed all, save for me, Muñoz, Ramírez, and Bitters, who climbed into his rig, untied the reins and started toward Kansas, the clanging and banging of his pots and pans dangling from the side becoming the music that accompanied us to Abilene. The noise beat listening to a politician the day before an election, but little else. Muñoz and Ramírez rode to the remuda of thirty-three additional horses and turned them north.

The cook's and wranglers' chores were easy compared to starting a trail herd on the first day. The steers bunched closely, many of them just waking as the hands worked the herd, whistling and yelling to get their attention, then slapping their flanks with hats or lariats. As the cattle bawled, bellowed and blubbered, they rose on their hind legs first and forelegs second, tossing their heads and occasionally clacking the horns of a neighbor. As the steers arose, so did the noise and dust as it had not rained since I had been on the Five-D ranch. Michaels and Errun started the animals north, taking their point positions.

Though Sainty eventually took the lead, he held back at first, making certain the swing and flank riders got in place and funneled the cattle after the others. I followed him around the rear of the herd where O'Henry, Muscher, and Dire rode drag. A few cantankerous steers bolted past the drags, and Sainty chased after them, cutting his mount in ahead of them and driving them back to their hoof-and-horn brothers.

"Don't let any of them get by you," the foreman yelled to the drovers as he forced the escapees back with the herd. "Your job is to keep 'em moving and stop 'em from straying."

Another steer bolted, and Dire took out after him, heading him off, drawing close enough to the runaway to slap him with the coiled rope he carried in his left hand.

"That's the way," Sainty yelled, as he watched the drag riders each take out after a fugitive and return him. "That's better, all of you. You'll make good cowhands."

By the time the shirker trio had chased several dozen deserters back to the others, the herd had stretched out over a mile. While they slept in a bunch, they strung out on the trail, the leaders and the strong ones moving to the front and the weaker or lazy falling to the rear. Sainty watched until all the animals moved north. "Show me the way to Kansas."

We rode at a lope to the front of the caravan, the foreman yelling encouragement to his hands as he passed. When we had put fifty yards between us and the herd, we slowed our mounts and visited. "Cattle are set in their ways," he explained. "We'll drive them hard today to get them as far possible from their customary ranges and to break them into a trail habit. I hope to make twenty miles a day for the first five days. That'll accustom them to the routine and tire them out so they're less likely to stampede."

"I can tell you've done this before."

Sainty nodded. "Never more than a hundred miles, though. I need you as the lookout, not just for Indians, but for prairie dog colonies, rattlesnake dens, coyotes, turkeys or any hazard that could harm or panic the herd. If you spot prairie dogs, we'll skirt the colony so none of our animals break a leg. If you see a flock of turkeys, flush them or they could spook the steers."

"I can manage that," I replied.

"Also watch for men that mean harm and recognize from a distance what kind of trouble lies ahead. Take riders, for instance. The sooner you identify them the more time you have to prepare for danger. A white man generally rides tall in the saddle and more straight-legged than an Indian, who's likely to lean forward more, his legs bent to grip his mount. Recognizing the difference can save lives. Reading sign of man and animal is important."

I looked back over my shoulder at cattle stretched behind us like a serpent that had swallowed a rat, the line narrow at the head of the herd and widening near the back where the dust was thicker, sometimes obscuring the men riding drag. We marched across a land of modest hills splotched with live oak and pecan trees. The late spring grass, thirsty for rain, was fading from green to yellow as it awaited the next thunderstorm. And the days were teetering between the pleasant temperatures of spring and the scorching heat of an unforgiving summer sun.

The befuddled steers bellowed and mooed as they walked, tossing their heads and twitching their tails. I hoped that Joseph G. McCoy remained a man of his word and vision. If not, Sainty might shoot me and negate my promise to return to Ruth. I had more than prairie dog holes and Indians to worry about.

The foreman circled the herd from time to time to check on and encourage his hands, leaving me alone to watch for all the hazards that could befall a herd on the move. I observed nothing of danger as we wove our way through the grasslands between clumps of trees. In Texas you saw more sky than I remembered in Arkansas among the tall pines. I came to enjoy the daytime heavens with their changing colors and moods and to appreciate on hot days those fluffy clouds that sailed overhead, occasionally floating in front of the sun and giving us blessed shade for a minute or two before moving on.

Sainty returned and apprised me. "We're doing fine. I told them to change their mounts one by one so the horses don't tire out. Other than that I had to tell the boys riding swing and flank not to let wide gaps develop between the cattle and ordered those on drag to keep them moving."

Shortly after high sun, I pointed north to a thin line of trees. "Water ahead."

"Looks like Bitters noticed, too," Sainty replied, aiming his finger at the wagon stopped in the shade of the live oaks. "We'll let the men eat in shifts and allow the cattle to graze and water before we head on. After lunch, you ride ahead and find us a place to bed down. The first night is the worst as steers grow skittish on unfamiliar ground. Always a chance they might run."

"How do you handle a stampede?"

"Every man rides to the front of the steers and turns the herd in on itself so the cattle circle up and mill. It's dangerous because the steers are a ton of terror on the hoof. Get in their way and they can trample you so there's nothing left but a greasy smudge in the grass."

After that unpleasant thought, I rode to the grub wagon and dismounted, tying my reins to the front wheel, not thinking a thing about it until I saw Bitters scowl.

"Move your damn horse, general. This ain't a livery stable."

"Sorry, admiral," I said, drawing a crazy look from the cook.

"Did you say admiral?"

"You're as much an admiral as I am a general," I said.

"Everybody's a general in my army because I can't remember names."

I untied my horse and took him along the creek to water, then hobbled him so he could graze. When I returned to the wagon, Bitters offered me a spoon and a tin plate with a slab of cornbread and a ladle of cold beans on it."

"Obliged for you moving your gelding."

"Don't mention it," I answered as I consumed his standard meal.

"A few of these boys lack manners," Bitters said.

"My momma taught me right," I replied.

"One of those sons of bitches called me 'Upchuck' behind my back."

"Which one?"

"The one I call general."

"You call everybody general."

"Oh yeah."

"Is it the fellow with the scars on his back or the roper that wears glasses?"

"Not them either. It's the taller one."

"The sorry fellow that always appears to be squinting down his nose at you?"

"Yeah, that's the one."

"His name is Chuck Muscher. Says he's from New York."

Bitters shook his head. "Should've known he was a damn Yankee."

"He must think it funny, him being named Chuck and you being the cook."

"Maybe, he thinks I don't hear him whispering to others and funning about me, but I ain't deaf. I hear insults, and I won't put up with them."

"Your cooking's fine, Charlie," I lied. "Without it, I'd starve." That was a true statement despite the poor quality of his fare.

"I'm obliged," Bitters said, nodding at Sainty as he approached. He retreated to the wagon and soon returned with a plate for the foreman.

The foreman frowned when he took his first bite.

"It's good, isn't it?" I asked.

Poor Sainty looked at me as if I was crazy until he realized Bitters stood nearby. "As fine a meal as I've ever had on the trail," he said, winking at me.

Bitters beamed. "Thank you, general, but that Yankee fellow don't agree."

"What's he know, being from up north?"

"Been calling me names, he has, general!"

"Like what?"

"Upchuck!"

Sainty choked and almost spit out his food as he tried to throttle a laugh. "I can't believe that," the trail boss sputtered.

"Put an end to it or I will, general," Bitters said as he returned to the wagon.

When cookie walked around his rig, Sainty looked at me. "Muscher may be onto something, but we can't afford to rile the cook if we want to eat. Why don't you ride out and tell him to knock it off? Tell him no more name calling for the cook. Hell, he could poison us. Intentionally, I mean." Sainty finished his plate as I walked toward the creek where I unhobbled Relee and headed to the rear of the herd, looking for our taste expert.

The steers had spread out along the creek, eating grass and drinking water. Michaels and Errun had driven many across the narrow watercourse to make room for others to graze and drink, then the point men headed for their grub, letting the swing riders watch over the herd. I passed the flankers and tipped my hat. At the end of the herd I found Dire, O'Henry, and Muscher, who wore a coat of dust. Even with bandannas over their noses and mouths, they coughed and hacked from the dusty fog that engulfed them.

Muscher worked on the opposite side from me so I aimed my bay around the caravan, wishing I didn't have to ride through a cloud of dust to reach him. I lifted my bandanna over my nose as I headed toward Chuck. O'Henry grumbled as I passed him, but I almost didn't recognize him as he had enough dirt on him to pass for a Mexican if not a white man. Reaching Muscher, I took off my hat to fan the grit from around my face, then yanked it back over my head so my hair wouldn't get any dirtier than it already was.

"What do you want, Arky?" York grumbled, glaring down his nose at me.

"I wanted to ride drag," I announced, "but Sainty says I'm too valuable up front."

"You best not chafe me, kid. I'm in no mood for it."

"That's kinda the message Sainty wanted me to deliver to you, York. He wants to find out if you've been calling Bitters 'Upchuck'."

"What of it?"

"Sainty says to stop it."

"The hell I will. Everybody's got a nickname the best I can tell. Irish for O'Henry, China for Mark, Sketch for Michaels, York for me. You're Arky. You know the rest."

"They don't have a hair-trigger temper like Bitters," I said. "He could poison us."

"He's poisoning us now with the slop he feeds us. I'll say what I want when I want to whoever I want. It's in the Constitution you Rebels tried to overthrow—unsuccessfully, I might add! You can't tell me what to say."

"I'll tell Sainty you're an authority on the Constitution and refuse to shut your loud mouth."

"You do that, Arky, and you tell Upchuck his cooking tastes worse than week-old dishwater. A starving dog wouldn't eat that puke."

I tipped my hat to Muscher and nudged Relee into

a lope so I could get away from York and the dust. I rode back to the wagon where Michaels and Errun were finishing up their lunch. They took their mounts and headed across the creek. As they did, Parsons and Mark came in for grub. I greeted them and whispered to watch their tongue around Bitters as he was sensitive to the Upchuck nickname. They were smarter than those fellows riding drag and knew not to insult—at least to his face—the cook.

I crossed the stream to report to Sainty on my exchange with Muscher. "York didn't take kindly to your instructions. Said something about the Constitution giving him the right to say whatever he wants to whoever he wants whenever he wants."

"I'm the law on this drive," the foreman shot back, "so it don't matter if he's got a copy of the Constitution in his pocket and a lawyer to represent him."

Shrugging, I replied. "Don't yell at me. I figure Upchuck will straighten him out on his Constitutional rights the next time Muscher shoots off his mouth."

Sainty laughed. "It is sorta funny, calling him Upchuck, but don't you tell anybody I said that." He turned his horse about and watched more cattle trickle across the creek after watering there. "We're making decent time for a first day. The creek's got a rocky enough bottom that Bitters can cross his wagon without trouble. Once those riding drag get their animals over, we'll let them eat and then reform the herd for the afternoon. You best hang around the wagon and keep any eye on Chuck and Upchuck. Report any problems."

Beeline and Banty were handing their empty plates to the cook, when I reached Bitters. They paused long enough for Toad to roll and light a smoke, then they mounted and returned to punching cattle, relieving the men on drag and herding the remaining steers across the creek. Cookie dumped their plates in a pan of dishwater as I dismounted and hobbled Relee. "You want me to wash those for you?"

Bitters looked at me like I had slapped him with a pound of rotten calf liver. He shook his head. "Nobody's ever offered to help before."

"I helped my girl with dishes back at the ranch, and I'd rather do something than nothing. Maybe I can wash off the dust."

"Ruth's a pretty gal," he said. "I'd help her with dishes, too."

I was cleaning tinware when O'Henry, Dire and Muscher came up. Chuck eyed me and shook his head. "You'd make some ol' boy a good little wife, Arky."

The trio of shirkers dismounted and led their horses to the creek to water where the men dusted their clothes with their hats, then bent and cupped water to their faces to remove as much of the trail dust as possible. When they returned, their cheeks and foreheads were streaked with mud, making them look like Comanches in cheap war paint.

Muscher sat Indian style on the ground. "What's for lunch, Upchuck?"

"The same thing you had for breakfast, general."

The food was cold, but I could tell the cook was hot.

Dire and O'Henry laughed as they joined Muscher.

Bitters walked over with a plate in each hand and gave one to Irish and the other to Dire. He returned to check on me at the dishpan.

"Where's my plate, Upchuck?" York demanded.

"Coming up, general," Bitters responded. The cook grabbed the ladle from the pot, dropped it on the ground, picked it up, let it fall in the dirt again, then retrieved it holding it up to the sun before scraping out the last serving of beans from the pot. What beans and grit hadn't fallen onto the plate, Bitters scraped off with his finger and stirred the confection with the same digit. "I need to fetch seasoning from the wagon," Bitters told Muscher. With the plate in his left hand, the cook marched to his wagon seat and yanked his pistol from the holster he'd nailed to the sideboard. Hiding the weapon beneath his apron, the cook strode over to York and offered him lunch. As his tormentor reached to take the plate, Bitters yanked the pistol from under his apron and aimed it between the Yankee's legs.

BOOM! roared the revolver.

Nearby cattle panicked, some bolting into the stream.

Clump went the plate as it landed face down on the ground.

"I've been killed," Muscher screamed, clutching at his groin.

Chapter 20

Chuck Muscher rolled on the ground, grasping his groin as Bitters stood over him, smoke wafting from the barrel of his pistol. Dire and O'Henry threw their plates aside, leaped up and dashed to the other side of the wagon, peeking around the tailgate to see if they were safe and if York was dead.

By the creek, Banty and Beeline struggled to calm the cattle as Sainty galloped toward the commotion, hitting the water at a gallop and splashing spray higher than his head. The cook lifted the pistol barrel to his lips and blew the smoke away. He shoved his still hot revolver in his apron pocket. "Looks like you spilled your plate, general," he announced as he squatted and grabbed the tinware. With his hands, he scooped up the food—dirt, twigs, grass and all—and splatted it back on Muscher's dish as Chuck writhed on the ground. Sainty reined up hard and leaped from his horse.

"We've had a little trouble," I informed the foreman.

Muscher thrashed about, but for all his commotion, I spotted no blood.

"What's going on, here?" Sainty yelled.

"Sorry, general," Bitters explained, "I swore I saw a snake and shot at him."

I looked at Sainty. "Chuck called him Up—"

The foreman lifted his hand. "Say no more."

"Chuck, I sent word for you to mind your manners around Bitters."

Muscher still squealed on the ground, unbuttoning his pants and sticking his hand inside to check if anything was missing. "He shot me," York screamed, even when he pulled out his bloodless fingers and saw not a spot of red.

"Dammit," Bitters cried, "I missed him. The next time I'll aim better and gelding that damned snake for sure." He extended the plate to his tormentor. "Here's your lunch, general, with extra seasoning."

Muscher ignored the cook's offering and kept checking his manlies.

Rebuffed, Bitters dropped the plate on the ground. "Hope you enjoy your grub, general. I made it special for you." The cook retreated to his dishpan, flushing Dire and O'Henry from behind the wagon as they scurried around the mule team to check on their compatriot.

I decided Bitters's bullet had missed flesh, but struck close enough to his groin to throw up dirt and rock that must have pinged him good.

Calming when he figured out the bullet had not hit him, Muscher sat up.

Sainty pointed his finger at Muscher's nose. "Next time I send you an order, York, you better obey or I'll be helping Bitters with his aim. Now eat your lunch, then get back to work."

Muscher took his plate, looked at the stew of beans, dirt and grass, then sat it aside.

"I said eat it, Chuck, or draw your pay and ride off."

"There's no spoon."

"Use your fingers."

Taking a deep breath, Muscher dipped his hand into the conglomeration and scooped it into his mouth, grimacing as he chewed and eventually swallowed.

"See, York, it's edible."

Muscher sat his plate on the ground. "I'm full."

"And I'm full of your defiance. Do what you're told, or I'll cut you loose. Now carry your plate to Charlie and get back to work."

Muscher took the plate to the cook. "Thank you, general," Bitters offered, grabbing the tin dish and flinging the food to earth, then plunging it in the soapy water. Dire and O'Henry decided they were full, retrieving their discarded plates and delivering them to the wash pan. Bitters scraped off their leftovers and dunked the dishes into the suds. Then the pair joined Muscher, all three mumbling to each other as they rolled and shared a match among their cigarettes.

Still standing with his arms across his chest, the foreman studied the shirkers' smoking routine. "Your shucks are lit, so mount your horses and return to work." The trail boss watched them head off to the cattle.

Only after the trio rode away did Bitters return his pistol to the holster nailed to the wagon.

Sainty turned to me. "As we form up the herd, help Bitters across the creek, then ride ahead with him to find a place to bed down for the night. We'll need level ground with decent grass and handy water. Another five hours until we stop for the day. That'll give us an hour before dark to let them settle. First night on the trail's always the worst."

"Yeah, boss," I answered.

"And," Sainty whispered, "don't call Bitters Upchuck or he might make you a steer."

"I learned that lesson," I replied.

"I hope Muscher has," Sainty said as he picked up his mount's reins. He climbed into the saddle and rode away to push the steers northward again.

Strolling to the cook, I offered to help. He pointed to the blister end of an ax poking up above the sideboard. "Go to the creek bed and cut me wood for tonight. When I finish up here I'll drive by to load it."

Nodding, I pulled the ax free, marched to my grazing bay and led him among the trees and brush along the stream. With plenty of fallen branches and dead wood to choose from, I chopped away. I had a nice stack of firewood when I heard the clatter of the cook's approaching wagon. He stopped beside me and jumped from his seat. I returned the ax and loaded the wood in the tarpaulin sleeve Bitters had tacked under the wagon bed.

When we finished, I unhobbled Relee and mounted as Bitters walked to the edge of the creek, studying the water. "It don't look too deep or muddy so we should be able to cross without trouble. It won't compare to crossing one of those streams in Mississippi or Tennessee. A lot of water in those places, not enough in Texas." He climbed back in his seat, and I directed Relee ahead of the cooking rig and into the water. Bitters' assessment had been right, the water was eighteen inches deep, not enough to wet our firewood. The creek bed was firm enough that the mules pulled the wagon effortlessly to the other side. "All our crossings won't be this easy," Bitters told me.

After we cleared the slight embankment, I saw the steers stringing out along the trail and spotted José Muñoz and Pedro Ramírez with the remuda. "Did the Mexicans get lunch?"

"They ate ahead of you and the boss. They don't complain about my cooking so I feed them first. Too, the wrangler is good at finding wood, breaking it up if he can and pointing it out so I can pick it up on the trail. His helper's okay, too. Even if he don't care for my food, he doesn't know enough English to tell me otherwise. I get along fine with people as long as they don't insult my food."

"I think York's learned his lesson."

The cook chuckled. "He did or he'll be a steer the next time."

"Let's put some miles behind us, Charlie, and find a camp site."

Bitters rattled the reins and his team moved into a comfortable trot. I rode beside him, until we neared the remuda, then I headed for the wrangler. As I approached, Muñoz broke away from the horses and trotted my direction.

"Señor Lomax," he smiled, "what was the gunshot? Snake or a skunk?"

"Both. Chuck Muscher insulted Bitters' grub, and the cook shot between his legs."

José frowned and made the sign of a cross over his

heart. "¡Señor, es mejor que nada! It's better than nothing," he translated.

"The cook didn't take too kindly to being called Upchuck."

His face contorting, Muñoz shrugged. "I know Spanish, English, a little German and a lot of Indian, but I don't know the word upchuck."

"When you eat food that won't stay down, you throw up or upchuck."

Muñoz laughed. "Vómito," he said.

"Bonito?" I repeated.

"No, no. Vó-mi-to, not bo-ni-to. Vómito means upchuck. Bonito means pretty."

"The difference between bonito and vómito in this outfit is the difference between being a bull or a steer," I observed. "How'd you learn to speak so many languages, José?"

"Just came easy to me, like working horses. I's born Mexican and lived with my family until I was twelve when the Comanches killed them and captured me. Three years I stayed with the tribe as a boy, picking up their language until I escaped. Then I lived a couple years with German folks that took me in. I was always around Spanish and English. Spoken words came easy. I don't read them as well as I speak them, but I didn't have much schooling."

"I had more schooling than I wanted, but I don't speak anything but English and probably not too smartly at that," I admitted.

"Words are like tools," Muñoz said. "You don't need to own every one as long as you have enough to build what you need."

I thanked him for his Spanish lesson and told him I needed to catch up with Bitters to find our evening camp.

"Remember, the difference between vómito and bonito if you want children!" He laughed.

Reaching the cook, we crossed a couple shallow creeks as we sought a spot to bed down. We finally came to a broad meadow, well grassed and with a little creek trickling along the perimeter. Far from the perfect location, the site was adequate to spend the night with plenty of room to rest the animals, sufficient grass for grazing and tolerable water for Bitters' cooking and cleaning needs if not the herd's drinking requirements. The cook aimed his wagon toward a small copse of trees for shade.

As Bitters unhitched his team, I unsaddled and hobbled Relee, then found a spot thick with grass where I could make my bed for the night. I dropped my gear there and assisted Bitters with the team. After the mules were hobbled, Bitters tossed me a shovel and pointed to a spot to dig a shallow fire pit. As dry as the grass was, a stray flame could start a prairie blaze. While I dug, Bitters unloaded crates and sacks of food, positioning pots and Dutch ovens around where I worked. Walking over and inspecting my hole, he nodded his approval and returned to the wagon to fetch firewood. I replaced the shovel and toted to the pit enough kindling and logs for both supper and breakfast. Bitters started his fire, then hammered stanchions into the ground on either side of the flames and slid the crossbar in place to hang his pot hooks and utensils.

"What was it like cooking for the army?" I asked him.

Bitters shook his head. "You ever cut flour with saw dust or tried to make coffee with hickory nuts?"

"Nope."

"That's what it was like. Even the generals ate poorly. The fellows that've been complaining about my cooking don't know what poor eating is. Hell, we lost the war because we didn't have enough to eat. Soldiers were too tired to fight and generals couldn't think straight for the hunger in the Army of Tennessee. Don't know about Robert E. Lee's army, but we starved on Confederate rations. Never enough other than what we could steal, mostly from our own people, old folks, women and young 'uns just as hungry as us."

Bitters pointed to the southwest and the cloud of dirt kicked up by our herd and tinting red from the late afternoon sunlight. "Dust in the sky always meant trouble, an army was getting closer and you were gonna die. I don't care to live through it again, and I don't intend to take nonsense from any man that didn't endure it, especially from that Yankee that hates my cooking. I can respect the trail boss and the one that's always reading his Bible, because I know they fought. Not so much the others. Enough about the war," he concluded and started a pot of coffee, then used the wagon tailgate as a table to make biscuit dough which he put in the bottom of a greased Dutch oven. After that he pulled out a slab of saltpork and sliced bacon to fry.

I helped Bitters by adding wood to his fire, pouring him a cup when the coffee boiled and dragging firewood from the creek. As the shadows lengthened, I saw a lone rider come over a rise and recognized Sainty. Shortly, the remuda came into view.

"It's time to start cooking, general," Bitters announced. He checked the biscuits and confirmed they had risen, then covered the Dutch oven with the lid. Bitters carried the container and the shovel to the fire, breaking up the burning wood and placing the pot on the coals, then scooping a batch of embers out to cover the lid. Next the cook dropped a metal grill across the fire pit, took a skillet and placed it on the iron to heat while he fetched the bacon, which he tossed in the pan and listened to it sizzle.

I was chopping wood when Sainty approached. He looked over the camp and my unsaddled horse.

"Lomax," he said, "we don't unsaddle our mounts until the day is done. Never know when we'll need them."

"It won't happen again," I said, as I walked over and re-saddled Relee.

"General," called Bitters, "I told him to unsaddle and help me. It's my fault."

Glancing at Bitters, I saw him wink, though I didn't know why he was taking the blame.

"I give the orders around here, Charlie, not you. And, another thing, I don't want you firing a gun around the cattle again. We were lucky you didn't start a stampede."

Bitters nodded. "Yes, general, but don't inform that

Yankee you told me such. I damn well want him believing he's one insult from singing soprano."

Sainty laughed. "He learned his lesson. If you'd fired your gun at night, we'd had a stampede, Charlie. Cattle spook easier in the dark when they can't see what's going on. This being our first night away from familiar pasture, the steers will be skittish tonight."

As Sainty looked over the grounds, he nodded. "This'll do. Not as much water as I'd like, but grass is plentiful, though yellowing, and there's plenty of room for bedding."

As he finished, the remuda approached, Muñoz leading and Ramírez trailing the horses. The wrangler angled the mounts toward the creek, letting them water and graze. Satisfied they were calm, Muñoz rode over and dismounted, acknowledging Sainty.

"No problems with the horses, el jefe," he announced. "Everyone but you and Lomax exchanged horses at least twice today, two of them doing it three times."

"Good work, José. Is the chow ready yet, Charlie?"

"I've got plenty of bacon. Let me check the biscuits." The cook grabbed a pot hook and lifted the lid from the oven. "Just a couple more minutes," Bitters announced, then resumed frying pork before fetching tin plates. "Cups are on the tailgate if you want coffee."

Muñoz grabbed one for himself and one for Sainty, who remained in the saddle, occasionally standing in his stirrups. "Here they come," he announced before the rest of us could see the herd. He dismounted and let his horse graze.

Bitters brought over three plates with four slices of bacon and two biscuits apiece. We squatted and ate. His biscuits were better than I expected and the bacon was crisp and tasty. Feeling mischievous, I waited until Muñoz had a mouthful of coffee, then called out "Vómito, Charlie, vómito!"

Munoz spewed coffee halfway to Austin, then stifled a laugh.

Our cook spun around. "What did you say, general? My hearing's not what it once was."

I said, "Bonito, Charlie, bonito!"

"Tell him what it means, José. Tell him what bonito means."

"It means pretty. Bonito means pretty." Muñoz stared at me, shaking his head.

Bitters rubbed his chin. "No one's ever called my food pretty before. I'm glad someone respects my cooking."

Sainty grinned. "We all do, Charlie, some of us more than others."

"You having trouble holding down your coffee?" I asked Muñoz.

He shook his head again and looked at the ground.

About the time we finished, Martin Michaels and Tom Errun guided the bellowing steers past us to the creek.

"José, you and Pedro mount up and spell the point men so they can grab a bite while the herd waters and grazes. When everybody's eaten, we'll settle the cattle."

"Si," said Muñoz, who climbed atop his horse, whistled for Pedro and waved him over. They trotted off together and soon Martin and Tom came to the wagon and dismounted, taking off their hats and slapping their clothes to remove the dust.

"We've had a good day, twenty-two miles by my estimate," Sainty said. "Any problems?"

Michaels shook his head. "Nothing major, save for Eye Patch. He's skittish and's been annoying our lead steer, a brindle we call 'Corkscrew'."

"Yeah," said Errun. "His horns are so crooked a snake couldn't crawl from end to the other without getting dizzy."

"Let's watch Eye Patch tonight in case he frets," Sainty said, looking up at a sky, tinted with the dust kicked up by the thousands of hooves. "This land could sure use rain, but I'm pleased we've got a cloudless sky and no chance of thunderstorms this evening."

"What was the gunshot during the lunch stop?" Michaels asked.

I replied, "York called Bitters 'Upchuck.' Bitters put

a bullet between his legs to let him know such aliases were unwelcome. It's safest not to criticize him."

"No," Errun whispered, "it's safest not to eat his food."

"Don't let Bitters hear you say that," I warned.

Charlie brought over two plates, oblivious to the earlier conversation, and offered the bacon and biscuits to the point men.

"Bonito," I said to Bitters as Michaels and Errun took their supper. "Bonito means pretty in Spanish," I informed the pair.

"We know," they replied, sitting to consume their grub.

"Bonito, Bitters," called Michaels.

"Bonito," echoed Errun.

"You fellows are smarter than Muscher," Sainty observed.

"Never insult a man that can spit or worse in your food," Errun answered.

As they finished their supper. Sainty explained that we'd ride double guard on the herd this night so the steers would grow accustomed to bedding together on the trail and having riders circling them. After a night or two, Sainty said the shifts would be handled by two men unless weather was stormy. The foreman instructed us to lay out our bedrolls while it was still light.

When the point men were done, Sainty sent Michaels and Errun back to the herd with instructions to send José and Pedro to spell Jurdon Mark and Trent Parsons so they could eat. The two swing men approached camp, talking as if they enjoyed each other's company.

Sainty told them the evening plan as Bitters brought over their supper. Parsons bowed his head and spoke a prayer, the rest of us looking uncomfortably from one to the other before bowing our heads until Parsons was done. Mark and Parsons ate the bacon and biscuits with their fingers as Bitters returned with their coffee.

Sainty asked, "Did you boys notice any problems with the cattle?"

"There was one steer I thought was jumpy, a splotched

222

animal, tossing his head and shaking it. I thought he was a troublemaker, but his head swelled by afternoon. I suspect he got bit by a rattlesnake."

"Keep close watch on him, like Eye Patch," Sainty replied. "We'll take care of any problem animals in the morning."

When he was done eating, Parsons walked over to his horse and rolled a cigarette. He opened a saddlebag and pulled out his Bible, which he read until Sainty instructed him and Mark to toss their bedrolls. When they finished, they returned to the cattle. After he and Mark rode away, Silas Banty and Toad Beeline approached the food wagon and dismounted. Both men were laughing, but Banty was doing most of the talking, something about when he was a kid riding in a cart he had tied to a milk cow's tail. He'd enjoyed the ride until the cow went through a gate and the cart got hung, yanking off the animal's tail. He said he chased that cow for an hour trying to catch her and nail the tail back on so his master wouldn't find out and whip him. Banty cackled as he told the story. I wondered if Silas had scars on his back.

They ate their meal as Sainty explained the evening plan, then fixed their bedding. When they were done, they returned to the herd. A few minutes after they departed, the drag riders came to camp, sullen and edgy, like they were walking on crates of dynamite. Bitters filled plates with bacon and biscuits for each of them, but didn't deliver them to the trio, leaving them on the ground by the fire. "Come and get it if you want it," he said, returning to the wagon and lingering by the seat for a moment. When he stepped away, I saw the holster on the sideboard was empty and spotted the butt of the pistol stuck in his britches.

Once again, Sainty explained the plan for the night as the shirkers ate their food. The three were as enthusiastic as the devil at prayer meeting, eating their supper sullenly and then rolling their smokes and unrolling their bedding before heading back to the herd.

After they left, Sainty informed me I would ride watch the first shift with him, Michaels and Errun. The first and last watches were the best because they offered you uninterrupted sleep. The middle shifts had to work their rest around their watch. Once the cattle were accustomed to the trail—and it could take one night or a dozen—the dark hours would be broken into four two-hour, two-man stints.

By dusk the four of us on the first shift were circling the herd, me and Sainty riding clockwise and Michaels and Errun moving counter-clockwise. While that procedure left gaps in the coverage from time to time, it meant that the riders were less likely to fall asleep in the saddle because they passed and spoke to each other periodically.

With most of the cattle resting after an exhausting day, a few remained upright, bellowing their disgust. The loudest of these was Eye Patch, who bawled, dipped his head and hooked another animal with his horns. The victim blubbered and instantly several animals jumped to their feet and milled around.

"Easy," cried Sainty, who hummed a song as loud as he could to calm the steers.

Michaels, Errun and I trotted over to help keep the cattle from running, and we finally got them to lie down again. When most of the animals had bedded, Michaels and Errun cut Eye Patch from the herd. They drove him a hundred yards away where both roped him. They dragged him a mile off and tied him between two trees before returning to Sainty and me. Without Eye Patch nearby, the steers calmed, and the rest of our shift passed peacefully. The foreman returned to camp for our replacements and soon, Banty, Mark, Parsons and Beeline took over.

Back at the wagon, I removed my boots and collapsed on my bedroll. I had survived my first day as a trail cowboy. I fell asleep dreaming of Ruth.

Chapter 21

Charlie Bitters walked around the camp, kicking everyone's feet and letting them know it was time to rise. I stretched and yawned, wishing for more sack rest, but this was life on the trail, something I had to adapt to. After tending my business, I fixed my bedroll and tossed it in the back of the wagon, then grabbed my gear and headed to the remuda. José Muñoz met me there, twirling a loop in his lariat and tossing the rope among the forty horses milling about. He snagged my bay. Generally, the hands had to catch their own mounts, but the wrangler knew I lacked roping experience and helped me so I wouldn't delay the start of the day's drive.

"Bonito," I offered.

"Vómito," he replied, snickering. "Don't repeat that again when my mouth is full, or I'll rope and hog-tie you before telling Bitters what you actually said."

"The cook and I get along fine," I replied as I slid my bridle over Relee's head.

"Not if I offer an accurate translation!" Muñoz laughed, leaving me to saddle up while he watched others catch their morning mounts.

By the time I got back to wagon, Mark, Michaels and Banty were chomping on dried apricots and cold biscuits from the night before. We took a jolt of coffee to help us regain our senses. Trent Parsons was still rolling up his bedroll when I swallowed my first sip of the black water. We learned that Reb, our heaviest sleeper, remained the hardest hand to wake up. He wasn't lazy or a slacker, he just rested soundly, perhaps from sleeping so many nights on battlefields during the war or maybe from reading his Bible nightly so he toted less on his conscience than most of us. Even so, once Parsons got up, he packed his bedding hurriedly and trotted to the remuda. Despite being the last to get up, he was never tardy for the start of work. Reb caught his mount and saddled it quickly, returning to camp with Errun and Beeline. As we awaited instructions, the smokers rolled cigarettes and the rest of us consumed our coffee. Sainty, arrived astride his horse, issued orders for the day while the men on the final watch came in to eat and change horses. Once O'Henry, Dire and Muscher finished, we started the cattle on another long day, twenty or more miles.

Sainty said, "Lomax, I want you to go with the wagon to Eye Patch so Bitters can take care of him. I need you to return the lariats to Martin and Tom." Turning to the cook and pointing to the northeast, he said, "Charlie, you'll find him tied to a tree in that direction."

"We'll have plenty to eat tonight," Bitters said as he divided up the remaining biscuits for the three shirkers on last watch. He grinned at me. "That Yankee and his pals are not getting fruit this morning." With that, he tied the bag of apricots and tossed it in the back of the wagon as the shirkers returned.

"Your biscuits are on the tailgate," Bitters told each as he arrived, paying no more attention to them as he packed. I noticed the holster nailed by the driver's seat was empty, so I knew the cook would deflate any criticism with a well-planned shot, in spite of his promise otherwise to Sainty. Muscher, though, was as quiet as a puppy sleeping in sunshine. The shirkers left their plates by the dish pan and stepped far enough away that Bitters couldn't hear their talk while they fixed their smokes. Once they lit them and took a couple drags, they started for their horses, getting ready to join others.

The cook placed his hands on his hips and shook his head. "Generals, if you want bedding tonight, you better roll up your blankets and toss them in the wagon. I don't care if you do draw last watch, it's still your job to handle your bedrolls."

The trio grumbled, but followed his instructions and tossed their gear in the back of the wagon. They mounted and rode away, glad to be out of range of Bitters' pistol and dreaming of the day they'd be out of range of his cooking. Once the three departed, I saw Bitters pull the pistol from his pants pocket and return it home.

Over the next half hour, I helped him finish loading as Muñoz and Ramírez started the remuda north. Then I hitched up the mules. Bitters climbed aboard and guided the wagon in the direction Sainty had pointed. In a few minutes we saw Eye Patch lying on his belly beside a firm oak tree. That animal's neck was bloody where he had fought against the rawhide lariats tied between two trees, but he had only tired himself out so much that he barely stirred when we stopped beside him. Bitters set the brake, pulled his pistol from the holster and jumped from his seat, landing nimbly on his feet. He walked around the wagon, aimed the revolver between the steer's eyes, cocked the hammer and pulled the trigger. BOOM! exploded the gun.

I untied the ropes from the two trees as Bitters lifted them over the animal's horns and coiled them. He handed me both. "Take these to the generals riding point." I trotted away, the lassos in my hand as if I knew how to use them. The cattle had started their morning trek so it took me a spell to deliver my cargo.

I found Michaels first. "Thanks, Lomax. I felt naked without it," Martin said.

"And I felt like a cowhand with it."

He shook his head and laughed. "Whatever your talents are, they damn sure aren't cowboying. Maybe it's speaking Spanish."

"What?"

"Bonito or was it vómito. I always get those words mixed up. I pray I don't confuse them in front of the cook. If I do, I'm blaming you."

"You wouldn't do that to a fine fellow like me, would you?"

He laughed. "Not unless I had to. Out of my way

because I've work to do." He rode off.

I spotted Sainty in front of the herd and galloped to him, asking if he could deliver Errun's lariat so I could return to Bitters. He nodded and instructed me to scout ahead after helping the cook. When I reached the cook, he had skinned Eye Patch's side and chopped a hind quarter off with the ax. He was working on meat easy to cut under the ribs, tossing chunks on a tarp he had thrown on the ground beside the carcass. When he completed that, he took a long butcher knife and slashed into the innards, pulling out various organs.

"Bring me that pot," he said, pointing to a blackened utensil sitting by the cow's head. I dismounted and walked over, grabbing the handle and grimacing as I saw a mess of brains in the bottom. I looked at Eye Patch's head, and Bitters had chopped his skull open to extract the gray mush. Taking the pot from me, the cook dropped the liver inside, then cut out the heart, kidneys and sweetbreads. "We'll have son-of-a-bitch stew tonight, general. You'll like it."

After seeing what was going into the concoction, I wasn't sure I could stomach it. "I bet Muscher will enjoy it"

Lifting his bloody knife at me, Bitters grinned. "He won't trouble me again, unless he wants to ride sidesaddle the rest of his living days."

I turned away as the cook put things in the container that were turning my stomach. Finally, Bitters quit excavating the remains of Eye Patch and stood up, wiping the knife on his britches before heading to the wagon and drawing a pail of liquid from the water barrel to wash himself and his blade. As he did, I found the lid to the pot and dropped it in place so I wouldn't have to look at supper. I put the container aside for Bitters to load, then pointed to the tarp. "What's to be done with the meat?"

"Fold the tarp over it. We'll load it and be on our way, general."

"Sainty wants me to take up the scouting and find places to lunch and supper."

"That's fine, general, but I'll need extra time tonight to cook the stew."

I started folding the tarp over the meat. "I know you don't remember folks' names, but why did you start calling them general instead of something else?"

"Habit, I suppose. I didn't care for John Bell Hood, an officer that was too proud of his position and rank, neither of which he deserved. I did it just to tweak his nose and let him know he wasn't as smart as he thought. It seemed more honorable than spitting in his food. After that, it became habit." Bitters dropped the pot on the floorboard under his seat, then came over to help me throw the fresh beef in the back of the wagon. As he took his place atop the rig and picked up his reins, he said, "I'll see you down the trail."

I mounted Relee and put him into a lope, taking my position as guide, always looking for potential hazards. Coming upon a large prairie dog colony mid-morning, I changed the course of the herd to bypass the rodents, but that was the only event of note that day until the son-of-a-bitch stew that evening. That was generally the way trail-driving developed, long, tiring days of dust, noise and monotony broken only by dangerous or comic events that relieved the boredom. In later years I heard old cowhands say that a man who worked cattle for twenty-four hours would desire to do it for the rest of his life, but I never found that much romance in cow-boying, and I had an easy job compared to those doing the real work, especially those riding drag.

For lunch that second day on the trail, Bitters handed out strips of jerky and more dried apricots, only boiling a pot of coffee for fellows to drink since he needed to get well ahead of us in time to cook the stew for supper. It became a habit for everyone to say "bonito" at some point in the meal, even when we ate dried beef and fruit, which were hard to screw up. Every "bonito" left our cook smiling that his food was loved, and the rest gagging that little had changed with his fare.

By evening I had found a stopping place with good grass and a shallow stream with adequate water for men and animals. The first thing Bitters did was dig a pit and start a fire so he could boil his stew. As the fire burned down to gray, glowing embers, he got out his butcher knife and began to cut the organ meats into small pieces. He added water, flour and pepper, then hung the pot over the embers to cook. While it simmered, he worked on more biscuits. In a while, Muñoz and Ramírez rode up with the remuda to let them graze. When Muñoz discovered fallen tree branches along the creek, he tied his rope around the limbs and dragged them to the wagon.

I left them and rode out to find the herd. About a half a mile ahead of the lead animals, I met Sainty.

"Glad to see you haven't unsaddled," he said.

"Don't take me long to learn a lesson."

"The herd's settling into a routine. If they rest well tonight, we'll drop the double guard and take our chances. I'm hoping things are better without Eye Patch."

"He's our supper," I announced. "Son-of-a-bitch stew as Bitters calls it. It's everything Eye Patch had, save for his hide, tail and horn!"

"Bonito," Sainty said. "Or was it vómito?"

I shook my head. "One of you is going to get me killed, if you keep that up."

"How's our camp tonight?"

"Plentiful grass and good water."

"How far ahead?"

"A couple miles."

"I figure that'll put us at nineteen for the day. Not as much as yesterday, but a good day at the start of the drive. Another long day or two and we'll slow to a dozen or so miles daily."

"By my thinking we are two days out of Austin," I announced. " We'll cross the Colorado there. That'll be our first major water crossing. It won't be the worst."

"We'll bed down on this side of the river and cross early the next morning. I'll send Bitters into town to buy any supplies he thinks we'll need between there and Waco."

Sainty and I waited for the head of the herd to reach

us. The brindle Corkscrew led the way with Michaels and Errun riding point on the perimeter. The foreman nodded. "They're getting trail broke."

"Men or cattle?"

Sainty laughed. "Both. We did okay on drovers. They're good until you get to those riding drag. Irish and York are trouble, Dire to a lesser extent, though he clings to them."

"Should we give them the Eye Patch treatment?" I offered.

Chuckling, Sainty shook his head. "No, we'll need them to reach Abilene. Let's help get the herd settled so we can eat." He trotted his mount over to Errun while I rode to Michaels.

"It's time to bed them," I announced.

Michaels nodded. "Bonito," he said, grinning and laughing.

Once again, I could only shake my head. "By the way, I gave your drawing to Ruth. She loved it. Said it looked just like me."

"I'm glad she approved. She's a pretty girl," he said.

His comment got me thinking. "Do you think you could draw a picture of her from memory? It'd be nice to have."

"Can't guarantee it'll be a good image, but I'll try," Michaels answered.

"I'd appreciate it."

"Give me a couple nights," he replied.

Sketch rode back toward the swing riders and helped them spread the herd out as the cattle approached fodder and water.

Deciding it best to get out of way, I returned to the food wagon, hobbled my horse and pulled the ax from the wagon bed. I headed over to the tree branches that Muñoz had dragged up earlier in the afternoon and began chopping firewood, uncertain if I wanted to be the first to sample the son-of-a-bitch stew.

As the cattle settled in, Sainty, Muñoz and Ramírez came for supper. I watched as they got up and returned to their horses to spell the point riders. None of them

staggered to their mounts so I decided supper was tolerable—or a slow-acting poison! I finished the wood,
leaving a supply by Bitters' fire pit and putting the remainder in the tarp belly under the wagon bed for later.
When Martin Michaels and Tom Errun came over, I
decided to join them. Bitters served us a tin of stew and
a biscuit. We fetched a spoon each from a can on the
tailgate. I stalled, pouring me a cup of coffee, until Michaels and Errun had taken their first bite. When they
didn't go blind or start howling at the moon, I took a
nibble. It was better than I expected, but far from home
cooking.

"Bonito," Michaels said, grinning at me.

"Bonito," echoed Errun.

"Si," I answered.

Bitters beamed as he continued his chores.

Like the night before, we ate in shifts until the herd
bedded. The only noise other than the bellowing of
the cattle was the call of bonito as those with any sense
consumed the stew.

Supper became one of the few times the hands had
occasion to relax, that and bedtime, which varied depending upon guard shifts. To break the boredom when
they had a few moments in the evening, the cowhands
amused themselves with different diversions. Martin
Michaels, or "Sketch," spent his time drawing in his
notepad, while Tom Errun, who we nicknamed "English," pointed out the shortcomings of English as we
Americans used the language. What he called a "waist-
coat" was a vest to us. Our suspenders were known to
him as "braces." Errun left us scratching our heads at
his definitions of our words. Jurdon Mark, or "China,"
played marbles, taking on any opponent, but it was little
fun when he won all the time. Trent Parsons, who we
called "Reb," read his Bible and griped about the pain
from the Yankee bullets still in his chest. Even though
he had been a slave, Silas Banty told funny stories of
growing up in bondage, like the time he tried to eat the
reddest apple he'd ever seen. Just one problem, it was
a wax apple. José Muñoz always wore a smile, except

around Irish, and laughed a lot. Toad Beeline never said much. Pedro Ramírez didn't know enough English to talk, and Harry Dire practiced rope tricks in camp when he wasn't using his lariat on cattle. Bartholomew Henry O'Henry and Chuck Muscher, moaned over everything except Bitters' cooking, at least within the cook's hearing range. Sainty tolerated the distractions as he had none of his own, save focusing on getting his herd to Abilene with minimal losses of cattle—or men.

Except for the son-of-a-bitch stew, the night passed without incident, the steers resting peacefully after two days and more than forty miles on the trail. I rode an uneventful watch with Sainty, Sketch and English, then retired to my bedroll. After checking with the hands at breakfast the next morning, Sainty said the herd was settling into the routine, and we'd start regular shifts that evening. "Bonito," cried the fellows as they rolled up their bedrolls and grabbed a quick cup of coffee and a couple biscuits. The smokers fixed and lit cigarettes before everybody saddled their first mounts for another day.

By the third day, the steers understood the routine and rose with less complaint than before. Corkscrew took his position in the lead and headed north on his own, the other cattle tramping behind the brindle. Sainty smiled. "It's what we want. The animals are adjusting to the routine. That's our first challenge."

"What's the next?"

"Getting them across the Colorado. I'll need you to scout a manageable crossing. Come morning I'll want you to ride Austin and find a good spot to swim the river."

"Sure thing, boss."

By Sainty's estimate, we made sixteen additional miles, making camp a six-hour ride from Austin.

After supper and before watch, Martin Michaels pulled out his sketch pad and began to draw. When I edged his direction, he closed the notepad and eyed me like a hen studied an egg-sucking dog. After I moved away, he opened the pad again and resumed his pencil work, but issued me a warning. "No peeking until I'm done or I'll tell Bitters how bonito rhymes with vómito!"

"Hey," offered Jurdon Mark, "how about a game of marbles?"

I hesitated. "It's a kid's game."

Mark shook his head and made marbles sound as adult a game as chess. "There's a lot of arithmetic in marbles, like playing the angles in billiards."

About the only arithmetic I could figure in marbles was counting up totals after the game.

Mark scratched a circle in the ground and dumped his bag in the middle. "We play for fun, Arky, not for keeps. There's fifty-one marbles there. Pick your shooter."

I grabbed one of the heftier glass pieces and watched Mark take a smaller one as he told me to shoot first. Cradling my shooter in the crook of my forefinger, I went knuckles down and I flipped it toward the clump of marbles, scattering them, but failing to knock one from the circle.

"Learn by watching," Mark said as he leaned over, put his fist on the ground and shot the glass orb. His shooter struck four marbles, knocking two out of the earthen ring. I suspect he could've banged all forty-nine out of the circle without a miss, but he quit trying and let me shoot after his seventeenth marble. I knocked out three, before missing. Mark claimed seven more before a half-hearted miss. When we finished, I counted up my marbles to save him time counting his. "Eleven," I announced, as I realized the arithmetic in marbles was subtracting mine from his winning total.

"Thirty-eight," Mark announced. "Care to play again?"

I agreed, thinking I might do better if he shot before me. "Only if you go first."

Mark herded the marbles circle's center.

Taking aim, Mark knocked two from the circle on his first shot, then ran the table, claiming every marble without me getting a shot.

"You're too good for me, China."

Mark shook his head. "You're setting me up to swindle me out of my marbles on another day. I know your type, Arky. Since we can't gamble on the trail, you're waiting until Abilene to claim all my marbles."

China's smooth talking made me feel like the victor, but I vowed never to play him in any game where my money was on the line. As we finished our second contest, Michaels and Errun headed out for the first shift, then O'Henry, Muscher and Dire, came to supper, their faces sweat-stained and gritty, their flesh powdered with the grime of the trail. They strode to the creek to wash off the filth.

As they returned, Bitters greeted them with the warmth of a corpse, "Evening, generals, son-of-a-bitch stew for supper."

"Bonito," Muscher said, glancing at me with a snarl.

Bitters fill three dishes with the potage, but left them on the tailgate with empty coffee cups for them to fill. Next he lifted the lid on the Dutch oven he'd cooked biscuits in. He cursed and shook his head as he bent over. Using his apron as a hot pad, he pulled out six biscuits charred so black we called them "O'Henrys." Standing back up, he returned the lid to the pot and marched over to the tailgate, dropping two biscuits each on the tins.

As the three shirkers approached the wagon for their supper, they grimaced at the sight of the blackened biscuits.

Bitters smiled. "I hope you enjoy your biscuits well done."

"Bonito," said Irish sullenly.

"Same," answered Muscher.

Dire just nodded.

When the three on drag finished their meal, including the charcoaled biscuits, they took their plates to the wash pan and left them without a derogatory comment. After that Dire and Muscher, rolled smokes, but O'Henry held back.

"I'm out of tobacco," Irish said. "Can anybody loans me some?"

Reb, who rested on his bedding reading his Bible,

looked up. "Long as you repay me."

"You can trusts me," answered O'Henry as he walked over. As Reb opened his saddlebags, Irish stared at the contents. "Damn, you gots a dozen tobacco pouches in there."

"Thirteen to be exact," Parsons announced. "It's a long way to Abilene. I'll give you a pouch if you'll buy me a replacement the next chance you get."

Irish nodded. "Deal!"

Parsons pitched him a bag, as O'Henry, his mouth agape, stared lecherously at his stock.

The pouch hit O'Henry's chest, then slid to the ground as Parsons latched up his saddlebag and resumed reading his Bible.

Tobacco, it turned out, became a big problem in the coming days.

Chapter 22

Come morning, Trent Parsons was as hard to wake as a fossil, but he finally broke out of his slumber, stretched and got up, quickly fixing his bedroll and tossing it in the back of the wagon. He walked over to his saddle and bent to pick up his bridle, pausing a moment as he studied his saddlebags. The flap on the tobacco side was unhooked. Reb looked at it, scratched his head, and started to tie the leather. He hesitated.

I approached. "What's the matter, Reb?"

Parsons ignored me as he flung back the flap and stuck his hand inside, pulling out his tobacco pouches. "I'm certain I secured this last night." He counted the patches, "Two, four, six, eight, ten, eleven," he said. "I'm missing one."

"You loaned O'Henry a pouch, remember?"

He nodded. "I had thirteen, I swear. After loaning him one, I should have twelve." He counted the pouches again. "There's only eleven."

"Lomax and Parsons," cried Sainty, riding up on his gelding, "quit lollygagging. We've got cattle to move."

"Yes, sir," I answered.

Reb nodded, yanking the strap and tying his saddle-bag, then picking up his lariat and bridle and jogging to the remuda.

I followed, listening to Reb mumble to himself.

"Something ain't right. Things don't square up."

Muñoz saw me approaching and roped Relee from

the milling horses. I thanked him, slipped the bridle over my bay and led him back to camp to saddle up. As I put the gear on my mount, Parsons returned, angrily shaking his head. "Somebody stole a pouch."

"Are you sure?" I asked.

Reb glared at me. "I don't make mistakes on something as important as tobacco."

His voice rang as taut as a lynch rope in use, and I dropped the subject. I ate the plate of bacon and biscuits Bitters offered me, but Parsons shoved his away, gulping down a cup of coffee, mounting his horse and trotting off.

"What's the matter with him?" the cook asked.

"He thinks somebody stole tobacco from his saddle-bag."

"It's the generals riding drag. I encountered their type in the army. Their kind lost our war for independence."

"I thought it was your cooking that freed the slaves," I joked.

"I'd've cooked better if I'd known some were as embittered as the one on drag."

We saw Sainty staring at us, tapping his fingers on his saddle horn, so we stopped talking.

While Bitters finished breaking camp, I hitched his mules for him, then climbed atop Relee and rode out to the foreman to discuss plans. The trail boss had slowed the pace to reach the Colorado the next afternoon. We would bed down on the river's south bank, letting the steers graze and water, then cross the river the following morning. Corkscrew proved himself a fine lead steer, maintaining a steady pace as set by the point men, making travel easier for us all.

For that night I found an expansive meadow where the cattle could eat. Though it lacked convenient water, the animals could manage a thirsty night as we would hit the Colorado River the next afternoon with time to sate their thirsts.

I got an early start the next day and made it to the banks of the Colorado before noon, plenty of time to locate a solid water crossing. Though I worried most over getting Bitters' wagon across, I found a pontoon bridge that traversed the water onto Brazos Street, which led to downtown and the stores where he could buy whatever supplies he needed. Then I worked my way east along the water course but encountered banks too steep for the cattle to manage. Retracing my steps, I passed the pontoon bridge and moved west, finding a crossing where Shoal Creek flowed into the river from the north. A wide flood plain provided a place to stage the animals before herding them up through a broad embankment cut that funneled onto West Street, the westernmost thoroughfare in Austin. Though the street was sparsely built, we would have to pass a dozen residences and stores before we reached open territory. Satisfied we could do it without causing too much damage to the houses, I turned back and found a pasture to spend the night near the crossing. I rode south toward the pinking sky that told me the herd was approaching. I met Sainty and directed the caravan to our evening home.

We set up camp as the animals grazed. The afternoon was cloudless and hot, but everyone enjoyed the slower pace as Sainty let the cattle graze unattended for an hour or two as we ate together. He informed the hands that Charlie would go into town for supplies and to provide him a list of things they needed and the money to pay for it. Most of them were too broke to buy anything, but I still had fifty Joseph McCoy dollars. I quietly offered those I trusted a loan, if they needed anything. Trent Parsons wanted six more sacks of tobacco, but he had the money to pay. Jurdon Mark asked for a bag of rock candy to get the taste of trail dust out of his mouth. Errun declined a loan, as did Silas Banty, saying he didn't care to be indebted to any man now that he was free. Muñoz and Ramírez said they were fine. Martin Michaels requested no purchases, but I decided to have Bitters secure him another sketchbook or a bundle of stationery plus added pencils to use for his drawings. For those that declined a loan, I opted to buy each rock candy. As for O'Henry, Muscher, Dire and

Beeline, they were on their own.

We ate a tasty dinner of canned stew and when everyone said "bonito," I believed they truly meant it this time since Bitters merely opened the tins and heated our meal. Before Michaels and Errun took first watch, Sketch said, "I have something for you, Arky." He tore a page from his pad and offered it to me.

I jumped up and raced to the wagon where Bitters was washing dishes by lantern light. Catching my breath, I studied the drawing, a perfect likeness of Ruth from the waist up. "I can't believe you did that from memory."

"A pretty face lingers in your mind," he replied.

By that time, everyone wanted to see and walked over to inspect.

"You captured her fine tora-loorals," English said.

"What the hell are tora-loorals?" China asked.

Errun looked at Mark as if he were so stupid he couldn't dot an "i" if his brain was all ink. "You know, bosom, breastworks."

Tom should've offended me, talking about my girl that way, but English's wide-eyed disbelief that we had no idea of the slang word's meaning disarmed me.

"Tora-loorals?" Michaels asked, scratching his head.

"Yes," Errun answered, stomping his boot. "Don't you Americans know anything?"

"Hey, Sketch," cried Muscher. "How about drawing me a girl? I don't care what her face looks like as long as she has big tora-loorals."

Coming from York, the comment hacked me, and I glared at him as I yanked the sketch away from everyone's sight. It angered Bitters as well because he marched over to the wagon, yanked his pistol from its holster and strode over to Muscher, who was still laughing at his own joke. Yank's hilarity died when he felt the cold barrel of Bitters' pistol sticking in his right ear.

"Don't be insulting Miss Ruth, general," Bitters ordered, "or you won't have brains enough to suckle on paper tora-loorals, much less real ones."

"Bonito," Muscher answered meekly.

"Did you say bonito or vómito?" Bitters snarled.

I gulped. The cook had heard my original insult after all, leaving me wondering why he hadn't given me the Muscher treatment.

"Charlie," cried Sainty. "Put that gun away and attend your chores. And Chuck, you keep your mouth shut. Your words have a way of grating on folks."

"You're all mad you lost the war," he said, looking down his nose at the foreman.

"See what I mean, Chuck. I figure the reason you're in Texas is that your allies couldn't stand you up north. Say another word, York, and I'll have Charlie clean your ears out with his pistol lead. Surely, your head's not so hard that it'll stop a bullet."

Muscher sulked away with Beeline, Dire and O'Henry to their bedrolls. They smoked and complained of the unfairness of trail life, Charlie's cooking, my easy job and their persecution by the boss.

As Martin Michaels and Tom Errun walked over to their horses to start the first watch, I ran over to them, waving the paper at Sketch. "Thanks, Martin. The drawing's perfect."

He grinned. "It created a stir."

I pointed at Errun. "No, it was Tom's tora-loorals that caused the row!"

"You Texans don't understand proper English."

I corrected the first half of his statement. "I'm from Arkansas."

He shook his head. "At least I'd heard of Texas."

Both point men laughed as they headed out for their two-hour shift. I folded the sheet and put it in my shirt pocket, then returned to camp, figuring we'd settle down peacefully after the earlier confrontation, but I was wrong.

As I sat down on my bedroll, O'Henry approached Parsons, who was lying on the ground reading his Bible by the light of a candle he had stuck in the soil.

"Reb," O'Henry announced, "I wants to repay you." Irish extracted what looked like a full bag of tobacco from his pants pocket and offered it to Parsons.

Placing his Bible on his bedding, Reb sat up, measuring O'Henry. "You said you had no tobacco, Irish."

O'Henry shrugged. "I dids, but I founds a bag—"

"Where? In somebody's saddlebag?"

Irish paused. "Yeah, in my saddlebag. Now I owes you nothing." He tossed the pouch at Parson's feet and turned around.

"I better not catch you in my things again, Irish—"

"Don't you accuses me of getting in your saddlebags."

"—or I'll gut you like a hog."

Now I had to admit it was a clever if sneaky thing to do, stealing a pouch of tobacco and repaying your loan with the stolen goods. O'Henry possessed the larcenous qualities sought in a good Democrat."

"You're a thief, O'Henry, a lying thief."

Irish spun around, his hand dropping to the butt of his revolver.

Parsons grabbed for his gun belt beside his bedding and yanked his pistol free.

Sainty jumped between the two. "Stop it, boys," he commanded, as he pulled his own revolver. "Put your guns away or I'll plug you."

Both antagonists warily complied.

Sainty was angrier than a buzzard circling a motionless mule only to discover the jack was just sleeping. "Boys, we haven't gone a hundred miles out of over seven hundred and everybody's at each other's throat. I'm telling you to stop to it, if you intend to draw my wages."

"How about a game of marbles?" Jurdon Mark suggested. "Settle this with your thumbs rather than your trigger fingers." His comments drew snickers from everyone, even Sainty.

The trail boss studied the drover. "Those that are wearing gun belts, take them off and leave them in the floorboard under the wagon seat."

I groaned. We might need a gun as we were on the outskirts of Austin where more mischief was accomplished in the statehouse by elected bandits than by all the self-appointed outlaws in the rest of the state, and Texas covered a lot territory. "What if we need to shoot a rattlesnake—or a Republican?" I asked, drawing a few snickers.

"I'll be first," Mark said, unbuckling his belt and starting toward the wagon.

"Take mine," said Parsons, handing his gun and scabbard to Mark.

With Parsons defenseless, I saw O'Henry slide his fingers to his pistol. Sainty noticed, too, and swung his revolver at Irish, who realized it as well, lifting his hand to his mouth and coughing into his fist. "You next, Bart," Sainty instructed, and Irish stepped to the wagon.

Muscher strode by the trail boss, unbuckling his gun. "What about Upchuck's pistol?"

Bitters glared at York as he marched past.

"Charlie's gun stays where it is, where everyone can see it. If it's not in the holster, you'll know to be on your best behavior. And I don't want to hear the word 'upchuck' again!"

"What about upward or upcoming or upend or upset or uplifting?" Mark grinned. "Are those words permissible?"

Sainty laughed as did everybody but the shirkers. "You understand what I mean, China."

Mark nodded. "A little levity cleanses the soul. I've never known a man to die laughing or playing marbles. Anyone up for a game?"

The tension broke—for the night at least—as everyone disarmed and retreated to their beds. Parsons resumed reading his Bible, the three shirkers griped about everything and Mark laid on his back looking at the stars while the rest of us crawled atop our bedrolls.

Sainty visited with Bitters, giving him money to restock foodstuffs and other gear. Next the foreman moved among his hands, asking if they needed anything from the store. When several complained they were broke, Sainty offered to take it out of their pay at the end of the drive, but they declined. The foreman gave his list to Bitters, as did I plus the money to cover my purchases.

"Generals," Bitters said. "I'm leaving early for Austin in the morning. For breakfast and lunch, I'll leave jerky and dried apricots, then fix you a fine meal for supper."

Still gazing at the stars, Mark answered, "Thank you, Upstanding," drawing a chuckle from everybody but the shirkers.

I drifted off to sleep and awoke the next morning as Bitters made his way through camp, kicking everyone's feet, reminding them to rise. As I pushed myself up, I told the cook I'd take care of Reb. I slid on my boots and grabbed him by the shoulder, shaking him vigorously. Parsons gradually rejoined the world. "It's crossing day," I said.

Reb batted his eyes, then turned over and reached for his saddlebags, unfastening the tie and lifting the flaps over the pouch where he kept his spare tobacco. He counted twelve sacks. "That son of a bitch still owes me a pouch. I loan him a sack, and he repays me with one he's stolen from me. You try to do the decent thing to help a fellow, and he spits on you."

"Forget it, Reb. I'll buy you a replacement pouch of tobacco. You know to watch him from now on."

"I can't let you do that, Arky."

"It's worth it, Reb, to put this behind us. He's mean enough to shoot you in the back. I'd rather buy you a pouch than see him bushwhack you."

Parsons shrugged, pushed himself up from his bedding, then grimaced. He bent and grasped his chest. "Ohhhh," he moaned.

"You, okay, Reb?"

He nodded and exhaled slowly. "It's that Yankee lead in me. It pains me sometimes, like the shrapnel is shifting. I can't explain it. Doctors couldn't either. It just up and surprises me some days." His breath came labored as he rolled his bedding. When he caught good air, he grabbed his bridle and lariat, then jogged to the remuda, roped his mount and returned to camp to saddle his horse. He took a couple pieces of jerky and three dried apricots from the wagon tailgate and ate them as he rigged his mount for the day. Even though he had arisen last, he rode out of camp first. I helped Bitters pack and hitch his team. Seeing I was running behind, Muñoz caught my mount and led him over, even saddling him as I finished harnessing the mules.

"Gracias," I said.

"Bonito," he replied.

The drag riders came in and took care of their bedding, then grabbed jerky and fruit and returned to the herd, which was rising and forming up to cross the Colorado. When the cook and I finished packing, Bitters hopped in the driver's seat and started north for Austin. I rode with him to a rise where I could point him to the pontoon bridge. He shook his head. "Never cared for them floating bridges," he said. "My feet got wet many times crossing them during the war."

"It beats swimming the river," I answered.

"Indeed, general, as I can't swim."

"You're likely not alone among this bunch. We'll see you on the other side of town."

"Bonito," Bitters smiled. "Or was it, vómito? I'm not that deaf." He laughed.

"Thanks, Upright," I offered, as he grinned and rode away.

After seeing the cook off, I caught up with Sainty. "Rough time last night. What started it with Reb and Irish?"

"Parsons thinks O'Henry stole a pouch of tobacco from his saddlebags."

"Didn't Reb loan him tobacco?"

"Yeah, but he thinks Irish slipped in during the night, filched a bag and repaid him that evening with the stolen pouch."

"Wouldn't surprise me none about Irish. He's got a chip on his shoulder the size of a granite boulder."

"Yeah, and the scars to go along with it. I'd like to know if the stripes down his back turned him rancid or his bitterness earned him those lashes to begin with."

"Can't say, Lomax, but we must watch him the rest of the way."

"Muscher and Dire, too," I added.

He nodded. "It's a long damn way to Abilene. But first, we've got to cross the Colorado. It's deep enough the cattle will have to swim. A horse might not have to, but the steers will."

"You expecting problems?"

Sainty shrugged. "Corkscrew's proving himself a good leader. I think after he gets his fill of water, he'll lead them across. I talked with Sketch and English. They indicate we'll be okay."

And, we were. It took three-plus hours to get the cattle over, but the crossing proceeded as smoothly as a drover could hope and without any losses. As it developed, our real problem was getting Bartholomew Henry O'Henry across the Colorado. When the last of the steers cleared the river and took to grazing on the flood plain skirting the water, O'Henry sat on his horse on the opposite bank, shaking his head.

"What's the matter?" Sainty yelled.

"I can't swims."

"You don't have to, your horse will."

"Don't trusts no horse."

"Hell, let's leave him."

Sainty shook his head. "Tempting as that is, we need all the men we've got."

"Why don't we send Reb over to help him across?"

"Damn, Lomax. You're stirring the pot."

"Call me Uppity."

Sainty spat and yelled at O'Henry to stay where he was while he ordered the others to drive the cattle up the draw and out of town as quickly as they could so as not to antagonize the fine citizens of Austin. As the others formed up the herd for the next leg of the journey, Sainty returned, and we swam our horses back across the river.

O'Henry sat on his mount shaking more than a drummer boy with hiccups. "I's afraid."

"You've got to cross if you want to get paid."

"I never learns to swims. If I falls off my horse, I drowns."

Even though I knew I shouldn't, I had to speak. "Before you try, Irish, you ought to confess your sins,

246

get right with God before you head to the other side, whether that side's on earth or in heaven. Admit to God if you've stolen anything over the last two days, Irish."

Sainty chided me. "Quit stirring the pot."

"I steals nothing unless I hungers or feels I'm owed something."

"Shut up, both of you," the trail boss said, instructing O'Henry on how to manage his horse in the river, telling him to dismount and loosen the cinches so the horse could breathe easier during the swim. Rather than use reins in the water, he should release them and splash the side of the horse's face to guide him. If the horse is a poor swimmer, he should slide off the back of the horse and hang onto the animal's tail as the reduced weight will help the animal float.

O'Henry mounted again. "I don't cares to grabs his tail. I needs to stay in the saddle. I'll crosses the bridge the wagon tooks and meets you later."

Sainty shook his head. "There's more rivers than bridges between here and Abilene."

"I fears I'll falls off. Can't swims."

"Hell," I said, "let's tie him in the saddle, if he's afraid of getting wet."

"That's about the dumbest idea I ever heard," Sainty said. "As scared as he is, his backside may pucker enough to secure him to his saddle."

"Tie me down," O'Henry cried

Sainty shrugged. "Okay, Lomax, have at it."

I jumped off Relee and untied O'Henry's lariat from his saddle. I tied one end around his left boot and stirrup, tossed the rope under the animal and affixed it around the right boot and stirrup. Next I took the lasso and loosely looped it over the horse's back several times to keep the animal from getting tangled in the line when he stepped from the water. I handed the loose end to Irish.

Even when he was secure, O'Henry balked. "I don't want to do it."

"You've got to, Irish," said Sainty.

Irish sat there, trembling like a rabbit in a coyote's

back pocket.

The trail boss assured him he would be okay, and we would be by his side. Sainty showed more patience than me.

I walked behind O'Henry's horse and slapped him on the rump. "Yeeehaaa," I screamed to give the mount extra incentive as he bolted into the Colorado River.

Chapter 23

"Aaarrrrrrggghhhh!" O'Henry screamed loud enough to be heard in Indian Territory.

"Damn, Lomax, why'd you do that?"

"You weren't getting anywhere with him."

Sainty slapped his horse and charged into the Colorado. I stayed out of the way to enjoy the fun.

As his horse hit the waves, Irish squealed like a girl, his mount plunging into the current. O'Henry flung his reins aside and grabbed the saddle horn as his mount fought the water and the terrified man astride him. At first the animal stayed on its feet, but either slipped on the bottom or stepped in a hole and sank, his head submerging as water reached O'Henry's chin. He threw his hands in the air as he straightened to keep his own nose above waves.

The foreman shouted for O'Henry to remain calm, a command as effective as telling a man with his hair afire to stay still. But Sainty, bless his heart, wanted to save O'Henry. I, however, opted to teach Irish to swim, even if it drowned him.

"Lordy, helps me," Irish cried, grabbing the saddle horn again when his mount's gasping head reappeared over the waves.

I told myself that besides tying him to his horse the next time we crossed a river, we might also gag him, as he was sure to stampede the herd if he put up another such ruckus.

"You'll make it," Sainty yelled. "It'll be okay."

Despite the flailing idiot atop him, his mount made it halfway across the watery expanse and found his footing, but O'Henry kept shrieking as if he were certain to drown. If I'd known Irish presented such a spectacle, I'd have sold tickets to the fine citizens of Austin for the show he was putting on.

Two-thirds of the way over the river, the horse climbed the ascending bottom, but the terrified O'Henry didn't notice, even when the water receded from his saddle horn to his stirrups to the horse's belly. He screamed for help and cried for deliverance, even as his horse stepped on the bank and shook moisture from his hide. The animal stopped and blew, likely too embarrassed to ride through Austin with an idiot on his back.

"You made it, O'Henry," Sainty shouted.

At that point Irish realized he had truly embarrassed himself. Sainty was so humiliated by O'Henry's cowardice he loped off for the herd rather than ride with O'Henry or wait on me. I tugged my hat snug over my head as that was where I kept Ruth's sketch when crossing the river. I swam Relee across the Colorado.

When I reached O'Henry, he was as mad as a jumping frog in a prickly patch. "You son of a bitch," he cried, "unties me and don't ever spooks my horse again."

Stopping and dismounting, I cinched up my saddle then climbed back aboard my bay and started up the cut. I smiled as I passed him.

"Unties me, dammit!"

"Not when you defamed my mother," I informed him. "I'll release you on the other side of town, but only if you mind your words. My momma would've washed my tongue out with soap, if I had used that kind of language."

"They solds my momma off before I could remembers her." He spat, shook his head and followed me up the draw that opened on West Street. The steers had reached the far end of town. In their wake people came out of their houses and business, shaking their heads at the droppings in the street and raising their fists at us. I smiled and tipped my hat, drawing their further wrath. One man, standing by a downed picket fence, picked up a cow patty and flung it my direction. I ducked and it flew over me, striking O'Henry on the shoulder. I had expected a better reception if not thanks for the fertilizer our herd had deposited on the streets of Austin.

Midway through town we passed to the west a castle-like structure with a stone sign identifying it as the Texas Military Institute. Fifty young cadets lined up outside the building, staring at us. I tipped my hat to them and found them more neighborly than the city folks as they flung neither cow dung nor shot bullets toward us.

As we reached the north side of Austin, the prairie widened and the herd drifted away from the fine folks and the crooked politicians of the Texas capital. When we finally rode out of sight of Austin, I offered to untie O'Henry.

"Hurries," he said.

"Quit your carping," I yelled as I jumped from the saddle and walked over to his mount. I untied the knot and then unwound the loops around the horse's torso, freeing Irish's right boot and stirrup before walking over and loosening the left leg and stirrup. As soon as his lariat fell free, O'Henry swatted the gelding's behind and bolted ahead.

That was a bad idea, I thought, because I hadn't cinched his rig. As he galloped away, his saddle tottered to the left, O'Henry tilting with it. He yanked on the bridle to stop the horse, but not in time to keep from sliding to the ground. Spooked by the loose saddle, O'Henry's mount bolted for the herd, leaving him afoot. It had been a rough day for Irish. Slowly, I coiled his lariat and remounted Relee, riding at a leisurely pace past my river-crossing pal.

"Hold up, Lomax," O'Henry cried.

"You didn't wait for me to cinch your saddle, so you're on your own, Irish."

He cursed me. "If I hads a gun, I'd shoots you."

"In the back, I suspect, like you thought about plugging Reb last night."

Leaving him to ponder his own stupidity, I rode on, accompanied by his curses. Not once this time, despite the colorful language, did he call me an S-O-B.

Halfway to the herd, I met Muscher riding out with O'Henry's gelding.

"Whoa!" I cried and York reined up. I handed him Irish's lariat. "He forgot this."

"What are you doing with it, Arky?"

"I planned to lasso his mount, but you caught him first. O'Henry neglected to tighten his saddle cinch after he crossed the river."

"That's your story. I'll see what Bart says." He slapped the coiled rope against his gelding's neck and the animal trotted off, leading O'Henry's horse, the saddle still ajar.

Reaching the dusty end of the cattle, I swung wide and rode around the animals, aiming to report to Sainty. I took time, though, to tell the heroic story of O'Henry crossing the Colorado to Silas Banty on flank, Jurdon Mark on swing and Martin Michaels on point. They enjoyed my account. Fortunately for Irish, he rode drag and remained at the caravan's rear until supper.

Beyond the point riders, I saw Sainty sitting on his horse, looking back at the Five-D herd. The smile on his face curdled as I approached. "You could've drowned O'Henry."

"You'd still be begging him to cross, if I hadn't inspired his mount to help."

"Maybe so, but you and he won't be chewing tobacco off the same plug anytime soon."

"It don't matter. He's got a big cow chip on his shoulder."

"I never heard it put that way."

"No, literally. He's got a fresh Five-D cow patty on his shirt. A fellow standing by a downed fence threw it at me. I ducked and it splattered Irish."

"Was it a picket fence?"

"Yeah."

"One of our steers hooked his horn in the pickets and knocked over a section. I paid the fellow five dollars."

"He was still mad when I passed."

"I can't afford to buy more fences between here and Abilene, Lomax. I need you to find future river crossings a mile or more from town to avoid damages."

"Next is the Brazos in Waco. I'll find us a crossing farther from civilization, if you can call Waco civilized."

Sainty laughed, then turned his horse northward and pointed that direction. "Why don't you ride ahead and locate our camp." The foreman glanced up at the sun. "Bitters should've had plenty of time by now to get out of town and start fixing supper."

"Bonito," I said.

"Vómito," he laughed.

I put Relee into a lope and rode five miles until I spotted a wisp of smoke from a distant campfire. Eventually, I spied the wagon and Bitters cooking supper. I heard him jabbering to himself well before he saw me. My approach startled him, and he jumped toward his pistol until he realized it was me.

"If I was a Comanche, I'd have your scalp by now, Charlie."

"My thinning hair'd make a poor catch. The wrangler has a fine head of hair to hang from the end of a lance, general. Any problems crossing the river?"

"Cattle and remuda made it fine. Had trouble with Irish. He can't swim and needed a little encouragement."

"I thought the foreman prohibited liquor."

Shaking my head, I told Bitters of how I assisted O'Henry across the Colorado.

The cook slapped his knee and doubled over laughing by the time I finished the tale, especially the part where Irish got plastered with a fresh cow patty.

From atop my horse, I surveyed the camp site and nodded my approval. "Good grass."

"No water, but I figured they'd had their fill crossing the Colorado, and we could wait a day before the cattle got desperate."

"Likely so," I responded. "I best get back to Sainty so we can drive the herd your direction. Everybody's eager for your supper. You promised something special."

"Chicken and dumplings. The foreman gave me enough money to buy three chickens from a butcher. We'll eat well. How do you say it in Spanish? Bonito or vómito?"

"You knew all along what I said, didn't you, Charlie?"

He nodded.

"How come you didn't put a bullet between my legs or a gun barrel in my ear?"

Bitters averted my gaze, then slowly exhaled like the last puff from a dying steam locomotive. He sighed, then looked up at me, his eyes moistening and not from the wood smoke. "I lost my only boy at Franklin. He was with the Texas Brigade under General Granbury and died with Hiram in a pointless charge ordered by John Bell Hood." He spat at the memory.

"I'm sorry, Charlie."

"You remind me of him. Vómito is something he would've said and found funny. Nothing malicious in his humor, just a kid wanting to have fun. John Bell Hood ended his laughter forever and much of mine."

"I'm sorry," I repeated.

"Weren't your doing, general. Please don't tell the others."

"I won't."

"You best find Sainty so the herd can find me because I won't go looking for them.

I left Bitters with his sorrows and retraced my route to the cattle, directing Sainty where to find Bitters and supper. "Chicken and dumplings," I informed him.

He smiled. "Ruth makes good chicken and dumplings."

Thinking of her, I pulled Ruth's sketch from my hat, looked at her smile and returned the drawing to my shirt pocket. I missed her. And her cooking! I wondered what she was fixing for supper, and if she was still wearing my blue calico apron only when she wasn't doing chores.

"Ride back to camp, Lomax, while I tell Sketch and English where to find dumplings."

Turning Relee about, I retraced my tracks to camp.

254

That evening Sainty let the herd graze on their own so all the drovers could eat together. As the cattle bedded down, one drover came late, greeted by everyone's smiling, dust-creased faces. O'Henry attempted to hide his own.

"Evening, Irish," said Jurdon Mark. "Is it true you swim like a duck?"

O'Henry grimaced.

"And squeal like a pig," Parsons added.

Irish spat at Reb. "That ain't funny."

"Neither's breaking the Eighth Commandment."

I couldn't remember the Ten Commandments by heart, though my mother had tried to instill them in me, but I suspected the eighth was do not steal. If the mandate was do not swim, Irish had obeyed God's law to the letter that very morning.

"Don't be preaching at me, Reb. I knows the Good Book for years. I reads it often."

Parsons walked over to his bedroll and picked up his Bible, shaking it at O'Henry. "After you eat, read from the scriptures."

"Yeah," China said, "read about Jesus walking on water to cross the Colorado."

"Come and get it," Bitters called, inviting everyone to grab a tin plate and step to the fire, where he stirred two pots.

Having eaten his food for days now, we didn't trample each other in the rush to secure a plate, though his dumplings smelled good. Perhaps it was a trap!

Parsons offered a prayer before Bitters ladled out a serving to Tom Errun, Silas Banty and me. The others stood and watched as we took our first bite. When none of us keeled over dead, the rest marched to the cook and received their rations. The chicken and dumplings melted in my mouth, so much tastier than I expected. I didn't know whether it was his cooking that had improved or my sympathy for him after learning of his son.

As dinner progressed, our cook drew genuine and rave compliments for his meal instead of the bogus "bonitos" that had showered him after most earlier meals. "Thank Sainty," Bitters said. "He gave me money to buy the chickens and extra time today to cook it. It's a challenge to cook three good meals a day when we've got to keep moving."

As we ate, Bitters retreated to the wagon and brought a gunnysack around, distributing all the purchases he had made for the hands while in Austin. He gave Trent Parsons his six tobacco pouches and most everything else to me. Everyone looked enviously at my pile as I distributed my goods. I pitched Jurdon Mark the rock candy he wanted. I surprised Martin Michaels with a bundle of stationery and pencils for his drawing.

Sketch cocked his head in surprise. "I don't have money to pay for it."

"It's a gift," I said, "for the fine pictures you drew of me and Ruth."

"I can use the paper."

Then I passed out the remaining bags of rock candy to Silas Banty, José Muñoz, Tom Errun and Pedro Ramírez, ignoring the glares of Dire, Muscher, O'Henry and Beeline, as they sullenly ate their supper. By the time we finished eating, darkness enveloped us, the only light coming from the campfire and the lantern Bitters had set on the tailgate while he cleaned dishes.

Parsons hadn't forgotten his debate with O'Henry and marched over to his bedroll to retrieve his Bible. "Before supper you said you could read, Irish. How about stepping over to the lantern and reading us a passage?"

O'Henry scowled. "I'll do that." He arose and grabbed the Bible then strode to Bitters. Turning to face us, he opened the book to the middle and announced the Twenty-third Psalms. He lifted the volume up to his face where I could just see his eyes over the top. He began.

The Lord is my shepherd, I shall not want.

He maketh me to lie down in green pastures; he leadeth me beside the still waters.

He restoreth my soul; he leadeth me in the paths of

righteousness for his name's sake.

Yea, though I walk through the valley of the shadow of death, I will fear no evil; for thou art with me; thy rod and thy staff they comfort me.

Thou prepares a table before me in the presence of mine enemies; thou anointest my head with oil; my cup runneth over.

Surely goodness and mercy shall follow me all the days of my life; and I will dwell in the house of the Lord forever. Amen.

I had to admit that O'Henry gave a perfect reading as I remembered the Bible verse. Then I realized he was holding the Good Book upside down. He wasn't reading, but reciting from memory.

Parsons nodded, "Well said, Irish." Reb winked at me.

When he did, I knew he, too, had noticed the wrong side up Bible.

"I bet you can't read the Lord's Prayer, even if I tell you where to find it," Parsons challenged.

O'Henry scowled. "I knows the Lord's Prayer."

"Matthew Chapter Six, Verses Nine through Thirteen," Parsons instructed.

Irish flipped pages in the Bible, then glared at Parsons, cleared his throat and spoke. "Now I lay me down to sleep—"

Muscher slapped his knee and hurrahed Parsons. "He found it, Reb."

"—I pray the Lord my soul to keep," O'Henry continued. "If I should die before I wake, I pray the Lord my soul to take." He shut the book. "I reads Bible verses for years."

Parsons shook his head, but didn't refute O'Henry's claim. He knew O'Henry was lying and illiterate, but didn't care to embarrass his enemy in front of others. "I've never heard the Lord's Prayer read as you did."

O'Henry returned the Bible to Parsons. "I knows my scripture readings."

Irish rejoined his buddies, who clapped him on the shoulder and congratulated him on his scriptural prowess.

"Next time, O'Henry," Parsons offered, "I'll have you read something from the Book of Consternations or the Book of Aggravations."

Those were new books to me.

"I proves my point tonight," O'Henry shot back. "No need to proves it again."

"Okay, men, enough preaching for the night," Sainty cried. "You've had a good meal, but now it's time to start night watch. Those that've got first shift, mount up and head out. The rest of you get some shuteye."

I stepped over to Parsons and slid onto my bedding.

"You noticed Irish holding the Bible upside down, didn't you?" I whispered.

Reb held his hand at his mouth, biting something between his fingers. He dropped his hand for a moment and whispered. "Irish can't read. He spoke from memory." Reb returned his fingers to his lips and gnawed on something.

I watched until my curiosity grabbed me. "What are you doing?"

Parsons remained silent as he bit on something I made out to be a bullet.

"Are you chomping on a bullet?" I whispered.

Reb nodded, then pulled his hand from his mouth. "My chest's been paining me. I'm trying to yank the lead slug out, give me something to bite on when the pain's excruciating."

"What are you gonna do with the powder?"

"Use it for medicine," he replied.

"You're more of a man than me, if you're taking gunpowder to ease the pain."

"The Bible eases my pain. The gunpowder exposes sinners."

Now Parsons was talking in riddles that confused me, like the Good Book he read nightly, as I had to admit I didn't understand it all, though I knew it'd make me a better person if I did.

I fell asleep that night uncertain what Reb was up to. Three nights later it became clearer as we were again preparing for bed.

"Somebody stole another pouch of my tobacco," Parsons whispered as he lit one of his candles by his bedding to read his Bible.

"Why didn't you say something?"

"It did no good last time. The thief denies it, but I'll find him."

"You think it's Irish?"

"Sure as I'm lying here." He paused. "You remember how God works in mysterious ways?"

I admitted I did.

"So does Trent Parsons. I'll peg the thief."

"You sleep too soundly to catch anyone stealing from your saddlebags. Some morning's I'm not sure a cannon could wake you."

"I can't deny that."

"And you think you'll catch him?"

"I guarantee it, Lomax."

Parsons returned to reading his Bible. When he finished, he rolled himself a smoke, lit the papers from the candle flame and enjoyed the tobacco after he blew out his candle. He lay there smoking until his cigarette was little more than a nub. He crushed the remnants of his smoke, then turned over and went to sleep.

Then next day we kept driving the cattle northward. I rode out front, marking the trail and watching for impediments that might slow our travel. After Austin we made ten or twelve miles a daily, giving the herd more time to graze and water since they were trail broke.

Come supper that night, we had bacon and beans, which had become our regular fare since Austin. After eating and sending out the first watch, we reclined on our bedding, Parsons reading his Bible. The shirkers complained about riding drag, about eating Bitters' food, which had worsened since the chicken and dumplings, and about life as a whole. The only thing they enjoyed was their tobacco.

After airing their complaints to each other, Dire, Beeline, Muscher and O'Henry swatted at their shirt pockets and pulled out their fixings, intent on enjoying final smokes before hitting bed. They passed around a match to light their cigarettes. When the match reached Irish, he touched it to the tip of his cigarette, which flared up and popped in a cloud of white smoke. O'Henry sat there dazed and confused by his exploding cigarette.

Parsons dropped his Bible, sat up and pointed at O'Henry. "There's my thief!" he shouted.

Chapter 24

Perplexed, Bartholomew Henry O'Henry shook his head and swatted at the white fog enshrouding his face.

Parsons stood up and pointed at Irish. "Thief," he shouted.

Sainty strode from behind the wagon. "What's going on?"

Reb wagged his finger at the crook. "He stole my tobacco."

O'Henry shook his head. "I didn't steals nothing."

"Ye shall not steal, neither deal falsely, neither lie one to another, Leviticus Nineteen-Eleven," Parsons replied. "Care to read it yourself, Irish?" Reb thrust his Bible at O'Henry.

"What are you talking about, Parsons?"

"I dumped gunpowder in a pouch of my tobacco, and waited for the thief to light up."

"That so, O'Henry? Did you steal another tobacco bag?"

"I never does that," he said, spitting the remains of his cigarette to the ground.

Sainty stepped toward him. "Give me the pouch."

He refused. "I owns this."

The foreman lifted his right hand. "I intend to check for gunpowder in your tobacco."

"Two cartridge loads," Parsons explained, as O'Henry jumped past the trail boss.

The thief dashed to the fire yanked the pouch from

his pocket and flung it into the flames.

"Damn you, Irish," Sainty scowled.

The blaze took hold of the pouch, which flared, then exploded in a cloud of white smoke.

"You're fired, Irish. Gather your belongings, saddle your horse and leave," Sainty yelled.

"Hold on," cried Muscher, stepping forward and glaring at the foreman. "If you fire O'Henry, I'm pulling out to. What about you, Harry, and you, Toad?"

"I'm with you," Harry answered, barely audible. Toad nodded he would leave as well."

"Fire him, you're firing four of us," York challenged, crossing his arms over his chest.

Tempers flared like the gunpowder in the flames, so I was glad our pistols remained in the wagon. Sainty faced a dilemma. He'd lose four needed hands, if he fired O'Henry. If he didn't, he'd keep a thief and his allies among us to start more trouble.

Parsons stepped to the foreman. "You don't have to let him go on my account, Sainty. As long as he stays ten feet from me and my belongings, I'll be fine. Everyone knows he steals."

Sainty looked at those with me. "What do you say, men?"

We shrugged. Nobody cared for a thief in our midst, but firing O'Henry and his pals meant more chores for the rest of us,

Jurdon Mark cleared his throat. "Maybe next time Irish needs a smoke, he can just light up a cartridge."

While O'Henry and Sainty stood stoic, everyone else laughed, including Irish's gang.

"It'd save time and trouble," China finished.

Sainty cracked a smile. "You can stay, O'Henry, but from now on you, Muscher, Dire and Beeline pitch your bedrolls on the opposite side of the wagon from us. Don't any of you go near Reb, his belongings, his bedding, his Bible and especially his tobacco."

For a problem with no answer, Sainty's decision was acceptable as hundreds of miles remained between us and Abilene.

"Is that clear to everyone?" the foreman called out.

We nodded.

Sainty pointed at the shirkers. "Move your bedding and belongings right now."

"Why do we have to move our bedrolls?" Muscher demanded.

"Yeah," O'Henry echoed.

"Shut up, Irish. You started this problem," Sainty answered. "Now move."

The troublemakers grumbled as they toted their possessions across from ours. While we would maintain a full crew to Abilene, the tensions remained. Jurdon Mark tried to ease the friction, alternating nights sleeping with each crew, but gave up after one night with the shirkers. "There's a lot of bitterness and resentment on the other side of the wagon," he explained.

Despite the dissension, we kept moving, averaging ten to twelve miles a day. The herd reached the Brazos early afternoon and we crossed a couple miles southwest of Waco while Charlie took the wagon to town to replenish our supplies. Everyone was more interested in watching the thief swim the river this time than in getting the herd across, but Sainty forced their attention on their jobs.

The Brazos ran deep and all the animals had to swim. By the time we'd gotten two thirds of the cattle across, the foreman asked me to accompany him to the rear of the caravan. As we approached those riding drag, he aimed his mount for Irish.

"O'Henry," called Sainty, "we've got another river crossing."

His eyes widened. "You bindings me to my horse again?"

"Nope, you're on your own."

Irish gulped.

"Cross on your own or stay here," Sainty said. "The choice is yours."

Irish yanked down his bandanna and glared. "Lomax didn't helps much last time."

"He's more than you'll have today. It's sink or swim

263

for you."

Sainty reined around and galloped away.

I grinned at O'Henry. "See you on the other side or never again."

Irish aimed a string of curses at me as I caught up with the trail boss.

"You hoping he stays on the south bank?" I asked.

"Or drowns."

Reaching the Brazos, we dismounted and loosened our cinches before remounting and plunging into the muddy waters, urging the cattle across. Our horses swam it easily.

We let the steers water as much as they needed, then bedded them in a broad pasture with good grazing. Eventually, O'Henry crossed the river and joined us, his clothes sopping wet.

"Damn," Sainty said when he saw Irish, "I was praying for a better outcome."

Bitters found us a half hour before sundown and set up camp, complaining about the high toll he had to pay to ferry across the Brazos. While everyone was hoping for chicken and dumplings again, Bitters fed us more bacon and beans, though he brought back a bushel of apples. He gave us one each with our meal and announced a treat later as he peeled apples, mixed them with water, sugar, cinnamon and dough. He put the concoction in his Dutch oven and cooked an apple cobbler, which he served in an hour.

"Bonito," everyone cried on my side of the wagon.

From the gang of shirkers, we heard complaints they were being served last and their portions were smaller than ours.

"They always get more or better food," Muscher bitched.

"Yeah," O'Henry agreed. "We works harder because we rides drag. We deserves more."

"You get what you get," Bitters replied.

"Treat us like you treat them," Muscher demanded, pointing to us.

When we finished our cobbler, each man on our side

264

of the wagon got up and carried his plate to the dishpan. The shirkers just stacked theirs in a pile at the foot of York's bedroll. Dire walked over to his gear and picked up his lariat, widening the loop and twirling the rope. As Bitters started for the plates, Harry tossed his lasso, hitting the stack and scattering the dishes.

To my surprise, Bitters grinned, bent and gathered the plates. As he returned to the dishpan, Dire pulled in his rope, twirling it again and tossing it over the cook's shoulders. Yanking the rope taut, he stopped Bitters in his tracks. Dire and his three companions laughed while the rest of us wondered if we should get involved. I expected Bitters to retrieve his six-shooter and give Harry Dire a dance lesson, but once the roper loosened his lariat, Bitters pushed the loop to the ground, stepped out of it and went about his business. Instead of reacting, he washed the dishes, mumbling to himself. The next morning as we arose for breakfast, Bitters surprised everyone with his politeness when the shirkers came in from last watch. Believing they deserved better treatment, those boys took to his newfound courtesies like kittens lapping at a bowl of milk.

Having cowed Sainty and Bitters, the shirkers next picked on the two Mexicans. Seeing no consequence to his lassoing Bitters the night before, Dire grabbed his rope, twirled a quick loop and tossed it at Pedro Ramírez's leg as he walked in for a coffee refill. Tightening the lariat around Pedro's left calf, Dire yanked on the lasso and Ramírez tumbled to the ground. Pedro cursed in Spanish as he yanked the rope off his boot and threw it back at Dire. Muñoz rushed over to check on his buddy. As he passed, Dire created a new loop and snagged Muñoz around his torso. The shirkers hooted as Muñoz fought the lariat and flung it back over his head. The wrangler turned around and stared at the four.

"Stop it," cried Sainty from the other side of the wagon.

"Just funning, boss," Dire said, his voice barely audible. "No harm to the greasers."

"If you rope another hand, Dire, I'll hang you with your own lariat," the foreman scowled. "That wasn't fun; that was plain meanness."

"You know I was just playing, don't you, José?" Dire whispered.

Muñoz shrugged. "No hablo ingles," he said, then helped Ramírez to his feet. Both men spoke heatedly in Spanish as they continued to the coffee pot for Pedro's final cup. When they passed back by the shirkers rolling up their bedding, Ramírez spat at their feet, but Muñoz chastised him, then grinned and tipped his hat at their tormentors. "Solo espera hasta que montes tus caballos," José called as returned to the remuda.

Sainty laughed like he understood what his wrangler had said.

All I knew was caballos, which I thought meant horses.

Sainty pointed his fingers at the shirkers. "No more kid's play. José's worked for me longer than any of you. He's a good man. You'll not abuse him or Pedro any more. Do you fellows understand?"

They nodded with a smirk. Since they faced Sainty down over his threat to fire O'Henry, they had grown emboldened, like they ran the outfit. They would learn over the next week that the people under the boss could be more dangerous to their well-being than the head man.

After having their fun at the expense of Muñoz and Ramírez, the shirkers went to the remuda to saddle fresh horses. Muñoz surprised me, paying more attention to the troublemakers than normal, helping Beeline and O'Henry with their mounts and sending them on their way. After Muscher mounted and Dire finished cinching his saddle, the wrangler slipped something out of his britches, then held one arm out and pulled the other back. Just as Dire put his boot in the stirrup, José released his back arm. Instantly, the gelding screeched and bolted forward, yanking Dire off his feet. Harry bounced on the ground, screaming, "My foot's hung," as his mount raced away.

I ran toward the commotion, less interested in helping than in seeing what Muñoz was holding. As I neared José, I saw him slide his slingshot back in his britches.

"Bonito," I called as I raced by, intent on seeing if Dire survived.

Muscher raced by on his mount, closing in on the horrified animal. Drawing beside the spooked horse, York took the runaway's reins and yanked him to a stop. Jumping from his saddle, Muscher fought Dire's frightened horse still rearing and stomping the ground, jerking Dire up and preventing him from freeing his foot. Sainty raced up on his mount and grabbed a bridle strap, shaking the gelding's head to get his attention. As the animal calmed in the foreman's grasp, York released the reins and dashed to Dire, working his friend's boot from the stirrup. With his leg free, Dire rolled away from the horse as Sainty led the spooked cow horse off.

Dire crawled onto his hands and knees, shaking his head and cursing as I jogged up.

"Good riding, Harry," I said.

"Shut up, Arky," Dire groaned as Muscher dusted dirt and grass off his pal's shirt and pants. "What happened?"

"Bee sting," I offered. "I heard one buzz past."

"Arky spooked my horse out of spite," Dire sputtered

Muscher helped him stand. The roper limped around in a circle, grimacing with each step and grabbing his buttocks. His shirt hung in tatters and his back showed bloody red and purple swatches from scrapes and bruises.

Sainty returned with both Dire's and Muscher's horses in tow. "Are you okay, Harry?"

"I've been better," he answered.

"Climb your horse and see if you can ride," the foreman ordered.

Dire took the reins and inserted his foot in the stirrup, pulling himself atop the saddle and settling gently onto his seat. He nodded. "I can."

"It's a good thing, because Bitters would ban you from his wagon after the way you roped him last night."

"I'd rather rot on the prairie than ride with the man that's been poisoning us daily."

Muscher remounted and studied his partner. "You sure you can ride?"

"Damn right, I can," he answered.

"Riding drag must have a new meaning for you now, Harry," I observed.

Dire cursed me again and rode toward the herd. When they were beyond hearing us, Sainty laughed. "Stung by a bee? You and I both know better than that."

"What did José tell them in Spanish?"

Sainty snickered. "Wait until you mount your horses."

"The bee was a stone from Muñoz's slingshot," I revealed.

"José always keeps a slingshot in his britches, and he's a solid aim. Those four best not toss their bedrolls under a wasp nest. I suspect those boys will have a few more remuda problems in the coming days. Now let's get back to work."

Sainty was correct. Next morning yet another bee spooked Muscher's horse and threw York to the ground. Stunned, Muscher lay sprawled in the grass, his nose bleeding and his forehead sprouting a knot on the side. After shaking the cobwebs from his mind, he rose to his hands and knees, then wobbled to his feet, grasping his saddle and mounting in a daze. Twenty-four hours later thorns caught in the cinches pricked his horse's belly when O'Henry tightened his saddle. Irish's horse stomped his left foot and kicked his right thigh, hobbling him. The day after that, something startled Beeline's horse, which tossed Toad on his shoulder.

"Bonito," Muñoz said as he watched Beeline ride away, holding his left arm and shoulder.

"Been a lot of insects in the air the last few mornings, José," I offered.

"Si," he answered. "Stone bees."

We both laughed and continued on to Fort Worth, me thinking all scores were settled, but Charlie Bitters still seethed from the poor treatment by the shirkers.

I figured by now he would've crumbled cow dung into their food, but I gathered he saved that recipe for later. So, we kept moving north with me in the lead, directing the herd around prairie dog colonies, log cabins where settlers had gardens coming to fruit, wayward skunks, and a rattlesnake den so filled with serpents you could hear their buzzing tails twenty yards away. We remained attentive to keep our horses from getting bit. We had a dozen or more cattle with swollen legs or heads as they had been bitten while walking or grazing. Three of them finally died. At night we stayed skittish about rattlers as we laid out our bedding, took a leak or started a watch.

Just like the steers, we had gotten into our own routine in the evening. Jurdon Mark played marbles for fun with any taker while Martin Michaels continued his sketching, drawing profiles of every drover. Silas Banty regaled us with stories from his childhood, and Tom Errun defined more British words than we cared to learn, but none topped tora-loorals. Trent Parsons read his Bible each night, occasionally smoking a cigarette. Muñoz and Ramírez bedded with us, though their chores meant they were the last in bed and the first to rise along with Bitters.

As for the shirkers, they kept to themselves, bitching and moaning over how unfair they had it riding drag and how they got the dregs of the meals and what they would do when they were paid and how rich they would be. When they weren't complaining, they were smoking their cigarettes, a habit Sainty had to caution them about for fear a misplaced cigarette might start a prairie fire and stampede the herd. We'd been lucky so far, not to have a major stampede.

Eight or nine days after we left Waco, we ended a long day with the steers bedded and us hungry for a supper. Charlie Bitters greeted everyone proudly. "Generals," he announced, "I made chicken and dumplings for tonight."

Everybody clapped and whistled.

"Don't startle the cattle," Sainty warned and our celebration fizzled, even more so when our cook continued.

"Problem is I only got one chicken, a prairie chicken I guess it was, and there's not enough to go around."

Everyone groaned.

"Since the drag riders question my fairness, I'm letting them have the prairie chicken and dumplings. I believe bygones should be bygones."

The shirkers stuck out their chests, damn proud to be rewarded for their intimidating behavior.

"Bonito," O'Henry shouted.

"Bonito," Muscher echoed.

All four of them gloated as they awaited Charlie to serve the plates. He put the regular allotment of beans and bacon on our plates, then turned to the trouble-making quartet. "I made cornbread tonight, too, but it's in short supply. You fellows don't mind forgoing the cornbread since you'll get the prairie chicken and dumplings?"

The shirkers agreed it was a fine tradeoff for us lesser hands to eat cornbread as long as they got the cook's specialty.

Bitters split up the cornbread among our plates and told us to come and get our grub. He then lifted the lid off of his Dutch oven and filled the troublemakers' plates, piling the biggest helpings on them of any since San Antonio. The rest of us looked at each other like our own mothers had slapped us. Bitters told the ingrates to sit so he could serve them coffee.

"Eat up, boys. Enjoy your supper. You deserve it," he told them.

As the shirkers gobbled down their meal, our side of the wagon stared at our same old bacon and beans. Nobody understood why the shirkers deserved such kingly treatment, especially after how they had mistreated Bitters.

"You boys got everything you need?" Bitters asked as they attacked their plates.

They nodded, chomping on their chicken and dumplings.

"Great," he replied. "I want to tell the other generals

a story." The cook turned his back on them and visited with us.

"Funniest thing, this prairie chicken," he said. "I killed it with my shovel as it tried to get away."

"I never heard of someone killing a chicken with a shovel," I said. "How'd you get close enough to swat him?"

"Fair question, general. He was flapping his wing as fast as he could, but I didn't see a second wing. Maybe he lost it, but he couldn't take to the air."

"Hey," cried Muscher from the other side of the wagon. "What kind of bone is this?" He held up a thin curved one.

Bitters ignored him and continued. "Odd thing is, he'd lost his legs, at least that's what I figured when he tried to skedaddle. I knew then it was a chicken because he was scared yeller and was retreating. He was darn sure chicken."

"This is an odd little bone," called O'Henry, holding up another thin one. "More chick than chicken it looks to me."

Bitters ignored them. "Then I just chopped his head off and skinned him."

"You didn't pluck him?" Martin asked.

"Odd thing was, general, he didn't have feathers, but he must've been a chicken because he was trying to slip away on the prairie."

"Well, Charlie, I'm damn sure confused by this," Sainty said.

"I'm telling you it had to be a prairie chicken, coward that he was, but I clipped his wing. Let me show you."

By then the malcontents stared nervously from their plates to Bitters.

The cook reached in his pocket and extracted a diamondback rattle, then held it above his head and shook it.

"Son of a bitch," cried Muscher, tossing his plate aside. "He fed us rattlesnake."

"Prairie chicken," Bitters corrected as he made the rattle buzz.

The shirkers jumped up, flinging their supper away, running from camp. We listened to them gagging and retching as we laughed, glad we'd eaten an inferior ration.

"I never cooked a more satisfying meal," Bitters shouted as he picked up their discarded plates and took them to the wash pan. "Remember the Alamo!" he called.

"Remember the prairie chicken!" I answered.

"Remember the prairie chicken!" the hard workers cried to the sounds of the shirkers puking.

Chapter 25

The "prairie chicken" supper clipped the wings of O'Henry, Muscher, Dire and Beeline as they behaved tolerably well afterwards. They carried their plates to the wash pan and complimented the cook on his meals, even when they thought otherwise. The foul four never figured out their troubles with their horses, as none ever saw Muñoz aiming his slingshot at one of their mounts, but their difficulties stopped after each had encountered a bucking horse.

Everybody had learned their lesson with Bitters and didn't complain about his cooking, even though the sameness of bacon and beans had worn on us and our stomachs as we were often bloated. Some evenings around the wagon, we avoided striking a match for fear our britches—or one of O'Henry's cigarettes—might explode.

Fact was, the only thunderclaps we heard between San Antonio and Trinity River came from Bitters' cooking and our backsides. The land thirsted for rain as much as we craved a breath of fresh air. About a day south of Fort Worth, thunderheads built to the west before noon. Giant clouds of gray and pink towered over the horizon, occasionally showing a flash of light, followed seconds later by a soft murmur of thunder.

The steers fidgeted and tossed their heads, bellowing and bleating as if they smelled trouble. Sainty circled the herd, informing everyone we would skip lunch to calm the steers if the weather spooked them. He said one by one we should peel off from the cattle and ride to Bitters, who would pass out strips of jerky and the last of the apples from Waco so we could eat in the saddle. The trail boss also ordered us to pick up our slickers as we would need them.

Sainty fretted as he rode with me. "That thunderhead looks bad," he said as he studied the roiling mischief-maker on the horizon. "Every upside has a downside," he postulated. "The country's dry and needs rain. A little water will enliven the grass and make better fodder for the steers, but if they stampede, we'll lose a bunch. The lightning and the thunder can spook them, but so can hail." A slash of lightning zigzagged through the distant cloud, which towered like a sinister tombstone over the horizon. Seconds later a low rumble washed over the land.

That growl of thunder scared me. Twisting in my saddle, I looked for cover, but we crossed level prairie land with only isolated trees that might protect us from hail, but not lightning. Glimpsing Corkscrew, I saw the imperturbable lead steer walking, tossing his head in the air. He was as confused as a preacher in a whorehouse. "What can we do?" I asked.

"Pray, if you're in good standing with the Lord," Sainty replied.

"Reb's got better connections than me upstairs with all his Bible reading and quoting."

"If they bolt, race to the front of the herd and turn them in on themselves, that'll confuse them and start them to milling until they slow to a walk. If you can't get ahead of them, ride the flanks to keep them from scattering."

"There are more of them than us. You sure they'll stampede?"

Sainty nodded. "Don't see any way to avoid it. Too many uncertainties with the weather, and it just takes one to spook, then boom they're off like they were shot from a cannon. Michaels is experienced, and Errun's picked up things fast so they might turn them, but they're in the most danger too. If either point rider goes down, we've got problems."

An uneasy feeling crawled in my stomach, not from Sainty's warnings as much as from days of trail cooking. My belly was tying itself in knots and paining me more than at any time since leaving the Five-D Ranch. I grimaced.

"You okay?" the foreman asked.

"Bad pains in my belly," I replied.

"Well, you gotta gut it up because we need every hand we have in the saddle this afternoon." Sainty issued a final warning. "If they run, watch out for their horns. If you think you've got a bellyache now, wait until you're skewered on the end of one of those things. Get your slicker and your lunch, then take up a position mid-herd."

"Sure thing, boss." I turned Relee toward the cook wagon.

Charlie Bitters reined up as I reached him. I leaned over and pulled my rain gear from the back. The cook gave me four strips of jerky and an apple. "We're in for a long evening. Anything could stampede the jittery cattle. Where's Sainty positioning you?"

"Mid-herd," I replied as I tucked the fruit in my britches pocket

"Good," he answered. "That's safer than in the lead. You be careful, general."

"Thanks, Charlie. You watch out for yourself." I grimaced at a shooting stomach pain.

"You okay?"

"My stomach's been paining me"

"Hold on," Charlie said, tying the reins to the brake lever, then crawling in the back of the wagon. He dug around among his crates of supplies and pulled out a handful of prunes. He returned to his seat and offered me the dried fruit. "Eat these. They'll clear your bowels."

I thanked Charlie as he picked up the reins and started forward.

"Remember the Alamo!" he called.

"Remember the prairie chicken!" I answered as we both headed on. I ate the prunes and jerky as I rode, saving the apple for later.

By early afternoon, we were positioned for the calamity we knew was to come. We watched the southwest as the thunderstorm moved closer. The cattle — and us men — grew tense the nearer the storm came. Lightning cracked the clouds. Thunder that once rumbled now boomed. Normally steadfast, Relee danced on nervous hooves, flinching with each crescendo of the turbulent heavens. "Easy boy," I said as much to myself as him. I stood in my stirrups and looked ahead, spotting Jurdon Mark and Trent Parsons in the swing positions, but unable to see Errun and Michaels on point. On the opposite side of the herd, I saw Sainty had taken his position. Behind me, I observed Silas Banty and Toad Beeline on the flank, but not Dire, O'Henry and Muscher on drag because of the dust.

The storm drew nearer, the lightning more frightening, the thunder even louder. Steers recoiled with each clap of the sky. A cool, then cold breeze washed over us. Shortly, the wind carried the fragrance of rain. I tugged my hat tighter, freed my bandanna from my neck, rolled it up, strapped it over my war bonnet and tied it under my chin to secure it from the blow. Putting on my slicker, I made sure it covered my shirt pocket and Ruth's sketch.

Next the sky flashed. A dagger of light hit a tree within a hundred yards of me. KA-BOOM! The thunder blasted over the drovers and steers. Men and animals cringed.

"Now I lay me down to sleep," I called out, trying to calm the cattle—and myself. "I pray Thee Lord, my soul to keep. If I should die before I wake, I pray Thee Lord, my soul to take. If I should live for other days, I pray Thee Lord, to guide my ways."

Flash, KA-BOOM went the sky. I gritted my teeth as I looked over the panicked herd. "Easy, easy," I cried, trying to calm us all. To keep my mind from thinking of my impending demise, I changed the words to the childhood prayer.

"Now I ride this herd to keep and wish instead that they were sheep. If they should bolt before I'm done, I pray their hooves that I outrun. If I should live for other days, help me outgrow my cowboy ways."

Joseph G. McCoy had it right. It was better—and safer—to be a cattle buyer than a cattle puncher.

Flash, flash, boom, boom thundered the sky as the roar of approaching precipitation enveloped the herd, then the rain itself, drenching us with buckets of water and splattering the land with drops by the millions. The cattle began to trot. We were losing them!

I repeated my impromptu prayer, calling it out as soothingly as I could, hoping to calm the steers. The roar of rain and wind muzzled the flashes of lightning and the blasts of thunder. The cattle slowed and stopped, looking heavenwards, some opening their jaws and letting the raindrops moisten their mouths. Time after time I repeated my prayer, hoping the animals remained calm. I looked around for other drovers, but the rain was so heavy I saw no one, only the confused steers that flinched with every slash of lightning and every crash of thunder.

Through it all, I battled stomach pains, uncertain how much longer I could stay in the saddle, but terrified that I might be trampled afoot. I repeated my new prayer and hoped the cloud would pass. The downpour lasted a half hour, drenching my hat and my head before slackening an hour before dusk. My slicker kept my shirt and Ruth's sketch dry, but the lower third of my britches and my boots were soaked. The lightning and thunder receded to the northeast. We had managed okay, largely because the storm had hit during daylight when the steers could see their surroundings

I recited my impromptu prayer one last time, thinking it had worked and calmed the cattle within hearing distance of my voice. My roiling stomach needed a heavenly entreaty as well. I grimaced and clutched at my gut, shaking my head as if that might allay the ache.

To make matters worse, Bartholomew Henry

O'Henry rode over. "Lomax," he scowled, "the trail boss sent me to check on everyone." He studied me. "Are you okay?"

I shrugged. "Don't know." Contorting, I grabbed at my belt. That's when I broke wind.

And that's when the cattle startled!

"What?" cried O'Henry, yanking off his hat and waving it at the steers, scaring them more.

The animals' pent up fears exploded. Nearby steers bolted ahead, further frightening their neighbors that raced forward, panicking others into running. Instantly, pandemonium shot through the herd. Thunder from above was replaced by thunder from below, as the earth vibrated and roared as thousands of hooves hit the ground in a mad dash to escape O'Henry and me.

In the instant I took to realize what had happened, the cattle in front of me charged northward, while those behind me hesitated, uncertain what to do. O'Henry raced after the stampeding half of the herd, waving his hat and frightening them even more. The trailing animals trotted forward, bellowing and shaking their horns. Suddenly, they started to run as well. I whipped Relee in beside them, attempting to turn these steers before they caught the others.

At my urging, Relee shot ahead, keeping me but inches away from the dangerous horns that might impale me. I heard the click and clatter of horns bumping against each other. That sound was the noise of the herd compacting so that the cattle had less room to maneuver and avoid each other. Gradually, I turned the stampeders in on themselves as the lead steers reached the drag animals and slowed. Silas Banty galloped behind me to help tighten the circle, while Toad Beeline on the opposite side, spun his horse around and made sure no cattle escaped from the growing vortex of hooves, hides and horns. Remaining drag riders Chuck Muscher and Harry Dire kept the laggard steers from scattering. We took until dark to settle the steers in our half of the herd, then spread them out so they had room to rest. The cattle grazed and drank water from the rain puddles scattered across the landscape.

The last dregs of daylight slipped away as Sainty approached. I spotted him and trotted over, figuring to update him rather than let him ask questions. "We turned this half of the herd and kept them together."

"Anybody injured?"

"Not to my knowledge. Everybody pulled their load."

Sainty nodded. "Nobody hurt on our end, but we weren't so lucky with the cattle. We got them turned but not before they scattered. I counted thirteen with broken legs or other injuries. We'll have to kill them and round up the others tomorrow. It'll cost us a day or more."

"Do we need to bring these up?" I asked.

"Not in the dark. Wait until morning and get them moving first thing. All the animals are jumpy, and we must ride guard on two herds tonight. Everyone. No supper, either."

I was thankful I had saved my apple in my britches, though I wasn't sure how hungry I'd be with my stomach bothering me. Darkness hid my pain from Sainty. "Want me to tell the others?"

"I'll do it. Nobody's sleeping tonight. I want every man in the saddle, even if he's asleep, to ride and calm the herd. After one run, they're more likely to make another."

I nodded.

"And I'm telling them you're in charge of this herd while I oversee the other."

"They'll love that."

"I don't give a damn what they think. That's the way I want it."

I'd never been in charge of men before, and I hated the idea. Just more things to worry over. My stomach cramped, and I leaned over in the saddle.

"Your belly still bothering you, Lomax?"

"Yep," I managed. "All the beans and bacon's caught up with me."

"We'll have fresh meat tomorrow when Charlie butchers one of the injured steers. Be careful tonight." Sainty left to ride around the herd and tell the hands the plan for the evening.

As for me, I desperately wanted to relieve the pressure, but I feared I'd start another stampede. I rode away from the cattle far enough not to startle the animals when I broke wind once, twice, three times. Fortunately, the steers ignored my indiscretions and kept bedding down. I was back in position by the time Sainty completed his rounds.

"We're three miles north of here. See you in the morning." The foreman rode away.

I circled the herd in the opposite direction of the other hands, then swung in beside Banty.

"Evening, boss man."

I laughed. "No one's ever called me boss before, Silas. I don't feel like much of one."

"All I feel right now is hungry," he countered.

Unbuttoning my slicker, I reached in my britches pocket and retrieved the apple that Bitters had issued me hours ago. Uncertain my stomach would handle anything, I offered it to Silas. "Want my apple?"

"No, sir. I not be wanting to be indebted to any man."

"It's not a loan, but a gift. Take it. Didn't Charlie give you one for lunch?"

"That he did," Silas answered, "but I be feeding it to my horse. He be enjoying it. My master always be telling me if you be eating fruit out of season it be killing you."

"Perhaps he didn't want you chomping another of his wax apples."

Silas laughed. "Worst apple I ever be eating. Now I be understanding why master be saying such."

"If I'm the boss man, I'm ordering you to eat my apple."

"Only if you splits it with me."

I offered him the apple. He took a bite and handed it back to me. I nibbled at it, wondering how the apple would affect my stomach, and returned it to him. We alternated bites until only the core remained. Silas nudged his mount ahead of mine, leaned over and fed the remnants to Relee.

"When we was kids and finished an apple," I related, "we'd say 'apple core' and someone would answer 'Baltimore.' Then you'd say 'Who's your friend?' and you'd throw the core at whoever they named."

"I'd be throwing it at Bart O'Henry," he said. "He be keeping his stinger out all the time."

"Chuck Muscher'd be my target. He's proof there's more horses' asses than horses in Texas."

Banty chuckled. "Never be thinking of it that way."

"Now tell me this, Silas. You were a slave and Irish was a slave. How come you're not embittered?"

"He always be looking over his shoulder at what be behind him. I be looking ahead to what be in front of me. I can't be changing my past, only my future. We all be needing something to be looking forward to."

"I'm anxious to return to Ruth. How about you?"

"I be supposing when I be returning to Texas, I be using part of my money to hires me a teacher. I always be wanting to read the Good Book for myself, like Mr. Parsons be doing each night. As a kid I be dreaming of opening a book or be holding a newspaper and be reading what it says like I be an educated man like you be."

Never had I been called a learned man until then. His awe of my simple education made me regret the times I'd fought against my mother's insistence on my school learning. Something Silas Banty desperately desired, I had taken for granted. "Maybe I could help you, teach you your A-B-Cs. That'd be a start."

"I be obliging to you, boss man, if it not be too much trouble."

"On one condition, Silas."

"What be that?"

"Quit calling me 'boss man'."

"Yes, sir, boss man," he said, then caught himself and laughed.

I grinned and rode on, checking on Dire, Beeline and Muscher as they worked to soothe the steers. As I suspected, they were angrier than a preacher with the devil for a neighbor because Sainty appointed me their foreman. They sassed me and told me they didn't need my mother-hening them. That evening as I circled the herd, confirming that all the riders were awake and attune to the cattle, I spent extra time with Silas each round, going over the alphabet. Not remembering how I learned to read, I figured the alphabet was the only logical place to begin, since I didn't have a book to show him letters. Acting as his teacher helped pass the time on an exhausting night when we all needed rest. By sunrise, both Silas and I slurred our letters as we recited them, and Dire, Beeline and Muscher slumped in their saddles, their energy and their sass depleted.

As sunlight bled over the horizon, I made a final round ordering my hands to get the cattle up and moving to rejoin the main herd. The way everyone slouched in the saddle, I figured we might have an easier time getting the steers to herd us instead, but gradually we got the cattle moving. We took it slow, not wanting to spook any nervous animals.

Mid-morning we reached the main herd, still bedded down or grazing on grass invigorated by the rain. The wagon was set up beyond the herd and Bitters had a campfire going. Sainty rode out, ordering us to ease the cattle in with the others and let them graze or rest. After that he pointed to the wagon and told us to fetch coffee and grub. He gestured at Muscher, Dire and Beeline, telling them to throw their bedrolls and get a couple hours of shuteye. "Lomax is no longer in charge, is he?" Muscher asked. "He's a worse foreman than you."

"Glad to hear that," Sainty answered. "Now I know I chose the right man."

The malcontents trotted over to the wagon for food and rest. As for me and Banty, Sainty told us to fill up on coffee and grub, then head out in search of as many of our cattle as we might find. He said he had sent Martin Michaels and Tom Errun to northeast and Jurdon Mark and Trent Parsons to the north searching for strays. Now he wanted Silas and me to move northwesterly to look for lost steers, while he and O'Henry kept watch over the herd.

I was expecting more bacon and beans, but Bitters

had butchered a steer injured in the stampede, and he had fried strips of beef and boiled a pot of prunes, figuring everyone's bowels needed more attention after weeks of trail cooking. Silas and I filled out canteens from the water barrel on the wagon, ate some fried beef, and stuffed a handful of dried apricots in our pockets for lunch. We led our exhausted horses to the remuda and swapped them out for new mounts. It felt odd riding away from camp on a dun instead of my bay, but he needed the rest more than I did. Our search for strays gave us more time to go over the A-B-Cs, and Silas was a better student than I was a teacher because he picked up things quickly and could recite the alphabet by the time we returned that evening with forty-seven of our lost steers and no dried apricots.

We were the last team to reach camp and Sainty added our finds to those returned by the others for a total of a hundred and eighty-three recovered. The foreman calculated and shook his head. "It's a damn shame," he said to himself as much as to anyone else.

As the last to return, Silas and I were only two drovers without sleep since the stampede so we spooned down the food as fast as we could, planning to crawl in our bedrolls and get blessed rest. While we ate, Sainty mounted his horse and rode out to bring Parsons and Mark to the wagon, leaving the cattle unguarded. Then he motioned to the remuda for Muñoz and Ramírez to join us. I finished my plate and carried it over to Bitters, then went to fetch my bedding, but Sainty told me to rejoin to the others.

"Men," he announced, "we lost a hundred and thirty three steers by my herd count plus another thirteen that had to be shot due to injuries. We can't afford more losses that size."

Everybody nodded.

"Your pay and the Five-D Ranch's survival depend on reducing our losses and making as big a profit as we can."

"Hold on," said Muscher. "You're not cutting our pay because of the stampede, are you?"

"No, Chuck, but if we don't have cattle when we get to Abilene, there'll be nothing to pay anybody with."

"Cattle or no cattle, you'll owes us a dollar a day," cried O'Henry."

"You owe me a full day's work, which I don't always get, Irish. We're in this together, whether we like it or not. That's why I need to know what started the stampede so it won't happen again.

O'Henry spun around and pointed at me. "Lomax started it. He farted!"

Chapter 26

I spat out the son-of-a-bitch stew I had been chewing. "Don't blame me," I cried.

"You farted," Irish shouted back.

"The cattle were fine until you waved your hat like a maniac."

"It stanks bad," he declared. "I neededs fresh air, or I was gonna passes out."

"Lomax started it," Chuck Muscher called.

"Yeah," said Harry Dire.

Sitting supper aside and pushing myself to my feet, I lifted my fists, ready to teach O'Henry a lesson. Irish crouched in a fighting pose, but Sainty stepped between us.

"Knock it off," the foreman ordered. "What's done is done."

Jurdon Mark stood up and removed his hat. "Sainty," he started, "you've prohibited cards, dice and liquor on the trail. You outlawing fist fights and farts as well?"

Muscher cried, "Why not ban Bitters? His cooking's curdling our bellies."

The cook dashed for the wagon to fetch his pistol and offer Yank a serving of lead.

"Easy, all of you," shouted Sainty. "Charlie, get back to your dishes. I'll let the cause of the stampede slide."

"Sure you will," continued York, "since Lomax started it. You've been favoring him the whole trip. No night duty, no time on drag, making him boss of our herd yesterday. If it'd been one of us four, you'd let us go or take money out of our due. Arky gets it easy."

"I hired him as a guide, not a drover. That's what Colonel Dillon wanted."

"The colonel ain't here so his opinion don't matter," Muscher argued.

"It does when these are his cattle you're working," Sainty shot back.

"There's fewer cattle today because Lomax pooted," Muscher continued. "If he keeps breaking wind, you won't have any steers to sell in Kansas, and we won't get paid."

"I'm not the only one around here to break wind," I shot back.

"You is the only one stampeding cattle with your farts," O'Henry butted in.

Tom Errun shook his head. "You Texans are so crass. In England we refer to flatulence as a bottom burp."

Everyone just stopped and scratched their heads before Trent Parsons turned religious.

"The scriptures tell us," said Reb, shaking his Bible, "that he who has sown the wind shall reap the whirlwind."

Walking to me, Mark threw his arm over my shoulders. "What have you to say for yourself?"

I nodded solemnly. "It was an act of God."

"We can all breathe a little better now that this has passed," Mark responded, dropping his arm from my shoulder and removing his hat. "It's time to take up a collection to help our brother Lomax, who henceforth shall be known as 'Whirlwind'."

Though his hat came back empty of donations, Mark's nickname stuck.

Sainty sighed and shook his head. "We'll stay the night and tomorrow to rest up. Give us all a chance to sleep after so little over the last thirty-six hours. Even after you call it a day, keep a night horse saddled nearby in case they run again. Once a herd's stampeded, the animals are more prone to run. We've can't let it happen again."

"As long as Whirlwind doesn't fart again, we'll make it," Muscher said.

"Bottom burp," Errun corrected.

"But Irish's gotta keep his hat on his head," I answered.

"I gots to breathe," O'Henry said.

"Drop it, boys," Sainty ordered.

"Don't call me 'boy'," Irish shot back.

"Then act like a grownup." The foreman turned to me. "Lomax, you and Banty get some shuteye. The rest of you return to your chores."

I melted into my bedroll, so tired I felt like I had been run down, run over and wrung out. Next morning, I slept so soundly I was as hard to rouse as Trent Parsons. I awoke to the aroma of frying bacon and biscuits baking in the Dutch oven. Since he didn't have to pack up and move that day, Bitters took time to cook a large and satisfying breakfast. We ate our fare and smiled when the cook pulled a jug of molasses from the wagon and let us soak our biscuits with the syrup.

Having the time off eased the building tensions. When not on watch, the drovers hung around the camp, lost in their own thoughts or pursuits. By day's end Jurdon Mark had played marbles with every one save Bitters and Sainty. He won every game, but nobody cared. Trent Parsons read his Bible, occasionally rolling a smoke and complaining of chest and stomach pains. O'Henry restlessly paced about, fickle fires burning in his tortured soul, while Muscher and Beeline lay on their blankets burning tobacco and bitching. Dire displayed his lariat prowess with rope tricks, though none risked a meal of prairie chicken.

Martin Michaels sketched the campsite, the cattle, the countryside and, when he was bored, the rest of us. Tom Errun kept scratching his head as he compared the English of his upbringing with that of America. He explained a "loo" was an outhouse and the molasses we had poured on our biscuits that morning was "treacle." Errun taught us that "gainsay" was to take exception to, like I had gainsaid O'Henry's accusations the previous day. If I had hung around English much longer, I might have become an educated man in England, though likely an idiot in Texas. While Errun was giving any who would listen a vocabulary lesson, Silas Banty recited his A-B-Cs, and I drew letters in the dirt with a stick for him to recognize.

At one point, Bartholomew Henry O'Henry eased over to watch. Figuring I'd offer him an olive branch, I said, "I'll teach you the alphabet and how to read."

"I knows my letters, and I reads," he answered.

"Then spell 'fart' for us," I challenged.

Irish spun around and strode away, avoiding me the remainder of the day.

"He don't be knowing how to read," Banty said, "and he be too proud to be admitting it."

As Silas was taking to his A-B-Cs like a politician to a bribe, I fretted how to teach him once he got the alphabet down pat. When I wasn't helping Silas, I admired Ruth's sketch.

While the rest of us took it easy, Charlie Bitters slaved over the campfire all day, fixing us hearty and even tasty meals, fried steak, boiled potatoes and cinnamon-and-sugar slabs rolled in dough and fried. For supper he fixed a pot of beef stew with as much cornbread and molasses as we could eat. As I took my supper plate to the dishpan, I complimented Bitters on the day's fine meals. He smiled. "Thank you, general. I do better when I've got time to cook."

We again slept with our night horses saddled nearby, but the herd grazed and watered peacefully. By the time we headed out, the following morning things were back to normal, save the grass was greener and the ground was softer from the rain. As we moved the steers north that day, we picked up three dozen lost head, reducing our losses to ninety-seven steers. That evening we reached the south banks of the Trinity River, but found it too high and fast to cross. I felt better about the stampede and the lost time because the flooding would have delayed us a couple days any way. We rested another day east of Fort Worth by the Trinity, though we didn't eat as well because Bitters took the wagon to town to replenish supplies and pick up any needs for the rest of us. Still being flush with Joseph G. McCoy's money, I gave cash to the cook to buy more rock candy for all but the malcontents, more drawing paper and pencils for Martin Michaels, and a McGuffey's Reader for Banty, if Charlie could find one.

Bitters returned before sundown, but too late to fix much of a meal. He made up for it by informing us he had bought four pies from Fort Worth's fine Methodist ladies who were holding a bake sale to benefit their local church. Now I was a Baptist by inclination, though I declined to hold it against the pies, especially if one was cherry. He divided the two pecan, peach and cherry pies among the fourteen of us. Bitters let me choose first, so I got my piece of cherry pie. Though it wasn't as good as Ruth's, I enjoyed it and thought more highly of Methodists afterwards.

Trent Parsons ate a slice of pecan pie, but retired melancholy saying it reminded him of pies his late wife once cooked. He went to bed early that night, complaining of stomach cramps, neither smoking a cigarette nor reading his Bible. He accepted my offer to take his watch on the herd. Shortly, Bitters distributed the purchases he had made for everyone, dropping a tow sack in front of me. I handed out sacks of rock candy to those on my side of the wagon, and gave Michaels more writing paper and pencils. From the bottom of the bag, I pulled out McGuffey's First Reader. I handed it to Banty.

"This book, Silas, will help you learn to read."

Banty held the thin volume to his chest. I couldn't be certain, but in the dim light I thought I saw tears brimming in his eyes. "Thank you, Whirlwind. You're a good man."

"We'll work on your reading tomorrow," I told him. "I need rest as I'm riding watch for Reb. His stomach's paining him. I'd hate for him to break wind and start another stampede."

As Parsons rode swing, he took the second night shift. It seemed I was barely asleep before I heard Tom

Errun saying, "Wake up, Reb, wake up."

I shook my head and arose. "I'm riding for Parsons tonight."

"Wish you rode for him every night as he's so hard to wake," English said.

I sat up, rubbed my eyes, pulled on my boots, yanked on my hat and stood up, stretching a moment before walking over and untying my night horse."

"You ready, Whirlwind?" Jurdon Mark asked.

"Yep," I answered as I pulled myself atop this strange horse and headed out to watch the herd. We relieved Martin Michaels, who returned to camp. Mark and I circled the herd in opposite directions, humming to ourselves to keep awake as much as to calm the steers. The cloudless night hung over our heads like a dark blanket pricked with pinholes, the stars twinkling like distant diamonds in the heavens. The periodic yelp of a coyote broke the silence and once I heard a varmint—perhaps an armadillo or a skunk—scrounging for food nearby. I tried to count the number of times Mark and I passed each other, but eventually lost track of all time. Mark, though, had been watching the stars revolving around the North Star and knew when their position had advanced two hours. When we met on the final round, he asked if I wanted to go wake up the flank riders for their watch. Not caring to deal with Toad Beeline, I told Mark I'd stay with the cattle until they showed. After a quarter of an hour, Banty rode up and relieved me, thanking me again for buying him the reader. Toad ignored me when I passed him.

Back at camp, I tied my horse and retreated to my bedroll, removing my boots and hat, then dropping on my bedding and falling asleep. Come breakfast, Bitters came by and kicked my feet. "Time to get up, general. See if you can wake Reb. He's getting harder to rouse every day."

Yawning and stretching, I arose and put on my boots, then headed off behind the wagon to attend my business, figuring a few more moments of sleep might profit Reb and his stomach. When I reached camp, Parsons hadn't moved so I toed his feet. "Time to get up," I implored him. He remained motionless, not a muscle twitching. I squatted and grabbed his arm, shaking it. Nothing! "Reb, wake up," I cried. He lay as still as a downed tree. I shook his shoulder. Next I yanked his blanket off, uncertain why he was even covering himself on such a warm night. He never flinched, though his eyes were wide open. They never blinked. "Reb," I shouted, the desperation rising in my voice, "quit funning us."

By then Bitters, Banty, Mark and Michaels had gathered, everyone fearing the worst, but afraid to say so. Michaels pointed to Errun returning from the bushes. "Go get Sainty. Quick!" Errun bolted toward the remuda.

I put my forefinger beneath Reb's nostrils. While I hoped to detect the faint kiss of a shallow breath, I felt nothing. He was dead. Grimacing, I lifted my finger to each eye and closed his eyelids, sorry to have to do that. Parsons remained in my mind a good man dealt unlucky blows by the war. I knew he rested better beyond the golden gates with his wife and children. Up there no one would steal his tobacco.

Errun rushed over with the foreman. "What's a matter?" Sainty called.

"Reb's dead," I answered as I pulled the blanket over his face.

"Oh," Sainty whispered.

"Last night he complained of feeling poorly. That's why I rode his watch."

"He may have been dead when I tried to rouse him?" Errun said. "He never moved."

"Could be," Sainty said.

"What do you think killed him?" Michaels asked.

"Anyone that says my cooking was at fault is getting a skillet up the side of the head," Bitters made clear.

"I be wondering if Irish smothereds him for his tobacco," Banty mused, then answered his own question. "No, even O'Henry's not be that mean a person."

Sainty shook his head. "It must've been his war wounds caught up with him. It could happen with all the bullet lead he said was in him, a bullet shifts, cuts or blocks something."

"Where we gonna bury him?" Errun asked.

"Bury who?" called Muscher, riding up with O'Henry and Dire from the last watch.

As we stared at the trio, Sainty said, "Trent Parsons died overnight."

"I wants his tobacco," O'Henry shouted.

Even Muscher and Dire took offense at his comment. "Damn, Irish, don't you have a smidgen of remorse for Parsons?" York demanded.

"Hell, I didn't cares for him, but I didn't wishes him dead," O'Henry answered, "Lomax maybe, but not Reb."

"Nobody else is dying on this drive," Sainty said, "and quit talking such."

"What are we gonna do with him?" Errun repeated as Muñoz and Ramírez rode over, confused why no one had come out to saddle mounts for the day.

"We're close enough to Fort Worth we'll see he's buried in town in a decent grave."

The remuda hands made signs of the cross over their chests.

"Remember Trent Parsons," Michaels said.

"Remember Trent Parsons," everyone repeated.

"Lomax," said Sainty, "let's take him to town." He turned to Muñoz. "You and Pedro saddle up Parsons' horse and Lomax's, too, so we can get moving."

Muñoz fetched my night horse and led him away, returning shortly with Relee and Reb's saddled mount. We pitched in and reverently lifted Parsons from his bedroll and draped him over his saddle and tied him in place with his lariat.

Sainty rode over as I mounted my bay and took the reins to Reb's gray. Stopping beside the others, the foreman eyeballed his bedroll and saddlebags. "This has been a hard day. Don't make it worse by scavenging Reb's belongings. We'll figure out what to do with them when I return. Until then, keep an eye on the cattle."

We rode slowly away from camp, leading Reb on his last earthly journey, stopping occasionally to make sure he was still secure over his saddle. We reached town in forty-five minutes, drawing attention from everyone on the streets, many pointing at us, women covering their children's eyes, a few fellows taking their hats off and holding them over their hearts as we passed. Sainty asked a bespectacled spectator for directions to the undertaker.

"Flenner Brothers undertakers and embalmers," he said. "Two blocks down, turn right and you'll see it three blocks north on the left."

Sainty tipped his hat. "Obliged."

"You'll need the sheriff, too," the spectator called.

Sainty sighed. "I didn't think about that. It'd been simpler to bury him on the prairie."

"Maybe," I said, "but it wouldn't be right."

"I know, but I hate dealing with the law."

"Sounds like you've had past encounters with a badge-toter."

"It's over," he said, "and I don't care to recall it."

I wondered if I was riding with a horse thief, a swindler or a killer as the pedestrians stared at us, discomforting me as if they might think I had killed Reb. It worried me I had eaten another slice of cherry pie and a man had died, just like in Davis Tutt in Springfield. I smiled after remembering everyone had survived when I ate Ruth's cherry pie.

At the end of the block, I saw the funeral parlor, sporting a sign identifying the building as that of Flenner Brothers whose offerings included undertaking, embalming, coffins, and hearse and carriage rentals. Our mournful journey stopped outside the structure where Sainty dismounted and gave me his reins while he went in. Pedestrians gathered, asking who he was and what happened.

"Trent Parsons, a man of faith and a veteran of the late war," I answered.

"How'd he die?" asked a woman beneath an umbrella shading her from the sun.

"We're not sure. He never woke up this morning."

"That's the way to go," said another woman. "Just go

to sleep and never wake up."

I suppose that was a decent way as long as it didn't happen to you, but I wearied of answering questions. To avoid more, I lowered my head and closed my eyes like I was praying.

"The Good Lord can't help him now," observed a fellow.

Maybe not, I thought, but perhaps the Good Lord could strike down the man that made that comment. My appeal went unanswered. Instead of God's voice, I heard Sainty calling.

"Lomax, let's ride around to the back of the building." He took his reins and led his horse to the rear, me leading Reb's horse. We stopped at the funeral parlor's back door where two narrow men wearing narrow black suits with wide black ties held a stretcher. By the resemblance of their mustaches and their gray eyes, I assumed they were the Flenner Brothers. I dismounted and helped Sainty untie Reb, then slide him over the saddle onto the stretcher.

"We must notify the sheriff," one mortician said as they carried Reb inside.

I rolled up Parsons' lariat, tied it to my saddle and secured the reins to all three mounts to a hitching ring. As I turned around, a lanky fellow wearing a badge approached.

"You the fellow that brought in a body?"

"Yes, sir, one of them. Trent Parsons was the dead man's name."

"How'd he die?"

Shrugging, I answered as best I could. "Can't say. He never woke up this morning."

"I'm Sheriff Sanders Elliott," he said as he dismounted and tied his horse beside ours.

"My trail boss is inside. He can tell you more."

"Why don't you join us?"

Having nothing better to do, I entered the funeral parlor. On the left side of the hallway was a room filled with coffins and on the right was an embalming space where the two undertakers had lifted Parsons on a wooden table with a sheet metal top. They stripped him. Elliott walked inside, but I stood in the doorway.

"Glad you're here, Sheriff," said the taller of the two. "We were about to send for you."

"Word travels fast when two men ride in with a body strapped over a horse," he replied, turning to Sainty. "You the trail boss?"

"Yep. Sainty Spencer's my name."

"What happened, Sainty?"

"Can't say, Sheriff. We found him dead in his bedroll this morning. Last night he complained of stomach pains. We didn't think much of it as we'd been eating trail food for days, and it doesn't always sit well on the bowels."

"Why didn't you bury him on the prairie?"

"Might have if I'd known the law would get involved, but we were close enough to town that I thought he should have a respectable burial like a good Christian man deserves."

"Your friend here says his name was Trent Parsons. That right? Any family?"

Sainty nodded. "Name's correct, but his family died in the war. I suppose that's true as he read his Bible daily and was sometimes melancholy."

"No odd circumstances surrounding his death?"

"Absolutely not," Sainty said.

Elliott nodded as he watched the undertakers, who were examining the body as calmly as they would a bolt of cloth. "Any signs of bullet or knife wounds or any bruising or scrapes?"

The shorter undertaker solemnly shook his head. "No recent wounds at least. There's three pucker scars in his chest from being shot in the past—"

"Parsons always told us he survived three Yankee bullets at Shiloh," Sainty volunteered.

"—and there's a scar like a doctor cut his side open, but no recent wounds, Sheriff."

"Thanks, boys," the sheriff said, moving toward me.

I stepped out of his path into the hallway, and Sainty followed the sheriff.

"Anything else you need to know, Sheriff?" he asked.

"Nope, not since there's no recent wounds, but it's something I had to check out. You boys have as good a day as you can, losing a pal like that. It's decent of you to bring him in for a proper burial. Most men would've left him in an unmarked grave, no monument to remember him by."

Sainty nodded. "Wait by the horses while I arrange to pay for the burial, Lomax."

I stepped outside with the sheriff, wished him good day as he mounted and left.

After a half hour, Sainty emerged with the taller of the two undertakers and pointed to Parson's horse. "That's the animal and tack."

The undertaker studied the gray, scratching his chin, then nodding. "Okay, the horse and tack plus twenty dollars ought to cover our services and a stone."

"I owe him thirty-nine dollars for work done, so throw in flowers and a preacher to say nice things over his grave, and I'll give you the extra nineteen dollars I owed him."

"We'll make it a fine burial."

"We're not staying for the burial as we've cattle to get to Kansas, but I'll be back in a couple months, and I'll check the cemetery to see that you've delivered what you promised."

"Our word is our bond, sir, especially for tragedies such as this. What do you want engraved on his stone?"

Sainty shrugged. "We don't know his birthdate or much else. Any ideas, Lomax?"

I thought for a moment. "How about Trent Parsons in big letters then, in smaller ones, died June 1867 trailing the first herd to Abilene?"

Sainty looked from me to the taller undertaker. "You got that?"

He nodded. "It will be how Mr. Parsons is remembered for eternity."

We climbed atop our horses and retraced our route through town, relieved that people no longer stared at us. Outside of Fort Worth we rode wordlessly for a spell.

"I expected dangers on the trail, but I never thought we'd up and lose a man in his sleep. Hell, if O'Henry can cross the Colorado tied to his horse and still survive, you'd think Parsons could live through a little shuteye."

Shrugging, I said, "Only God knows for sure, but I fear I killed him."

Astonished, Sainty removed his hat, leaned toward me in his saddle and just shook his head. "Pray tell, Lomax, how did you manage that?"

"Cherry pie," I answered. "Sometimes when I eat cherry pie, people die."

Sainty required an explanation, so I told him about Hickok and Tutt in Springfield.

"I read about that in Harper's Weekly," my foreman responded. "I don't recall them mentioning you, though I didn't know you at the time, but I damn sure know they never mentioned cherry pie."

"It's something I live with," I confessed.

"You ought to put notches in your plate every time you eat a slice of cherry pie and kill a guy."

I chuckled. "Silly, I know, but the thought pesters me."

"Perhaps it's only an Arkansas superstition," Sainty said as he tugged on his hat. "Superstition or not, I pray we don't lose another man, even a troublemaker."

"I'll lay off the cherry pie to help our chances."

Even Sainty's prayers and my abstinence from another slice of heaven on earth came in vain as others would die, and I would come close to it before we returned to Texas.

Chapter 27

Back at camp Sainty instructed Charlie Bitters to gather up Reb's belongings and deposit them in the wagon for safekeeping. That afternoon the foreman decided to push the herd across the Trinity despite our low spirits. As the river was still up, Sainty ordered the cook to ride to Fort Worth and cross the bridge rather than try to float the rig over the Trinity and risk losing it. Sainty also told O'Henry to accompany Bitters so Irish needn't swim the river. As Bitters was hooking up the team, Sainty gave him one last order. "Don't buy any more cherry pies." Bitters stared at the foreman as if he had been eating loco weed. Sainty glanced at me and shrugged. "I want to be on the safe side."

As the wagon headed to Fort Worth, we started the herd across the Trinity, which was high and fast but manageable. We handled our duties with a demeanor so somber you'd've thought we'd been named in grand jury indictments. All the drovers made it over, though a dozen steers didn't. Once on the north river bank, we re-formed the herd and continued toward Kansas, leaving Trent Parsons forever on the south side of the Trinity.

Bitters and Irish caught up with us by supper time, but the cook brought no treats. Muscher complained and asked about pies, but the cook said Sainty had forbidden them. That wasn't gospel, but close enough to make it worthless to explain the details. If the whole truth were known, I'd have been blamed for the dearth of pies. After we settled the cattle, Sainty called everyone to camp. As Bitters handed out strips of jerky and prunes for our meal, the trail boss explained he had bartered Reb's horse and tack for a funeral and marker, then paid the undertakers what Parsons was due to provide a fine burial with a preacher. Sainty told Bitters to fetch Reb's bedroll, slicker and saddlebags, and instructed me to get Reb's lariat from my saddle.

"Parsons had no next of kin that we know of," Sainty said, "so we'll divvy up his belongings among ourselves."

"I want his Bible," I announced, tossing Parsons' rope to the trail boss.

"Hold your horses, Lomax." Sainty chided.

"I need someone to take Reb's spot on the second watch. Whoever does, gets first pick."

Nobody volunteered, the middle watches being harder on your sleep than the first or last, until Dire finally, answered, though barely audible. "I'll take second watch if I get his lariat."

"Fair enough, Harry, but no rope tricks on the rest of us." Sainty tossed the coiled lasso to the roper, who was as happy as a kid pulling a puppy's ears.

"I want his Bible," I repeated.

"Didn't take you for the religious type," the foreman answered, digging it from the saddlebags.

"Few people do," I responded as he handed me the Good Book. I decided I'd give it to Silas if he learned to read. I tucked the book under my blanket.

Sainty distributed Parson's other belongings. O'Henry insisted on the tobacco sacks. Not even the smokers challenged Irish for the tobacco as they feared Parsons had doctored the pouches with gunpowder. That didn't bother O'Henry as he had survived one loaded cigarette.

I also claimed Parsons' supply of candles and matches. After distributing its contents, Sainty kept Reb's saddlebags, saying they would be perfect for returning his profits to Texas. After we divvied up Parsons' bedding and slicker, Muscher asked, "What about his gun, holster and bullets?"

"Yeah," shouted O'Henry, "when do we get our pistols back?"

Bitters had guarded them in the wagon floorboard ever since the confrontation outside Austin. "There ain't no bullets," Charlie announced. "Parsons pulled a bullet from his belt every day until they were all gone. Not sure what he did with them 'cause I never heard him fire one, and I never saw any of you with a bullet hole in your gizzard."

I figured I knew what had happened to the missing ammunition as did all the smokers, save for Irish.

"The guns stay where they are until we cross the Red River into Indian Territory," Sainty said. "Okay, back to work."

Martin Michaels and Tom Errun mounted their horses and rode out for the first watch while the rest of us prepared for bed. I told Silas to bring his bedding over near mine, and we'd go over his reader. A smile wider than any river we'd cross cracked his black face, his white teeth shining in the dying light. When we both settled, I took the book from Banty and flipped to the pages featuring the alphabet.

"You've learned to recite your A-B-Cs, but you need to recognize them. Here's two pages that'll show you. On the left are the capital and small letters like you see in this book. On the right are the large and small script letters you use writing." I pointed to the A in the first column of capital letters on the left page. "Slowly recite your alphabet, and I'll point to the correct letter as you read."

He listed off the letters from beginning to end on both columns of capitals. Then we went down the two lists of small letters. "You need to study these until you know them on sight," I told him, and he nodded. "Each letter makes a unique sound, Silas."

"Like birds," he said.

"Yeah, that's a good way to put it. And you combine those letters and sounds to make different sounds we call words."

"Like a mocking bird be imitating other birds?"

"Sort of, Silas. Now I want you to go down the list of capital letters in order, then start at the bottom and recite the alphabet backwards."

"No, sir, I be wanting to begin there first, see if I can be recognizing them."

Taking a deep breath, Banty made it from zee all the way to dee before he confused it with bee, his only mistake. I corrected his error and complimented him. Silas smiled. "You're a good teacher, Whirlwind."

"Thanks," I responded, though I knew he was a better student than I was instructor.

North of Fort Worth, the drive again fell into a routine of ten to twelve miles a day, our interactions more subdued, as losing Parsons lingered on our minds. I gave Banty more lessons, and he connected the letters to the sounds they made. The third night beyond the Trinity, Silas read his first sentence from Lesson I. "Theee ... doggg ... rannn," he said. "The dog ran."

"That's right, Silas. By the time we get to Abilene, you'll be reading better than me." Banty was so pleased he swelled up like a frog in a churn despite O'Henry glaring at him. "Irish is proud of you, too," I said, pointing at him.

Silas glanced at O'Henry and back at me. "He be wearing a mad because I be bettering myself. He's too bitter to be bettering himself. He be wallowing in anger like a hog be squirming in mud." With education, Silas had the makings of a philosopher, I decided.

A week out of Fort Worth, we came to Salt Creek, the tiny burg that had been my first stop in Texas, two miles south of the Red River. We bedded the cattle west of town that afternoon, giving them time to graze, but the grass was mediocre.

While the others tended the steers, Sainty ordered me and Charlie Bitters to ride with him to the little community. Charlie would purchase what supplies he needed, if he could find them in such a tiny town, while Sainty and I inquired about the best Red River crossings. Passing through the place I pointed out my first flyer still tacked to a tree. Not impressed, Sainty sought men who knew the river and its quicksands. One fellow indicated another herd had crossed east of town ten days earlier. He suggested we follow those tracks, and Sainty thanked him.

The information worried me if it meant an unknown herd might beat us to Abilene and cost me my bonus. Sainty and I angled east out of Salt Rock, easily finding the phantom herd's trail because rains had preceded the cattle, their wake leaving dried and crusted hoof tracks. We followed those pimpled indentions to the banks of the Red.

There we sat on our horses silently studying the muddy Red and inspecting the sandy banks bordering the river. The waters flowed lazily past us. Sainty pointed across the river. "Looks like they exited there." I followed his finger and nodded. "You head east," he said, "and I'll ride west, see if we can spot any bogs."

Parting, I rode fifty yards my way, coming to a location where the rotting heads and necks of three long-horns protruded from the mud and sand, flies buzzing around the lifeless forms. The trapped animals had suffocated or starved in the quagmire. I turned Relee for Sainty. We met where we had parted. I pointed to the dead steers. Sainty nodded. "There's quicksand two hundred feet west and a hundred and fifty east. Think we can funnel the herd in this gap?"

"We don't have a choice," I replied.

We sat there studying the river, then Sainty looked west to gauge the sun, examining the horizon so long I glanced that way and saw a festering storm cloud. The trail boss sighed. "I don't care for the looks of that."

"I figure it'll go north of us. Hard to say, though."

"That doesn't concern me now as much as a down-pour upstream flooding the Red and trapping us on this side for days." He studied the clouds and the river. "We're gonna cross the herd this evening. You fetch Bitters and tell him to find us east of town quick as he can, but not to cross the river himself until we can help. We don't gain any time if the river floods, and we can't get him and our grub across. I'll start the cattle moving and meet you here." We galloped away, me to Salt Creek and him to the drovers. I found Bitters in the little store, arguing with the proprietor on prices.

"It's too much," Bitters complained, "for what I'm getting."

"That don't matter, Charlie," I told him. "We've got leave. Now! Storm clouds to the west could flood the river. You don't want to be crossing a flooding Red River."

"It's still robbery," Bitters argued.

"Pay and load up. Meet us east of town."

"What if it's dark?" he protested.

"Light a lantern and hang it from the wagon. We'll find you. I've gotta run." I dashed outside, mounted Relee and raced south of town to intersect the herd, catching them a mile away as they trotted toward the crossing. The steers bellowed and spewed their anger over disrupted grazing. I joined the men on drag. With Corkscrew's help, Sainty, Michaels and Errun would get the herd to the crossing. For the rest of us, the challenge was holding the animals together so they wouldn't scatter or hit the river early.

The steers jogged ahead as I raced to the back, blocking a dozen from escaping and driving them back with the others. At the rear of the herd, O'Henry and Muscher understood the hazards, keeping the animals moving, pushing the strays back into the pack. Together we shoved the steers into a tight column, so close that their horns clacked against each other.

We first had to swing the animals away from the river, then point them north and squeeze them through the window Sainty and I had found between bogs. The closer they came to the water, the harder the task became to funnel them toward the safe crossing. The riders on point, swing and flank controlled the string of steers, sweeping well south of the river, before turning them north toward the water.

On drag we whistled and shouted, cursed and spat, waved our hats and slapped them with our lariats, trying to keep them trailing the others rather than breaking straight for the water. Occasionally, a steer bolted from the herd toward the Red. If we could cut him off without losing others, we did. If not, we let him run, as we had hundreds more to keep in line. Still the cattle bellowed and cried, wanting to seek their own paths, oblivious to the danger.

Nearing the river, the run became pandemonium on the hoof, turning dangerous when the trailing cattle glimpsed the leaders approaching the water. Instinctively, the cattle aimed straight for the river. The drags drifted while we pushed them back. More broke through our thin line and sprinted to the water as we battled them. At one point a steer in front of me bolted for the river. I yanked on Relee's reins to cut him off, but my bay stumbled. I feared Relee would throw me beneath the pounding hooves, but my sure-footed gelding caught himself and bolted ahead while the stray bogged in the quicksand's gritty grip.

If I'd had my pistol, I might have fired it a time or two to scare the drags back on course, but without it all we had were our hats, ropes and voices, which filled the air with blasphemy. I twisted in my saddle to look at the riverbank where a dozen anxious animals were trapped in the quicksand, fighting the quagmire, lifting their heads, tossing their horns and bawling in terror.

While we had casualties, O'Henry and Muscher fought the rawhide tide and saved hundreds of others from the same fate. Much as I disliked the pair, they flexed men's shoulders on this day. As the leading steers waded into the water and started across the wide Red, the swing riders Jurdon Mark and Harry Dire worked their way back down the herd, squeezing the animals closer to fit between the quagmires. Every drover understood the urgency, which sharpened each rider's senses and made him at that moment as good a cowhand as ever rode the Plains.

Each man grasped the implications of the sinister thunderhead pulsating with flashes on the horizon. Despite the lightning, we heard no thunder, either because of the distance or of the low rumble from pounding hooves and clacking horns beside us. Gradually, we turned the caravan's rear away from the water and into line behind their predecessors. Finally, we positioned the steers for a straight shot to the crossing and the opposite bank.

I waved my hat over - head and celebrate, "Yee-haw." While we had lost a few cattle to the quicksand, the bulk of the herd remained intact, because of solid cowboying. As the middle of the caravan plunged into the river, flank riders Silas Banty and Toad Beeline reversed course and rode back to help us push the final third of the string to water. No steer escaped after that.

I glanced from the steers to the river as Corkscrew led the leaders onto the far bank. As best I could tell, the water only came to the animals' bellies. Even O'Henry could cross the Red without breaking into a sweat or screams. "Yee-haw," I cried, as excited as I had been the whole trip, feeling everyone had toted his weight. Maybe Trent Parsons was upstairs, looking over us.

Across the river I spotted José Muñoz and Pedro Ramírez, who had taken the remuda over earlier and now entered the water to drive the cattle out. Behind me I glimpsed our approaching food wagon. As daylight faded, the lightning on the horizon grew more obvious and ominous, telegraphing a horrendous downpour upstream. As we pushed the final dregs into the river, we splashed in behind them, crossing the water easily. In the half hour we took to get the last of the cattle across, darkness enveloped the land like a sheet of coal. The water never reached our stirrups as we drove the cattle up the embankment into Indian Territory. I estimated the river was three hundred or more feet wide at the crossing. As the last steers emerged from the water, we chased them up the bank and out of the river plain to protect them from any flash flooding. Sitting atop the embankment on our horses, we rested a minute, O'Henry and Muscher rolling and lighting cigarettes, then blowing smoke into the air.

Despite the odor of cigarettes, I caught the aroma of new rain, though the clouds remained miles away.

Looking across the river, I observed Bitters and his wagon, engulfed in a globe of light from the lit lantern he hung from the front wagon bow. "I'm gonna give Bitters a hand." I trotted down the slope and plunged into the water, which now lapped at my boot and stirrups. The river was rising! Perhaps the scent of rain was really the smell of approaching flood waters.

I whistled, then yelled at Bitters, "Bring the wagon, hurry."

Charlie remained motionless, either not hearing or not seeing me.

I twisted in my saddle and screamed at the hands on the embankment. "Come on! The river's rising. We've got to get Charlie across."

All four bolted down the bank and raced toward me, as I swatted Relee on the rump, gigging him with my boot heels, pushing him as fast as he could go. With a river bottom mushy with sand, my bay struggled for footing. Walking across the bottom was manageable, but galloping was impossible. Making my way to Bitters, I screamed, "Water's rising! Come on! Hurry, dammit, hurry!"

Bitters finally waved he'd heard me, but instead of starting the rig toward the river, he leaped from his seat and ran around it. I listened to the clink, clang and bang of metal more than I saw him. He reappeared on the opposite side of the wagon and jumped back into his seat beneath the lantern glow. I sprinted to him. "What the hell were you doing?"

"Throwing my pots, pans and tools in the back in case anybody wants to eat between here and Abilene." He scrambled and untied the reins, released the brake and shook the lines, sending the mule team bolting down the embankment and into the water. The mules struggled against the sandy riverbed. "Move, you bastards, move," screamed Bitters.

As I rode in beside him, the water reached my ankle. I was terrified of what the darkness hid. A wall of floodwater might be roiling toward us. I directed Relee to the team, grabbing the harness and helping pull one mule forward. We inched along until the others reached us.

"Water's rising," I screamed.

"We know," cried Muscher.

"The wheels are sinking in mud," I answered.

"Rope the mules," shouted Harry Dire, who raised his voice for the first time, "and drag them."

I swatted my saddle, but couldn't find my lasso. "My rope's gone,"

Dire rode over, slapped his tack and yanked a rope free. "Use Reb's."

I unrolled enough to make a loop and slide it over the mule's neck, nudging my bay, letting the lasso play out and distance me from the team. I dallied the lariat around my saddle horn and kicked Relee in the flank. "Yee-haw," I screamed, water half way up my calf.

Somebody roped the other mule and tugged on the team with me, but the water kept rising and the current kept strengthening. We stalled and were going to drown in the Red. Unlike Trent Parsons, we would have no marker to designate our final resting place. As we pulled, the wagon lurched forward and our pace quickened, the water giving the rig enough buoyancy to lift the wagon slightly. The tail end of the rig began to float with the current.

"The back's drifting," Bitters screamed.

"I'll get it," Dire shouted. He tied his lasso onto the rear wheel then secured it to his saddle horn and pulled with us, steadying the rig so it wouldn't float away with our cook, food and bedding. The water reached my knee. As long as our horses maintained footing, we might make it. Once they lost their hold on the bottom, everything was lost as they couldn't swim the wagon to shore. If that happened, we must toss our ropes aside and swim ourselves and our horses to the bank as best we could. Despite the danger, the oddest wish raced through my mind. I prayed that O'Henry had not returned to help because of his terror of drowning. As I struggled to keep Relee moving and the wagon following, I thought of Ruth and wondered if I would live to return to her. Also, I thanked God that I hadn't eaten a slice of cherry pie on this or the previous day. It's funny the things that run through your mind when you are about to die.

Though we reached the three-quarters mark across the river, I still doubted we would beat the flooding, especially after I detected a low growl in the distance. Amid the water in the darkness I saw nothing beyond the swaying lantern's glow. The far rumble had to be the rushing waters of a flash flood. The tumult became a roar. Water crept halfway up my knee.

"Hurry," I cried. I knew we wouldn't beat the wall of water headed our way. I thought of Ruth again.

A horrific scream arose on the opposite side of the wagon. It was O'Henry.

"Hold on, Irish," I yelled. "You'll make it."

He shrieked again, drowning out the calls of approaching riders.

Martin Michaels, Tom Errun and Jurdon Mark splashed toward us and the lantern glow. An instant later, I saw two ropes land around the neck of my mule and another over the head of the opposite mule. The lines drew taut as the drovers tied them to their saddles and turned their horses to the bank. The wagon lurched forward thanks to the extra animals tugging us to safety.

"Pull, dammit, pull," cried Bitters.

The distant growl increased, and I again caught a whiff of what smelled like approaching rain. As the river bottom began to ascend toward the bank and the water level dropped from my knee to my stirrups, I thought the worst had passed, but the downriver roar grew louder. Fifty feet from safety, then twenty. Martin, Errun and Mark rode out onto the dry bank, but didn't stop. They kept tugging on the wagon like the rest of us, their footing giving them more strength. The roar crashed upon us as the wheels hit firm soil and the wagon lurched forward and up the incline toward higher ground. I glanced back, but failed to see the river for the darkness. We heeded the water crashing against the banks we had just evacuated.

"Irish," I yelled above the receding growl of the rushing floodwaters, "are you okay?"

Nobody answered.

"Bartholomew Henry O'Henry, where are you?"

I heard sputtering, then coughing on the opposite side of the wagon, followed by a trembling voice. "I swalloweds water, but I'm's fine. I'm damn glads I didn't sees the flood waters coming."

"Glad you're okay, Irish."

"Yeah," cried the others.

"None of us would've made it if Sketch, English and China hadn't pulled us out," I said. "We barely made it, even with their help."

Drawn to the lantern for a report, Sainty rode up. "Did everybody make it?"

"Best we can tell, general," offered Charlie Bitters.

"Hell," I said, "even Irish manned up and jumped in the river to save Bitters."

"The wagon may be a little wet," Bitters explained, "but nothing that won't dry out."

"What happened?" Sainty wanted to know. Between us all, we gave as full an account of what had transpired, even if our eyes perceived less than our ears. Our foreman seemed satisfied. "Good then," he said. "Charlie, you go fix us some supper. The rest of you go spell Muñoz and Ramírez, then help Banty and Beeline bed the cattle. They're still a little restless. We'll stay the day tomorrow, calm the herd. Once Charlie gets grub, let's eat together tonight." Sainty rode off to attend the steers, while we removed our lariats from the mules or the wagon, then coiled the ropes up and hung them on our saddles. I thanked Dire for the loan.

"Reb's lariat brought me—no all of us—good luck," I told him.

After that we rode to the cattle, our eyes adjusting to the darkness once we were out of range of the lantern. Gradually, I saw great, dark forms milling around or hundreds more laying on the prairie. The exhausted steers had lost their edge from the run and river crossing, but a few still danced about nervously. Us drovers circled the herd until, Bitters banged on the triangle, calling us to eat. With no campfire, we knew supper would be a cold one. We reached camp and dismounted.

Standing by the wagon in the lantern's glow, Sainty called out. "Gather around."

We did as ordered and stood waiting while Sainty counted us all.

"We're missing one," he said, then grimaced. "Oh, yeah, Reb's no longer with us." He seemed embarrassed. "I want to tell you, all of you, how proud I am of your performance today. If I'd lost anyone of you today, it'd been a much tougher journey to Abilene. What possessed ya'll to ride out into the flood?"

"Seemed the right thing to do," answered Michaels.

"They'd done it for us," said Errun.

Mark paused and stroked his mustache. "The thought of losing Charlie's grub was more than I could bear."

"Bonito," everyone cried in unison, drawing a grin from the cook.

"Jerky and prunes for supper, generals, as my wood's wet and it's too dark and late to find more."

"Vómito," everybody groaned. Bitters smiled again.

Chapter 28

We awoke the next morning more relieved than rested. Though the river had flooded, the rains missed us overnight. While we had barely gotten the grub wagon and cook across the Red, we slept in Indian Territory that night with the vast majority of our cattle and all but one drover we had started with. Charlie Bitters was chopping firewood when we arose so breakfast was delayed, though it didn't matter as Sainty wanted to let the steers graze and rest while we dried out our belongings from the river crossing. As we relaxed, I helped Silas Banty with another reading lesson, and he read lines such as "the cat is on the mat" and "the man has a pen."

Mid-morning Bitters had breakfast ready with all the bacon we could eat, two biscuits apiece and apple butter from Salt Creek for those biscuits. As we ate, four visitors—Indians—slipped up on us afoot. Their black hair in braids and their foreheads encircled by beaded headbands with dangling eagle feathers, the braves approached us with narrow eyes and clenched lips. Each carried a Henry repeating rifle and wore white man's boots and trousers plus store-bought vests over their shirtless chests. The leader displayed a red necktie knotted around his neck. We stood uneasy and uncertain if the braves had bought the clothes, received them as handouts from the government or removed them from victims.

When Sainty spotted them, he motioned for Muñoz

to parlay with them as José understood sign language and several Indian dialects. The wrangler motioned with his forefinger for me to join him. Together we approached them respectfully, but defenseless as Sainty had yet to pass out our revolvers. I suspect we were crossing the Chickasaw Nation land and assumed these men represented that tribe. At first they stood as straight and still as a pine tree on a windless day, but as we neared Red Tie pointed at me, then whispered to the others. They stared at me, then looked at one another, nodding their heads.

Muñoz whispered, "They're talking about you, Whirlwind. Have you killed any Indians around here?"

"Not a one. I just rode through the Territory on my way to Texas."

"You still wearing your Indian bracelet, the one the trader gave you?"

"Yep."

"Then pull up your sleeve."

Carefully, I reached across my chest and tugged slightly on my shirt until the worn cuff rose over the bracelet Jesse Chisholm gave me.

We drew up an arm's distance from the braves, and Muñoz greeted them in sign language. Red Tie answered, and the wrangler smiled. José understood the dialect and began to converse with the leader. They asked each other questions, then Muñoz turned to me, looking as confused as a boy who'd dropped his chewing gum in a chicken pen. "Lomax," he said, "are you known as 'Man Who Rides with Arrow in His Chest'?"

"I suppose so."

"Condenación," Muñoz exclaimed. "You don't strike me as that tough."

"It's a long story."

"Tell me later, but show 'em your bracelet."

I extended my arm so they could see Chisholm's gift.

As I lowered my hand, Muñoz talked their language. The Indians gestured back, often pointing at me. "They're amazed you're still alive after riding across Indian Territory with an arrow in your chest. One asks if your chest can stop rifle bullets."

My eyes widening, I shook my bracelet at them. They backtracked.

"Don't scare them," Muñoz whispered.

"Hell, they scared me. Why are they discussing shooting me with a rifle?"

"Because they stand in awe of your strong medicine, your powers."

I crossed my arms in front of my chest like they had angered me with their question. As they took another step backward, Muñoz talked to them. The discussion lasted several minutes.

"We are crossing their land, the land of the Chickasaw, a peaceful people attempting to learn the white man's ways," Muñoz translated. "For our cattle to cross their lands, eat their grass and drink their water, we must offer tribute for the privilege."

"Tell them men of such strong medicine do not pay tributes."

Muñoz glared at me. "Don't let it go to your head, Man Who Rides with Arrow in His Chest. We bargain with them. Otherwise they'll harass our herds, perhaps stampede them, no telling how many cattle we'll lose as well as men. I'll make them a proposal."

The braves murmured to each other until Muñoz spoke again.

He made a point and the Chickasaw discussed it before lifting their noses in the air and shaking their head so even I knew they had refused the offer. "They say the toll for cattle crossing their land is a hundred steers. I offered them one instead. You saw the reaction."

"A man of my powers should never be required to pay," I noted.

"When I ride with an actual god, I won't pay. Until then, we'll pay tribute," he responded, before resuming negotiations. After five minutes they nodded their agreement.

"What did they decide?"

"Since your medicine is so strong, they'll settle for ten steers. Go explain the deal to Sainty. Tell him it'll cost less to agree than to risk an attack or stampede."

"A man with my powerful medicine should not be relegated as a messenger boy," I replied.

Muñoz smiled, the whispered with grit in his words. "Do it or I'll kick your behind and change your Indian name to 'Boot in Butt'!"

Disappointed in José's failure to recognize my powers, I strode back to camp and explained the extortion, convincing the foreman that Muñoz believed ten steers was a good agreement compared to the alternative. Sainty nodded. "The deal's fine as long as I pick the steers." He turned to Martin Michaels and Tom Errun and instructed them to mount up. The two left with Sainty and moved into the herd, cutting the trade animals out from the others, picking the dregs, the slow and lazy animals that delayed progress.

I returned to the wrangler and told him the arrangement was acceptable. When Muñoz confirmed the understanding with the Chickasaw, they smiled. The one with the tie stepped forward and crossed his arms over his chest, holding his rifle between them

"You speak our language good, Man with Scalping Hair."

Muñoz and I stood stunned. This Indian spoke English. Not only that, he had understood everything we had said during the negotiations. "And your English surprises me," José answered.

Red Tie smiled. "Bargaining is easiest when you listen to the other side's plan. You should respect the one we call 'Man Who Rides with Arrow in His Chest.' His powers will not be dimmed by a boot in the butt."

"Thank you, Chief," I responded, never questioning his sincerity, until he chuckled, then turned to the others and told them something that drew laughter from them.

"What did he say, José?"

Muñoz snickered. "He said an arrow in your butt might diminish your powers."

"Make sure they understand a bullet in the butt won't prove anything either," I said.

314

Red Tie turned around. "We understand!" All the Indians laughed.

Now I was scared, remembering the ride through Indian Territory with True Shot, the one who had stuck the arrow in the haversack to begin with. Did he understand English, too? I'd said many a mean thing that might have gnawed on him if he had understood my words. I hoped I didn't encounter True Shot on the journey back to Kansas.

Sainty, Michaels and Errun drove the ten steers our direction. As they neared two more Indians came up from the river cut, leading six horses. The two new Indians wore breech cloths and leather vests, each with a bow and quiver of arrows hanging over their shoulders. As they neared, the negotiators stepped toward them, taking the lines for their horses and nimbly jumping atop their saddle-less mounts. All but Red Tie trotted over to their ransom and herded the ten steers away.

Red Tie came over, leaned over in his saddle and shook Muñoz's hand. "It was fun trading with you." He pointed at me. "The young one has powers among some in Indian Territory, though not all. Others of us know better."

"And some of you don't let on you understand English."

"As well as Spanish," Red Tie said. "It helps in the bargaining."

"I'm sure it does." Muñoz laughed. "You outfoxed me."

"One warning, Man with Scalping Hair," Red Tie advised. "Rains have fallen in the direction of the setting sun, but not on Chickasaw lands for two full moons. Thirst has driven animals mad, what you white men call rabid. We have killed many rabid coyotes and skunks. They will attack cattle, horses or man. They fear nothing on two legs or four."

At that moment, I feared no animal as much as I did a sneaky Chickasaw that spoke English and understood every insulting thing I had said. I stood beside Man with Scalping Hair and watched the braves ride away with ten of our cattle. When they sauntered out of rifle range, I turned back to camp with Muñoz, Sainty, Errun and Michaels.

"How'd you become 'Man Who Rides with Arrow in His Chest'?" the wrangler asked.

By the time we reached camp, I had explained the story.

"Maybe we should call you 'Pin Cushion' instead of 'Whirlwind'," Sketch suggested.

"Or 'Bottom Burp'," English offered.

When we rejoined the others, they asked what had transpired. Muñoz told of the negotiations and my special powers. Even though, Muñoz confirmed they were friendly Indians, everyone was spooked by how quietly they had slipped up on us.

"We want our guns," Muscher demanded.

Sainty dismounted and looked from face to face. "Don't turn them on each other. Does everyone agree?"

We all vowed to throttle our tempers, but the promise was only as solid as the paper it wasn't written on.

Sainty motioned for everyone to follow him to the wagon where he issued our revolvers and belts, noting that we should check and oil our guns. He prohibited us from firing them, except when threatened by others, not a member of his outfit.

We let the herd graze that day while we caught our breath from the flooding river and our near demise getting the wagon over. In the afternoon, Sainty and I rode over to the edge of the plain and looked at the river basin. The Red River flowed fast and wide, almost twice as wide as we had crossed the night before. We counted six of our cattle grazing or watering along the opposite side of the river, but they weren't worth retrieving now or when the waters receded. Though we hoped to get a count of the number that had bogged down in the muck, the high waters had already covered them and shifting sands had likely buried them. I guessed we had lost thirty-three in the bogs, bringing our total losses to thirty-nine, counting the ones still alive but on the other side of the Red. Sainty pulled out a tiny pad of paper and a pencil from his pocket and noted the estimated losses.

We returned to a late lunch of fried steak, pan-fried potatoes, canned tomatoes and cornbread. As we ate, the others hurrahed me about my Indian name, but the conversation soon turned back to Indians. Accustomed to Comanches that could attack at any time, the drovers remained skittish, uncertain that any tribe could be trusted. They became even more nervous when other Indians approached our camp, some with women and children. Muñoz walked out to talk, then pointed at me, waving his arm for me to stand up. When I did, the Indians stared at me, their jaws dropping, then flapping as they murmured among themselves. One Indian pulled a feather from his headband and offered it to Muñoz, who took the gift and nodded as he listened to the brave.

Shortly, Muñoz returned to camp. "They want to see Man Who Rides with Arrow in His Chest to tell their children and grandchildren in the years to come. They say you have strong medicine."

I shrugged, then grinned at my doubters.

"They believe you're a freak, Whirlwind," Muscher said, "and I agree with them."

"A powerful freak," I responded

Muñoz stepped over and handed me the eagle feather. "The Chickasaw brave asked you to wear this in your hat so they might know you from afar."

I removed my headgear and wedged the quill under the leather band.

"You think Lomax is one of them?" Muscher asked. "Is he wearing a feather so they'll know not to shoot him when they attack? If they attack, I'm shooting Lomax first."

"You're crazy, Chuck," I said.

"You haven't lived under threat of Comanches like we have."

"I've been face to face with Comanches and lived to tell the story," I replied.

"When?"

"The day I took Ruth to San Antone to get supplies

and pick up Charlie. I encountered four on the trail, all wearing war paint and drawing their weapons."

"You're lying." Muscher said.

Sainty stepped between us. "You didn't inform me of that, Lomax."

"You were rounding up cattle. Didn't think it was that important."

"It's always significant when they're near the colonel's ranch," Sainty continued. "How'd you survive?"

"I showed them the bracelet. They looked at it, then rode away."

"That's crazy," Muscher shouted.

Muñoz stepped into the conversation. "Maybe not. The bracelet is an amulet that ensures the safety of the bearer. I saw one once when I was in captivity, and all Indians held it in awe."

"I've never known José to tell a lie," Sainty said, "so I trust him."

Muscher shook his head. "I don't trust Lomax, and I don't trust those Indians, whether they're Comanche, Chickasaw or Cherokee."

"I agrees with Chuck," O'Henry said, as he rolled a cigarette, placed it between his lips and flicked a match. Our debate might have continued, but once Irish touched the match to the tip of his smoke, it fizzed, then popped, leaving his face in a cloud of white smoke.

"Reb sends his regards from upstairs," Jurdon Mark offered. "Said he hoped you are enjoying his smokes."

"Looks like Reb's tobacco is more of a hazard than the Chickasaw," I said.

"We'll see," Muscher shot back. "It's a long way across Indian Territory. Plenty of time for trouble."

We scattered after that. Michaels worked on his sketch book while Silas studied his reader. To help Charlie I took his ax and went out looking for more firewood. I found a clump of trees toward the river where branches had fallen. Cutting them free of the trunk, I turned around one time and flinched at a dozen Indians only thirty feet away, all staring at me. I never heard them slip up nor leave. They were there one moment and gone the next. They never threatened me, just stared, but their stealth left me with an eerie feeling, and I understood how Muscher might be spooked.

In fact everyone bore a case of nerves as evening encroached upon the remnants of our day. While the others worried about Indians, the thing that bothered me was the knowledge of another Texas herd more than a week ahead of us, eating the grass we needed and beating us to Abilene, depriving me of my reward. When we gathered for a supper of beef stew, Sainty told us to keep a night horse saddled and nearby in case the Indians tried to flush our herd or steal more of our animals. We ate our meal quietly. As we bedded down, Silas and I agreed that we would dispense with his reading lesson that night while others checked the loads in their freshly oiled pistols in case Indians attacked.

All that assaulted us when we crawled atop our bedrolls was the gentle breeze drifting from the west and carrying with it the stench of a frightened skunk.

"Damn, Whirlwind" cried Muscher. "That stinks. You better not stampede the herd."

O'Henry, Dire and Beeline laughed with Muscher on the opposite side of the wagon. It was odd how twenty-four hours earlier we had been working so well together, and now we were back to bickering and grating on each other's nerves. Soon I heard the snores of men around me before I drifted off to sleep. Near the end of the second watch, the sound of a horrific squeal awakened the whole camp.

"Aaaarrrrrrggggggghhhhhhhhh!"

"Indians, Indians," someone screamed.

"Shoot him, shoot him," cried another.

I sat and scrambled for my pistol, mad that Muscher's fears had proved right.

On the opposite side of the wagon, I made out a dark form dancing around and screeching like an Indian from hell.

I yanked my gun from my holster and pointed it at the commotion. A gunshot flashed in the night, then another. For a moment, I spotted Beeline fighting off an attacker. I couldn't see the assailant, but he and Toad wrestled as the drover cried for mercy and help.

The ground rumbled.

Three, four, five more shots rang out, then a sixth and a seventh.

The earth beneath me vibrated even more.

Damn the Indians, I thought. They'd started a stampede. I jumped up, shoving my revolver in my holster and grabbing my boots, then hobbling to the wagon to screen me from the Indian attacker on the other side. I could fight Indians or I could try to stem the run. I ran for my night horse, untying him from the wagon tongue and leaping into the saddle. As I kicked his flank, the gelding raced toward the roar of the herd and away from the camp and the attacking savages.

My sure-footed mount burst forward, gaining on the herd while I heard the shouts of Martin Michaels, Tom Errun, Silas Banty and Sainty as they followed me. Jurdon Mark and Harry Dire were riding second watch so they were somewhere up ahead, trying to turn the herd. Mark made a decent hand when he wasn't playing marbles, and Dire performed miracles with a rope, so they stood a chance of turning the steers before they scattered across Indian Territory.

"Ride, boys, ride," cried Sainty as we split, Martin and Tom angling off to the west while the rest of us raced down the east side of the herd. Our main goal was to compress the animals and prevent their scattering over half the country. As I neared the racing steers and their pounding hooves, I felt the heat generated by their exertion and smelled the dust that they kicked into the night air.

"Whoa, boys!" I yelled.

The steers kept running.

My stampede prayer came to mind. I recited it to the cattle just as I had on the first stampede that I had survived. "Now I ride this herd to keep and wish instead that they were sheep. If they should bolt before I'm done, I pray their hooves that I outrun. If I should live for other days, help me outgrow my cowboy ways."

No matter what I called the cattle kept bellowing, bawling and running, but their pace slowed. I prayed that Mark and Dire had turned them. As the cattle tired, I lowered my voice still repeating my prayer time after time. I moved away from the slowing animals as I sensed the head of the herd was turning back on me. Moments later sure enough, Corkscrew and the other leaders doubled around on the rest of the pack as the animals slowed to a walk, then milled against each other. Shortly, I encountered Mark riding toward me.

"Is that you, Lomax?" he called.

"Yeah!"

"What was all the firing?"

"Indians attacked camp," I said.

"Thought you said they wouldn't bother us."

"I've been wrong before."

"Anybody hurt?"

"Beeline was one, but I'm unsure about the others. I raced to help with the cattle."

"Dire and I managed okay, if I say so myself," Mark said. "It was as easy as playing marbles."

"Hell, I'll let you go back and play marbles with the Indians, if you can convince them not to attack us."

"Who else chased the herd?"

"Best I can tell, it was Sainty, Michaels, Errun and Banty."

"I glimpsed Muñoz and Ramírez. That leaves Bitters, Muscher, Beeline and O'Henry back at camp. You think they could hold off the Indians?"

"Can't say," I answered. "I don't remember much shooting after I got on my horse. We may not know until morning."

Mark and I split up after that, riding around, trying to keep the herd contained and driving strays back with the others.

I recited my impromptu prayer as much to calm my nerves as to settle the cattle. I had nothing against the Indians, like I did the malcontents, but even so I'd rather sacrifice a Chickasaw life than one of our men. Though Mark was the only other hand I saw for a spell, we went about our jobs knowing our assignment was to contain the herd, then bed them down and ease their fears. We spent the night settling the animals, and about dawn Sainty reached me. He sighed heavily when he drew up beside me. "Everyone did a fine job best I can tell in the darkness. "We didn't lose any men with the cattle," Sainty informed me, "but I don't know about those in camp. I haven't seen O'Henry, Muscher, Beeline and Bitters."

"Those are the names that Mark and I came up with."

"The cattle'll be fine now as we've enough hands here to contain them. Let's you and I ride back to camp. You got a gun on you?

"Revolver, no carbine."

"Same with me. I don't carry one on my night horse to cut down on weight."

We started back for camp, passing Martin and Errun, advising them of our plan.

"Good luck," Martin said.

"I wasn't expecting an Indian attack. Your medicine must have worn off with the Chickasaws," Errun observed.

"Yeah," Marin noted, "that bracelet of yours isn't worth a damn stopping attacks."

"Or, stampedes," English added.

We rode two and a half miles and light was just pushing the darkness away when we came within sight of camp. A lantern hung from a wagon stave, casting a yellow glow around the rig. I stared without spotting movement."

"Do you see anyone?" Sainty asked.

"No. You think they're dead?"

He shrugged. "Nothing surprises me anymore, not with bad luck we've had lately."

Drawing within a hundred yards of the camp, three shadowy figures jumped up from the ground.

Sainty and I yanked our revolvers, ready to mow down those sneaky Chickasaw.

"Don't shoot, it's me, O'Henry and Bitters!"

"Who's me?" called the trail boss.

"Muscher," came the answer.

"Where's Beeline?"

"He's dead?" O'Henry noted.

"What happened?" Sainty asked.

"Look for yourself, general. You'll find him under his blanket."

Chapter 29

As we neared camp, we understood why Bitters, Muscher and O'Henry had evacuated. The pungent odor of skunk musk attacked our noses. Sainty and I pulled our bandannas over our faces and advanced past the abandoned bedrolls and dying campfire on our side of the wagon to the four bedrolls on the opposite side. We found Beeline sprawled on the ground amidst the bedding, his socked feet protruding from beneath the blanket drawn over him. The stench stung our nostrils, and we gagged as Sainty dismounted. He stepped to the wool cloth and lifted the corner. We gasped at the sight.

Beeline had fallen on his back, the left side of his face unrecognizable, a gory mess. Nothing made sense until Sainty yanked the covering away. Eight bloody bullet wounds peppered his torso. Even worse, Beeline clenched in his right hand a dead skunk. Nauseous like me, the foreman dropped the blanket across the body, mounted his horse and turned him around to rejoin Bitters, O'Henry and Muscher.

The trio awaited us. "Damnedest thing I ever saw," Sainty said, "though I'm not putting all the pieces together."

"Remember the scream?" York asked quietly.

"Who could miss it?" I answered, and Sainty nodded.

"Way we've figure it," Muscher continued, "the skunk came into camp—"

"We believes it rabid," Irish said.

"—and bit Toad on the nose or cheek and gnawed on his face."

"Toad fights that mad varmint, trying to yanks him off," Irish continued.

Muscher grimaced. "Toad's fighting or strangling the skunk. We wake up to the commotion—"

Sainty finished his explanation for him. "—and think he's an Indian."

Both Muscher and O'Henry nodded.

"The way he screams," Irish said, "I knows he's an Indian."

"We emptied our revolvers in him," York whispered.

Silently we looked at each other, shaking our heads.

"God rest his soul," Sainty said.

"We didn't mean to kill him," Muscher added softly.

After a long pause, the foreman replied. "Much as it pains me to say, you may've done him a favor, Chuck. You, too, Bart. The skunk had to be rabid. Toad would've had the hydrophobia and faced a lingering and horrible demise. This way he died quickly."

Muscher shrugged. "Maybe you're right, Sainty."

"I watched a man die with hydrophobia, general," Bitters said. "He turned mean and crazed as if he had a demon in his brain. He craved water, but feared drinking it, and finally twitched and shook himself to death. Not a pretty sight or a decent way to die. It was worse than the broken bodies I saw in the war."

"What's done is done," Sainty said, "and nothing'll bring Toad back."

"What can we do for him?" Muscher asked.

Sainty stroked his chin, then pointed toward camp. "Let's pack up and move away from the stench as fast as we can. When that's done, why don't you and O'Henry dig him a grave?"

Sainty turned to me. "Drive the mules here, while the rest of us load the wagon."

I rode to the remuda, which had scattered during the excitement. After a half hour I had found the mules and rounded up the horses, including Relee. I drove them north of the rig and separated out the two jacks. Occasionally, I glanced at the others, who were rolling up bedrolls and tossing them in the wagon. The fellows worked hurriedly, all of them gagging and Bitters even retching once. I herded the mules to camp and hopped down, harnessing the team and noticing the collars were both beginning to fray and show their stuffing. That was something to fix later. At that moment, we needed to hitch the mules and drive the rig away from the odor.

"What about Toad's bedding?" York asked. "It stinks worse than a sheepherder's socks."

"We'll wrap and bury him in it," Sainty said as everyone scurried to finish packing.

The mules balked at being hitched to the wagon, fighting against the skunk's perfume and perhaps the scent of death. The foreman rode over and used his horse to intimidate the mules into backing up to the rig for hitching to the doubletrees and wagon tongue. As Bitters and I finished hooking up the team, Sainty trotted around the campsite, making sure we had picked up everything. As far as I could tell, only Toad's body and belongings remained. As I climbed onto my night horse, Sainty instructed Irish and York to get in the back of the wagon. As soon as they crawled aboard, Bitters jumped into his seat and started north.

We stopped a thousand feet from the site and breathed the air untainted by the pungent odor, but the stink had perfumed our clothes. After a spell, we came to tolerate it because we couldn't escape it.

"What do I do now, general?" the cook asked. "Do I set up camp or not?"

"All we're doing here is digging a grave and burying Toad. Soon as that's done, we'll move on. Grub may be late today."

"The fellows'll be hungry, riding all night and no breakfast."

"They'll manage better than Toad," the boss replied.

As Muscher and O'Henry jumped from the wagon, Bitters crawled in the back and extracted his shovel and ax. He tossed them on the grass. "Dry as the ground is, you boys'll need them both."

"Find a spot you think Toad would've liked and start digging," Sainty ordered. "Whirlwind, fetch horses for Irish and York, then you and I'll retrieve the body."

I didn't mind bringing the animals back, but I dreaded bringing Beeline to his grave as I smelled bad enough already. Riding to the remuda, I observed Muñoz and Ramírez approaching from the herd. As they neared, I grabbed the reins of the night horses that had been saddled for Muscher and O'Henry.

"Buenas dias," Muñoz said, his smile drooping when he caught a whiff of me. Both he and Ramírez yanked off their hats and fanned their noses. "You stink like a skunk, Whirlwind. Stay away from us."

"There's no escaping it," I said, explaining the sad story of Toad Beeline's demise.

Muñoz stopped fanning himself and did the sign of a cross with his hat. He turned to Ramírez and explained in Spanish my miserable tale for Pedro, who plopped his headgear on and made signed the cross over his chest. "Muy triste," Ramírez said.

"Very sad," Muñoz translated for me. "What does the boss want us to do? We came back for the horses as the cattle are settled."

"Though he didn't say, I'd suggest you drive the remuda up with the herd, and we'll join you once we bury Toad. No sense in all of us stinking."

"Gracias," the wrangler answered.

I turned my horse around and started for the wagon, leading the two horses. Reaching the others, I informed Sainty of my instructions to Muñoz.

"Good. Nothing he and Pedro can do here except stink, and the five of us smell bad enough for the whole outfit. Let's fetch Toad."

I asked Bitters to tie the reins of Muscher's and O'Henry's horses, then accompanied Sainty to the death site, pulling our bandannas over our noses as we neared the body. Our mounts fought against us, backing away when we halted them over the corpse. Dismounting and handing me his reins, Sainty stepped over and yanked back the blanket. He kicked at the skunk, trying to knock it from Toad's hand, but the fatal grip was too tight.

"It'll have to stay," he said. "I'm not touching that damned varmint because I don't want the hydrophobia."

"Don't blame you."

The trail boss spread the blanket beside Beeline, then marched to the opposite side and stuck his boot under the body and lifted his foot, trying to roll him onto the wool spread. It was slow work, moving from his torso to his legs to push Beeline to the middle of the blanket. "That'll have to do," Sainty said to himself as much as to me. Throughout the ordeal, Toad's dead fingers remained frozen around the varmint's neck. The foreman bowed his head, saying a silent prayer, then pulled the blanket over the bloodied face that would never feel sunlight again. He tugged the cloth across Beeline's body. With his boot he nudged Toad's arm closer to the torso and kicked at the skunk again. Poor Toad, it seemed, would carry that skunk to the Pearly Gates. Sainty picked up the other side of the cover and draped it over the corpse.

Next Sainty took his lariat from his saddle and tied it around the blanket at Toad's feet. He uncoiled the rope as he backtracked to his horse, mounted and secured the lasso to the saddle horn. I handed him his reins and pointed at Toad's boots, bedding and belongings? "What about his things?"

"Leave them there. They stink to high hell, and we'll have a hard enough time ridding ourselves of this stench without bringing more of it into camp."

"Good by me. We started for the wagon, dragging the body behind us. You should've let me help bundle him up," I offered.

"Felt I had to do it on my own. I had a responsibility to get Parsons and Beeline back to Texas safely. I failed."

"Way I look at it, Sainty, neither died because of you. Parsons expired in his sleep. A rabid skunk killed Beeline, even if the others shot him."

"But if I hadn't returned everyone's guns yesterday

evening."

"You told York and Irish he'd died a more horrible death from hydrophobia than bullets."

"Maybe so, Lomax, but their deaths weigh on my mind."

"The losses are a burden on everyone, but no one blames you."

We dragged Toad's mortal remains back to the wagon where Muscher and O'Henry had hewn a grave out of the stubborn ground. The hole looked barely three feet deep, but both York and Irish sweated from the effort.

"Is this good enough?" Muscher asked Sainty.

"It'll have to do," the foreman answered, "because we've got to catch up with the herd."

"Good," said Irish. "I'm tireds and I didn't hires on to be doing slave work."

"Toad'd do the same for you," Sainty replied as he slid off his horse.

I dismounted as well and joined our trail boss as he strode to the blanket-wrapped body. He yanked on the rope so his mount backed up and gave him enough slack to loosen the loop around Beeline's feet. We bent to lift him but before we could, Muscher and O'Henry came over and helped us. Together we carried Toad Beeline to his last resting place and eased him in his grave, sorry that fate had dealt him so poor a hand.

After we placed him in the ground, we surrounded Beeline and removed our hats, standing silently, lost in our own thoughts about his mortality and ours. The presence of death humbles any man of sound mind. None of us knew what to say. Sainty cleared his throat, shifting his hat from hand to hand at his waist. "Toad Beeline made a good drover, and we're sorry to lose him." He paused, casting his gaze one by one upon us. He shrugged. "I'm ashamed to say I know little about Toad other than that. I wish we could give him a better burial like we did for Reb."

"We should say a prayer," I offered. We shifted on our feet and looked at each other, shrugging at our loss for words that matched the grandeur of death. "Perhaps

Irish could say his Lord's Prayer," I suggested.

O'Henry grimaced, then nodded and recited the childhood plea. "Now I lay me down to sleep. I pray Thee Lord, my soul to keep. If I should die before I wake, I pray Thee Lord, my soul to take. If I should live for other days, I pray Thee Lord, to guide my ways."

"Amen," we said in unison as we put on our hats.

Sainty grabbed the shovel and scooped dirt back atop Beeline. As the foreman covered Toad, the cook retreated to the wagon and pulled a slat off of a crate and with a butcher knife carved Beeline's name in the wood. "It's not much," Bitters admitted, "but it beats nothing out here on the Plains."

In a half hour the trail boss had mounded the grave over and tamped it down with the back of the spade. Bitters walked over and shoved the impromptu marker into the soft dirt.

"We'll buy a decent one in Abilene and provide a more fitting memorial. I want you to look around and remember this place so we can find his grave on the return trip. I doubt this wood will last."

After a couple minutes of staring at landmarks in relation to the Red River cut, we branded our memory with the location and mounted our horses, riding off and leaving Beeline alone. I don't know about the others, but I wondered if I'd wind up in a lonely, unmarked grave in the vastness of the Plains. The thought was sobering.

When we reached the herd, we found the animals at ease and grazing. The other drovers wanted the particulars of Beeline's death until they got close enough to whiff us. Then they retreated, deciding details would wait. What couldn't wait was food as nobody had eaten since the meager offerings the previous night. Bitters passed out jerky and dried apricots, though the fellows who had stayed with the cattle had to hold their noses to take it from him.

"What's the plan, boss?" asked Martin Michaels.

"I'm not sure. Lomax, how far are we from water."

While I had tried to remember the next watercourse,

I stood confused. "I'm thinking there's a creek a half day from here."

"We need water for drinking, washing and bathing," Sainty noted.

"I could use a bath," Sketch said, as several others nodded their agreement.

"Okay, men, let's mount up and get the herd moving. Charlie, you ride ahead as fast as you're comfortable and find the water, if you can, and set up camp there. Fix as big a meal as possible. Lomax, you'll take Beeline's place on the flank opposite Silas. Any questions?"

"Yeah," answered York. "Have we got time for a smoke?"

"Sure, Chuck."

Muscher, Dire and O'Henry pulled out their tobacco and rolled their smokes, Irish even offering Banty tobacco for a change.

Silas waved his offer away. "I not be wanting to be indebted to any man, evens for a smoke."

O'Henry smiled, glad to save Parson's tobacco for himself.

Muscher struck a match and lit his, then Dire's and O'Henry's. As Irish inhaled, his cigarette fizzed and popped, shrouding his head in a puff of white smoke. Once again Trent Parsons had reached from beyond the grave to slap Irish in the face.

Everyone snickered, including O'Henry, who pulled the tobacco pouch from his shirt pocket and tossed it away. "Another bag ruined," he said.

By then Bitters was driving the wagon north, and Muñoz and Ramírez had retreated to the remuda. The rest of us got on our horses and headed for the cattle to get them moving. Some steers balked, but most arose, their heads pointing toward Kansas as if they knew the direction to go if not the fate that awaited them. Point riders Martin Michaels and Tom Errun managed Corkscrew and the leaders, getting them up and walking. Jurdon Mark and Harry Dire followed in the swing position while Banty and I eased into the flank posts, leaving only Muscher and O'Henry riding drag. As they were the lesser hands, I worried that they would lose too many strays, but they handled the steers well, never letting one escape that I saw, perhaps because the cattle had grown accustomed to the routine or perhaps because they wanted to wring the guilt out of their minds for shooting Toad Beeline.

As we headed north, we sometimes noticed clumps of Indians standing in the distance, watching us. I removed my hat to confirm the eagle feather had remained in place. It had. Who was I to deny the Indians a chance to see a man with my powers? Whatever medicine I carried I prayed was strong enough to frighten off animals. After losing Toad, we advanced with more fear of rabid skunks and other varmints than we did of Indians. I noticed signs that another herd had preceded us. We tramped a trail littered with the dried dung from a thousand or more cattle, I estimated. While that was half the size we started with, that would still be enough to ruin any bonus I was due from Joseph G. McCoy. Riding flank beat working drag, but it fell far short of scouting the route ahead of the herd. I had to admit I'd had it easy until then, but I now had to prove my worth to everyone.

As the day lengthened, the sunlight lessened, and I feared my memory had betrayed me in finding the next creek. The sun slipped behind the horizon and the twilight brought a silky light that softened the sky as it faded to darkness. I kept the cattle moving, but looked for any rabid skunks that might attack me or my mount. When night enveloped us, and I feared my recollections were askew, I spotted glow in the distance that had to be our cook's campfire. We drove the animals toward the fire. Sure enough, Bitters was tending the flames and even better I noted beyond him the dim line of trees snaking along the creek.

Sainty rode up, ordering us to let the cattle graze but keep them from spreading out too far if they went to water. The herd slowed and the steers foraged while the thirstier among them caught the aroma of water and headed for the stream. Since we arrived after dark, we ate in shifts so someone was always attending the steers. Bitters had fixed cornbread and the saltiest beans I'd ever eaten. The cook apologized for the beans, offering regrets he didn't have better fare, saying nothing had gone right since he had set up camp. He said he had walked to the creek to get a bucket of water, then slipped and fell in up to his waist. Back at the wagon he had picked a sack of salt up by the wrong end and spilled most on his pants and some of it in a pot of beans he was cooking. We accepted his contrition as we were too tired to complain.

More than our salty fare or Indians, we worried over another rabid skunk slipping into camp and attacking. "What are we gonna do about skunks?" Muscher asked as he ate. "I'm damn sure gonna sleep with my face covered from now until to Abilene."

"Don't know there's much we can do," Sainty responded, looking at Bitters. "How are we on firewood?"

"Plenty here with more by the creek."

"Then stack it by the fire. We'll keep it burning tonight. I don't know if the fire'll scare them away, but at least we'll be able to see. Every time we change a shift, the fellows that come in to sleep can add wood to the fire and maintain it. We'll have plenty of occasions tomorrow to chop more wood since we'll be cleaning up and ridding ourselves of the skunk stench. As for food, I've picked out a steer Charlie can kill for meat."

Riding flank meant I rode the third of four watches. I would not enjoy another uninterrupted night of sleep until Abilene. As I returned that first night from watch, I roused O'Henry and Muscher, tossed logs on the fire and tried to catch two more hours sleep before a new day and the same old chores. Bitters had bacon and biscuits waiting when we woke up. We worked in shifts to wash our clothes and bathe in the creek with the lye soap Bitters provided. We scrubbed away, trying to eliminate the skunk stench that had seeped into our garments. None succeeded, though we cut enough of the odors that those who hadn't buried Beeline could stand to bed beside those who had. Our cook heated water for shaving if we were tired of our whiskers, and he pulled a pair of scissors from his sewing kit to trim our hair.

While we were getting clean and civilized, Bitters shot the steer the foreman provided, then butchered it for meat to last the next two days. Returning to camp, he started a pot of stew before heading to the creek to bathe and wash his clothes. He stripped first and bathed, draping his pants and shirt over a bush. While he was bathing and singing to himself, Corkscrew came to water. After drinking his fill, he passed Bitters' pants, sniffed the salt and grabbed the britches in his mouth, trotting away without Charlie ever noticing. Things might have ended well except another steer whiffed the salt and bit onto one of the denim legs. After that the two longhorns tugged and fought over the pants. By the time they settled their disagreement, the trousers had been shredded into a dozen pieces and that many steers were walking around the herd, soaking up the salt from scraps.

When Charlie emerged from the creek, he discovered his britches were missing, but figured it was a prank by one of us. He washed his shirt, socks and long johns, then jumped back in the stream while his clothes dried. After an hour of enjoying the cool water, he got out, put on the remaining garments, pulled on his boots and walked to camp, promising to shoot whoever stole his trousers. Everybody denied it and thought it a big mystery until Jurdon Mark rode up.

"Anybody lose his britches?" he asked.

"So you're the no good dog that stole 'em," Bitters cried, reaching for his pants.

Mark dropped a denim remnant into the cook's fingers. "It wasn't me, but Corkscrew. I saw him and another steer fighting over them. Your britches were ripped to shreds."

"Damn," Bitters said. "I don't have another pair."

"Must've been the salt you spilled," Sainty offered. "Cattle get salt thirsty after a while."

Bitters mumbled curses as he grabbed his bib apron from the tailgate, hung it over his head and tied it around his waist. "You fellows will have to put up with a cook without pants."

"We can accept that, Charlie," Mark responded, "but don't fix our meals if you lose your drawers."

Chapter 30

Once I was riding flank and taking the third watch, the days ran together, one inseparable from the other with the constants of stifling dust, bellowing cattle, lingering animosities among the drovers, and food that went down poorly but, even so, better than it came out. In what spare time we had, Michaels still produced pencil drawings; Errun still lectured us on the ways of English life; Banty still worked on his reading lessons; Muñoz and Ramírez still managed the remuda; Sainty still tried to keep the drive moving; and Bitters, still pantless, cooked our meals, mostly beans, which he had taken to calling "Arkansas strawberries" in my honor. Muscher, Dire and O'Henry still bitched about everything.

As we passed through Indian Territory, folks still came out to see me for my strong medicine so I kept the eagle feather in my hatband. Somehow word of my approach moved faster than the herd so most days saw men, women and children awaiting us. I always looked for True Shot but never spotted him among the folks lining the trail to watch me. Occasionally, one of the Indians begged for a steer on behalf of his family. If they looked hungry, Sainty obliged with a malingering animal. By my count he lost a dozen steers this way. Sainty was more benevolent than the Indian agencies that served the various tribes. The Indians left us alone, and we tried to do the same for them, steering our cattle away from their modest homes and crops as they adapted to the White Man's ways. We also skirted those agencies and the Army forts to avoid any trouble with the government as we remained uncertain how officials viewed our trespassing on tribal lands.

We traversed more creeks and rivers than I could count, but we had become so jaded we no longer saw any humor in O'Henry's water crossings. When we reached the Salt Fork of the Arkansas, O'Henry faced his greatest challenge since plunging into the Red to help the wagon. He had tired of riding in saturated britches after so many water crossings and took off his pants and tied them around his neck. The water proved deeper than he expected with both him and his horse going under before he grabbed the horse's tail, allowing his mount to swim out. Unfortunately, his pants came loose, and he held onto the tail to save himself rather than his pants. His britches floated away, then settled to the bottom of the Salt Fork.

When Sainty checked on the drags, he spotted Irish and shook his head. "Is anybody in this outfit gonna have pants by the time we reach Abilene?" He huddled with Muscher and O'Henry to count the losses other than garments. They estimated twenty had drowned or floated away with the current.

A few days shy of a month we entered Kansas. We knew it to be true because the Indians disappeared and we faced a meaner tribe of people—homesteaders. They were a stingy and suspicious lot so we tried to swing wide of the sod homes they protected like mansions, though the dwellings were made of dirt and straw. When they saw us approaching, the men rode out on their bareback mules with a double-barreled shotgun resting across their legs and informed us we weren't welcome anywhere near their places or crops because the longhorns carried Texas fever that destroyed Kansas livestock. Sainty offered them a steer for beef, but even then they declined the gift for fear of the malady spreading from the longhorn to their own stock. After riding all the way from the Lone Star State with this herd and crew, I questioned whether the cattle even caused the disease. Instead of the longhorns, I figured it was the mangy Texans themselves that spread the fever.

The homesteaders threatened Sainty with the law since he was inside the dead line, though I had assured the foreman that Joseph G. McCoy had fixed it with the governor for lawmen to look the other way. Sainty called their bluff, saying he would bed his cattle down right there until the settler summoned the sheriff to arrest him. Not wanting the dangerous herd parked near their own stock, the nesters caved and waved us on with instructions to get out of their sight immediately. Sainty tried to bargain with every settler for an old pair of britches to clothe his outfit, but the pioneers cared more about their property than they did the decency of Bitters and O'Henry. Those fine, upstanding Kansans were mean enough to slip rattlesnake in your pocket and then ask to borrow a dime. And those were just the women!

Somehow we zigzagged around the various homesteads and stirred up no more trouble than was manageable, except in camp where tensions grew each day. We tired of each other's company, and we needed something to release steam before we killed each other. After crossing the Arkansas River without human casualty, though we lost another thirty-six head of cattle, Sainty found Jesse Chisholm's trading post and purchased pants for Irish and Bitters. I regretted not going to thank the old fellow for the bracelet that had eased my way with Indians, but I was too tired to accompany the foreman.

That evening, Bitters and O'Henry put on new denim britches, each man as proud as a billy goat with four horns. The next day we continued our journey to Abilene. We had been three weeks in Kansas and as we neared our destination, I no longer worried if Joseph G. McCoy had built his dream railhead. By then I was so tired of trail dust, cow dung, monotonous food and the same old chatter we'd heard since leaving San Antone. Tom Errun ran out of British words after supper one night when he announced, "I'm still peckish."

"Did you say you were a pecker?" I inquired.

"No, peckish. How would you Americans say it? Hungry I suppose."

"Oh," I said.

"What's a pecker?" he asked.

For once, I shocked Errun that I knew a word he didn't and incensed him when I defined it for him. Errun didn't speak to me for a whole day after I expanded his vocabulary. As for all his prattle, his definitions had diminished in value after tora-loorals way back in Texas.

Jurdon Mark grunted his displeasure when no one played marbles any more as we'd all lost to him dozens of times since starting the drive. Silas Banty grumbled that, despite his superb teacher, he wasn't reading as well as he would like, though he was better at it than the average Democrat. Martin Michaels complained that he was running out of paper for his sketches. Even the unflappable Jose Muñoz turned grumpy and Ramírez, too, though we never understood his Spanish enough to know why. Dire, Muscher and O'Henry bitched about everything as usual.

Exhaustion set in from it all, the past weeks being the worst of my young life. The medicine I'd had in Indian Territory didn't serve me well in Kansas so I yanked the eagle feather from my hatband and threw it in the remnants of an evening fire. Cowboying was hard work. I'd had it easy the first half of the drive, but after Parsons' and Beeline's deaths, I rode flank and took the third watch each night. Only thoughts of Ruth pulled me through, that and the drawing Michaels had sketched for me, though it was worn, faded and smudged. Some evenings after supper, I'd pull it from my pocket and stare at it, looking at the lips I'd kissed and longing for the day when I would caress her again, but that day was still weeks away. Thoughts of her and the pot of gold beneath the Abilene rainbow got me through the tedious days remaining on the trail.

Each new morning we put aside our differences and drove the steers toward Abilene. Along the trail,

I noticed we were catching up to the herd we had been tracking since the Red River. The tracks and the cow dung looked fresher and the grass was eaten closer to the ground, meaning it hadn't had time to grow since the preceding longhorns had grazed it. I figured they were two maybe three days ahead of us at most. Unlike us, they had likely slackened the pace to give the animals a chance to put on weight before reaching Abilene.

One evening as we were bedding the cattle, three men approached on horses from the north. They stopped to blather with Sainty, who invited them to share our camp. When I came in the trail boss motioned for me to come over and introduced me to Colonel O.W. Wheeler and his associates Wilson and Hicks. They had driven longhorns from Texas ahead of us and sold all twelve hundred steers. My hopes of the bonus fell flatter than a miser mistaking a chicken dropping for a quarter.

"How'd you learn of Abilene?" I asked.

"Saw it on a flyer in Austin."

Damn, I thought. I'd killed my own bonus. "How were the facilities in Abilene?"

"Didn't see any," Wheeler said.

Sainty gave me a look that would've scorched granite.

"What do you mean, you didn't see any?" Sainty asked them, but glared at me.

"We never made it to Abilene, the three of us. Our hands did, but not us."

"How do you explain that?" Sainty asked, the exasperation rising in his voice.

"Some northern buyers met us two days this side of Abilene, men representing Smith, McCord and Chandler. They offered us a good price in cash right there, and we sold the herd, never laid eyes on Abilene. We paid our hands, and the buyers hired them to finish herding them to Abilene."

Satisfied with the answer, Sainty cocked his head and stared at Wheeler. "Why didn't you ride into Abilene after such a long, hard drive?"

Wheeler twisted in his saddle and patted his saddle bags. "It's hazardous to herd cattle seven hundred miles, but not nearly as dangerous as getting your money home, especially when folks know about it. You're aware of how drovers think, aren't you? I didn't want one or two of them deciding I owed them more than their wages. By the time they got the herd to Abilene and celebrated, we'd have a four-day lead on them. Driving cattle to Kansas is only half the job."

Sainty grimaced. "I never considered that."

"Honest men seldom do," Wheeler said.

The foreman invited the three to stay for supper and spend the night at our camp. They accepted the hospitality and even complimented Charlie Bitters on his beans, bacon, cornbread and syrup. "I wish our cook had been this good," Wheeler said.

We hands stared at each other, wondering if the cattleman had a defective tongue or an appetite for misery. "Bonito," I said.

"Remember the Alamo!" Jurdon Mark cried.

"Remember the Alamo!" Wheeler, Wilson and Hicks replied.

The next morning, our guests headed south and we pointed north as we had every day for almost three months. Our spirits rose as we started, certain our journey was nearing completion, eager for hot baths and shaves, and maybe even liquid refreshment to cut the trail dust from our throats. In fact, we might play something other than marbles if we found a saloon with a square dealer. Two days later, Abilene appeared in the distance. It resembled nothing I remembered. Stock pens with lumber still slick from newness gleamed in the sun and loading chutes lined the railroad tracks. Next to the stockyards stood a new barn with an attached pen for a hundred horses. Nearer town was a three-story hotel that promised feather mattresses and clean sheets. McCoy had fulfilled his dream and not only saved my hide but also fattened my wad of cash, assuming he still remembered me.

Sainty directed us to a crook in the Smoky Hill River where the watercourse limited the steers' options to run on three sides, and we set up camp behind them to block that side. It was the best campsite on the trip because we realized it was our last before we sold those damnable longhorns.

After we settled the steers to grazing, we gathered for lunch. As we ate, Sainty told us he intended to head into town and find Joseph G. McCoy to strike a favorable deal. The foreman planned to take Bitters along to buy more grub for the next day or two, depending on how the sale proceeded.

"We want town time this evening," Muscher announced.

"Yeah," said O'Henry.

"Me, too," Dire whispered.

"Not tonight," Sainty replied, stomping his foot. "This is the first night we've camped so close to town. There are a lot of strange noises the cattle aren't used to. Everyone is to keep their regular watch and sleep with night horses saddled."

The malcontents grumbled, but the rest of us understood. I wanted to bathe in the Smoky Hill River and make myself presentable before I visited McCoy and got the remaining hundred dollars he owed me plus my per head bonus for leading a herd to Kansas.

After Bitters finished washing the dishes, he mounted a horse Muñoz had saddled for him and rode with Sainty into Abilene. We decided among ourselves who would watch the cattle and Dire, Muscher and O'Henry insisted they would handle the afternoon chores. The rest of us understood their uncharacteristic offer was merely to keep their evening free so they could sneak into town and celebrate, Sainty be damned.

Silas Banty and I retreated to the river with lye soap and a razor and spent thirty minutes washing out clothes and another hour in the river washing ourselves and shaving off our whiskers. All the time, Silas wanted to work on his reading so I would call out words like "talk," "horse," "church" and "poker" for him to spell. We enjoyed dreaming about the future. My future had Ruth in it, and his was owning a ranch like Colonel Dillon. I figured his dream was less likely than mine to come true, him being a former slave, but I didn't say that, not caring to demean his hopes. He talked about finding a decent woman to marry, explaining he wanted a literate wife so they could buy and read a Bible together.

I remembered Reb's Bible in my saddle bags. "When we get back to camp, I've got something I want to give you, Silas."

"No sir, Lomax. I be indebteds to you enough for you educating me to read. I can't be taking nothing more from you, no sir."

"My gift didn't cost me a thing, and it won't cost you a cent either."

"If that be the truth, so be it."

We splashed around in the water until we figured our clothes were dry, climbed out, dried off and returned to camp, feeling as fresh as a newly printed greenback. While Banty grabbed his bedroll from the wagon and threw it on the ground, I went to Relee and extracted Trent Parsons' Bible from my saddlebags. By the time I reached Silas, he was reclining on his bedding reviewing his McGuffey's Reader.

When he looked up, I offered him the Good Book. "This was Reb's. I wanted it as a gift for you when you could read."

"But I ain't be learned yet as I don't be knowing all the words."

"You never will, Silas. Reading is like life. You learn something every day. Take it."

Banty dropped his reader on his blanket and jumped up, hugging me first, then taking the Bible. "I'll be taking good care of it. I be promising you that."

"I know you will."

Reverently, he took the book and looked up at me. "You be thinking I can read it now?"

"Try."

He opened the Bible to the first chapter. "Ge … gen—"

"Gen-e-sis," I helped.

"Genesis," he said, then continued. "In the be-gining God creeee—"

"Created."

"—created the hee-ven—"

"Heaven."

"—and ear-th."

"Earth."

"—earth."

"You did it, Silas, you did it," I bragged. "You'll get better with time and practice."

"Thank you, Whirlwind, thank you," he answered, prouder than Adam without a fig leaf. "I never be expecting my own Bible so soon. Maybe one day I be having my own ranch."

I left him alone and walked over to Michaels, who was making another sketch. "You've been drawing a lot, mind showing me some of your pictures?"

"Sure, but they're not that good."

He flipped through his pad, and I shook my head in disbelief. His drawings struck me as unbelievable. How could a man who did such rough work with ropes and cattle have such a delicate hand for art? Not only that, he labeled each drawing, not with a cursive handwriting but with letters so precisely drawn that they looked like they had been printed by a press. "You ever done anything in ink?" I asked him.

"Can't afford ink and pens," he answered.

"I'll buy some for you if you'll do another one of Ruth in ink as my pencil sketch is getting smudged."

Michaels smiled. "I'm not surprised as much as I see you pulling it from your pocket each evening. I'll even do you a couple other ink sketches if you like."

"Let me think about it."

Sainty and Bitters rejoined us late afternoon, both carrying gunny sacks and smiling as if they had dead Republicans in the bags.

The cook lifted his gunny sack. "Fried chicken to-night. Bought five from the butcher."

I couldn't believe the Abilene I had visited in the spring now had a butcher's shop.

Sainty pointed at his bag. "Potatoes, canned tomatoes and green beans plus oatmeal cookies or biscuits as the English general calls them. We got butter as well."

344

The foreman looked at me and nodded. "Too, I've sold the herd for more than enough to save Colonel Dillon's ranch and even buy more land. Lomax, you were right about Abilene and McCoy."

I was just relieved that McCoy had lived up to his word and not sent me on a fool's errand.

Sainty informed us, we'd cross the river in the morning and take the herd to the stock pens to get a count and determine the final total at twenty-two dollars and fifty cents a head. "You'll get paid tomorrow afternoon once I receive the cash from McCoy. I suspect it'll be around three o'clock. Even though Drovers Cottage, as McCoy calls his eighteen-thousand-dollar hotel, isn't finished, I've arranged for us to spend the next two nights there on feather mattresses, two to a room. It's on me boys. One more night sleeping on the ground and tending cattle, then it's mattresses for two nights before we start back to Texas."

We cheered, even the three shirkers. Sainty checked the longhorns while Bitters asked me and Silas to build a fire as he cut up and floured the chicken and peeled the potatoes for boiling. Everyone pitched in to help with supper, but with the late start, it was near dark when we finished eating, and Bitters had done the dishes. O'Henry, Dire and Muscher tossed their bedrolls on the opposite side of the wagon from the rest of us as usual. Then they made a big deal about swapping out their mounts for their night horses, but all save Sainty and Bitters suspected they planned to sneak into town and celebrate before returning in time for their watch.

Sainty never caught on as he was so excited about the price he was getting for the beef. The three shirkers put their saddle bags and gear under their blankets to make it appear they were sleeping as normal. They even left their hats at the end of their beds to further the ploy.

After the first watch had departed for the herd and the rest of us had reclined on our bedding, they led their night horses around the herd and toward the river, mounted and crossed into Abilene to celebrate. When Jurdon Mark woke me for my watch, he was angered

Dire hadn't returned in time to take his shift. "I doubt they'll relieve you," Mark said, "but I'm heading back out until you and Silas arrive since no one else is watching the cattle."

Arising, I awakened Banty, who put on his boots, his gun belt and his hat and was soon atop his horse, riding out with me. I explained that Dire had already missed his shift, and I doubted O'Henry and Muscher would relieve us.

"No surprise," Banty replied. "Can't be depending on them for nothing."

We relieved Mark. "I hope they return in two hours," he offered.

"We're not counting on it," I said. "Even if they come back, who knows what shape they'll be in."

"Rouse me if you need more help," Mark replied as he rode off to bed.

As we expected, the malcontents didn't return until dawn. When they did, they were drunk and arguing, O'Henry cursing the loudest, furious about something and threatening to kill someone.

Banty trotted over. "Think they'll spook the cattle?"

"It's light enough the cattle can see. They're the jumpiest in the dark."

We angled our horses over to intercept them and direct them around the cattle, but before we reached them, O'Henry jerked out his revolver. He fired three times at the cattle before Muscher knocked him out of the saddle.

The cattle jumped to their feet and tossed their heads, but held steady. The next thing I heard was from the wagon.

"What the hell's going on?" yelled Sainty.

Chapter 31

With enough daylight to inspect their surroundings, the longhorns looked around, then settled down. I trotted my night horse to the river, inspecting the herd and finding by the water three dead animals. Jogging to the wagon, I answered Sainty. "I'll tell you what happened," I shouted. "Irish, York and Dire went out tom-catting last night and missed their watch. And O'Henry shot a trio of steers."

Dire and Muscher rode up to camp, leading O'Henry's horse and singing "Camptown Races."

"Where's Irish?" Sainty demanded. "Why'd he kill three steers?"

The duet continued crooning as they reined up and saluted Sainty. "Reporting for duty, general," Muscher giggled.

"You're drunk," the foreman stated. "I ordered you to stay in camp until we got the cattle to the pens."

"We had certain urges," Dire snickered, his normal soft voice strengthened by liquor.

"Whiskey and wine," York said, but corrected himself. "I mean whemen and 'iskey."

" 'Fancy Nancy,' she called herself," Dire announced boldly.

"More like 'Big Mouth' Nancy," Muscher chuckled. "She could talk the loincloth off a wooden Indian."

I decided that was a useful skill for her profession.

"She was a dollar a bedding," Dire proclaimed.

"Old enough to be Methuselah's girlfriend," York added. "Claimed to be the only harlot in town."

Dire sobbed. "Poor Bart. He didn't get none. Big Mouth said she wouldn't bed his kind."

"We felt so bad for the Irish we did Fancy Nancy twice," York explained, yanking his hat off, "but you know what? That didn't cheer Irish at all. He was so mad, he shot those steers to put them out of his misery."

Sainty had heard enough. "Clear out," he commanded. "Swap your night horses for your own mounts, gather your belongings and leave."

Dire and Muscher hesitated, looking at each other with uncomprehending eyes.

"Find me in town this afternoon to collect your pay, less the cost of three steers. No stay at the hotel either. I'm done with you fellows and O'Henry."

Muscher's and Dire's celebration fizzled, their minds muddled by their revelry and their firing.

"Get out of your saddles and get out of here," Sainty demanded.

The pair remained as still and dense as the wooden Indian Big Mouth could charm.

"Let me help," Sainty said, stepping beside their mounts and jerking them out of the saddle. They hit the ground like a ton of stupidity, struggling to get to their feet.

By then all the hands were up and listening. Martin Michaels said, "I'll swap out their horses." He walked over and grabbed the reins.

"I'll help and good riddance," spat Tom Errun.

Jurdon Mark volunteered to tie up their bedrolls while Muñoz and Ramírez cut the trio's horses from the remuda.

Sainty turned to me. "You're mounted. Find O'Henry and throw his revolver in the river so he shoots no more of my steers or one of us."

"Sure thing, boss," I said, turning my mount toward the Smoky Hill River and Abilene. I found O'Henry sprawled on the ground, a big goose egg growing on his right forehead where York had slugged him. Dismounting and spotting his empty holster, I walked around until I found his pistol. I grabbed the revolver and flung it into the river, enjoying the splash as it disappeared beneath the ripples. I damn sure wasn't going to carry O'Henry back to camp, so I took off my hat and filled it with water and returned to Irish. Standing over him, I dumped the liquid over his face. His eyes opened, full of bewilderment. I swatted his cheeks with my hat.

"You're crossing the river, Irish," I shouted. "Don't fall off your horse."

O'Henry screamed and flailed his arms as if he were drowning.

I grabbed him and yanked him to his feet. He was as confused as a steer at mating time.

"Slide off your saddle and grab your horse's tail so you don't drown," I yelled as I walked him over to my night horse. I lifted the tail and stuck it into his hands, his dazed mind still muddled by liquor and the ample knot on his forehead. As his fingers tightened around my mount's tail, I jumped in the saddle, wondering if my mount would put up with O'Henry pulling on his tail or just kick him to be done with it. Night horses didn't spook easily so he plodded toward camp, never unleashing the flashing hooves that O'Henry deserved.

"Hang on, Black Bart, so you don't drown," I yelled. Irish was so dazed, he never realized I'd called him by the nickname he detested.

As we neared camp, he screamed, "I'm drowning. Get me to land."

Everyone but Dire and Muscher chuckled.

"You can't do this, Sainty," York repeated several times.

Behind me, I heard O'Henry mumbling. Twisting in my saddle, I laughed. He was shaking like a wet dog. "You made it to the river bank, Irish."

He released my horse's tail and fell to the ground sobbing.

Michaels and Errun returned their horses. I dismounted to help Mark tie their bedrolls atop their mounts. We all boosted them back on their horses.

"Lomax, make certain they get across the river," Sainty said, turning to his former hands. "Find me in Abilene this afternoon and we'll settle your wages."

Muscher shook his head of the whiskey-induced cobwebs. "You'll get your due, Sainty, both you and Lomax."

Sainty swatted Muscher's horse on the rump and the animal trotted toward the river.

I clicked my tongue and started O'Henry and Dire moving the same direction as I herded them to the Smoky Hill. When we reached the water, Dire plunged right in, but Bartholomew Henry O'Henry hesitated as usual. Deciding to help him along, I yanked off my hat, swatted his mount on the rump and whistled. The gelding bolted into the river, Irish screaming like a hungry baby, though the water was at most three feet deep. O'Henry made it across.

I returned to camp, excited about payday and shedding Dire, Muscher and O'Henry from our outfit. Back at the wagon, I had never seen so many smiles. Everybody was grinning like possums eating persimmons. While Charlie Bitters packed the wagon, we swapped the night horses for our own mounts, then hitched the mule team to the rig and watched the cook start for the rock-bottomed wagon crossing.

Sainty examined the rig as Bitters pulled away. "The harness and collars are mighty worn. I may have to buy replacements."

"I've repaired harness leather before," I told him. "I can help."

Sainty nodded. "José has too. Maybe you can work on them tonight. I've arranged to shelter and feed our horses in McCoy's barn for two nights. We'll give them plenty of hay and oats so they'll be stronger for the return home. Can you believe it, Lomax? We made it!"

"I'm ready to get back to Texas," I said, as we mounted up to move the herd for the last time. We drove the longhorns across the river where I had spooked O'Henry's horse. When we got the final steer out of the water on the Abilene side, we shouted to success. Martin

Michaels, Tom Errun, Jurdon Mark, Silas Banty, José Muñoz, Pedro Ramírez, myself and even the foreman whooped and hollered with delight. We trotted the steers to the stockyards, directing them into the pens, Sainty and McCoy's representative counting the animals as they trotted in.

When the last steer ran inside, and the yard hands closed the gates, Sainty and McCoy's man huddled while us drovers gathered to await the total. Sainty joined us, a huge smile on his face. "Eighteen hundred and thirty-six head," the foreman announced.

"Remember the Alamo!" Mark cried. "Eighteen thirty-six is the year the Alamo fell."

"Why are you fellows always remembering the Alamo? You lost."

"It's the Alamo," Mark explained. "Sure it was a failure, but failure breeds success, and success breeds greatness. Texas is destined for greatness."

What escaped me at the moment was that by getting the first herd to Abilene, I had pioneered the path for the state's greatness as the cattle trade would make Texas a wealthy state. And instead of getting any credit, the trail came to be known as the Chisholm Trail. I never got a penny for my work beyond what McCoy paid me before and after the drive. Though I had a debt to Jesse Chisholm for giving me the bracelet that warded off the Indians, I didn't owe him the fame that went with the trail I blazed to Abilene. At the time, I wasn't bitter because I thought I had made a fortune as it was, and I had Ruth to return to. The only thing I learned that day was not to spit on the Alamo's memory, at least when Texans were around.

After the herd was penned, Sainty rode with the yard man to McCoy's office to finalize the sale. At the small building beaming with a fresh coat of white paint, our foreman dismounted and removed from atop his own saddlebags the ones that once belonged to Trent Parsons. As the other hands headed toward the barn, I directed Relee to McCoy's place as it was time to renew our acquaintance. I tied my bay to the hitching rail and waited in the shade until my boss finished.

Sainty emerged from the office with the saddlebags hanging over his shoulder and a grin as wide as the Red River roiling across his face. The horse satchel was bulging with the profits from the trail drive. "We did it, Lomax." He patted the saddlebags. "In here's the money we'll need for the Five-D to survive and prosper. We are indebted to you, and I suspect the colonel will give you a bonus when we return."

"Ruth will be bonus enough."

"Have you been thinking as much about her as I have Madlyn? Since Colonel Dillon can't deny my wish now, I plan on asking her to marry me as soon as I get home."

I nodded. "That thought's entered my mind with Ruth."

Sainty smiled as he climbed atop his horse. "I gotta find the boys and pay them."

"They're at the barn, tending the horses."

"You care to ride over with me?"

"I've got business with Joseph G. McCoy first. He still owes me money for plastering flyers all over Texas."

"Join us when you can, and inform me if you see the three I fired this morning. I want to settle up and be shed of them for good." Sainty turned his mount toward the barn and ambled off, his shoulders held high with pride despite the cash weighing them down.

Dusting off my clothes, I entered the building to be greeted by a snarly clerk, who eyed me from boot to hat. He was sitting in a small room behind a big desk that blocked the door into the owner's office. "This ain't a saloon, cowboy, so be gone."

"Before I go, tell me the date."

"It's August thirty-first," he said. "Now leave."

"Tell Mr. McCoy, that H.H. Lomax has returned to collect his hundred dollars and his bonus."

"Joe McCoy doesn't pay that kind of money to anyone. I ought to know. I keep his books. Now, get out of here."

Smiling, I pulled my revolver from my holster, cocked the hammer and pointed the barrel at the clerk's nose. "Unless you want a third nostril, you better fetch him or he won't have to pay you ever again. H.H. Lomax is the name."

The clerk arose from his chair and meekly knocked on the door, opening it, slithering in like the snake he was and closing it. I released the hammer on my pistol and shoved it back in its berth, waiting for Joseph G. McCoy. After a minute, the clerk opened the entry and stepped out. "My apologies, Mr. Lomax. Mr. McCoy will see you now."

"Remember the Alamo!" I said as I marched past the desk and into the owner's office. The clerk shut the door behind me.

"Welcome back, lad," McCoy said, walking over and throwing his arm around my shoulder.

"I've come for my hundred dollars."

He pulled me toward the window overlooking his pens and sidings. "Can you believe it? Have you seen how much Abilene has changed since you were here in the spring?"

"You must be proud to see your dream come true."

"It's not come true yet, lad. Next year's when I'll be rolling in money."

"Once word gets out I paid over twenty-two dollars a head, herds will stampede to Abilene. I'm paying high prices now to draw more cattle here. Once they're here in greater numbers, purchase values will fall."

I feared he was preparing to welsh on the money and bonus he owed me.

"You know those other fellows I sent to distribute flyers?"

"Never met them."

"They never delivered a one, but you made it clear to San Antonio and back."

"With a herd of Texas steers, and I arrived before September first."

McCoy pulled his arm from my shoulder and pointed to a plush chair on the opposite side of his desk, which was bigger by half than his clerk's and a lot fancier than the apple crate he once called his desk. He stepped to the corner that cradled a safe four feet high and sturdy as a locomotive.

"Let me get your hundred," he said as he walked the steel box. He spun the dial and entered the combination, then yanked on the lever and pulled open the heavy door. He counted my money, returned the surplus and started to lock up.

"Don't shut your safe yet. You're forgetting my bonus. A dime a head if I got the first herd here."

"I bought another herd from Texas five days ago, lad."

I shook my head. "Not from what I picked up on the trail. I ran into Colonel Wheeler a few days back. Was it his herd you bought?"

"Absolutely! That's the Texan. I'm glad you met him."

"I know that before he reached Abilene, he sold his herd to northern buyers, Smith, McCord and Chandler. They're the ones that brought the cattle to your stockyards. So, it was a Yankee herd when it reached Abilene, not a Texas herd."

Leaving the safe unlocked, McCoy stepped around his desk with my hundred dollars in greenbacks. I stood up and extended my left hand, while letting my right hand fall to the butt of my pistol, my fingers tapping on the grip.

"Wheeler's was a Texas herd," McCoy insisted.

"It wasn't Wheeler's when it got to Abilene. He sold it to Yankees. That makes it a Yankee herd!"

McCoy shrugged.

My fingers slid around the handle of my revolver.

His eyes widening, McCoy licked his lips, then backed away. "I'll give you five cents a head."

"You promised me that anyway, if I brought a Texas herd to Abilene. Sainty Spencer, the man whose cattle you just bought, can confirm I led the cattle here."

"Six cents apiece?"

I shook my head.

"Seven-and-a-half cents?"

"I'll settle for eight cents a head, no less." My fingers tapped impatiently on my sidearm.

McCoy took a deep breath and sighed. "Fine, lad.

You drive a hard bargain."

"You still come out ahead."

"That's always a sharp businessman's goal. Now that's eight cents a head for fifteen hundred steers."

"There were eighteen hundred and thirty-six cattle," I corrected him.

"Oh, yeah," he said as he turned back to the safe to extract more of his precious money. While he was counting out my due, I grabbed the pen from his ink well and a piece of paper to cipher out what I was owed. By my arithmetic, it came to twelve cents shy of a hundred and forty-seven dollars.

"Okay," McCoy grinned as he turned. "Here's a hundred and seventeen dollars."

I dropped the pen on the paper and pointed to my calculations. "Your figures and mine don't add up the same."

McCoy stepped over to his desk and inspected my ciphering. When he realized I knew my multiplication tables well enough to calculate my earnings, he nodded. "A hundred and forty-seven dollars and eighty-eight cents it is then. My head calculations were a little off," he admitted.

"Let's round it off at a hundred and fifty dollars, and you'll never see me again." I let my right hand fall to my gun again for emphasis.

"That's an excellent idea," McCoy said. "I've got business to take care of and a traveling photographer's in town I need to show around." He took out additional bills from his safe, added them to what he had left on his desk, then counted out in my hand my payment and bonus.

After I recounted it to make sure he hadn't shortchanged me, I shoved the money in my pocket, tipped my hat to Joseph G. McCoy and exited. His dream had put considerable cash in my pocket. With the new money, what Ruth and I still had from McCoy's initial payment and what Sainty owed me, we would end up with close to four hundred dollars back in Texas. As I passed through the front office, I growled at the clerk and strode outside, slamming the door behind me as if I could get away with anything now that I was almost rich.

I mounted Relee and headed to the barn to join the others. They were celebrating when I arrived as Sainty was handing out their earnings. The foreman had hung his saddle bag over the stall wall and opened a flap to take out the bills for our pay. By his calculation he owed the drovers a hundred and seven dollars for the days we worked rounding up and branding cattle before the drive and the days on the trail. He'd counted out cash to everyone but Bitters and me when I joined them at the rear stall where the Mexicans had carried the harnesses, collars and lines for the team. Bitters stepped up to receive his earnings, which were twice that of the drovers, then I took mine, sliding the cash into my pants pocket, careful not to let anyone see how much money I was really carrying.

"Now, fellows, don't go drinking your earnings up and wasting it on wild women like our three troublemakers last night," Sainty chided.

"Sounds more like wild woman," Jurdon Mark said.

"Don't care to meet Big Mouth," Tom Errun said, "though if there's a wooden Indian in town, I would like to watch her talk his loin cloth off."

"I wouldn't mind sketching her—" Martin Michaels said, then added "—from afar."

Silas Banty shook his head. "I not be interested in plowing any field Irish be thinking of plowing. I be buying me another reader."

"You don't have to worry about us," Mark said. "Perhaps a drink, but no gambling, unless someone wants to shoot marbles for nickels."

"Remember the Alamo!" I shouted.

They cheered.

"You're welcome to ride back to Texas with us. There's some safety in numbers since we've all got considerable money."

"We're agreed to stay together," Michaels said. "We don't trust Irish, York and Dire."

"Great," Sainty answered, pointing to Banty, Mark, Errun and Michaels. "You four find and escort them here so I can pay their wages. I'd like you around when I do." He turned to Bitters. "Find us an eatery, and I'll buy everyone's supper." He looked at me, Muñoz and Ramírez. "You three work on the harnesses and let me know what tools or parts we'll need to repair them enough to get home."

We went about our assigned tasks, while Sainty marched back and forth, waiting for the troublemakers to arrive. Muñoz and I inspected the rigging and found worn places in the reins, a rip in one of the stomach girths and a tear in a breeching band. The collars were in the worst shape with the seams split and the stuffing slipping out, so much so that the collar was unbalanced and likely to strain the mule's necks.

After comparing thoughts with José, I informed Sainty we'd need a stitching awl, a punch, leather laces and straps, a rivet mallet and rivets plus time to repair everything, especially the collars as the leather coverings must be opened and the old padding balanced or replaced. Sainty grabbed the saddlebags from the stall partition and started for the barn door when Irish, York and Dire entered, followed by Banty, Mark, Michaels and Errun. He returned to the stall and draped the saddlebags over a plank, then untied a flap. Sainty pulled out money enough to pay Dire, O'Henry and Muscher, all reeking of liquor.

"We found them in the saloon," Mark said.

"That's what got them in trouble in the first place," Sainty said.

"Being borns was what be getting them in trouble," Banty noted, as the trio glared at him.

"Just because you reads don't makes you our betters," answered O'Henry.

"Shut up," Sainty said. "I'm tired of your mischief, and I'm not taking any lip from you, if you want to get paid."

They were sober enough to understand they best be quiet, if they wanted their money.

"Ya'll worked a hundred and seven days for me at a dollar a day, but I'm charging each of you twenty-two dollars for one of the steers O'Henry shot."

"What?" cried Muscher. "Dire and I didn't shoot any steers."

"No," shot back Sainty, "but if you'd obeyed orders, you wouldn't have been out tom-catting around, so you're all responsible."

"Did you charge Whirlwind for all the cattle lost because he farted?" York demanded.

"No, because I never ordered him or anyone in this outfit else not to bottom burp."

"It ain't fair," Dire cried loud enough for everyone to hear.

"Work it out with Irish," Sainty said. "Take it from his pay."

"Nobody takes any money from me," O'Henry scowled.

Like the snakes they were, they silently watched Sainty count out eighty-five dollars apiece. He offered their pay one by one, and each snatched the bills from his hand.

"We want the rest," Muscher demanded.

"I've paid you what you're due."

"But not what we're owed. We'll get ours and more," York threatened, shaking his pay in Sainty's face. "It's a long damn way back to Texas."

Sainty turned to buckle the strap on the saddle bags.

O'Henry raised his fist and stepped toward the foreman until he heard a metallic click. He looked around, and saw Jurdon Mark holding a pistol aimed at his gut.

"You face all of us if you attack Sainty," Mark said. "You've been paid, so skedaddle and stay out of our sight."

Irish backed away, then spun around for the barn door, Muscher and Dire following in his wake, blessing us with more profanity than I'd ever heard in such a short time. Fancy Nancy wasn't the only person in Abilene with a big mouth.

"You best be careful," Mark told Sainty.

"They're not so stupid as to rob me."

"I wouldn't be so sure," Michaels affirmed.

"I'll state it outright," I said, "they are that stupid and mean. The sooner we can get out of Abilene, the better we'll all be."

Sainty looked at me. "If I hurry, I can get to the store before closing and bring back what you need for the harnesses."

"Whatever you can do to get us back to Texas sooner pleases me more," I replied.

Sainty lifted the saddle bags from the partition, draped them over his shoulder and walked with the others outside. He returned alone forty-five minutes later and handed us a gunny sack with our supplies. Looking back several times over his shoulder, Sainty said, "I suspect they're following me and planning to waylay me."

"I told you they would," I said.

He removed the saddle bags from his shoulder and tossed them on the partition. He looked at me, then Muñoz. "José, send Pedro outside to watch for Muscher, O'Henry and Dire. If he spots them, tell him to come running, but otherwise to stay there until you say it's okay to return."

Muñoz issued instructions in Spanish, and Ramírez scurried away.

Once he left, Sainty studied me and the wrangler. "I can trust you two, so I want you to hide the money somewhere because everyone in town knows I've been carrying it around in the saddle bags. You can tell me later, but keep it hidden where no one would think to look. He opened the flaps on the pouches and hand-ed us stacks of money tied with string. Sainty kept a couple hundred dollars in his pocket, then studied the door. When he was certain no one was looking, he bent and grabbed hands full of straw to stuff the saddlebags pouches like they still carried the money.

"I know I promised you a meal at the eatery and two nights in the hotel, but if you can get the cash hidden and the harnesses repaired tonight, we'll leave tomorrow."

José and I looked at one another, nodding. "We're fine with it," I said.

"Good. As for rooms in Drovers Cottage, José you're sharing a bed with Pedro and you with Silas, Lomax."

I nodded.

Muñoz said, "Let's get to work." When Sainty disappeared outside, the wrangler looked at me. "Where are we gonna hide the money?"

"Let's think about it while we start the repairs," I said. We worked until dusk dimmed the barn. Muñoz stepped to the wagon, pulled out a lantern and lit it. We continued by lantern light on the harnesses, when the perfect hiding place dawned on me. I told Muñoz. He laughed.

"You're smarter than folks think, Whirlwind," he said.

We hid the money and finished our repairs around eleven o'clock. We headed to Drovers Cottage with Ramírez, who had remained on guard while Muñoz and I worked. As the hotel was unfinished, we found no clerk, just a lantern on the front desk with a note listing the room numbers for each pair of drovers and Sainty, who had a room of his own. Muñoz lit a match and led me and Ramírez down the hallway, checking the door numbers until we came to their room. As the doors still lacked knobs, Muñoz pushed theirs open and Ramírez stepped inside. Muñoz lit another match and escorted me along the hall. We passed a cracked door and detected moaning.

"Think that's Big Mouth at work?"

"I hope not," I said. "I'd hate to see her at work from the tales about her."

"Oooohhhh," came a low groan, sounding more like pain than pleasure.

Muñoz glanced at me, and I nodded that we needed to investigate. The wrangler lit another match as I pushed open the cracked door. Muñoz slid the match inside.

There on the floor lay Sainty.

Without looking, I knew the saddlebags had disappeared.

But not the money!

Chapter 32

Instead of pulling out for Texas the next morning, we stayed an extra day in Abilene as Sainty needed time to recover from the knot on his head. His assailants had entered his room through a window, clubbed him and taken the saddlebags. I wish I had been there when Muscher, Dire and O'Henry opened the flaps and found straw rather than money. As the hotel was under construction, workers still hammered and sawed upstairs, contributing to Sainty's discomfort. The beds in our rooms remained unassembled so we slept on sheetless feather mattresses on the floor, though that beat sleeping on the ground.

Except for mealtime, we stayed around the hotel to guard Sainty should his assailants come back, though Muñoz, Ramírez and I visited the store to buy a few clothes, ammunition and supplies for the return. I also bought a bundle of flyer-sized paper, three bottles of ink and two pens to give to Martin Michaels to replicate his initial sketch of Ruth with a pen-and-ink drawing.

When I returned to the hotel, I gave the pens, ink and paper to Martin and handed him his original drawing of Ruth. In less than fifteen minutes, he had replicated the first, and Ruth looked as beautiful in ink as she did in pencil. To pass the time away, I suggested he produce portraits of O'Henry, Muscher and Dire.

"What do you want with pictures of those saddle tramps?" Michaels asked.

"We know who blindsided Sainty, but the law doesn't. We'll have these to show what the assailants look like."

Sketch grinned. "That's a great idea, Lomax."

He started working, but insisted no one watch over his shoulder while he created the first drawing. When he finished with Muscher, he even put a caption over the fellow's head. We laughed, slapping our knees when he showed us his masterpiece, and we suggested what should be printed beneath the likeness, elbowing each other in the hilarity. Michaels drew pictures of Dire and O'Henry, listing his "Irish" and "Black Bart" aliases. We chuckled, until Sainty moaned.

"Not so loud," he pleaded from his mattress.

Michaels showed the trail boss the three drawings, and Sainty even laughed through the pain. "That's funny, boys," Sainty grimaced and rolled over on his side. "I want to start home in the morning, even if I have to ride in the wagon."

"Fine by us, boss," I said. "We're ready to get back to Texas."

Michaels handed me the three drawings of the saddle tramps and I folded them and put them in my shirt pocket with both pictures of Ruth. Come noon, me, Silas, Charlie and Jurdon went to lunch at the new eatery and returned to guard Sainty while the rest dined. Barely had they brought back soda crackers and cheese for the trail boss, than a well-dressed fellow with an unruly beard poked his head in our room.

"Pardon me, gentlemen," he said in an odd accent. As we looked at each other to confirm he was talking to us, he continued. "My name is Alexander Gardner. I'm a traveling photographer. I am setting up my camera to make a likeness of Drovers Cottage. Might I impose upon two or three of you to have your picture made?"

"You're not from these parts, are you?" Tom Errun said.

"Scotland originally," Gardner said.

"I came from Manchester," English informed him.

"My sympathies," the photographer replied. "You must be the spare. Am I right?"

English laughed. "Father was military. He had no title to bequeath." When Errun saw the confusion on our faces, he explained that British nobility bequeathed titles and estates to the firstborn son, the heir. A second son would assume the title only if something happened to the oldest. "Thus, the heir and the spare." We still scratched our heads, but Gardner grew impatient.

"Will you gentlemen assist?"

"If you take my likeness," Jurdon Mark asked, "can you promise me it won't show up on a wanted poster anywhere?"

Everybody chuckled except Gardner. "It'll be far enough way that no one will recognize you. I need a couple or three men to stand on the front porch. A lady will join us to make this appear as a distinguished hostelry."

"Sure," Mark said. "I'll go along, but I want Lomax with me. He's more likely to appear on a wanted poster than me."

"I'll help a chap from across the pond," Errun volunteered.

"Three will suffice," Gardner announced. "Please follow me."

We walked out on the porch with Gardner and encountered a woman so ugly that a freight train would take a dirt road before crossing her path. She was rouged, wrinkled and painted up so much that she looked like a carousel horse. "Morning, boys," she said. "My name's Nancy, though my close friends call me Fancy."

"Nancy's good enough for us," I replied. Errun, Mark and I couldn't gaze at her long for fear of going blind. She was wearing a black dress with a billowing skirt, a high collar that would've served humanity by choking her, and a top that couldn't hide the pronounced sag of her tora-loorals. If she had been Eve, mankind would've stopped with Adam. Of course, Adam had more sense than Dire and Muscher, and he hadn't been three months on the trail herding longhorns either. I questioned whether I wanted my photo taken with a woman of her limited charms and abundant ugliness.

"We're delighted to make your acquaintance," Mark said, "but we're broke."

Nancy lost all business interest in us, but she jabbered like she was paid by the syllable. Our ears begged to surrender, but Big Mouth fired words like a cannon spewed grapeshot. Nancy told us she had worked the goldfields of California in her earlier years and had done right well in San Francisco, too, but pickings were poor in Abilene, though likely to get better next year, when she hoped to open a cottage of her own, so to speak.

I debated if I wanted my likeness made with such a hideous woman. "You sure we won't be recognizable, Gardner?"

"Your faces will be the size of a fly speck," he said as he positioned us with me beside Nancy. I almost passed out from her perfume. The photographer stepped off the porch, backing away and stumbling over construction debris.

He joined his assistant and lifted the black cloth behind his camera and stuck his head under it. Gardner reappeared. "Now be still so there's no blur." Then he shoved his head back under the cloth and removed the lens cap to shoot us. I twisted my head from side to side to distort my face so posterity could never prove that I had been this close to Fancy Nancy and her drooping charms, which I had to be careful not to trip over when the photographer dismissed us.

After what seemed like an eternity, Gardner replaced the lens cap and popped up from beneath the cloth. "Thank you, lady and gentlemen. You may attend your business now."

Nancy took him seriously. "If you boys find money, I'll make you a two-for-one deal."

"I'm joining the priesthood," Mark said, "and have vowed to stay celibate."

The painted slack puller, grinned with a play on words. "I can sell-a-butt before you turn steer on us," she replied.

Mark, Errun and I dashed inside the hotel to tell the others of our encounter with Fancy Nancy. They ran to the front to glimpse her before she waddled away, holding up her skirt and maybe even her tora-loorals to navigate the construction debris.

After that run-in with Nancy, we agreed that we were leaving Abilene in the morning, even if we had to bind up Sainty and throw him in the back of the wagon. The sooner we got away, the less likely we would encounter Big Mouth or the three saddle tramps that attacked our foreman. Fortunately, we didn't see Nancy, Dire, Muscher or O'Henry again in Abilene.

We arose early the next morning except Sainty. While Jurdon Mark stood guard with him, the rest of us ran over to the stockyard barn and saddled our horses and helped Bitters harness the wagon. He inspected the repairs, complimenting us on our work. "It's as good as my cooking," he said, "especially the collars. They should get us to Texas."

Michaels and Errun saddled Sainty's and Mark's horses while Muñoz and Ramírez rounded up the six spare mounts Sainty would take back to Texas because of their good cow sense. When we were ready, we returned to Drovers Cottage to put the foreman in the wagon.

"I can ride my horse," he argued.

"Give it a day more," Bitters said. "Besides I need someone to talk to."

"You got the marker for Toad Beeline, didn't you, Charlie?" Sainty asked as we helped him into the rig to rest on the bedrolls.

"It's back there somewhere," he answered. "His name's burned into the wood."

We tied Sainty's horse to the rear of the wagon and began our trek back to Texas, first crossing the Smoky Hill River and heading south, all of us richer than the last time we crossed that watercourse. We took it slow the first day and picked up the pace the second as much as the wagon would allow without jarring the cook out of his seat. What slowed us down, however, was Charlie Bitters, who felt obligated to fix us a time-consuming meal in the evening, starting a fire, then getting the coals right and baking something in his Dutch oven, rather than frying fare faster in a skillet.

So anxious was I to return to Ruth that I decided to speed our journey up. After he had finished supper that night and washed the container, I volunteered to hang it on the wagon and had him confirm I'd placed it on the correct hook. He nodded his approval. When he wasn't looking, I pulled the shovel from the back of his rig and slipped off fifty yards to dig a hole in the hard earth. Leaving the spade, I returned to the wagon and waited for the right moment to steal the Dutch oven and bury it. The more I thought about it, though, the more I liked the idea of putting something in the pot that would ensure my future, though I feared it would betray a friend. I lingered around the wagon and the mules, trying to stay invisible, and when no one was looking, I pilfered my quarry, lifted the lid of the Dutch oven and slid it inside. When the drovers were occupied, I raised the cast-iron pot from the sideboard hook and toted it over to the hole where I gently lowered it into the ground and quickly covered it up with dirt. I put the shovel in its place and me to bed.

"You be okay?" Silas Banty asked. "You being restless tonight."

"Eager to get back to Ruth," I said.

By the next morning, Sainty was well enough to ride so we saddled up to leave, but not without a commotion. "Dammit to hell," Charlie Bitters cried. "I've lost my pistol."

We inspected the holster nailed to the sideboard and confirmed his loss. "You must've hit one too many holes with the wheels," Sainty said. "I'll buy you a new pistol in Texas."

"On the bright side," Mark observed, "we can gripe about your food without getting shot."

"Bonito," I said as the others, save for Bitters, echoed me.

"There'll be plenty of chances to poison you between here and Texas," Bitters said.

"I was joking," Mark explained.

Bitters shook his head. "I wasn't."

As we rode away, I looked behind me at the gravesite of the Dutch oven that had caused us so much misery on the trail, but would no longer slow our sojourn back to Texas. "Adios," I said.

A half hour after we left, we crossed a stream lined with cottonwood trees and a gravelly bottom that made the crossing easy. Come lunch time, we reached another watercourse with sloping banks, a brush thicket and scattered trees.

That's where they surprised us! As we started down the incline to the water's edge, Chuck Muscher, Harry Dire and Bartholomew Henry O'Henry emerged from behind the brush, their carbines leveled at us.

"Morning, boys," said York. "We came to collect the rest of our pay."

"And the other money you carries, Sainty," Irish said.

"Yeah," said Dire.

"First, throw your carbines on the ground," Muscher ordered. Anybody that tries something gets shot."

We did as ordered as we weren't gunmen.

"Get off your horses," Muscher commanded and we obeyed. "Now, one by one, pull your pistols and toss them on the grass."

"And, Charlie," Muscher said, "I haven't forgotten about you. Get out of your wagon and pitch your pistol in the stream."

"I can't."

"You better."

"That's impossible. I lost it on the trail yesterday."

"If I find you're lying, I'll shoot you," Muscher said, then turned to Sainty. "Okay, boss, hand it over."

"Hand what over?"

"The money you made off the herd," York demanded. "And this time we want the cash, not straw."

"So it was you that buffaloed me. I figured so, but now I know."

"Quit stalling, Sainty. Where's the damn money?"

"I have no idea."

"What do you mean you have no idea? You better

hand it over or we shoot folks, Lomax first."

Sainty sighed. "I gave it to Lomax and Muñoz to hide in case you returned. I don't know where they put it."

"Where is it, Meskin?" Muscher asked.

"Yo no hablo ingles," Muñoz said.

"He says he doesn't understand English," Sainty translated.

"That's a lie," said Muscher, "but that leaves us with Lomax, and he speaks English. Where is it, Whirlwind?"

Everyone stared at me, but only Muñoz knew where we had hidden the cash. He looked at me, the wagon and back at me, wondering if I would divulge the hiding place.

I sighed. "I'll lead you to the money, if you let everyone else ride away unharmed."

"Show me where it is," Muscher demanded.

"It's not here."

"What?" said Sainty, lunging for me.

I shoved Sainty away as he tried to choke me. "I had to do it," I said.

"¿Qué estas diciendo?" Muñoz asked as bewildered as a woodpecker in a petrified forest.

"Start explaining, Lomax, or we start shooting,"

Taking a deep breath, I exhaled slowly. "Last night I took the money and buried it in Charlie's Dutch oven."

Everyone looked from me to the wagon and the empty hook where the pot usually hung.

"You bastard," cried Sainty. "I can't believe I trusted you."

"Bastardo," Muñoz shouted.

Muscher laughed. "You sly dog, Lomax. We're trying to get what's owed us—"

"And more," Sainty broke in.

"—and you're taking everything. You're the biggest crook of all."

I hung my head. "It's not something I'm proud of."

"You bastard," Sainty repeated.

I shrugged. "It had to do it. Let the others go, Muscher, and I'll split the money with you." I looked at the other drovers. "Sorry, fellows, I couldn't resist that much cash."

Sainty raised his finger and pointed it at my nose. "If I ever see you again, I'll kill you."

I grimaced at his words, but what he said next cut me to the quick.

"When I see Ruth, I'll inform her of the lying, thieving scoundrel you are."

"If I had my pistol," Bitters said, "I'd shoot you in the back for stealing my Dutch oven."

"I took what I needed to secure my future," I explained. "Nothing personal, fellows."

"Damn, Lomax," laughed Muscher, "you're despicable, the kind of guy to dip an old maid in honey and stake to an anthill."

Shrugging, I said, "Let's ride so I can get on with my life."

Muscher shook his head. "You don't have many hours left in your life, Whirlwind."

"If they don't kill you," Sainty said, "I'll hunt you down and do the job myself."

"Why should I find the money if all you plan to do is kill me?"

"Get him out of here," Sainty sighed. "I can't stand the stench of the lying skunk."

Muscher nodded. "Bart get down and collect their carbines and pistols. I don't want them shooting us when we leave."

O'Henry jumped from his saddle and collected the revolvers, tucking half the pistols in his belt and offering the others to Dire. Then he retrieved all the carbines and split them among Dire and Muscher.

"Let me take a carbine," I offered.

Muscher laughed. "After we find the money, you'll take a bullet instead."

"Let me shoots him," O'Henry begged.

"No," said Dire with his soft voice, "let's hang him. Use Trent Parson's lariat."

"You can't leave us without weapons, not with Indian Territory and Texas ahead of us," said Sainty.

"Let's do a little horse trading, Sainty," York offered.

"We'll sell you back your guns and your horses for what you owe us and everything else you made on the drive. Is that a deal?"

Sainty stood silent.

"I'll take that as a yes. We'll drop your guns and leave your horses a mile from here. You can come after them once you hear my gunshot."

Standing silent, Sainty scowled at Muscher and glared at me, hate oozing from his eyes.

Turning my back on the trail boss and the drovers, I retraced my steps for the day. Soon, the three saddle tramps rode beside me, ejecting all the bullets from the carbines, then removing the cartridges from the pistols. After more than a mile, they threw all the weapons on the ground and released the horses. Riding off at a canter, York lifted his revolver skyward and fired.

I wondered if the Five-D men would come for me and the money once they retrieved their weapons. After my betrayal, I figured they'd rather plug me than find the cash. We rode at a gallop and made it to the gravel-bottomed creek lined with the cottonwoods in an hour. A half hour beyond the creek was the buried Dutch oven and its treasure. As I had hidden the pot in the dark, I hoped I could find the spot because I figured this trio would show me neither patience nor mercy. I wanted it to end quickly.

"Where is it?" Muscher demanded.

"We're getting close," I stalled, trying to place the landmarks I remembered from when we broke camp. To buy time, as I looked about, I offered a suggestion. "I figure there's some forty thousand dollars there."

"No matter until we find it," Muscher said.

"When we do, we can split it four ways, ten thousand apiece. What do you say?"

"I say you're crazy," York responded. "Besides, you won't be in any condition to spend money."

"You'll be deads," O'Henry added.

The land became familiar. I tugged on my reins and slowed Relee, then stood in my stirrups, looking left and right. What I thought was my mound on the left turned out to be an animal burrow, so I changed course and pointed east. "Maybe it's over there." As I was about to turn that direction, I spotted a pile of freshly spaded dirt thirty feet ahead of me. "There it is."

Reaching the spot, I jumped from Relee and looked up at my captors. "Did any of you bring a shovel?"

"Use your hands," Muscher ordered as he slid from his horse, followed by Dire and O'Henry. Gathering around me, they grinned like small dogs about to dig up a big bone.

I fell to my knees and scraped the dirt aside, making a hole about a foot deep before my fingernails rubbed against the cast-iron pot. The three closed in, peering over my shoulders as I gradually brushed the soil away. "Back up," I said, "and give me room to pull this out of here." Their eyes widened, and they licked their lips.

"Let's sees the money," O'Henry begged, almost drooling.

I grabbed the handle and pulled the pot out. Muscher bent to grab it, but I slapped his fingers away. "I need room," I scolded. They inched back. I sat the oven on the ground and lifted its lid, just enough to slide my right hand inside. "Who wants the first bundle of money?"

"Lets me have it," answered O'Henry.

With that, I yanked out Charlie Bitters' wagon pistol and pointed it at my captors. "Don't make a move, or I'll shoot you." I stood up, my revolver aimed at Muscher. "You die first, York."

They stared with disbelieving eyes that a guy as dumb as me had snookered them.

"You bastard," shouted Muscher.

"Seems I'm everyone's favorite bastard today."

O'Henry bent forward and looked in the cast-iron pot. "It's empty," he cried.

"You're smarter than you look, Irish. Now one at a time, I want you to unbuckle your gun belts. You first, Chuck, then Irish and Harry."

They followed my instructions, though not without chatting.

"We'll get you for this, you double-crosser."

"No honor among thieves, isn't that what they say?"

One, two, three gun belts fell to the ground.

"Now back away, fellows." I waved my pistol at them, and they retreated as I went to their horses and yanked the carbine from each scabbard. I carried the long guns to Relee and squeezed two into my empty scabbard, then slid Bitters revolver into my holster and used the third carbine to manage the saddle tramps. "Lift your hands where I can see them and back up until I say stop." They hesitated and I fired a shot into the ground at their feet. "Do what I say."

As they inched away from me, I bent and grabbed their holsters, buckling them so I could hang them over my arm as I retreated to my bay. My antagonists kept backing toward Dakota Territory.

"This far enough?" Muscher asked.

"Nope, keep going until you reach Canada."

I hung the gun belts from my saddle horn, took my bay's reins and led him over to the Dutch oven, figuring I should take it to make amends to Charlie for stealing both his pot and his pistol. I draped the pot's handle on the saddle horn of O'Henry's horse, then tied the reins of the other two horses to Irish's saddle, all the time waving the carbine at the three troublemakers as they backed away. I mounted Relee. Once I settled atop my gelding, I nudged him toward the south. "I'll leave your horses a mile from here."

"What about our guns? Don't leave us defenseless," Muscher yelled.

"No deal. You planned on shooting me with them so I can't trust you."

I put the horses into a lope and soon left my enemies running after me and shouting every profane word they could come imagine. I smiled, confident I had out-smarted them and could outrun them to camp. Even if I didn't, they had no weapons and I had plenty. A mile or so from the spot where I had outwitted the saddle tramps, I untied the three trailing horses from each other, then lifted the Dutch oven from O'Henry's saddle and started back to rejoin what I hoped were still my friends. At once a frightening thought hit me. I knew where the money was hidden as did Muñoz, who had helped me put it there. What if José, played dumb and convinced Sainty I was indeed a thief and had stolen the cash? If that happened, I was as good as dead once Sainty spotted me. After that, Muñoz would be rich.

That thought worried me so much that I lowered my guard, as I approached the gravelly creek lined with cottonwoods. I dismounted and let Relee drink. I tossed the shirkers' three gun belts and pistols in the water, then ejected the shells from two of the carbines and tossed them in the drink, leaving the third carbine in my scabbard. As I secured the Dutch oven to prevent it from chafing Relee's neck, I heard pounding hooves from the north. Checking out the noise, I saw Harry Dire barreling toward me and twirling a lasso. Damn! A rope became a weapon in Harry's hands.

I fumbled to untie the Dutch oven, then tossed it aside as Relee reared. Fighting him, I shoved my boot for the stirrup and missed, stumbling and almost losing the reins. Dire came closer. Relee raised on his hind legs again, and I yanked the reins, trying to control him and mount. Finally, I got my boot in the stirrup and hauled myself atop my gelding. Dire raced at me, twirling a loop. Behind him charged York and Irish, screaming. I bolted across the stream, but realized Dire would rope me on the open ground, so I headed east along the creek bank, riding among the cottonwoods, ducking beneath low branches.

When I looked back, I saw Dire charging within throwing range. I drove my bay toward a cottonwood tree with a low branch. That's when Dire tossed his lariat. I instinctively dipped my head as Relee raced under the limb. I heard the whirl of the loop as it soared over the branch and then dropped behind me. I grinned and looked over my shoulder at my assailant. In the damnedest thing I ever saw, Dire rode under the limb and the loop snagged under his chin and went tight because of his saddle dally. When Dire hit the end of that lasso it yanked him from the saddle. I heard a snap, a scream and a moan. The rope tore loose from his tack, and Dire collapsed on the ground.

O'Henry and Muscher drew closer as Relee veered from the trees and hit the water, dashing for the other side of the stream. But my surefooted gelding, stepped on a rock or in a hole, stumbling and crashing into the creek, tossing me on the bank, knocking my breath out. I gasped for air as O'Henry leaped off his horse and pinned me to the ground, punching me in the face, three times.

"Don't kill him yet," yelled Muscher. "Let me help Harry." York dismounted and cried out. "Damnation, Harry's dead! Looks like he snapped his own neck as crooked as his head is."

Slowly I drew in air, though O'Henry's weight on my chest impeded my breathing.

"Lets me shoot him now," Irish said.

"Don't do it, Bart. Let's hang the bastard, that's a slower way to die. And Lomax deserves to strangle."

My mind swirled as O'Henry yanked me to my feet. I looked across the stream and saw Muscher loosening the loop from Dire's neck and pulling it over his head. Next he tossed the rope over the same limb that had killed Dire as Irish shoved me toward the water.

"You wants me to be brings his horse?" O'Henry asked.

Muscher shook his head. "No, we'll hoist him ourselves. Lomax deserves to strangle slowly for lying to us about the money. I plan to enjoy every minute of his dying misery."

As O'Henry pushed me to the water, I said. "You could drown here, Irish."

He shoved me again. "I can wades this stream. It doesn't comes to my knees. You won't mocks me ever again, Lomax."

With Irish nudging me forward, I feared I was crossing a river for the last time on this earth. The next river I crossed would be on the trail to eternity. At least I'd see the brothers I had lost to the war.

York awaited me as I stepped out of the creek. He took my arm and jerked me toward the cottonwood limb with the rope draped over it. Still dazed from the fall, I stumbled forward.

"Where's the money hidden, Lomax?"

"I'll be damned if I tell you. You're gonna kill me either way."

Muscher nodded. "I'll take more pleasure in hanging you than I would in spending forty thousand dollars." He secured the loop over my neck and tugged it snug until I couldn't speak. I tried to loosen the rope remove until O'Henry slugged my jaw. I dropped to my knees, too stunned to react as Irish retreated to his horse and brought over a length of tie-rope to bind my hands behind me. He yanked me to my feet and positioned me beneath the limb.

"One last time, Lomax, where's the money?"

"Go to hell, both of you."

"You'll be there in a few minutes," Muscher said.

I'd had a rope around my neck back during the war when Yankee bushwhackers tried to hang me, so I wasn't looking forward to repeating the experience. Irish grabbed the strand, and tightened it further so I couldn't breathe. O'Henry grinned at hoisting me all the way to the Pearly Gates, my preferred destination, not his.

As they tugged on the line, the prickly lasso dug into my neck and snagged my jaw under the left ear. Against my will, I rose until only the tips of my boots were on the ground. I fought for breath.

That was the moment that James Butler "Wild Bill" Hickok rode back into my life.

Chapter 33

"Afternoon, boys," said a voice I recognized but couldn't place.

The lariat fell slack. I dropped to my knees, shaking my head and trying to loosen the loop enough to breathe.

"What seems to be the trouble, boys?"

Gasping for breath, I swung around and saw a fellow in a frock coat sitting in his saddle and pointing his carbine at my hangmen. Watery from strangulation, my blurry eyes failed to focus at first. He wiggled his carbine, and Muscher and O'Henry backed away from their end of the rope. As my sight cleared up, I noticed the rider had long, flowing hair of a chestnut hue.

"Now tell me what's going on, boys," he demanded again.

"We were hanging a horse thief and a killer," Muscher yelled, pointing to Dire's crumpled body. "What business is it of yours?"

I looked at my savior as he lifted his left hand and pulled back the lapel of his coat. My eyes focused on a shiny tin star pinned to his chest. I glanced up at the man's face and recognized Wild Bill Hickok.

"This badge makes it my business. I'm Deputy U.S. Marshal Bill Hickok."

With my hands tied behind my back, I struggled to arise and explain myself.

Hickok looked at me and asked, "What do you have

to say for yourself?"

I opened my mouth to speak, but my words came out raspy, so much so that even I couldn't understand them.

Hickok's eyes widened as he stared at me. "Lomax? H.H. Lomax?"

I nodded.

"What the hell, Lomax? You're too dumb to be a thief, though you did beat the Rattle Jar." He grinned. "How are you, Lomax?"

"You know each other?" Muscher cried.

"Know him?" I wheezed. "I've combed nits out of his hair."

Hickok's smile soured. "That's not a matter we discuss around others."

"Sorry, Marshal. It's hard to think straight with two scoundrels hanging onto a rope around my neck and my hands tied."

Wild Bill nodded at O'Henry. "Untie his wrists."

Irish walked over and worked the bindings loose. "You knows each other?" He stared in disbelief.

"We grew up together," I lied. "Best friend I ever had."

O'Henry groaned. "We was about to hangs you."

"You should've spent more time hanging and less talking, Black Bart."

He shoved me to the ground. "I hates that name, Lomax."

"What's going on?" Hickok shouted, as I pushed myself up and removed Reb's rope. "You two keep your hands where I can see them. Explain yourselves."

Muscher complained that I had stolen their mounts and shot Dire before they could catch me and play judge, jury, and executioner.

Hickok studied Dire's corpse. "No blood or gunshot wounds on your pal, and I damn sure don't see extra horses." He looked at me. "What's your story, Lomax? You didn't run out on them like you did on me before the Tutt trial, did you?"

"Bill, you know I always liked you, but my wanderlust got the best of me. As for these two, they're thieves. We drove cattle together up from San Antone, but the foreman fired them in Abilene, and they were trying to rob him of his profits on the way back home."

"He owed us money," Muscher screamed, but realized that hurt his alibi. "I mean we were trying to get what was ours."

"And everything else," I explained, elaborating how the three had gotten the drop on our outfit and exaggerated how I had decoyed them away from the others with the Dutch oven until I turned the tables on them and escaped. "You'll find the cast-iron pot and lid up the creek."

Hickok pointed at Dire.

"How'd he die?"

"He was chasing me, but his horse tripped and threw him, breaking his neck," I said, figuring Hickok would never believe what had actually happened.

"That's a lie," Muscher shouted. "He was lassoing Lomax when his rope hung over the tree limb, snagging himself and snapping his neck."

"That's the damndest story I ever heard," Hickok said.

"You can't believe a thing they say," I countered.

"Believes us, it's true," O'Henry pleaded.

"These may explain things," I said as I reached in my shirt pocket and pulled out Martin Michael's pen-and-ink drawings. As I approached his horse, I culled Ruth's pictures from the other three and handed Wild Bill the ones of O'Henry, Muscher and Dire.

Hickok looked at the first sheet, then at Muscher. "What's your name?"

"Chuck Muscher."

The deputy nodded and studied the next sheet before glancing at Irish. "Your name?"

"Bartholomew Henry O'Henry."

"That's a mouthful," Hickok said. "Now who's the dead man."

"That's Harry Dire," York answered.

"Okay, boys, you fellows are under arrest."

"What?" screamed Muscher.

"Why's you arresting us?" O'Henry yelled.

"You want the crimes or the reward money?" Hickok asked.

"Reward money?" York shouted in exasperation.

Hickok turned the papers around and showed them their likenesses. They gasped as Hickok read the wording

"This one offers a five hundred dollar reward for Bartholomew Henry O'Henry, alias Black Bart, alias Irish for murder, robbery and rape, Kansas City, Kansas."

Outraged, O'Henry charged Hickok, who leveled the carbine at him. "Stand back, Bart."

"That's a fraud," Muscher cried. "There was a cowhand on our drive that could draw pictures and letters. He did that."

Hickok looked at me.

I shook my head and shrugged. "Says Dire hung himself and now claims a cowhand can draw wanted posters. These fellows must think you're dumber than I am, Marshal."

Wild Bill turned to Muscher. "You're only worth a hundred and fifty dollars, Chuck."

"I didn't do nothing," he insisted.

"Says here you're wanted for bribery, larceny, forgery and buggery."

"What?" Muscher said, pointing at the papers as Hickok folded and slipped them in his pocket. "Those posters are the forgeries."

"You fellows are going with me to Kansas City," Hickok announced.

"What the hell is buggery?" Muscher asked.

Hickok laughed. "You'll learn in prison." The marshal turned to me. "Gather their horses for me, Lomax, starting with Dire's. We'll begin with him, but if he gets to stinking too bad, we'll bury him. Hell, he's only worth fifty dollars."

"Sure thing, Bill." I ran across the creek to get Relee, then rode back past Hickok and fetched Dire's mount.

"Do me a favor, Lomax. Go through his saddlebags and remove any guns, knives and ammunition."

I jumped down and rummaged through each pouch in the tack, throwing a knife and a carton of bullets in the stream.

"Check his bedroll, too, as I want his accomplices to wrap him up in it to cut the smell."

Muscher and O'Henry stared wide-eyed at Hickok, bewildered by their upcoming trip to Kansas City.

When I finished inspecting Dire's belongings, I tossed the bedding by his side and led the other horses to the creek bank where I rummaged through Muscher's possessions, throwing into the water two cartons of bullets, two knives and three pouches of tobacco for spite. O'Henry had nothing in his saddle bags worth keeping, much less throwing away. By the time I was done, Hickok's two prisoners had bundled up Dire and tied him over the saddle.

As I helped Hickok bring justice to Kansas, Muscher and O'Henry bellyached about the unfairness of their arrest and how they planned to get even with me when they were released. They called me a liar, a conniving skunk, and a worthless piece of cow dung, though I had to admit two out of three wasn't bad, coming from them.

"Both of you shut up," Hickok said, "my ears are full, and we haven't started east."

"We ain't wanted, marshal," Muscher protested.

"Those is true words," O'Henry interjected. "We is innocent."

"That'll be for a judge or jury to decide," the marshal responded and nodded to me. "Look in my saddlebags for two pairs of wrist shackles, then clamp them around their hands."

I unbuckled the horse satchel and fished about until I found the irons.

"Just as well Dire died as I only have two sets of manacles," Hickok told me. "I might have had to shoot him anyway to be safe."

Irish and York looked at one another, shaking their heads. "You'd've been killing an innocent man," Muscher spat.

"I never arrested an outlaw yet that failed to say he

380

didn't do it."

"Truer words were never said," I noted as I walked over to O'Henry with the shackles.

"Hold your arms straight out in front," Hickok ordered.

O'Henry balled his fingers into fists and raised his arms. I clamped the irons on his wrist and locked them in place. He lifted his fists, intending to club me with his chain bracelets.

"Don't do it," Hickok commanded.

"I's a slave again," he lamented.

"You're a slave to your own crimes," the marshal told him.

"I's done no crimes," he protested.

"Back away from, Lomax," Hickok ordered, "so he can put the restraints on buggery boy."

Like York, I wasn't sure what buggery was, but I didn't show my ignorance by admitting it.

"This is the biggest outrage since I left New York," Muscher proclaimed, lifting his arms.

"Maybe you should've stayed up north," I suggested, clamping the manacles around his wrists. Eager to get them out of my sight, I walked over to their horses, grabbed their reins and led them over to the two prisoners.

"Help them in the saddle," Hickok ordered.

I tried to assist Muscher, but he shoved me away. "I'll do it myself, but one day I intend to find you, Lomax, and throw you over a horse like Harry there."

"I intends to finds him first," O'Henry said, as he also refused my aid.

"Hell," said Hickok, "you two are gonna talk him to death before then." He grinned at me. "You care to ride to Kansas City and share the reward?"

"There's no reward," protested Muscher. "Those wanted posters are fakes."

"Shut up," the marshal ordered.

"No, Bill. I've got a girl waiting for me back in Texas. I'm eager to see her. Hope these criminals don't cause you as much trouble as they caused us on the drive to

Abilene."

"Best of luck to you until our trails cross again."

I wasn't sure I cared to meet Hickok again, once he discovered the wanted posters were forgeries, but I said otherwise. "Like you, I'll look forward to it."

"One more thing, Lomax," the lawman said. "Tie Dire's horse to one of their saddles, and we're Kansas City bound. Good luck with your girl."

"Ruth's her name. She's as cute as a speckled puppy."

I hitched Dire's mount to Muscher's saddle, and Hickok started his little caravan east for Kansas City. Retrieving Trent Parson's lariat, I rolled it up as I watched them disappear in the distance. I never saw Muscher or O'Henry again, though Hickok and I would run into each other nine years later in Deadwood. As for Irish and York, I heard varying stories of their fates in the ensuing decades. By one account, O'Henry found religion and settled in Nicodemus, a northwest Kansas community established by former slaves. Another story said he had gone to the mining country in Colorado and had the misfortune of lighting a cigarette too close to a dynamite wagon. That day, he just up and disappeared. If that story is true, Reb's loaded tobacco pouches had prepared him for his fate. As for Muscher, the stories varied as well. In one he was hung as a horse thief. By another, he married Fancy Nancy for her honey and her money, but smoked a cigarette in bed and burned themselves and half the town. In a third telling, a Baptist preacher in Kansas City assassinated him to purge him of his buggery demon. At least the preacher didn't catch him dancing or York's fate would've been even worse. Whatever the truth, I never encountered either of them again, and I was much the better for it.

As my troubles disappeared over the horizon, I assessed my situation. I still had a good gelding plus Charlie Bitters' pistol in my holster and one of the shirker's carbines in my saddle scabbard. I bent and grabbed the lariat Irish and York had hoped to hang me with and began to coil it, thinking I would throw it in the creek with their weapons until I realized it had belonged to Trent Parsons. So, I tied it to my saddle as a reminder of Reb. Now I had to catch up with the Five-D outfit and hope Muñoz had told Sainty the truth about the hidden money. To enhance my chances of being welcomed back rather than shot by the Five-D bunch, I mounted Relee and retraced my tracks until I found the Dutch oven and lid I had discarded in my flight from the malcontents. Though the pot slowed me down, I turned south to begin my Five-D quest.

Two days later about noon, I spotted outfit. Uncertain of my reception, I pulled the carbine from its boot and tied my bandanna around the barrel, signaling I approached in peace. Too, if things went bad, I'd have my carbine ready to defend myself. So focused were they on getting back to Texas, the fellows never realized I was gaining on them until I whistled. They turned their mounts around and Charlie reined up the wagon. As I neared, Sainty whispered something to them and every one pulled his pistol from his holster and aimed it at me.

That skunk Muñoz hadn't told Sainty where the money was stashed. I couldn't believe it. I lifted the Dutch oven as a peace offering, but still they scowled at me. One by one they dismounted and strode my way. Charlie Bitters jumped from the wagon, scurrying with them. Instead of a pistol, he pointed his finger at me as he stopped just in front of Relee.

"I returned your pot," I said, leaning over in the saddle and handing it to him, then straightening and cradling my carbine barrel in the crook of my left arm, wondering which of my former friends I'd have to shoot first.

Sainty waved his pistol at me. "What do you have to say for yourself, Lomax?"

I shrugged. "I didn't steal your money."

The trail boss's face quivered, then broke into a huge smile as he shoved his gun back in his holster. "I know. José told me."

Everybody replaced their pistols and hurrahed me, coming over to welcome me back. When I dismounted, they slapped me on the back and announced how glad they were to see me.

"You should've seen the look on your face," laughed Jurdon Mark.

They all hugged me, enjoying my confusion and relief.

"How the hell did you escape?" Tom Errun asked.

"Michaels' ink sketches saved me!" I told them the whole story leading up to the timely arrival of my old friend Wild Bill Hickok, deputy U.S. marshal. "The fake wanted posters convinced the lawman they were lying instead of me. By the way, what's buggery?"

They all laughed again.

"Mount up," Sainty ordered. "There are things, Lomax, you need not know."

Bitters hugged me. I pulled his revolver from my holster and gave it to him.

"I couldn't believe I lost the pistol or the Dutch oven, general. Why'd you take it?"

"I wanted to get home to Ruth as soon as I could. Cooking in it took too long. I stole the gun because I figured you'd shoot me if you found out about the pot. I wanted to guarantee my future back to Texas."

"Why didn't you tell me, general? I'd've sped up things for you and your girl."

I smiled as Bitters walked back to the wagon to return his pistol and his Dutch oven to their regular places. Completing that, he reached in the wagon bed and extracted my carbine and pistol. "We picked these up for you."

Sainty rode over and grinned. "Sorry, for the names I called you, Lomax. I couldn't believe you'd stolen the money. José told me the truth. Stuffing the mule collars with the cash was clever. Now every day I look at the harnesses and know our future's secure."

His apology pleased me, but one thing stuck in my craw. "Why didn't you send men to rescue me?"

Sighing, Sainty answered slowly. "I thought about it, I did, but I realized as shrewd as you were, you'd figure how to get out of the bind. And, I was right because here you are."

"Thanks to Deputy Marshal Hickok. If he'd been a minute later, I'd been swinging from a cottonwood tree."

"You're like a cat, Lomax, always landing on your feet. Besides that, I wanted to see Madlyn."

Then I understood. I'd have sacrificed Sainty to return to Ruth.

We rode away from that spot, glad not to have to look over our shoulders for O'Henry, Muscher and Dire. The days added up as we headed south, making good time out of Kansas and entering Indian Territory. Bitters didn't use the Dutch oven again on the trip, saying its burial left a residue that ruined the flavor of his cooking. I knew he was favoring me, so we could get home faster. The novelty of seeing Man Who Rides with Arrow in His Chest had worn off, and few Indians came out to see me pass on my third journey across the Territory. Even better, we never spotted a rabid skunk, though near the Red River we found the mound of dirt where we had buried Toad Beeline. We spent an hour there as we planted at the head of his grave the wooden marker Sainty had bought in Abilene. With his name burned into the face, Toad would no longer be an anonymous grave to those passing.

When we had set the marker, we removed our hats and said a silent prayer before Jurdon Mark suggested we say the real Lord's Prayer for poor old Toad.

"I gots my Bible," Silas announced. "I be reading it if we be finding it."

Mark borrowed the volume and thumbed to the New Testament. "It's in Matthew somewhere," he said as he scanned the pages. "Here it is, Matthew six nine." He returned the Bible to Banty and pointed the place to begin.

Silas read slowly, hesitating at new words but making it through the entire passage.

"Our Father, which are in heaven, Hallowed be thy name. Thy kingdom come. Thy will be done in earth, as it is in heaven. Give us this day our daily bread. And forgive us our debts, as we forgive our debtors. And lead us not into temptation, but deliver us from evil; For thine is the kingdom, and the power, and the glory, forever. Amen."

"Amen," we all said in unison.

Even though it took Silas a long time to finish the passage, I stood proud, having had a hand in helping him learn to read.

We donned our hats, mounted up and headed south, crossing the Red River without the drama of our first crossing. When we pulled out of the water and onto firm ground, we whistled and waved our headgear, glad to be back in Texas again.

"Remember the Alamo!" we shouted.

Without the bellowing of balky cows and the cloud of dust they kicked up, the journey was pleasant, made even more so by the cooler breezes of early fall. When we reached Fort Worth late one evening, Sainty paid for us a night in a hotel so we could get a bath, change clothes and leave early enough to go by the funeral parlor for one of the Flenner brothers to take us to Trent Parsons's grave.

Come morning, we felt better after a bath and a night's rest on a feather mattress. We were at morticians' office when the proprietors arrived in their buggy. "Mr. Spencer, isn't it?" the tall brother asked Sainty, while the short one hopped out of the rig.

"That's right. We've come to see the arrangements for Trent Parsons."

"I thought so," he replied. "I'll leave my brother to open the parlor, and you can follow me to the cemetery." Rattling the reins, all of us, including Charlie Bitters in his wagon, followed the mortician down the dirt streets of Fort Worth. We covered a mile before we reached the graveyard, and the buggy turned and passed through the open gate. Our procession snaked among a hundred graves with markers of wood and stone, in various shapes and colors, some simple crosses, others elegant stone statues in honor of the deceased. At the far edge of the cemetery, the tall mortician stopped his buggy and pointed to a gray granite stone that marked the last resting place of Trent Parsons.

"I hope the headstone and plot are to your liking, Mr. Spencer. It was a nice service, though sparsely attended."

Sainty dismounted, strode over to headstone and walked around the site, careful not to dishonor Reb by stepping on his grave. He turned and nodded to our cemetery guide. "It is fine, very fine. Thank you."

"Will you be needing anything else, Mr. Spencer?"

"No, sir, Mr. Flenner."

"Then I'll head back to my office. Please stop by on your way out of town, if something should come to mind." He clicked his tongue, and his horse pranced out of the graveyard.

We dismounted and joined Sainty. Silas brought his Bible and found the bent page corner that marked the Lord's Prayer. We removed our hats. As he read the passage, I smiled at the memory of Reb and his decency, then chuckled at him spiking his tobacco with gunpowder to identify the thief among us. When Silas finished the scripture, we said "amen." We walked somberly back to our horses, and I saw Parsons's lariat tied to my saddle. I removed it and returned to the gray stone and hung the lasso over the corner of his monument. "We got the first herd to Abilene. We wished you were with us, but I know you're happy with your wife and boys. I'm leaving your lariat should the Lord need a good cowhand." I retreated to Relee, mounted and soon caught up with the outfit, glad we need not visit any more graves.

Southward we continued, fording the Trinity, reaching Waco and crossing the Brazos. From there we reached Austin and crossed the Colorado, the last major river before we reached the ranch. I spent much of my time, pulling the ink drawing of Ruth from my pocket and smiling at her as I rode. The closer we came to the Five-D, the longer it each minute took to pass. Our final night on the trail I was so anxious I slept poorly, longing to see Ruth again. I arose even before Charlie Bitters and saddled Relee.

José Muñoz joined me. "You eager to see her?"

"Wouldn't you be?"

"Si, ella es muy bonita," he responded.

I smiled, knowing he had called her beautiful. "Thank you," I said. "Thank you for complimenting Ruth and for telling Sainty where the money was hidden."

"It was the honest thing to do," Muñoz said. "My mother always told me to do the right thing."

"Mine did too," I said, "though I don't know that I always have."

"I suspect you have," he replied, "and I know you and your woman will teach your children the same values."

Soon all the drovers arose, tending their business and packing up. Once the horses were saddled, we mounted and headed for home. We were over thirty miles from the place, but eager as we were we paced our horses so as not to wear them as we didn't have enough to switch out everyone's mount. Sainty often rode up to the wagon and mule team, leaning over in his saddle and patting the harness collars resting on the shoulders of the two mules. His success would earn him Colonel Dillon's permission to marry Madlyn. I supposed I should ask the colonel for Ruth's hand as well, since he was the closest thing to kin she had on earth.

As the sun was dying on the western horizon, we rode into view of the ranch house, the barn and pens. I saw smoke coming from the kitchen stovepipe, and I knew Ruth was preparing supper. The foreman and I trotted our horses ahead of the others.

"We're back," Sainty yelled and whistled.

"Ruth," I shouted. "I promised you I'd return. I'm back!"

Sainty whistled again.

The front door opened and Colonel Dillon stepped out, then darted back inside, returning moments later with Madlyn. She grinned, waved her hand and bolted off the porch to meet Sainty. We reined up twenty feet from the house. Sainty leaped from his horse and ran into Madlyn's arms.

I jumped from Relee.

Madlyn hugged Sainty, then cried, "Lomax, wait."

I couldn't wait. I bounded up on the porch, swung open the door and darted inside, headed straight for the kitchen, ready to sweep Ruth in my arms and give her the first of many kisses to follow. I jumped into the kitchen, "Ruth? Where are you?" I couldn't find her. I glanced out the back door, making sure she wasn't outside, then retraced my route through the place, calling her name. "Ruth! Ruth!"

Not finding her, I ran back out onto the porch. The colonel, Madlyn and Sainty awaited me, their shoulders slumped, their demeanors dark and helpless. "No," I said.

Madlyn answered with a sad smile. "Come with me, Lomax. I need to show you something."

She took my arm and escorted me around the house and toward the giant tree that shaded the Dillon family cemetery plot.

"No, no," I said. "It can't be."

Madlyn patted my arm as she accompanied me to the graveyard. A new grave had been dug and filled. A nameless white cross marked the head of the mound of dirt.

I pulled my arm from her hand as my knees grew mushy, and I fell upon them.

"We're sorry, Lomax, we really are."

I waved her away. "Please, I want to be alone with Ruth."

Silently, Madlyn retreated.

Confused, I took off my hat and tried to comprehend the loss. Nothing made sense any more except tears.

I wept and wept. Then I wept some more.

Chapter 34

I stayed the night with Ruth, telling her of the money I'd earned and how I had planned to spend it with her. While there was still light, I looked at her newest drawing, but a tear fell upon it and smeared the ink so I put it away. I told her of the funny things that had happened during the trail drive, and how much I enjoyed our brief stay together, and how I wished I could swap my life for hers. But she never answered, and she never came back. Placing my hat on her grave and using it as a pillow, I slept with her for the first and only time.

Come morning, I arose exhausted and hungry. I'd irrigated her grave with my tears, and I hoped the moisture would spawn a beautiful crop of bluebonnets in the spring. That night is where my hatred of Texas and Texans sprouted. They should have saved a fragile young flower like Ruth. Surely, there was a Texan who could have cured her. All Texas left me with was a painful memory forever. It was so confusing. I didn't know where to go or what to do.

Finally, I got up, swiped at the dust from her grave on my clothes and picked up my hat. Starting for the house, I saw Relee in the corral with the other horses and knew somebody had tended him for me. As I walked toward the kitchen, I noticed the drovers scattered around the barn and corral. They came up and hugged me or patted me on the shoulder or stated condolences. Jurdon Mark, Martin Michaels, Tom Errun, Silas Banty, José

Muñoz, Pedro Ramírez and Charlie Bitters escorted me to the house and offered to help me through my grief.

I thanked them, telling them I would let them know if I figured anything out, but nothing could lessen the pain in my heart. Thoughts and the drawing of Ruth had helped me survive the cattle trail, and now I could never even thank her for that, much less marry her. As the men returned to their chores, I entered the kitchen where Madlyn worked over the stove.

She turned around when I entered. "I'm so sorry, Lomax."

I nodded. "What happened?"

"About six weeks after you left, she got sick. Typhoid, we think."

"Was it painful?"

"It was a slow death, but she lingered, thinking of you. She asked me to place your unfinished painting at the foot of her bed. Ruth smiled at it, despite the discomfort. She held the pencil drawing of you in her hand when she died. Your likeness was the last thing she saw on this earth."

My eyes moistened. "I was going to marry her."

"I know and so did she. That's what kept her smiling in spite of her sickness. After her passing, we used money you had left her to buy a coffin and a dress, the fanciest she had ever owned. We fixed her hair and put on that fine dress with your blue calico apron over it. We left the drawing of you in her hand. Even in burial, she was beautiful, and your likeness was with her."

"Thank you," I said.

"She was one of us so we buried her in the Dillon plot."

"I'm grateful for that. I want to buy her a stone."

"We'll purchase her one now that we have money."

"No! I intend to buy it."

"Sainty brought in the mule collars last night and explained how you saved the money. We owe you a lot, Lomax."

"I owe Ruth a decent headstone, and I will buy her one."

"How can we repay you?"

I thought for a moment, then nodded. "I want the portrait you did of me."

"Certainly, Lomax. It's still in her room at the foot of her bed where she last saw it. I covered it after she passed."

Leaving Madlyn, I made my way to Ruth's tiny room and took the painting off the easel, never lifting the cover to look at it. Sadness overwhelmed me, standing where she had died and wondering what her last thoughts were, wishing I had been present to comfort her in her final moments. Tucking the canvas under my arm, I carried it back into the kitchen.

"Ruth thought it was a fine likeness and had me bring in my paints to incorporate her suggestions. She spoke of a kindness and decency in your eyes. Have you looked at it?"

Sighing, I shook my head. "I need coal oil and a tin of matches."

Madlyn's hand flew to her lips. "You're planning to destroy it, aren't you?"

"It's mine, you said."

"But why?"

"I want her eyes to be the last that ever gaze upon it."

Madlyn fidgeted, both confused and disappointed at my decision. Perhaps it was illogical or the wrong thing to do, but I had never felt such a hurt in my life. My hardened demeanor either frightened or wore Madlyn down. She moved to the cabinet and retrieved the matches, then stepped to the corner and picked up a gallon coal oil can with a spout.

"Sorry," I said as I took them from her and marched outside. I strode to the Dillon family plot. "Good morning, Ruth. I've brought the painting you liked." I laid the artwork on the mounded dirt and poured the fuel over it until the cloth cover and the canvas were soaked. After backing away from the pyre, I dropped the can, lit a match and tossed it on the canvas. The portrait whooshed and burned violently, sprouting azure flames that reminded me of bluebonnets. My mind flashed back to that cottonwood tree in Kansas when Wild Bill had saved me from a lynching. If he'd been a couple minutes later, I would have already been with Ruth. I cursed Hickok and Texas, and damned Texans and my luck. Then I sobbed. When the blaze died and nothing remained but ash and the smoldering remnants of the charred frame, I picked up the oil can and returned to the house. I saw all the hands at the barn standing and staring silently at me.

When I entered the kitchen, Madlyn hugged me as Dillon and Sainty walked in. "I'm so sorry," she whispered.

I freed myself, tossed the matches on the counter and put the fuel can in the corner, then stood there, uncertain what to do.

She asked, "Do you want breakfast?"

"Whatever you've got that's quick," I answered, taking a seat as the two men joined me.

The colonel spoke first. "You saved our ranch and earned our perpetual gratitude. Stay here for as long as you like. We'll make a cowboy out of you yet."

"The memories are too painful."

"Would you at least stay for the wedding? The colonel's agreed to give me Madlyn's hand, and she's promised to marry me."

"Congratulations, Sainty" I offered. "I know you'll be happy."

Madlyn walked over with a plate of biscuits and a jar of wild plum preserves. "The biscuits are cold but they'll hold you over until lunch," she said.

"I'll be gone by then," I said, eating my breakfast in the awkward silence of people uncertain what to say.

"Where you heading, son?" asked the colonel.

"San Antone to hire a stone mason to carve her headstone. After the stone is set, I'll be leaving."

"For where, son?"

"Anywhere outside Texas. I've come to hate this state."

When I was done, I thanked Madlyn and shook hands with Dillon and Sainty before exiting out the back and heading for the barn where the fellows were tending their horses.

"We cared for your bay last night," José Muñoz offered.

"Thank you."

"We're all sorry," Martin Michaels said as everyone gathered around me.

"We left your belongings in the wagon," Tom Errun added.

"I'm leaving Texas in a few days."

"We wouldn't have made it without you," Jurdon Mark offered.

Silas Banty marched up and hugged me. "I be reading now. Thanks be to you."

Charlie Bitters swatted my back. "General, you're a fine boy, like my son would've been if he had survived the war."

Even Pedro Ramírez said something in Spanish that Muñoz translated. "He says you're a good man to cross rivers with."

Not knowing what to say and or do, I stood there motionless.

"I'll saddle your horse," Muñoz offered.

"Thank you." To escape my friends, I entered the barn. I found my carbine, bedroll, canteen and saddlebags in the wagon bed.

The wrangler brought Relee into the barn, and I hugged the animal's neck and slid the bridle over his head as Muñoz saddled him. As I loaded my saddle satchel, José retreated from the barn. I added my other gear to Relee's back, though I couldn't find my canteen even though I had just seen it.

Muñoz returned, holding up my water flask. "I filled your canteen, Lomax."

Taking it from him, I tied it to my rigging and mounted Relee. "Thanks, José, for everything." I turned my gelding and rode out of the barn past my saddle pals. They offered their goodbyes and waves, but I trotted off, crying much of the way to San Antonio.

Once in town I found an old stone mason that would

sell me a fine tombstone for fifty dollars, but he said it would take two weeks to engrave it. I told him I'd pay him double if he completed it in three days. He balked until I offered triple his going rate for a carved, delivered and installed headstone. My money was persuasive, and he agreed as long as I paid half up front and half on delivery. I pointed out the pink stone I wanted, and he brought me a pencil and pad to write the inscription. As I wrote "Ruth" on the paper, I realized I had never known her last name. So, I added my surname behind hers. I didn't know her birthdate either, but remembered she was near my age so I put "1850-1867." Such an inscription seemed so sparse. Then I added two more words: "Beloved Companion."

I handed the sheet to the stone man, who said such a brief dedication could be done in two days for the same price, of course. I fished out my money, and placed seventy-five dollars in his hand. "See you day after tomorrow," he said.

Watching his reaction to my cash, I stepped around to the opposite side of Relee, pretending to adjust my saddle bags, but actually hiding all but twenty dollars of my cash inside. Then I found a cantina and bought a bottle of whiskey to help me kill the next two days. I'd heard that liquor helped you forget, but when I sobered up I still remembered the pain and had a headache to boot. On the second day, I returned and found the mason and his Mexican helper had already loaded the monument in his cart ready to ride out to the ranch. He showed me the inscription:

RUTH LOMAX
BELOVED COMPANION
1850-1867

I bit my lip, fighting back tears, and nodded my approval.

"Such a shame for one so young," he noted.

Again I nodded as he and his helper climbed into

the cart and followed me to the Five-D. We arrived in a couple hours, and I directed the workers to the burial plot. As we unloaded the stone, Madlyn joined us.

"It's a beautiful stone," she said, drawing close enough to read it. She wrinkled her nose.

"I didn't know her last name," I explained. "It would've become Lomax, if she'd lived."

Madlyn smiled. "I understand."

The two men wrestled the stone out and struggled their way across the plot, gently lowering the marker to the ground. The mason fetched his shovel from the cart, and walked to her grave.

"What do you want done with the cross?" he asked as he pulled it from the mound.

"I'll take it," I said.

He handed it to me, then dug a hole in the undisturbed dirt at the head of her resting place. Satisfied with his spadework, he and his helper worked the headstone into the excavation, set it and filled in around the marker. As they finished placing the stone, I dropped the cross at the foot of the grave and retreated to my saddlebags to get the remaining seventy-five dollars I owed the craftsman.

As I counted out his pay, he smiled. "Are you pleased?"

"Yes, sir," I replied as I handed him the money, "But let me borrow your spade for a moment." I took the shovel, picked up the cross and marched behind the stone. Touching the cross to the back of the tombstone, I pounded it into the ground with the spade.

"Why, Lomax, that's such a striking stone, you don't need the cross," Madlyn said.

"Yes, I do," I answered, handing the tool to the mason. "I plan to leave her a gift."

Madlyn shrugged as the mason climbed into the cart with his helper and left.

"I want to do this alone," I told her.

She smiled, walking over and giving me a hug. "Would you stay to eat with me? I'm the only one here as all the men are out working cattle or have left the colonel's employ."

"No, I'm riding on."

"The wedding's in a couple weeks. I wish you'd stay."

"My best to you and Sainty, but it's too painful to linger here, too many sad memories."

Madlyn nodded, hugged me again and retreated to the house.

When she disappeared, I stepped to Ruth to offer my final goodbye and my final tears. "I never gave you a ring, Ruth, so I want to leave you my bracelet." I pulled the amulet from my wrist and held it up for her. "It's silver. You deserve gold, but this is the best I have. I planned to have it melted down into our wedding rings and a necklace for your wedding gift. Since I can't do that, I want you to keep it forever." I slid the bracelet over the top of the wooden marker until it rested on the crossbar. "I love you." I turned, mounted and rode away, looking back once over my shoulder and remembering the last time I had seen her the morning we left on the trail drive. She stood in the golden glow of the lantern light, a soft halo circling her beautiful brown hair. This day, the sun cast a glint off the silver bracelet, and I took it to be a heavenly smile from Ruth. It was decades later before I could mention her name again.

Nor did I see any of the Five-D owners or hands after that, though in the coming years I soiled myself several times returning to Texas, though not always by my choice. Along the way, I encountered people that knew them. Colonel Dillon died a couple years later and willed his spread to Madlyn and Sainty Spencer. After the colonel's death, Sainty parlayed the inheritance into one of the great ranching fortunes in South Texas. Madlyn continued her art, becoming a portrait painter highly sought after by ranch families, her paintings valued in the thousands of dollars. I always wondered what my portrait might have been worth had I not destroyed it. Together Sainty and Madlyn became major Texas philanthropists.

As for the drovers, José Muñoz became Sainty's ranch foreman and Pedro Ramírez his second in command. They both married and did well. Silas Banty and Tom

Errun both bought their own ranches. Silas worked on the Five-D for six years, taking only a quarter of his pay and having Sainty invest the rest in cattle for him. Silas accumulated enough money and smarts to buy a ranch in Mitchell County. Some said by the turn of the century, he and his literate wife were the wealthiest and most respected former slaves in Texas. I knew they enjoyed reading their Bible scriptures together.

Errun got funding from his English connections and started the Man U Ranch in Tom Green County with a cattle brand unique throughout West. On the left stem of the U he added a circle at the top and a diagonal a quarter of the way down and a longer diagonal half way down. The image resembled half of a stick man on the left side of the U, creating the Man U Brand. Martin Michaels gave up cowboying and turned to artistry, earning a fine living and a reputation as the Leonardo of the longhorn, with his pen-and-ink sketches and later his paintings. Some said he rivaled cowboy artists Charlie Russell and Frederic Remington, but a fire in his studio destroyed most of his work, leaving little of his legacy for posterity.

As for Charlie Bitters and Jurdon Mark, I never learned their fates. The best I could tell from Charlie, he'd lost all his kin and was likely alone in life, much like Trent Parsons. Like Reb, I suspect he died in his sleep, especially if he ate his own cooking. As for Mark, I never found out what came of him. If I were guessing, I suspect he charmed his way to success or finally lost all his marbles. Whatever the outcome, the fellows that survived the drive without being arrested seemed to have done better in life than me, largely because I bounced around the West too much. Even old Jesse Chisholm came out ahead of me. While he died of food poisoning four months after we returned to the Five-D, my trail wound up carrying his name, a fact that galled me for years.

Though the trail-driving chapter of my life ended when I departed the Five-D, my cowboying legacy followed me for years the farther north I went to escape

Texas. The more I introduced myself on the Plains, the more people associated my name—in a bad way—with that of Wild Bill Hickok, who was becoming a Dime Novel hero from the fake adventures writers concocted in fancy New York or Chicago offices.

Word was that Hickok had told folks if he ever saw me again, he would shoot me for all the humiliation I had caused him. He started spreading stories I'd defiled his hair and embarrassed him. The first time I encountered such a lie, I ignored it, but more and more lies reached my ears, all involving something I'd done to his tresses. I finally decided he was still smarting from my comments to Chuck Muscher and Bartholomew Henry O'Henry about us being such good friends that I had combed nits from his locks. Hickok was as fussy about his hair as he was about his clothes and his appearance.

Over the years the stories worsened. When I introduced myself I'd be asked if I was the Lomax that did this or that to Wild Bill's mane. The accusations claimed I'd stuck thirty pieces of chewing gum in his hair or tarred and feathered his locks or poured coal oil on his tresses and set them on fire. Other stories declared I braided his hair to a bedpost when he was drunk and yelled "fire" into his room, almost scalping him when he jumped up. Some declared I peed or took a dump in his hair while he was dozing. Still others suggested I'd thrown acid or dripped a quart of molasses on his head. My two favorite tales reported me shaving his head and selling his hair to a wig maker and me tying firecrackers in his curls and lighting the fireworks to watch him dance.

At first it was amusing to hear those stories and imagine myself a villain in one of the Dime Novels, but after years of putting up with those slanders, I finally had had my fill of them and decided I would one day put an end to the lies Hickok was spreading. By a set of unfortunate and deadly circumstances I wound up in Bismarck, Dakota Territory, in July of 1876 and learned that Wild Bill was in the Black Hills in a town called Deadwood. I vowed to find him and end those lies once and for all. By then in Bismarck, I was riding an army mule I'd named Ciaha, in honor of my late acquaintance Colonel George Armstrong Custer, a man who deserved the enduring infamy at the Little Bighorn. In fact, Ciaha was an Indian word I'd made up to stand for "Custer is a horse's ass." In my mind Custer, like Muscher, was one of those horse's asses without four legs.

Me and my mule were fortunate enough to catch a steamboat headed south from Bismarck with some injured survivors of the Little Bighorn battle. Ciaha and I got off the boat in Pierre and rode west into the Black Hills toward Deadwood. Along the way, I had plenty of time to consider whether or not I wanted to settle my difference with Hickok. I'd seen what he had done eleven years earlier to Davis Tutt in Springfield, and I wasn't certain I had the speed or the nerve to face him, but I was tired of his falsehoods demeaning my family name. I figured the only sure way to beat Hickok was to shoot him in the back with a twelve-gauge shotgun, but that didn't seem the sporting thing to do although it would certainly have been safer for me than taking chances against him in a fair fight. Over the years, I came to believe that survival trumped ethics in the West.

I arrived in Deadwood the last week of July. The place was a scab of a town squeezed between the mountains like a festering pimple. Men claimed they could get rich panning gold and some did, but most went through life like me, always missing out on the big bonanza and being left with the tailings of the lucky ones. Knowing I might risk my life in confronting Wild Bill Hickok, I decided I would go out clean and in new clothes. After purchasing a fancy suit in a dry goods store, I found a place that offered cheap baths. After I'd paid my dollar I found out why. The four tubs were out back of the little building surrounded by a puncheon fence with little privacy. I undressed out in the open like the other fellows, bathed and shaved in lukewarm water with strong lye soap. I got out, dressed and paid a nickel for a splash of tonic water because I had plans to relieve a little tension with the ladies before I sought Hickok. Though I wasn't proud of myself, I'd found out after San Antonio that for the right price, some women would be glad to spend time with you and work the kinks out of your muscles. I asked the bath house proprietor about a place where I might find such women.

"You want cheap or fancy?"

"I want fancy as long as her name ain't Nancy. These clothes are for a lady, not a harlot."

"Try the Ozark House. It's the fanciest place in town. Word has it most of the girls can even read." He gave me directions to an adjacent street, describing the brothel as a red clapboard building with a green door.

I tugged on my coat collar, straightened my tie and asked the fellow how I looked.

"Good enough for a funeral," he replied.

I hoped it wasn't my own as I left the bath house and climbed atop Ciaha, riding along the street that teemed with horses, wagons, miners, carts, dogs, pigs, chickens, oxen, bullwhackers and an occasional decent woman. However, I wasn't chasing decency on this day. I came to a building that matched the description I'd been given, though no sign identified the house as bawdy.

Sliding off my mule, I stepped on the muddy street and grabbed the door knob to enter, but the place was locked. I knocked, and momentarily I heard the entry being unlocked. Standing before me when the door swung open was a striking woman, maybe a decade older than me.

"My, my," she said, "don't you look as fine as a stud horse."

"I'm new to town. Is this the Ozark House?"

"It is. Won't you come in, handsome?" As soon as I stepped inside, she shut the door behind me and grabbed my arm before I could step away. She pointed to a bench. "Have a seat and remove your boots. It saves time later and doesn't muddy the carpets I brought from St. Louis."

I did as instructed, staring at her modest, high-necked blouse and billowing skirt, as I pulled off my footwear and dropped them by the three pair that had been pushed under the bench. Taking my hand as I stood up, the madam escorted me into the parlor where a single woman sat, staring through a stereoscope.

"It's still early in the afternoon, three of our girls are occupied with other visitors and the rest are sleeping. JoLeah, though, can take care of your needs. It's three dollars for an hour. Ten dollars for four hours, but no sleeping when you're done." The madam had soft brown hair and brown eyes that lacked the hardness of most in her trade. I'd worked in a brothel in Waco the year before and found the madam here to be as classy as Medusa had been in Texas.

When JoLeah lowered the stereoscope, she offered me a smile that would melt butter. She had golden hair, blue eyes, and luscious lips that begged to be kissed. She wore modest attire that hid her abundant assets. "You're a handsome fellow," she cooed. "What's your name?"

"Lomax," I said, "H.H. Lomax."

The madam gasped, and I watched the stereoscope slide from JoLeah's hands onto the carpet. Her hand flew up to her mouth. "You're not the Lomax that powdered Wild Bill Hickok's hair with crumbled cow dung, are you?"

Before I could answer, the madam grabbed my arm and jerked me toward the stairs. "This one's mine, Jo-Leah. Attend the entry while I take care of Mr. Lomax."

I climbed the steps in socked feet, and she never let go of me, leading me past five doors on each side of the hallway to the one at the end. She removed a key from her pocket, quickly unlocked the door and dragged me inside, locking up behind us. I would have preferred JoLeah as she was younger and her blond hair was more appealing, but I wasn't about to turn pass on a free romp. I yanked off my hat and put it on a chair, then pulled off my coat and hung it on the back of the seat.

"Slow down," she said as she walked in front of me, eyeing me from head to toe and smiling. "You turned out well."

Emboldened by her compliment, I reached for her tora-loorals!

Before I could touch them, she slapped my face.

"Do you know who I am?"

Rubbing my cheek, I nodded. "About the meanest whore I've ever met."

She slapped me again. "Never call me or my girls a whore!"

I stood as confused as a preacher in hell.

"Your name is Henry Harrison Lomax. You're from Cane Hill, Arkansas, son of George Washington and Abigail Lomax."

Not only was this woman the meanest madam I'd ever encountered, she was also the smartest. I wondered if she knew everything about all her clients.

"You have five brothers—"

I'd been told of people that could read minds or at least trick people into thinking they were reading your mind, but this woman was amazing. I nodded,

"—and three sisters."

"I don't remember my oldest sister," I said. "She ran away from home before I had firm memories of her."

"I'm Constance Louise," she said. "I'm your lost sister."

With that she threw her arms around me and hugged me tightly.

Now I was even more confused, much like a lawyer in heaven.

Chapter 35

"We always wondered what happened to you," I said as Constance led me to a maroon velvet sofa and sat me down. I looked around the spacious and well-apportioned room as I tried to come to grips with finding my long lost sister—in a whorehouse. "You never wrote."

"It would've broken Momma's heart to learn what became of me."

"You could've lied," I answered, shaking my head, trying to conjure up memories of her, but my recollections remained foggy.

"Momma taught us never to lie," Constance reminded me. "Like you, I was born with Pa's wanderlust. How are Momma and Pa?"

"Fine as far as I know," I shrugged. "I haven't seen them since leaving home eleven years ago to escape the war animosities."

"You haven't written them?"

"No, ma'am. I never knew what to write as I haven't amounted to much or done anything to make them proud. I'll get back to Cane Hill one day."

"I go by an alias now, so I don't shame the folks in Cane Hill."

"Actresses was what they called the working girls in Waco."

"I'm Annie Ozark. I couldn't forget the hills back home so I named myself after them. So please call me Annie instead of Constance or the family name."

"Since I left home, I've been called many things, but the closest I've come to having a nickname was Whirlwind or Lead Eye, a nickname Bill Cody gave me from our buffalo hunting days, saying my aim was so bad I wasted a buffalo's weight in gun lead to bring one down."

"That sounds like Bill."

"You know him?"

Constance smiled. "Let's just say he's been to the Ozarks." Her expression turned serious. "Speaking of tarnishing the family name, I keep hearing rumors of a Lomax fellow that did gawd-awful things to Wild Bill Hickok's hair. Is that you?"

Gulping, I nodded. "It's nothing like you've heard. Only thing I ever did was a favor to help him get rid of the lice."

"Then why's Hickok fabricating these lies?"

"I mentioned combing nits out of his hair to two fellows. He's a mite touchy about it."

"You know he's in Deadwood, don't you?"

"That's why I came to town. I intend to stop the lies."

"Don't get yourself shot and become fodder for another one of those Dime Novels that carry his name, nothing but outlandish lies those things are. Word is he's gotten married, and he's going blind."

"Any relation between the two?"

Annie laughed. "I wouldn't know in this business."

Then we updated each other on our lives. Constance left Cane Hill a few years before the war, but got married too young to a fellow that drank and beat her. He returned home drunk one night and collapsed on their bed. She threw the covers over him, took her sewing kit and spent two hours sewing him up in the sheets. With her broom she beat the hell out of him to teach him how it felt. Before he could tear his way out of the bloody cocoon, she packed her belongings and left. She despised work as a laundress, cook or waitress and took up the bawdy business because becoming a lady of commerce was easier on the spine and didn't leave calluses on the hands.

I told her about the war driving me from Arkansas

and taking our brothers John at Gettysburg and Van at Prairie Grove. She cried at the news of John and Van, even if it had been more than a dozen years earlier that they had left this earthly realm. I detailed meeting Wild Bill, riding with Jesse James, working on the railroad, leading the first herd of Texas longhorns to Abilene and accompanying the Seventh Cavalry on Custer's ill-fated Little Bighorn expedition.

My accounts enthralled her, though I'm not sure she believed them all. "I want you to stay here, Henry," Constance finally said. "I've got ten beds besides mine, but only eight girls working right now. I can give you a room. The room is much smaller than mine, but it'll have a feather mattress, and you'll be nearby so we can visit more."

"I've slept in worse, Constance—errr—I mean Annie."

"Yes, remember it's Annie."

I nodded. "Just call me Lomax to reduce chances of our doings reaching Cane Hill."

She smiled. "Wonderful then. I'll have the fellows stable your mule and bring up your belongings. We can spend the day visiting, and you can worry about finding Wild Bill tomorrow."

As she told stories, I vaguely remembered her among my childhood recollections. When we went downstairs, Annie informed her help that I was a family friend from Arkansas, and I would stay for a few days as I looked up another acquaintance in Deadwood. The girls tittered when they found out my name was Lomax.

A raven-haired woman asked, "Do you know Wild Bill Hickok?"

"I've eaten a meal or two with him, if that's what you mean," I replied.

A red-headed gal inquired, "Are you part Indian?"

"Or a barber?" JoLeah asked.

I shrugged. "What?"

"What they're getting at," my sister explained, "is whether you scalped Wild Bill Hickok."

"Gracious no, ladies. All I ever did was comb nits out

406

of his hair."

They squealed like they'd never had lice, which was probably true as Annie ran a clean and respectable bawdy house by the look of the girls, the furnishings and the carpet which had never been sullied by a muddy boot.

After the introduction to the ladies, Annie and I retreated to her room, spending the rest of the evening together, us leaving only to find an eatery where she treated me to a fine beefsteak dinner. By midnight we were both tired and the noise from the rooms down the hall had quieted enough for me to retire to a bed that offered me a fine feather mattress over bedsprings that had endured a lot of mileage and creaked whenever I turned. I slept well and late, knowing there was no need to be in any hurry as Wild Bill would not be in any condition to start his gambling and drinking before noon. Arising, I dressed in my new clothes and strapped on my gun belt. Lifting my Colt from the leather, I checked that all six chambers were loaded. I stepped out into the hall and knocked on Annie's room.

Shortly, she cracked the door and smiled at me. "Good morning, Lomax. Rest well?"

"After you've slept on the ground as much as I have since leaving home, it takes a day or two to grow accustomed to a soft mattress and creaking springs."

"They take a lot of use," Annie said. "I'll have a fellow see about oiling them, if you don't mind him being in your room."

"That's fine. I'm heading out to find Hickok."

"Don't get yourself shot," she implored me.

Marching downstairs, I stopped at the bench and pulled on my boots. One other pair remained so I assumed the owner had paid for the night. I announced I was leaving if someone wanted to lock the door behind me. JoLeah strode over to the entry. "You be careful, Lomax. Not everyone in Deadwood is as cultured as we are at Ozark House." She batted her eyes at me. "And, you're always welcome in my room, paying or not."

"That's mighty kind of you, Miss JoLeah. I may take

you up on that." Tipping my hat at her, I stepped into the muddy streets of the mining town. I marched a block to Main and inspected the saloons on the north side of the street, checking out the bar and the gambling tables for James Butler "Wild Bill" Hickok, the greatest pistoleer in the West if the Dime Novels and Wild Bill himself were to be believed. By my count, I inspected thirty-eight drinking establishments, which wasn't bad for a town with but a single undertaker, B.P. Smith, who advertised his trade in a sign over his funeral parlor. Most of the saloons carried their proprietor's moniker, though there was the Bella Union, Eureka Hall, Grand Central, Little Bonanza, No. 10, and Red Bird. With so many saloons, I thought Deadwood was more civilized than I had realized until I counted three newspapers and twenty-seven law offices. A single newspaper could do more damage to a town than a fire on a windy day. As for lawyers, they were simply bandits by other methods.

After I investigated the last saloon on the north side of Main Street, I started back on the opposite side of the street, entering each drinking establishment and looking around, occasionally asking the bartender if Hickok had been in. I entered Nuttall and Mann's No. 10 Saloon and studied the layout and the two dozen customers, none of them Hickok. Like most establishments along Main, the building had a narrow front, barely more than twenty feet wide, but lengthy sides stretching eighty feet to a back door. I counted six round tables, including one on each side of the front entrance and four more strung out along the west side of the establishment. A twenty-foot-long, ell-shaped mahogany bar jutted out from the east wall about fifteen feet from the front door. Unlike others I had searched, this saloon catered to the serious drinker or gambler, a simple room with few frills, save for the tin ceiling. Kerosene lamps cut through the dimness and warped wooden floors creaked when you walked.

I stepped up to the bar and greeted the bartender, asking if Hickok had been in today.

"Not yet," answered the barkeep. "Who's inquiring?"

"Who are you?" I asked.

"I'm Henry Young," he announced.

"My name is H.H.—"

"Lomax!" Young shouted.

"—Lomax," I finished.

"Hey everybody," the bartender cried. "This is H.H. Lomax, the fellow that Bill's always bitching about."

A customer with two half-full mugs of beer in his hands walked up, eyed me and shook his head. "He don't look that tough."

Another patron slid up to the bar. "It true all those things you did to Wild Bill's hair?"

"Lies," I cried, "all lies. I combed nits out of his hair, that's all, dammit"

Young interrupted. "I wouldn't say that aloud, Lomax. Hickok is a mite prickly about his hair and his cleanliness."

"Well, I'm plenty touchy about all the lies he's been telling for the last decade."

The bartender studied me and shrugged. "I don't get it. Hickok says you've got the steeliest nerves he'd ever seen on a fellow, something about outfoxing all comers on the Rattle Jar. That ring a bell?"

I nodded.

"No offense, Lomax, but you don't look that tough or that nervy," Young announced.

"Couldn't agree more," said the patron drinking from two mugs. "Bill's building you up as the toughest thing since shoe leather to make a better Dime Novel story when he kills you."

Young chuckled.

"What's so funny?" I inquired.

"Hickok said if he spread enough stories about you in his travels, you'd one day come to find him so he wouldn't have to look for you. Damn if he wasn't right 'cause here you are."

I studied the motley group of customers and started to ask when Hickok might return, but the front door banged open and a shrill voice scratched our ears.

"Where is he, that Wild Bill?" cried this ungodly

character in buckskins and a greasy hat.

I wasn't the only one looking for Wild Bill.

"We don't allow ladies in here, Martha Jane," Young called out.

"I ain't a lady so that don't matter," she shot back. "Is my feller here or not?"

"He's not your feller or beau or anything else," Young answered.

"He is, too," she cried. "He just don't know it yet."

"Well, he ain't here," Young said, "but another infamous character is. Care to guess?"

"Has General Custer's rose from the dead and come to ask me to scout for him again? The damn Sioux would never have massacred him if I'd been along."

"No, it's even worse than George Custer," Young announced. "It's H.H. Lomax."

The nearby fellows flushed like a covey of quail as Martha Jane exploded with enough cusswords to make Satan blush."

"Lomax, meet Martha Jane Canary, better known as 'Calamity Jane'," Young said

No nickname ever fit a person better than Calamity for Miss Martha Jane Canary. I dipped the brim of my hat and nodded at this tornado of a pest blowing through the No. 10 Saloon.

Her right hand fell to the gun belt she wore on her hip like a man. Calamity leaned forward and squinted at me. "I ought to kill you for the horrible things you did to my Wild Bill and his hair," she said, then paused staring at me. "But you're kinda cute."

"Don't believe everything you hear, Miss Calamity."

"Oh, and you've got manners!" She curtsied for me. "No one ever calls me 'miss'."

"And I ain't that cute."

"Sure you are, in a roughhewn way like me," she countered.

Cute was the last word I'd ever associate with Calamity as she looked like she'd been run over by a locomotive and reassembled by a blind man, who installed the train whistle for her voice. I turned to the bartender.

"Will Hickok be back tonight?"

"Return at seven o'clock, and you'll find him."

I tipped my hat at Calamity, raced to the far end of the room and bolted out the rear door, which opened onto a narrow street where most of the brothels, including Ozark House, were located. I hid behind a wagon for fear she might follow me. Sure enough, she tailed me out.

"Come back, Lomax," she cried. "I'd like to spend time with you, have a fallback plan in case Wild Bill and I don't work out." While she was standing on the stoop, somebody inside No. 10 Saloon slammed the door shut and barred it. Calamity spun around and pounded on the entry, unleashing a string of profanity that would've made a priest's ears wither.

While she attacked the saloon's rear entrance, I dashed from the wagon and hid building-to-building as I made my way to Annie's place. I pounded on the door, hoping to get inside before Calamity saw where I was staying. As my sister opened the door, I jumped in.

"You must've found Wild Bill," she said, shutting and bolting the door.

"Worse, a beast named Calamity Jane Canary."

"Beast indeed! She sought a job here as one of the girls and then as a bouncer. Either way, she would've killed our business with her wicked manners and tart tongue. Don't let her follow you here."

"I'm not letting her trail me anywhere, if I can help it," I said, sitting and taking off my boots, then accompanying Annie to her room.

As I sat on the sofa, my sister asked me if I'd like lemonade. I nodded, and she opened the door and called for two glasses. She looked at me. "Did you find, Hickok?"

"Nope, but I found where he'll be tonight."

"And that is?"

"Nuttall and Mann's No. 10 Saloon."

"Ah, yes, one of Deadwoods less elegant drinking establishments."

A knock interrupted my response.

"Come in," Annie called.

As the door opened, JoLeah entered with two glasses of lemonade in her hands.

"I've told you, JoLeah, when you serve drinks, always deliver them on a tray not in your hands. It's much more elegant and appealing to the gentlemen."

"Yes, Miss Annie. My apologies, Mr. Lomax." JoLeah smiled and offered me my drink.

"Thank you, JoLeah." My sister watched her leave the room and close the door. "She's taken a liking to you Henry. In fact, she asked me if she could treat you for free. I told her I was fine with it, if you didn't mind."

"I've never had so many girls take to me on the same day," I answered.

"JoLeah's a lady. Calamity Jane is a swine. She drinks, gambles, curses, smokes and fights, all bad habits to have when you're as stubborn and slow of mind as she is. Now tell me about Wild Bill."

After a big sip of lemonade, I said, "I'm supposed to return at seven o'clock. I'll go about seven-thirty, make him wait a spell."

"You know what you're doing?"

"No, but I always seem to get by!"

"There's more mean men in Deadwood than any place I've ever been, Henry, so don't overestimate yourself."

"Thanks for the warning, big sister, and for giving JoLeah the okay to take a go at me."

Annie smiled. "I've never known a man to refuse."

We visited about home for a couple hours until I could tell by the growing shadows out Annie's window that the day was dying. I stood up, thanked my sister for her hospitality and told her I wanted to eat supper before I met Hickok. She offered her company, but I declined it, saying I needed a little time to think. She saw me to the door and opened it once I wore my boots. I stepped in the doorway, looking both directions for Canary, then skipped outside when the way was clear. Deciding I would best avoid Calamity by seeking an eatery somewhere other than Main Street, I found a hole-in-the-wall place that fed me overpriced ham, turnips and burned biscuits. The food was so bad it reminded me of Upchuck's cooking on the old Lomax Trail years earlier. Even if the fare tasted horrible, the company—none—was perfect, allowing me consider how to handle Hickok if it came to a gunfight.

As it neared seven-thirty, I paid my sixty cents for the meal, took a last sip of my coffee and strode to Main Street. Word had gotten out that the despicable H.H. Lomax, now being called "the barber of Wild Bill," was headed for a showdown with the man he had denuded because people crowded on the plank walk outside No. 10, looking through the window. "Here he comes," someone called and everyone turned from the saloon to watch me. I unbuttoned my frock coat and hooked the right side behind the butt of my pistol. I glared at the crowd as if I was as tough as the calluses on a barfly's elbows. The throng parted, and I felt like Moses on the banks of the Red Sea. Someone inside opened the door, and I entered. The packed place echoed with the noise of more than a hundred customers until they realized I had joined them. The No. 10 Saloon fell so quiet you could hear hair grow. As everyone's gaze fell on Hickok, I spotted him seated at the third table from the door, his back to the wall.

"It's been a long time, Lomax." Hickok said.

"Almost nine years in Kansas. I'm here to stop all the slanders you've been spreading about me and your hair since then. None of them were true, were they?"

Hickok shook his head. "Not a one."

The crowd groaned, falling silent again after a sharp glance from Hickok.

"I fabricated the stories so you'd find me, and I could kill you."

The spectators gasped and grinned. They lusted for a shootout!

"What for, Bill? Combing nits and letting it slip?"

"Hell, no, Lomax! You cost me my badge as a deputy U.S. marshal."

"What?"

"Remember in Kansas when I saved you from the

lynching you deserved?"

I grimaced and realized Chuck Muscher, Bartholomew Henry O'Henry and Harry Dire might have the last laugh on me yet. "I recollect a little."

"Do you recall the forged wanted posters?"

"I never told you they were authentic."

"No, you let me make a fool of myself. A hundred and fifty miles I rode to Kansas City. Do you realize how bad Dire smelled by the time I got him there? The stench has lingered in my nostrils for years."

"You didn't get the reward money?"

Hickok slammed his fists into the table and stood up as those near him backed away. "There weren't any rewards because the wanted posters were forged. They accused me of trying to swindle the government. They not only let me go but blackballed me from the federal payroll ever again."

"Seems it didn't keep you from finding law jobs in Hays and Abilene, from what I heard."

"Pay wasn't as good."

I wriggled the fingers on my right hand. "Are you ready to settle it?"

"Not here, not tonight."

"You scared?"

He nodded. "Scared you'll shoot innocent bystanders when we make our play."

"From what I been told, Bill, you're going blind. That true?"

"Lies, lies," he cried. "I can see as good as ever, and I can shoot even straighter. We'll settle it tomorrow at high noon on Main Street, just like Davis Tutt and I resolved our differences."

"I'm game, Hickok. We'll do it like Springfield, seventy-five yards apart for the play."

Hickok hesitated, and that told me his eyesight was indeed deteriorating.

"Or do you prefer a hundred yards? That's fine by me," I said, calling his bluff.

He nodded his head. "Seventy-five yards it is. You'll be as dead as Tutt by high sun."

"See you then," I said as I backed out the door.

No sooner I had set foot on the plank boardwalk than spectators broke out in cheers.

"A gunfight," someone yelled.

"Let the betting begin," another man shouted.

"But who'd bet on Lomax," cried an obviously inebriated saloon patron.

I would, I thought to myself as I marched back to the Ozark House, ever alert for any sign of Calamity Jane.

Annie was standing outside on the stoop, her arms crossed over her chest as I approached. She smiled when she saw me.

"You trying to drum up business?" I asked.

"Mondays are always slow, but I was out here waiting for you. I'm glad you're safe. Did you get it resolved?"

"Sort of," I said.

"What do you mean sort of?" Her grin narrowed.

"We're meeting on Main Street at high noon tomorrow to shoot it out."

Annie gasped as her hand flew to her mouth and. "Henry!"

"His eyesight's going bad, I don't think he can even see anything at seventy-five yards, much less hit his target."

"He did in Springfield from what I've heard."

"I was there, but it was a lucky shot. His luck is about to run out."

"Your luck may be in short supply after your close call with the Seventh Cavalry."

Gulping, I nodded. "I'd forgotten about that."

"How could you? It was just last month. This is the last day of July."

"I'd lost track."

"What you need's a good night's rest and a lot of prayer. I'll put the girls on it."

"What? The rest or the prayer?"

"Both," she announced as we headed inside.

As I pulled off my boots and shoved them under the bench, I realized they were the only ones there.

"I told you Mondays were slow," Annie said, closing

and bolting the door.

Though early, I retired to my room for what might be my last night on earth. Lying on the pillow with my hands behind my neck, I stared at the ceiling lost in my thoughts until a soft rap came at my door.

"Come in," I said.

JoLeah entered, wearing a smile and a nightgown. "I thought you might like company."

She was right.

Chapter 36

I awoke the next morning as refreshed as a man could be on the day he might die. JoLeah had worked out my tensions three times before dawn. I arose mid-morning and dressed in the new trousers, frock coat and white shirt I had bought upon arrival in Deadwood. After strapping on my holster and pistol, I checked the Colt to confirm each chamber was loaded with a cartridge. I even knotted under my collar a tie that a customer had left in the room. The way I figured it, if Hickok killed me in fine attire, the undertaker B.P. Smith could throw me in a coffin and pitch me in a hole and save my sister some money.

JoLeah awoke. "Good morning, Lomax," she said. "You look as handsome as a stallion."

"I feel like a stallion after last night."

She grinned. "It was fun, wasn't it? But promise me one thing, will you?"

"What's that?"

"Don't die on me!"

"I'll manage. I always do." I walked over to the bed, kissed her on the lips. When I stood up, I ran my fingers through her straw-colored hair

"Is there anything I can do for you, Lomax?"

"Keep my mattress warm and pray for me."

"Do you think God listens to the prayers of a sporting girl?"

"I suppose he hears everyone's prayer, though I can't

say if he answers them all. But you don't worry because I'll return this afternoon. Now let me ask you something, JoLeah. Is there a bakery in town?"

"That's an odd question for a man about to face Wild Bill Hickok."

"I've a hankering for cherry pie," I said.

"Over on Main Street there's George Eggert's or J.A. Wilson's. They're the best bakers in Deadwood."

"Thanks," I replied, leaning over and kissing her a final time. I exited the room, wondering if I would see her again.

Downstairs Annie was pacing the floor between the parlor and the entry. She met me at the stairs and threw her arms around me. "Henry, I'm scared for you. This is Wild Bill Hickok you're facing."

"I've survived on my wits since I left home. I'll do so today." Walking to the foyer bench, I sat and pulled on my boots. As I stood up, I checked my pistol in my holster again and nodded at Annie. "Take care, big sister."

She opened the door, and I stepped out into a bright day, ready to eat pie and to meet my fate in the middle of Deadwood. I strode to Main Street and spotted Wilson's bakery. Going inside, I asked for cherry pie, but the baker told me he was sold out. I marched down the street until I found George Eggert Bakery. As I walked inside, I noticed folks pointing and whispering. The store, though small, exuded the fragrant aromas of bread and cinnamon and sweets. Two small tables with chairs waited empty by the window.

"You're new here," said the aproned man behind the glass case displaying his baked goods. "My name is George Eggert, proprietor. How can I help you?"

"Cherry pie, you got any?"

"Indeed I do. I'll slice you a piece right now. Twenty-five cents."

"I want the whole pie and a fork. I plan to eat it here," I answered, pointing to a table.

"My cherry pie is delicious, I admit, but it's too rich to consume in one sitting. Why do you want a whole pie? It's two dollars and fifty cents."

"For good luck. Last few times I've had cherry pie, men died. Today's Wild Bill's turn."

Eggert gasped. "You're not the infamous H.H. Lomax that did all those horrible things to Hickok's hair, are you?"

I nodded, no longer caring they were false because in less than an hour, one of us would be dead. Either I would no longer hear the lies or he would no longer spread them.

"And the one that will face Wild Bill in a shootout at noon, are you?"

"That's me."

He crossed himself and grinned. "The pie's on the house, Mr. Lomax!"

Eggert removed a golden brown pie from the case and handed it to me. I took it to the table closest to the window and sat as the baker scurried over with a fork. He placed the utensil by the pie pan and smiled.

"This is wonderful that you would stop by for my pie," Eggert said. "By this afternoon, I can advertise my dessert as the last supper of the late and despicable H.H. Lomax, the most recent victim of noted pistoleer Wild Bill Hickok. People will come for miles to eat my pie."

"Thanks for your faith in me, Eggert!" I said as I picked up my fork and took a bite. While Eggert didn't know how to make friends, he sure knew how to make a tasty cherry pie.

"Nobody in Deadwood has faith in you, Lomax. It's ruined the betting pool."

"What? People are wagering on the outcome?"

"Oh, yeah, ever since word got around last night. At first betting was slow because nobody thought you had a chance. But now I understand men are betting a dollar on you hoping to win five or ten, that's how steep the odds are. No, offense, but I'm going for the sure thing, Lomax, even if I only win a dollar. Should be a big crowd come noon. I'm closing the shop to watch."

"I hope you're disappointed in the outcome, Eggert," I responded. "Now let me eat my pie alone in these, my last few minutes on earth."

The baker wiped his hands on his apron and backed away, as if he feared I would shoot him in the back. I might have, if I'd known the odds.

As I ate, I realized I was dining across from the No. 10 Saloon. I watched it for any sign of Hickok. Thirty minutes before noon, bartender Henry Young emerged, carrying a small sack of flour. I wondered if he had taken up baking like Eggert. The barkeep waded into the street directing horses, buggies, wagons and riders around him. He marched west thirty-five yards, bent and poured a line of flour on the street. Next he put his heel on that powdery white mark and strutted back down Main toward the saloon and bakery. As he passed, I heard him counting off numbers, "—forty-three, forty-four, forty-five, forty-six—" with each step. He was measuring out seventy-five yards for the big showdown. I figured he wanted to save time with the preliminaries so he could sell more drinks to celebrants after the smoke had cleared. Traffic on Main diminished and folks gathered on the plank walks for good positions to see the gunplay.

When men realized I was sitting by the window eating cherry pie, a crowd gathered to watch me eat. "He's as calm as a kitten sleeping in spring sunshine," I overheard one say. "Or, as dimwitted as a possum," said another. That's when I realized glowing eulogies would not accompany my funeral. I continued eating my lunch as the spectators shouted my progress to those less fortunate ones unable to reach the window and watch a doomed man eat his final meal.

"It's five minutes to noon, Lomax," said Eggert, jittery as a Mexican jumping bean. "I need you to hurry so I can close and find a spot on the street to see you die."

I calmed Eggert down. "Nothing will start without me. Even if I'm late, you'll still get your dollar."

When I ate my last bite, I wiped my mouth on my coat sleeve while the spectators cheered, "He's done! He's done!"

I stood up, hooked my coat behind my pistol butt, scowled to intimidate Eggert and walked out of the bakery, the proprietor following me like an eager puppy and locking the door behind us. "Good pie," I told him.

"Good luck," he replied. "You'll need it."

I worked my way through the crowd to the street and stepped out into the clammy dirt that Deadwood called Main Street. Confidence drained from me after hearing comments like "There's the man that's about to be dead!" or "He's a walking target!"

As I stepped to the middle of Main, Hickok emerged from the No. 10 Saloon and squeezed his way through the crowd. He squinted and looked around. I soon realized coming from the dim drinking establishment into the bright sunlight blinded him. "If you can't see me, I'm over there," I called, waving my arms and pointing at Eggert.

"I see you," he scowled.

"Then quit talking and start walking to your chalk line," I said, trying to steady my nerves.

The bartender Young took it upon himself to announce the rules as he stepped between me and Hickok. "I'll stand between you until you take your places. Once I back out of the way, I'll count to three. When I reach three, you draw and kill Lomax—I mean, fire. After the festivities everyone is welcome to celebrate with drinks in the good old No. 10 Saloon, where Wild Bill Hickok, famed hero of Dime Novels, has agreed to sign autographs."

As the crowd applauded the announcement, Wild Bill and I turned our backs to each other and marched toward opposite ends of the Main Street. The swarm murmured with anticipation of my demise, another notch in Hickok's pistol, and more fodder for a Dime Novel, this one with me as the villain. I reached my mark and took an additional step behind the flour swash, figuring Hickok might get a lucky shot at seventy-five yards with Davis Tutt, but never at seventy-six yards with H.H. Lomax.

I turned around and Young still stood between us as Hickok searched for his spot. Finally, he spun about, and the bartender backed away. Wild Bill jutted his head forward and squinted.

"Hey, Bill," I yelled, pointing at my baker spectator George Eggert nearby, "there I am."

Several spectators laughed while others cursed that I would make light of such a serious moment. I brushed my coat back from my holster, wriggled my fingers and prepared to shoot it out with the deadliest pistoleer in the West.

"Quiet everybody," Young shouted. "They need to hear the count."

At that moment, I had a terrible fear that the bartender and Hickok had worked out a signal that would give Wild Bill an edge on the draw.

"One," cried Young.

At that point, I knew I should've asked for an impartial judge.

"Two," called the referee.

It was too late. I stared at Hickok watching for his move.

"Waaaaiiiiittttt," came the ungodly screech of Calamity Jane, pushing her way through the crowd, bolting to Wild Bill and flinging her arms around him. "He's younger than you," she cried. "If he killed you, what would I do, Bill?"

"Go to hell," Hickok said, trying to shove her away, but she clung to him like rust to metal.

The crowd booed Calamity. Young, bless his heart, stepped back in the firing line between me and my opponent.

I couldn't tell if Calamity was just nuts or both nuts and drunk.

"Leave me be, woman," Hickok screamed.

"Let me be your wife!"

Though folks had come to see a gunfight, they were viewing a marriage proposal.

"I'll be a great wife," Calamity said, "riding with you in life and in Dime Novels, side by side, killing outlaws."

Hickok lowered his voice and said something to Calamity. She released her hold and backed away, her hand over her mouth.

"What did he say?" yelled Eggert.

Somebody in the crowd near Hickok answered. "He said he got married five months ago."

"It don't matter," Calamity shouted, throwing her arms out like she was being crucified. "I'll marry you any way and skin and gut your other wife, just to make it legal."

"Leave me be, woman, so the shooting can commence."

Rejected and humiliated by the man she loved, Calamity cut loose with enough profanity to stampede a herd of angels. She lowered her head, stomped away from Hickok, scowling at Young as she passed him and heading straight at me. The crowd jeered and whistled at her. I thought about drawing my gun and shooting her to put us all out of our misery, but feared Hickok might misread my response and plug me instead. Either way would've been easier on our ears.

She drew up opposite of me and planted her balled fists on her hips. "I think I'll marry Lomax," she screamed for Hickok's benefit. "He's a lot younger and handsomer than you, Bill."

As I considered Calamity's motivation, I realized she considered Hickok the heir and me the spare. I didn't care for her thinking. "I'd sooner kiss a glowing branding iron than you, Calamity," I said.

"And listen to him, Bill," she cried. "He's so poetic, even when he's playing hard to get."

Everyone but the lunatics in the crowd, roughly a third of the spectators, knew she was trying to make Hickok jealous.

"I bet his gun barrel is longer than yours, Bill."

I hung my head as the crowd snickered. She could make an anvil blush. I considered shooting her again, but feared she'd come back to haunt me for the rest of my life. Calamity stepped toward me, but I dodged her outstretched arms and ran in a circle to avoid her.

For once, the crowd cheered me, but I was getting nervous that while I was dodging Miss Calamity, Mr. Hickok might shoot me and claim he was aiming at her.

I glanced at Wild Bill, who had approached Young to confer with the bartender, who nodded and walked to me while signaling for others to join him. As he neared me, Young snapped his finger and pointed at Calamity. His henchmen surrounded her, one grabbing her neck and bulldogging her to the ground. Next his allies each grabbed a leg or an arm and yanked the squirming, flailing and cursing Miss Canary up and escorted her to Deadwood Creek where they tossed her in the water. If ever someone needed a bath on that day, it was Calamity Jane, but the world couldn't produce enough soap to ever wash out her filthy mouth.

When Young was sure Martha Jane Canary would not break through and attack me or him, he looked at me. "It's over. Bill wants to parlay with you tonight in the No. 10 Saloon, if you're agreeable."

"Fine by me as long as there's no gunplay."

"Agreed," Young said. "Be there by seven o'clock." The barkeeper-turned-referee turned to the crowd and lifted his arms for silence. "Ladies and gentlemen, the festivities are concluded. Wild Bill and Lomax have decided to let their differences ride for the moment."

People hissed and booed. One man cried out, "Damnation, I came for a gunfight, and what I saw was a fun fight." Another fellow shouted, "What about the bets?"

"All bets are off," Young answered. "While I can't designate a winner, I can name a loser." He walked over and lifted my right hand in the air like a prizefighter. "I'm declaring H.H. Lomax the loser since Calamity has shifted her affections from Wild Bill to poor Lomax."

The crowd laughed and dispersed. As they did, I glimpsed a dejected George Eggert, unlocking his bakery for the lunch trade and grumbling that his Lomax-ate-here-last promotion would have to wait. After making sure Calamity wasn't waiting somewhere to ambush me, I rushed back to the Ozark House to announce that I was still alive, but the news had beaten me there. Everyone greeted me at the entry with smiles on their faces, save for JoLeah, who scowled.

I took off my boots, then escorted her into the parlor.

424

"What's the matter, Jo Leah?"

"It true that Calamity Jane made a play for you?"

"Nothing but a ploy. She's trying to make Wild Bill jealous so he'll marry her, even though he's already hitched. I'm speculating she wants to be a Dime Novel heroine. Why else use a name like Calamity? It's not nearly as pretty as JoLeah."

She sighed and gave me a kiss. I explained to the soiled doves what had transpired, from the cherry pie to Calamity's first bath since birth. After I finished my story and answered their questions, I whiled the afternoon away until time to return to the saloon for my powwow with Wild Bill.

I arrived a few minutes early to find Hickok, sitting with his back to the wall and winding up a poker game with a wild-eyed fellow I learned was named Bill Sutherland. He wore his brown hair to his collar and kept scratching his neatly trimmed mustache and the narrow goatee leaking from his bottom lip as he counted out his money and pushed it to Wild Bill.

"That's all I got. I'm short sixteen dollars," Sutherland told Hickok.

Hickok had either become a better poker player or learned how to cheat since his days in the Library at the Lyon House of Springfield. Hickok thumbed through the money that Sutherland offered him and nodded. "Your total's correct. You're short."

"I can pay you in a day or two. If not tomorrow, on Thursday."

"You need money to eat until then?" Hickok asked.

"Don't care to be any deeper in debt than I am now."

Hickok nodded and both men stood up. "Tomorrow or Thursday'll be fine," Hickok said as he eyed me. Sutherland spun about and strode out the front door, slamming it as he hit the street.

Wild Bill turned and frowned. "You're lucky Calamity saved your butt today, Lomax. If there's one person I loathe more than you, it's that woman. I despise her more than the devil hates holy water. Her loud mouth, her lack of shame and her face that looks like a tow sack full of turnips."

"She speaks highly of you, Bill."

He glared at me. "I intend to kill you before long because I don't trust you. It's just like you to ambush a fellow, so I won't turn my back on you. But as long as Calamity keeps pestering you instead of me, I won't shoot you as that's enough of a load for any man to carry, no matter my feelings toward him."

"If that's to be our understanding, Bill, so be it, but if I can help you and Martha Jane get back together, it would be one of my proudest moments."

"Scram, Lomax, now that we understand each other."

I figured it was a one-way understanding, one I disliked. To keep Wild Bill from shooting me, I had to tolerate a woman who was meaner and uglier than a bulldog on a gunpowder diet. If I shed myself of Calamity, then I faced a gunman with a grudge hotter than three shades of hell.

"You don't scare me, Hickok."

'Maybe not," he grinned, "But Calamity damn sure does."

We both knew he was right, because he was just as scared of her.

I left and returned to Annie's place, which was running busier than a normal week night by the nine pair of boots under and around the bench. I retreated to my room, ready to rest after a long and dangerous day, and hoping that JoLeah might join me, but she was popular that night. The next day I stayed in my room, afraid to get out on the street for fear of running into Calamity. Annie came in to visit, and I updated her on Hickok's latest threat. She told me I ought to leave, but I told her I didn't care to ride from Deadwood always looking over my shoulder. Annie sent food up for breakfast and lunch so I could stay hidden, but by mid-afternoon I'd had enough waiting and worrying. I got up and dressed, putting on my gun belt and revolver in case I needed to defend myself against Hickok—or Calamity!

Downstairs I put on my boots and asked one girl to lock the door after me. Before exiting, I stuck my head outside to make sure Calamity didn't lie in ambush. She didn't, so I headed out on the street, then up to Main and down to No. 10 Saloon. I walked in and found Hickok in a card game with Carl Mann, one of the saloon owners; William R. Massie, a Missouri River steamboat captain; and Charlie Rich, a local ne'er-do-well. As usual, Hickok sat with his back to the wall so no one could sneak up on him and so he could see both the front and rear entrances. His expression tightened when I stepped to the bar and ordered a whiskey. Paying for the jigger, I took it to an empty table by the front door. I moved the table to the corner and placed a chair behind it so I could sit in safety and watch Hickok from the side. Wild Bill wilted under my stare and turned to Rich, asking him to swap seats, but Rich refused until Hickok pointed to me and mouthed, "Lomax." Rich quickly changed his mind and his seat with Wild Bill, who now sat facing me and the saloon front.

He glared at me so much I was surprised he kept up with his cards. Two more customers entered, the second one being Bill Sutherland, who sat on a stool at the bar opposite Hickok's table. Sutherland purchased a beer. He tapped his fingers on the bar and looked over his shoulder several times, though Hickok never gave any sign of seeing him as he was so focused on me. While I noticed Sutherland, I figured he was there to inform Bill of a delay in repaying his gambling debt, otherwise why did he fidget so? After five minutes, Sutherland got up, leaving half his beer in the mug and heading toward the rear door. He'd taken maybe a dozen steps, when he spun around and started back to the front, angling over to Hickok's table.

When he was an arm's length from Hickok's chair, Sutherland yanked his pistol from his holster.

"Duck, Bill," I cried.

"It's Wild Bill not Duck Bill," he shouted, the last words he would ever utter.

BOOM! Sutherland's revolver exploded in a cloud of white smoke.

"Damn you, take that!" Sutherland cried as James

Butler "Wild Bill" Hickok collapsed dead on the table, his cards falling from his hands.

Across from Hickok, Captain Massie screamed and grabbed his left arm. "I've been shot."

I reached for my revolver, but the assassin swung his gun toward me. "Don't do it, Lomax," he ordered, then turned his pistol around to the rest of the customers. "Everyone move up front with Lomax," he said, his eyes wide with fear.

The bartender and patrons did as he said. Everybody held their hands in the air, save for Hickok and Sutherland. When we had congregated by the front, the killer waved his gun at us again. "Get out of here, now, or I'll shoot!"

We scrambled for the door, rushing outside. I jumped in front of the window and saw Sutherland running for the back exit. Yanking my gun from my holster, I shot through the window at the fleeing murderer. That, it turned out, was a big mistake.

Bartender Harry Young cried out, "Wild Bill's been murdered."

A passerby heard my shot and Young's words, then cried, "Lomax has killed Wild Bill."

Screaming people surrounded and grabbed me, crying, "Lynch him! Lynch him!" They yanked me into the street. I'll be damned if the same Wild Bill Hickok who had saved me from one lynching would cause my death by another.

I tried to lift my gun and defend myself, but a man tore my pistol from my hand. Half a dozen others ran into the saloon to check on Hickok.

"Here's a rope," cried one helpful vigilante.

"I didn't do it. Believe me," I cried. "I'm innocent."

"Calamity Jane can't save you now," yelled another voice.

One fellow inspected Hickok and came to the door. "He was shot in the back of the head."

"Murdering coward," they screamed. "String him up!"

The men tugged me into the street, but another hand

grabbed my arm and yanked the other direction. "He didn't do it," cried Young. "Bill Sutherland did it. He escaped out the back."

"Then let's find Sutherland," cried a vigilante.

The fine men of Deadwood shoved me to the dirt and darted off looking for the actual killer.

I fell to the ground. "Where's my gun? Where's my gun?"

Young offered me a hand and helped me up.

"My gun? My gun?" I asked.

"Don't know where it is," Young said. "Just be glad you're still alive." Together we marched inside and pushed our way to the table where Hickok lay sprawled across the green felt.

His exposed cards showed aces and eights. For years, folks claimed the "Deadman's Hand" caused Hickok's death. I knew better. It was the cherry pie!

Chapter 37

Excitement ran high in Deadwood as the fine, up-standing citizens of the mining town grappled with the blatant murder of Wild Bill Hickok. Much of that anger focused on Bill Sutherland, but part fell on me. Even though I didn't pull the trigger, my presence in the No. 10 Saloon made Hickok switch chairs to watch me rather than other potential threats. That was the pre-dominant belief, though a more sinister theory emerged that I had plotted with Sutherland to distract the Dime Novel hero so my ally might shoot him. Some even said they should've gone ahead and strung me up right after the shooting. The potential danger from those speculations, however, worried me little compared to the rumor that Calamity Jane blamed me for shooting her betrothed-to-be and planned to plug me in the back when she got the chance. I found a gun shop and bought a new pistol to replace the one taken from me during the lynching attempt. I prepared to fight her off.

Even though my life was in danger from several sources, I didn't abandon Hickok like I had in Missouri because justice, or injustice as it turned out, was much quicker in Deadwood than in Springfield. As there were no recognized lawmen, judges or other legal au-thorities in town, the citizens organized an impromptu court, selecting a judge and prosecutor from their own kind and then drawing lots to determine which dozen miners would sit as jurors. The trial started the morn-ing after the murder, and I witnessed the proceedings and even testified. Bill Sutherland turned out to be Jack McCall, who claimed Hickok had killed his brother, and he was only delivering the justice denied in his sibling's murder.

I was the second witnesses when the trial began at nine o'clock that morning in McDaniel's Theater, which was an appropriate forum for all the acting the defense attorney did. Fact was, the judge wasn't truly a judge, nor the prosecutor a prosecutor, and I wasn't much of a witness because I wanted to escape Deadwood as soon as possible after Wild Bill's funeral.

The prosecutor asked me to describe what I witnessed the previous day, and I told him everything from the moment Jack McCall entered the saloon until he escaped out the back. I thought testifying was a snap until the fellow defending McCall got up and badgered me.

"Is it true men tried to lynch you after the shooting?" he asked.

"That's true."

"And why did they consider lynching you?"

"They must've thought I shot him. They were wrong."

"Were they? Just the day before hadn't you and the deceased, James Butler Hickok, faced off in the street to settle an old score when the demure Martha Jane Canary, jumped between you two and stopped any gunplay."

The spectators laughed at his description of Calamity, and I burst into a smile.

The so-called attorney pointed his finger and me and scowled. "This is no laughing matter, Mr. Lomax. Isn't it true you've been called 'Lead Eye Lomax' for the bullets you put in dozens of victims?"

"No, that's not true!"

"You're denying you were ever called 'Lead Eye'?"

"Not that, but that—"

"So, you've lied to the court, have you?"

"—I killed people."

"So now you admit you killed people, and you connived to kill the beloved Wild Bill Hickok, everyone's favorite Dime Novel hero, did you not?"

"No, no, no," I cried out, looking at the judge for help. He shrugged.

"And so, killer that you are, you wanted to Mr. Hickok dead so he wouldn't steal your girl, the lovely Martha Jane Canary. But you were too much the coward to do it yourself, and connived Mr. Jack McCall to do it for you by lying to him that Mr. Hickok planned to shoot him over his sixteen-dollar debt."

"It's lies, all lies," I protested.

"That," this fake attorney said, crossing his arms over his chest, "will be for the jury to determine.

I stepped from the witness stand, furious that under oath I had to tell the truth while this fellow hadn't taken an oath and lied as much as he pleased.

Other witnesses followed me, claiming that the murdering McCall was a quiet and peaceable man unlike the noted shootists Hickok and Lomax, and that McCall was a decent man incapable of shooting Wild Bill unless put up to it by some despicable, low-down skunk with a grudge against Hickok. The attorneys, witnesses, and even the judge always looked at me when they blamed that skunk. When they accused me of such depredations, I always studied Calamity, sitting in her seat, seething at me.

What the trial lacked in legitimacy it overcame in propriety, adjourning in time for everyone to trek to the Ingleside Cemetery for Wild Bill's funeral service. Hickok's friend Charlie Utter had organized and paid for the services, including a handsome black coffin with ornamental silver trim and handles. Hickok looked as peaceful as any man alive with his brains blown out, his thinning and receding chestnut hair parted down the middle, his mustache trimmed and his face shaved. He wore a white shirt under a black broadcloth frock coat. His rifle lay by his side in case he needed to shoot his way out of heaven or hell as I was uncertain just what his preference might be. After many fancy words about what a fine man Wild Bill had been, they clamped the coffin shut and lowered his remains into the earthly embrace of the Black Hills. The moment remained a

quiet and respectable one until Calamity Jane wailed
and sobbed in her demure and lovely way, crying out
she planned to kill the son of a bitch responsible for
this, pointing my direction. So much for the "spare," I
thought, now that the "heir" was gone.

While Miss Canary was crying vengeance, those of
us that sought justice returned to the theater to continue the trial. The judge ordered the attorneys to speed
things up to finish in time for the theater proprietors
to prepare for the evening's performance. After the
testimony closed, the attorneys made hurried final
arguments and the judge gave the jury their charge.
Since the theater would be in use that evening, the judge
would reconvened the trial in the No. 10 Saloon when
jurors reached their verdict. While the scene of the
murder was an odd place to announce the verdict, the
real reason was a tree behind the saloon made a perfect
scaffold for hanging McCall as soon as the guilty verdict was announced.

However, it was not to be. I thought I was fortunate
to be among those admitted to the saloon for the verdict,
but I was wrong there, too. Even though one spectator
brought in a rope knotted in a hangman's noose, he
didn't have a chance to use it. In one of the great court-
room travesties of the ages, the jury declared McCall
not guilty. The tree out back remained unused. The
stunned crowd grumbled and glared my way. Though
no one said it aloud, I knew they blamed me for putting
McCall up to the dastardly deed. The fellow carrying
the noose whispered, "Let's hang Lomax, anyway."

A smiling Jack McCall walked out of that saloon a
free man, while I slipped out into the darkness trying to
avoid a vigilante noose or an encounter with Calamity
Jane. I strode to the Ozark House. Upon admission I
shed my boots, climbed the stairs and entered my room.
Shortly, my sister rapped on the door. "May I come in."

"Certainly," I said as I plopped down on the bed
drained from the day's events and the uncertainty of
what tomorrow would bring.

Annie parted the door, and left it open for the girls

433

that had followed her upstairs, including JoLeah. "Do you mind telling me and the others what happened?"

I shrugged. "Jack McCall was found not guilty and released."

Several girls gasped.

"The lawyers made it seem like I had put him up to it. The jury bought it, reasonable doubt, they called it."

"Oh, Lomax, what are you going to do?"

"Leave in the morning. I'm not safe around here with feelings running high and that crazy Calamity Jane threatening to skin and gut me for causing Wild Bill's demise."

"I'll go with you," JoLeah announced, pushing her way inside the room.

"Too dangerous," I replied. "I'd hate for you to get hurt. I lost a girl to death a decade ago. I'd rather leave one behind than lose another."

"That's enough, girls," said Annie. "Return to the parlor, and I'll meet you there in a few minutes." She closed the door as they backed away, then turned to me. "I hate to say goodbye, but it was inevitable. You and I got Pa's wanderlust in us, though I'm wandered out and settling here for good. If you visit our parents again, don't tell them what I'm doing. Say I'm an actress or something softer than a madam."

I stood up and hugged her, then broke free and stared into her eyes. "You're secret's safe with me, and you've done well for yourself."

She nodded. "I'm stashing money away, investing in mining and lumber properties. I plan to put this behind me in a few years and lead a respectable life for a change, probably here, so no one but you from Cane Hill would ever find me."

"You think you'll marry again?"

"If I found a man as decent as you, Henry, but likely not. I've been with too many to settle with one and put up with his flaws. I hope to die a rich spinster," she laughed.

"Thanks for your hospitality, including JoLeah. I have money so what do I owe you for my stay, Constance?"

"Why, Henry? Nothing. You're family, the only one I

can call family now. Please write if you get the chance, and I'll do the same for you, if you let me know where you are."

"I'm never sure where I'm headed until I get there."

"In the morning, I'll have a fellow saddle your mule and leave him tied outside."

"Visit me again, Henry, and write when you learn news of Momma and Pa."

Constance saw me off the next morning, and I left Deadwood, not to return for years. I promised to write her and I did, once every two or three years. I received a letter from her every five years or so. She may have written more, but I moved around so much that any other missives never caught up with me.

I had traveled to Deadwood to stop the annoying stories Hickok had been spreading. Fact was, the false tales continued for years whenever I introduced myself to others. Sometimes those lies became so entangled in the facts of his murder that the unfamiliar thought I had killed Wild Bill. Falsehoods are as hard to kill as a ten-headed rattlesnake and a hundred times more dangerous.

Leaving Deadwood, I escaped Martha Jane Canary and her possible vendetta against me, whether real or imagined. Wherever I went, though, I often encountered her, as she became a Dime Novel character in pulps featuring Deadwood Dick. I even found pulp publications with her name on the top and an illustration of her on the cover. Calamity Jane looked better in fiction than in real life. And, she cussed less in print than in person.

When I returned to Deadwood many years later, the territory stood on the verge of being admitted to the Union as two states, I never encountered Calamity or heard her name mentioned on that trip. I had hoped to visit Constance, but I missed her as she had journeyed to the capital for the statehood celebration. The Ozark House had burned, but she now lived in a fine stone house. By then Constance was respected as the town's most benevolent matriarch, though she continued to go by Annie Ozark or Miss Annie as she was called for her charitable donations. She was still leaving her mark on the town, only now in more reputable ways as her bawdy house savings plus her mining and timber investments had paid off handsomely. Before I left town, I slid a note under her door letting her know I had dropped by.

I also decided to visit Wild Bill's grave, but Deadwood had grown and changed so much from the rough-hewn frontier village I remembered that I couldn't find the place. When I asked around, I learned from an old geezer that the whole cemetery had been dug up and the deceased replanted on Mount Moriah out of the way of the town's growth. I rode up the mountain and found his grave with a fine stone monument listing his name and that of his murderer, Jack McCall. So many visitors hiked to his plot that nobody wanted to be buried next to him and have their plots trampled by the souvenir seekers who frequented Wild Bill's resting place.

After that visit I left Deadwood, never expecting to return, but in the summer of 1903 a letter from the faded mining town caught up with me. Annie's Deadwood lawyer, Chunky Gaines, wrote to inform me of my sister's death that spring. As I was identified as her only known family member, I was the heir to a substantial sum from her fortune and was invited to Deadwood to collect. Fortunately, I had money enough to buy a train ticket that would take me back a final time to the Black Hills.

I got off the train at the Deadwood depot and stood on the platform, inspecting the town for the first time in fifteen years. The boom had passed and the community was a frail monument to itself and might have died like other area mining towns except for the public fascination in Wild Bill Hickok. As I looked toward Mount Moriah where the legend lay buried, a freight man with the railway company walked over once my train pulled away.

"You here to see Wild Bill's grave?"

"Perhaps," I said, "but mostly on legal matters."

My new friend pointed to Mount Moriah. "He's buried up there so he's closer to the angels."

"I figured Bill would've been more at home in hotter climes."

"Heaven or hell," the railway fellow replied, "Wild Bill could've faced them all down. In fact while he was alive, the only two fellows that ever got the best of him were Jack McCall, who shot him from behind, and that villain H.H. Lomax, who always attacked his hair when he was asleep. But now they can't do a thing to him."

"He's been dead a quarter of a century."

"Not only that, he's stone, like a statue."

"What?"

"When they moved his grave, they opened his coffin and Wild Bill had turned to stone. His corpse weighed three or four hundred pounds, just like a statue he was."

"Then why don't they dig him up and stand him on a pedestal so he can bring a little life back to town, like the old days, when things were booming?"

"That'd be illegal."

An ore train was inching toward us on the tracks. I turned to look for my carpetbag, then go find the Gaines lawyer, when the railway man grabbed my arm.

"Want to view a legend from those boom days before law came to Deadwood?"

I shrugged. "Why not?"

Then train engine huffed by, pulling a dozen empty ore cars.

"Check out the last car, I thought I saw her climb in when the train stopped on the siding."

"Who?"

"Calamity Jane," he answered.

I patted the revolver at my side in case I needed it to defend myself. "You don't say?"

As the train crawled ahead, I spotted a figure with arms draped over the side of the ore car.

"That's her," my buddy informed me. He waved. "Howdy, Calamity, where you headed?"

"Going to Terry," she cried with that irritating voice that still grated on your nerves like chalk on slate. "There's money to be made there."

While her voice was recognizable, her looks had faded like old paint. Her stringy hair tumbled out from her greasy hat and years of liquor and dissipation had ravaged her homely face, which needed washing. Her eyes looked dull and sad, so much so that I thought about shooting her to put her out of her misery. As her car passed us, she lifted her right hand and offered a limp wave. For the first time in my life, I felt sorry for her.

"Being a legend must be tough," I said.

"Yeah," the railway man answered. "The only money she makes now is by selling her autograph. I understand she was a beauty back in her younger days."

"She wasn't that pretty," I corrected.

"You knew her?"

"Briefly," I replied and walked away in search of my sister's lawyer.

I found the law office of Chunky Gaines on a Main Street I no longer recognized. Fires and a major flood on Deadwood Creek had destroyed the town I had known a quarter century earlier. Destruction, it seemed, was the fate of all wicked towns since Sodom and Gomorrah, with the possible exception of Washington, D.C. I entered and introduced myself as H.H. Lomax. He didn't believe me. I had to confirm my identity by telling him where I grew up and the names of my parents and siblings. Then he asked me what was the one thing me and my sister had in common beyond family.

"We were bitten by Pa's wanderlust bug."

Constance's estate lawyer smiled and said, "Welcome to Deadwood, Mr. Lomax. Two imposters have attempted to claim your inheritance, so I am glad we have found the actual heir Miss Annie loved." This lawyer was a bloated fellow with a tight collar he kept tugging at and eyes that looked beady behind thick spectacles. He informed me that it required up to ten working days to finish the necessary paperwork and court filings to turn over my bequest. He reviewed his desk calendar and did a little calculating. As it was late afternoon on a Friday, July twenty-fourth to be exact, he couldn't initiate matters at the courthouse until Monday. So, he told me I might need to remain in Deadwood as late as

August seventh.

"I don't plan to stay that long," I informed him. "And I don't have lodging."

"Mr. Lomax," he intoned, "I think you can remain for whatever time the filings require as you are due to inherit almost twenty-six thousand dollars."

I exhaled so fast my breath whistled.

"That's right, almost twenty-six thousand dollars. And, you will have the key to her stone home, which is not quite a mansion, but plenty substantial for a Deadwood residence. Should you need funds for expenses until we settle the estate, please inform me and I will advance you the necessary monies, which will be subtracted from the final settlement. Is that satisfactory?"

I sat so stunned, I could only nod.

"Good, then let me accompany you to your sister's place," said the Lawyer Gaines.

We exited the office together, but I would have felt better if Chunky had locked the door behind us. After all, he was handling my money now, but Deadwood had changed. The less gold there was to be found, the more civilization encroached. If things didn't change, in another quarter century Deadwood would civilize itself to death.

Gaines escorted me south from Main Street, past the site where the Ozark House had been replaced by the brick building that looked vacant as I passed. We cross the stream and followed a street that curved toward Mount Moriah and ended at a stone house that overlooked Deadwood. It was a dark stone structure with a wide front porch that faced the site of her former brothel. Gaines didn't say much, just unlocked the front door and gave me the key.

"If you want to sell it, I have a buyer," he said, "but you can stay here as long as necessary. Drop by next week if you need money or an update on the probate process. Good evening, Mr. Lomax." He headed back to his unlocked office.

I entered and looked around, opening the drapes to let in afternoon light. Constance had lived well. The

floor was covered with thick Persian rugs, plush so-
fas and chairs, mahogany tables, cut glass lamps and
a pump organ. On one side of the parlor was a small
library and on the other side a music room with a piano
and harp. To the back of the house was a kitchen with
equipment I'd never seen before, a water closet and a
dining area with a table that seated twelve. Upstairs I
found her large bedroom with a canopied bed and three
smaller bedrooms. I tossed my carpet bag on a bed in a
room with a window overlooking the streets of Deadwood below and stood staring at the withering town.
Constance had known when to check out as I didn't give
the place another decade to survive.

Meanwhile, I had ten days to kill until I became
rich. I slept nights in Constance's castle and walked the
streets to waste time. Taking my meals at the best eatery on Main Street, I got acquainted with the local folks,
especially the old-timers who were intrigued when they
found out I was named Lomax. A lot of the same old stories about me defiling Wild Bill's hair came up as well as
new tales about me masterminding Hickok's murder or
shacking up with Calamity Jane. I told folks I was not
the H.H. Lomax, but a cousin with intimate knowledge
of him and his past. Most sensationally, I proceeded to
correct them on the facts and asserted that James Butler
Hickok and Martha Jane Canary were indeed lovers.
The locals loved the gossip.

During my dining sessions I got to meet and eat with
Hank and Charles Robinson, brothers and proprietors
of Deadwood's Robinson Funeral Home. Both fellows
sported fine heads of black hair and thick mustaches
while Charles was tall and lanky and Hank was shorter
and bespectacled. They reminded me of the undertakers back in Fort Worth when we buried Trent Parsons.
Both had a great sense of humor, but could look as somber as a defeated politician the day after the vote tally,
which made them perfect for their profession.

My second Saturday in Deadwood, I arrive late to
supper and found the eatery buzzing with people and
gossip. The tables were taken, and folks were even

waiting to be seated when Hank Robinson waved me over to a spare seat at their small table.

"Have you heard?" Hank asked.

"It's the biggest thing to hit Deadwood since Wild Bill Hickok was assassinated," Charles noted.

"What could top that?" I asked.

"Calamity Jane died this afternoon in Terry. They're bringing the body to town tomorrow for us to bury," Charles told me.

"I didn't know."

"Such a shame," Hank said.

"What's that?"

"That she doesn't have the money for the grand funeral she deserves," Hank informed me.

"She was a local institution, even if she only drank and begged for money."

"You should take up a collection, let folks pitch in," I offered.

"There's not that much money in Deadwood anymore," Charles said. "If Annie Ozark were still alive, she would help, maybe even cover the expenses. She'd make it a funeral to remember."

Hank shook his head. "We'll place her in a pauper's grave. Sad, isn't it, to bury a celebrity that way?"

As I had kept my business to myself and not explained the reason for my Deadwood visit nor my relationship to Annie to protect the family name, the Robinson brothers sat ignorant of my connections. A funny thought entered my mind. "How much would a fine ceremony cost?"

"Eight hundred should offer a respectable funeral," Charles said.

"Fifteen hundred would provide the splendor of Miss Annie's burial," Hank said. "It was a beautiful ceremony. Such a pity that none of her family attended."

Licking my lips at the thought of getting back at Wild Bill for all the shame his lies had attached to my name, I asked a simple question. "Would thirteen hundred dollars make a good show? I might be able to get money, though I wouldn't want to go fifteen hundred and top Annie Ozark as I understand she was a wonderful woman."

"She was indeed," said Hank.

Charles nodded. "Miss Annie was a delight and thirteen hundred would cover a wonderful service, embalming, coffin, clothing, flowers, hearse, grave and tombstone for Miss Calamity."

"What would possess you to be so generous?" Hank asked.

"It's my way of paying tribute to the pioneers that settled this part of the country, but I have only one stipulation."

"We'll certainly identify you as the benefactor of Miss Calamity," Charles said.

"Absolutely not," I said, hitting the table with my fist so hard that the dishes rattled. "Giving is the only satisfaction I need, but my stipulation must be met. I want her buried by Wild Bill Hickok. They were lovers, and he would've married her except he'd gotten hitched earlier in the year and couldn't get out of it before he was killed."

Both brothers leaned toward me. "Did you know Wild Bill?" Hank asked.

"Knew him well," I said, then whispered, "I'm H.H. Lomax."

They gasped. "The H.H. Lomax?" Charles asked.

"Shhsssss," I nodded. "I don't want my real name known. Too many grudges of folks that think Bill and I didn't get along. Untrue. You can't believe all the rumors about me, because Hickok and I went way back. I even combed nits out of his hair in Springfield. The day he was shot, he was gambling to win enough money for a lawyer to divorce his wife and start over with Miss Calamity Jane. It's the saddest love story I've ever run across in all my years out West."

The brothers looked at each other, and I thought I saw the glint of tears in their eyes.

"I'd always heard he hated her," Charles said.

"That's what Hickok wanted people to believe until he could file for divorce, but he was smitten with her. But that's past. If you want the money, secure permissions and make arrangements to dig her grave as close to Wild Bill's as possible. As soon as the grave is dug, I'll get you the money."

Chapter 38

So excited were Charles and Hank Robinson about the thirteen hundred dollars that would flow into their pockets to bury Martha Jane Canary that they advised me to be at their funeral parlor during church time the next day. The undertakers had hired a freighter in Terry to bring the body back to Deadwood to arrive during church services and avoid a spectacle. Apparently, the citizens needed an exhibition because most skipped church and lined Main Street to await Deadwood's celebrity corpse.

Those folks got a show as the teamster was two hours late, having stopped to killed off two bottles of liquor on the road. As this was not his usual freight, he didn't know how to transport Miss Calamity. Rather than throw her in the back and cover her with a blanket, he tied her to a chair, which he secured to his wagon seat. Calamity Jane rode into Deadwood for the last time back to back with the freighter, bound in a wooden chair, uncovered by blanket, her head bobbing at every bump in the road. When the teamster stopped in front of the funeral parlor, the Robinsons chewed him out for his stupidity. One of the wagon occupants had been drinking because the aroma of liquor permeated the air, but I wouldn't have put it past Calamity, with her affinity for whiskey, to have killed one of the two empty bottles that rolled around in the wagon bed by her chair.

Charles raced inside the funeral parlor and returned

with a silk cloth which he draped over Calamity's face as Hank worked to untie his latest client. The driver was no help, and Hank elbowed him out of the way. So unsteady was the teamster that he fell off the seat and onto the ground, never making a sound when he hit bottom. The crowd moved in closer, their morbid curiosity drawing them to Calamity like Democrats to a bribe. I helped the Robinson brothers wrestle the corpse out of the wagon and up on the plank walk.

"Please folks move out of the way," Charles pleaded. "Allow her dignity."

"Like your drunk driver showed," one Bible-toting church member said.

Somehow we got Calamity through the crowd and inside the door. Hank slammed it behind us as Charles pulled the curtains on the front windows. When they felt they had adequate privacy, they lifted the silk cover. I stared at Martha Jane. Death hadn't improved her looks.

"I'm leaving," I said. "Is everything arranged for the plot next to Wild Bill's?"

"We talked to the mayor," said Hank, "and he thought it was a grand idea. It would draw more visitors to Deadwood."

"They're starting the grave this afternoon," Charles continued. It should be completed by morning. We'll aim for the funeral day after tomorrow."

"I'll check the cemetery tomorrow," I said, "and make arrangements for the money, if I am satisfied with the plot. Hope to have the cash to you tomorrow afternoon." I opened the door, then slammed it shut behind me as curiosity seekers still thronged the walk, trying to peek at the late Calamity Jane.

After dining on an early supper at the eatery, I retired to Constance's castle and bed, arising at dawn to walk up to the cemetery. As I had requested and the Robinson brothers had promised, the grave had been dug beside Wild Bill's. I smiled. She might not be able to reach over and touch him, but she could tunnel to him in a week maximum. I grinned.

I walked down Mount Moriah and over to Main Street, waiting outside Chunky Gaines' office until he arrived.

"Good morning, Mr. Lomax," he said as he opened the unlocked door and walked inside. "How can I help you?"

"I need thirteen hundred dollars today."

"I can arrange that. May I ask what for?"

"It's a life-and-death matter," I replied.

"Then I shall get to the bank, and you can return later to collect the funds."

Shaking my head, I said, "I'd rather accompany you." I didn't like him getting my thirteen hundred dollars and leaving it in an unlocked office. We strolled to the bank together. Afterward, I delivered the cash to the funeral parlor and knocked on the locked door several times. The Robinsons ignored me until I shouted, "I've got the money."

Quickly, the door swung open and Hank pulled me inside as Charles slammed and latched it behind me. Both men looked haggard and tired, though they perked up when I counted out the cash into their hands. They stepped over to the coffin and lifted the lid for me to inspect the corpse.

I stood stunned. They had produced the greatest work of art I had ever seen. I remembered back to my trail-driving days how Madlyn Dillon had painted such beautiful pictures and how Martin Michaels had drawn such life-like sketches—and wanted posters as well—but this was artistic mastery. They had dressed her in a flowing virginal white gown and washed and set her hair, then tinted, powdered, rouged and massaged her face until she had an angelic and peaceful smile upon her lips. She smelled of lilac and embalming liquids.

"We worked all night," Hank said.

"And we're exhausted," Charles added, "but everyone wants to see her."

"That's why we didn't answer the door until we knew it was you," Hank said.

"You're arrival was timely," Charles noted. "You

must stay here and guard her, not let anybody in, so we can get home, clean up and return for the photographer. We want to memorialize her likeness."

"And," said Hank, "since you are paying for this service, we'd like you to drive the hearse with Charles, but you should buy a fine suit, shirt and tie befitting the occasion. The dry goods store across the street can fix you up."

"I don't need a suit."

"It's on us, sort of," Hank said, holding money I'd just paid in the air. "Tell the merchant to charge it to our account."

Charles and Hank rushed out the front door, locking it behind them and leaving me alone with Calamity Jane. Even though I knew she couldn't shoot, stab, bite or scratch me, I felt nervous standing there with her looking all presentable for the first time in her life. "You'll be reunited with Bill tomorrow," I told her. "He'll love it."

Periodically, people came to the door, shook the knob and knocked. I pulled a chair up to the front and told the curious to go away until the curtains were pulled. On a couple occasions to pass the time until the undertakers returned, I tried to imitate Calamity's screechy voice to make people think she was haunting Deadwood. One of those times, the fellow yelled, "It's me, Calamity, the photographer. I peeked out the window and saw two men carrying a tripod and bulky equipment. I let them in and told them to take care of Martha Jane themselves until the Robinson brothers came back.

"The undertakers wanted close-ups of her face and long shots of the full coffin, did they not?"

"Far as I know," I said.

"And they desired to be in one with Calamity?"

I shrugged. "I suppose so."

"Excellent," the photographer said.

"Now lock the door behind me once I leave."

They let me out and latched things down before anyone else slipped in. I crossed the street bought my funeral clothes, then marched home and rested, returning late in the afternoon for an early supper since I had missed lunch. I strolled over to the funeral parlor first and saw mourners lined for a hundred yards up the street. Charles stood at the door, allowing people in two at a time and reminding them this was a visitation not a circus. That struck me odd until I looked inside and saw they had tied chicken wire over the top half of the coffin.

"What's with the wire?"

Charles shook his head. "People kept snipping off locks of hair. If we didn't do something, she would've been bald by the service tomorrow."

That disrespect angered me as these were likely the same folks that had been incensed by all the false stories of the despicable things I had done to Wild Bill's hair.

After supper I retired to the castle and wandered around the house, looking for things that reminded me of Constance, but I found nothing that linked her to me or to Cane Hill, Arkansas, where we had both been born. I didn't believe that Constance was so heartless to disown her roots, but rather played it cautiously so no one might defame the family on account of her profession. I decided I would sell the place.

The next morning I dressed in my new funeral suit and walked to the lawyer's office, telling Gaines I wanted to sell the castle, as I called it, if the buyer were still interested. He said he was the buyer and offered me a fair price. We agreed he should add that to my final settlement.

Next I went to the funeral parlor where a hearse was parked outside with two matching black horses. The coffin had been loaded so it was just a matter of taking Calamity to the Methodist Church for the service and up to Mount Moriah for the internment. We drove her to the packed house of worship. As we carried Martha Jane inside, everybody rose in respect for a woman who gained little respect in life, but much notoriety. The pastor ignored her vices and praised her virtues of kindness and sincerity. If she wasn't always a saint, the preacher said, then she at least meant well. Amen!

After the service, the Robinsons opened the casket

and allow everyone to pass her mortal remains a final time, though without the chicken wire on this occasion. When the last mourner passed, Charles and Hank tightened the lid over her. The Robinsons, the preacher and I were the last to look upon her earthly face. "Say hello to Wild Bill for me, Calamity," I whispered. Maybe it was the shadow of the closing cover, but I could've sworn she smiled at me.

The four of us carried her out to the hearse, loaded her in the back and started for Mount Moriah. After a long climb, we reached Wild Bill's marker and her grave. After unloading the coffin and placing it on slats over the cavity, the preacher said a few last words and another prayer, then several men slid ropes under the box and lifted it so others could yank the slats free. The attendants lowered her into the ground and covered her with dirt.

I walked over to the Robinsons and told them I'd be walking back to my house as I thought it unlucky to drive an empty hearse. They laughed and thanked me for paying for the service. They asked me if they wanted a copy of one of Calamity's death photos.

"Yes, but place it atop Wild Bill's grave. I know he would appreciate it," I said with as straight a face as I possible. They agreed and shook hands with me. I walked from there down the winding street to town.

Four days later, I rode the train out of town, having more cash in my pocket than I deserved, thank you, Constance Louise Lomax or Annie Ozark to her Deadwood friends. As I looked up at Mount Moriah, I smiled. Hickok's lies about me might live for years to come, but they would eventually die away. Wild Bill, by contrast, would spend eternity with Calamity Jane at his side.

In fact, she was probably digging her way over to see him at that very moment.

Boy, would he be surprised when she broke through!

About the Author

Growing up in West Texas and loving history, Spur Award-winning author Preston Lewis naturally gravitated to stories of the Old West and religiously read his father's copies of True West and Frontier Times. Today he is the author of more than 30 western, juvenile and historical novels as well as numerous articles, short stories and book reviews on the American frontier.

Preston Lewis is a past president of WWA and WTHA, which in 2016 named him a fellow. He has served on the boards of the Ranching Heritage Association and the Book Club of Texas. He and his wife Harriet live in San Angelo, Texas.

READ MORE ABOUT PRESTON LEWIS AT: https://wolfpackpublishing.com/preston-lewis/